Praise for the novels of Katie MacAlister

A Girl's Guide to Vampires

"With its superb characterization and writing that manages to be both sexy and humorous, this contemporary paranormal love story is an absolute delight."
—*Booklist* (starred review)

"Fantastic! It's sensual, it's hilarious, and it's a winner! Ms. MacAlister is my favorite new author."
—Reader to Reader Reviews

"A book rich with humor, loaded with sexual tension, and packed with interesting, if sometimes slightly offbeat, characters."
—Romance Reviews Today

"Hysterically funny paranormal romance, oh my!"
—The Best Reviews

The Corset Diaries

"Reality TV has never been more entertaining than here as the wickedly funny MacAlister has her heroine record her hilarious experiences with a quirky cast of characters and her passionate encounters with Max in a laughter-laced diary that is a saucy, sexy delight."
—*Booklist*

"Offbeat and wacky. . . . MacAlister has outdone herself with this reality show run amok. Tessa and Max are funny, sexy, and slightly poignant—a true match."
—Romantic Times BookClub

"An enjoyable contemporary romance . . . The story line is fun to follow. . . . Fans will enjoy this entertaining anachronistic look at displacement as the modern crowd struggles with life just over a century ago."
—The Best Reviews

continued . . .

Men in Kilts

"With its wickedly witty writing, wonderfully snappy dialogue, and uniquely amusing characters, MacAlister's latest is perfect for any reader seeking a deliciously sexy yet also subtly sweet contemporary romance." —*Booklist*

"A fun, fast paced, and witty adventure . . . *Men in Kilts* is so utterly delightful, I read this book nearly all in one sitting."
—Roundtable Reviews

"Katie MacAlister sparkles, intrigues, and is one of the freshest voices to hit romance. . . . So buckle up, for Katie gives you romance, love, and the whole damn thing—sheep included." —The Best Reviews

"*Men in Kilts* is filled with warm, intriguing characters and situations, and the atmosphere is fiery as Katie and her silent Ian irresistibly draw you into their story." —*Rendezvous*

"Wonderfully witty, funny and romantic, *Men in Kilts* had me laughing out loud from the first page. . . . A definite winner." —Romance Reviews Today

"This book hooked me from the first paragraph and kept me smiling—and sometimes laughing out loud—to the last page. . . . I thoroughly enjoyed *Men in Kilts* and recommend it highly." —*Affaire de Coeur*

Katie MacAlister

Fire Me Up

An Aisling Grey, Guardian, Novel

A SIGNET ECLIPSE BOOK

SIGNET ECLIPSE
Published by New American Library, a division of
Penguin Group (USA) Inc., 375 Hudson Street,
New York, New York 10014, USA
Penguin Group (Canada), 90 Eglinton Avenue East, Suite 700, Toronto,
Ontario M4P 2Y3, Canada (a division of Pearson Penguin Canada Inc.)
Penguin Books Ltd., 80 Strand, London WC2R 0RL, England
Penguin Ireland, 25 St. Stephen's Green, Dublin 2,
Ireland (a division of Penguin Books Ltd.)
Penguin Group (Australia), 250 Camberwell Road, Camberwell, Victoria 3124,
Australia (a division of Pearson Australia Group Pty. Ltd.)
Penguin Books India Pvt. Ltd., 11 Community Centre, Panchsheel Park,
New Delhi - 110 017, India
Penguin Group (NZ), 67 Apollo Drive, Mairangi Bay,
Auckland 1311, New Zealand (a division of Pearson New Zealand Ltd.)
Penguin Books (South Africa) (Pty.) Ltd., 24 Sturdee Avenue,
Rosebank, Johannesburg 2196, South Africa

Penguin Books Ltd., Registered Offices:
80 Strand, London WC2R 0RL, England

First published by Signet Eclipse, an imprint of New American Library,
a division of Penguin Group (USA) Inc.

First Printing, May 2005
20 19 18 17 16 15 14 13 12 11

I am always grateful to a number of people by the time I'm done with a book—my editor and agent for encouraging me to continue to write, the readers who send me letters urging me to write faster (which make me giggle), and my friends and family who put up with my general crankiness while I'm writing. All of that is true with this book, but in addition, I'm also profoundly appreciative of Laura Toth's help with the Hungarian phrases and words used, and for being the inspiration for setting this book in her beloved Budapest.

1

"You'd think that Hungary would see the light as far as secondhand smoke is concerned, wouldn't you? I probably lost at least thirty percent of my lung capacity on the trip from the airport."

I didn't even glance at the massive hairy black form at my side as we disembarked from the train on a cloud of cigarette smoke. Instead, I said through my teeth, "Language!"

Two big brown eyes opened wide with surprise.

"Stop it," I hissed, glancing quickly around us to see if anyone had overheard. We were elbow to elbow with what appeared to be half the population of Hungary, all intent on going to the same place at the same time as us. Luckily, no one seemed to be paying attention to a huge black dog and its unexceptional owner. I took a firm grip on Jim's leather leash, wrapping it around the wrist on my left hand as I used my right to tug on the big suitcase on wheels that kept clipping my heels.

"Oh, right, I forgot. Ixnay on the alkingtay. Bowwow. Arf. Bark bark. Hummina hummina hummina."

I glared at the demon in Newfoundland dog form that stood beside me as we struggled through the huge crowds at Budapest's main train station. We moved slowly forward with the rest of the lemmings, part of the *shuffle, stop, shuffle, stop* pattern of movement that characterized a large number of people trying to pass through a narrow opening.

Jim's eyebrows rose at my look. "What?"

"You are talking," I answered, more or less grinding the words. "Dogs don't talk, so just *shut . . . up!*"

"Well!" Jim sniffed in an injured manner as we shuffle-stopped our way forward a few more feet. I knew from the experience of having lived with Jim for the past month that my furry little demon would have an expression of profound martyrdom on its face, an expression not at all common to most Newfies but one that Jim had perfected during our relatively short time together. "That wasn't a direct order, was it? Because you didn't say, 'Dammit, Jim, I said shut the farking haitch up!' which, of course, is what you normally say when you want me to shut up. And I know *that's* a command, because you only say 'farking haitch' when you're really PO'd. So I thought I'd better check whether or not that last 'shut up' was a direct order or just a hopeful desire on your part."

I stood in the center of the Keleti train station surrounded by hundreds of people—nice, normal people, people who never once thought about things like demons, and demon lords, and Guardians, and all of the strange beings that populated the L'au-delà, the Otherworld—and I wondered for the hundredth time whether if I tried really hard I could send Jim back to the fiery depths of Hell.

"No," it answered my unasked question before I could do so much as level another squinty-eyed glare at it. "You tried three times to send me back. The last time cost me a toe. My favorite one, too. How you can make a toe disappear right off my foot is beyond me, but the point is that I'm not going to risk another unbalanced paw just so you can play Junior Guardian. I'm staying put until you get yourself a mentor and figure out that whole sending-me-back thing."

"Will you stop answering questions before I ask them, stop telling me what to do, and above all, *stop talking*?"

As crowded as the platforms were, the air filled with fumes from the fast-food restaurants that lined the main section of the station, not to mention the ripe odor of a couple of hundred people who'd been crushed into a busy train on a hot August day, as well as the noise those very same hot, sweaty people made as they tried to escape the station—despite all that, my words managed to penetrate the miasma of sound and echo with a strange piercing quality off the tiled walls.

Several heads swiveled to look back at us. I smiled somewhat grimly at all of them. A hurt look filled Jim's brown eyes as it sniffed, with studied indifference, the butts of the man and woman in front of us.

We shuffled forward another few feet.

"So, *that* was an order?"

I sighed, my shoulders slumping in defeat. I was hot, tired, jet-lagged from the flight from Portland to Amsterdam to Budapest, and to be honest, Jim's presence—although annoying in many ways—was more than a little reassuring considering just who else was occupying the same continent on which I now found myself.

The memory of glittering green eyes filled with smoky desire rose with no difficulty to dance before me but was squelched with a much greater effort. "No, it's not an order," I said softly. "At least not until we're through this crowd. I doubt if anyone can even see you, let alone notice that your mouth is moving."

"I told you to get me that ventriloquist tape I saw on TV."

The mass of humanity rippled forward, then halted again. I stood on my tiptoes and peered around the big sun hat of the woman in front of me and caught sight of what was holding us up. At the far end of the platform, where the passage narrowed to one open exit to the taxi ranks and passenger pickup areas, several men in security uniforms had stopped the crowd as a couple of VIPs were escorted off the train.

"What is it?" Jim asked. "Dead body? Someone throw himself in front of the train? Are there splattered body parts everywhere? Did you remember to bring your digital camera?"

"You are a sick, sick demon. There are no body parts, splattered or otherwise. It's just"—I craned my neck— "just a woman and a couple of guys in really expensive-looking designer clothes. They're probably movie stars or politicians or something." The crowd shimmered as a second exit was opened up, the mass of travelers undergoing mitosis as one part of the crowd headed for the new exit. Sweat trickled down my back, dampening the tendrils of hair that had escaped my ponytail until they clung to my neck. I was starting to get light-headed from the heat, the pressure of so many bodies, and the lack of sleep during the twelve hours it had taken to get from Portland to Budapest. I had to get out of there.

"Come on. I think I see a break." I pushed Jim toward

the slight opening next to a couple of kids decked out in Goth gear who were sucking the tongues out of each other's head, jerking the suitcase behind me, apologizing under my breath as I jostled elbows, backs, and sides and squished forward. "Why I thought coming here was such a good idea is beyond me."

"Makes sense to me," Jim answered a bit distractedly as it smelled people, luggage, and the litter on the ground with the same unbiased interest. The crowd thinned dramatically as people scattered once they made it past the bottleneck of the exit. "You need training. Budapest is where it's happening. Hey, when are we going to eat?"

"I could have had a nice vacation in the Bahamas, but oh, no, I had to come—" My feet stopped moving. They simply stopped moving as my eyes bugged out of my head, my heart ceased beating, and my brain, usually a reliable and trustworthy organ, came to an abrupt and grinding halt. With no obstructing crowd remaining, the group of people standing just outside the floor-to-ceiling glass windows on the west side of the train station was perfectly visible to me.

Jim stopped and looked back at me, one furry black eyebrow cocked in question at my abbreviated statement. "You aren't using crude sexual slang, are you? No, you can't be, because I know for a fact you haven't been gettin' any since we left Paris."

Slowly, I blinked to make sure I wasn't seeing things, my stomach turning somersaults, my whole being riveted on the scene just outside the station.

Jim turned to see what held me in such thrall. "Wow. Talk about speaking of the great horned one. I must be psychic or something. What's *he* doing in Budapest?"

It hurt to breathe. It hurt to think. It just hurt, period. I felt like someone had used me as a punching bag for a few hours, every atom of my body pulled so tight I thought I was going to explode into a million little pieces.

Outside the window a small clutch of people stood before a long, glistening black limousine, evidently there to welcome the VIPs from the train. They consisted of three men and one woman—all Asian, all dressed in red and black. The men wore black slacks with open-necked shirts in different shades of red, while the woman looked as if she'd just stepped from the cover of Beijing *Vogue*. She was tall and willowy, had long, straight glossy black hair that reached to her waist, wore a black miniskirt and a red leather bustier, all carried off with an effortless grace that spoke of years spent in expensive Swiss finishing schools.

But it was one of the men greeting the VIPs who caught and held my attention. The wind rippled the dark forest green silk of his shirt so that it outlined the lovely curves of his muscular chest and arms. That same wind was responsible for his dark hair, longer than I had remembered it, ruffling back off a brow graced by two ebony slashes that were his eyebrows. Despite the heat of the August afternoon, he wore leather pants—*tight* leather pants—the garment glistening in the sun as if it had been painted on his long legs and adorable derrière as he made a courtly bow to the VIPs.

"Drake," I said on a breath, my body suddenly tingling as if it was coming to life after a long, long sleep. Even his name left my lips sensitized, the sound of that one word strange after its banishment from my life four weeks ago.

Four weeks? It seemed more like a lifetime.

Jim gave me a long, appraising look. "You're not going to go all Buffy/Angel on me, are you? Mooning around bemoaning the forbidden love that cannot be? Because if you are, I'm finding myself a new demon lord. Love I can take, but mooning is not in my contract."

I started toward the window, unable to help myself, my body suddenly a mass of erogenous zones that wanted more than anything on this earth to place itself in Drake's hands. His lovely long-fingered, extremely talented hands.

"Aisling Grey."

The sound of my name brought me out of the trance. I swallowed hard and looked around, my mind a muddle of desire and lust and erotic memories that damn near brought me to my knees. Names, as I have had opportunity to point out, have power, and Jim's invoking my name had the ability to snap me out of something I had spent every night praying for strength against.

"Thanks, Jim." Slowly I gathered my wits and determination, thankful that in the hustle and bustle of the train station no one had noticed a deranged, lust-crazed woman and her demon in talking-dog form. "I don't quite know what came over me."

It raised an expressive eyebrow. "*I* know."

I dragged my eyes from the sight of Drake and his men waving the VIPs toward the limo. I hauled my wheeled suitcase forward and out the doors, purposely turning my back to the scene that had held such interest, Jim pacing silently beside me. "I'm OK now. It was just a little aberration. I told you when we left Paris that things between Drake and me were over. It just took me by surprise seeing him here, in Budapest. I had assumed he'd still be in France." Safe. Several hundreds of miles away. In a completely different country, living out his life without me.

"Uh-huh. Right. Tell it to the tail, Aisling."

I ignored my smart-mouthed demon as we joined the end of a queue for taxis. The handful of people ahead of us laughed and chatted gaily, just as if their world hadn't come to a grinding halt, whereas mine . . . I glanced back at the limo. Drake was overseeing Pál, one of his men, loading the matched set of luggage in the back of the glossy car. Bustier Woman was speaking to one of her contingent, suddenly calling for Drake. I narrowed my eyes as he strolled toward her with the same fluid, coiled power that sent shivers of delight down my back.

Had. Once. Now, of course, it did nothing for me. Nothing at all.

I sighed. Jim stuck its snout in the bag of the elderly couple in front of us, saying softly, "That was a pretty pathetic sigh. It had a lot of meat to it."

"I know," I answered, trying not to grind my teeth as the woman put her hand on Drake's silk-clad arm, no doubt caressing his wonderful steely bicep. "It's really bad when you can't even lie convincingly to yourself."

Jim pulled its head from the bag to look at me, its eyes opening wide suddenly as it made an odd combination of a bark and a warning. "Behind you!"

I dropped its leash and spun around in a crouch, half expecting an attack of some sort, but finding instead that my suitcase had attracted the attention of three street gypsies, all of whom obviously had the intention of lightening the load of my possessions. "The amulet!" I screeched, throwing myself on top of the half-opened bag.

The biggest of the thieves, a young man who looked to be about nineteen, jerked the bag out from underneath me, his accomplices pulling on the outer flap so that it peeled back like a ripe banana. I lunged toward the small brown leather amulet bag that was stuffed into my underwear. "Hey! Let go! Police!" My fingers closed around the bag just as the youngest thief, a girl of about fifteen or so, grabbed it, but I had not survived my Uncle Damian's wrath concerning the loss of a valuable antiquity for nothing. I had to save this one at all costs. I jerked the amulet free just as someone behind me shouted. The street gypsies snatched up handfuls of my things—pants, shoes, and my cosmetic case—before racing off in three different directions.

The wind, coming off the nearby Danube, flirted with the opened suitcase, decided it liked the look of my newly purchased satin undies, and scooped up several pairs, sending them skittering down the sidewalk. The elderly couple who had been in front of us helped me gather the remaining clothes that had been knocked out as the gypsies made their snatch and grab, repeating soft assurances that I didn't understand. I left Jim to guard the luggage as I ran down the sidewalk, the amulet still in my hand. I plucked my underwear from a phone booth, a magazine stand, and a newspaper box. One last pair, trembling next to a garbage bin, suddenly spun upward in a gust and flew a few feet down the sidewalk, their flight coming to a swift end as the pink satin and lace material wrapped itself in a soft caress around a man's leg.

A man's leather-clad leg.

"Oh, god," I moaned, closing my eyes for a second, knowing exactly who owned that leg. Why me? Why did this sort of thing have to happen to me? Why couldn't anything in my life ever be simple? When I looked again, Drake was holding my panties in his hand, his head slowly turning as he scanned the crowd until he saw me clutching a handful of underwear.

Any thoughts of escaping undetected died in that moment. The woman who had been about to get into the limo paused and raised a beautifully arched eyebrow at him, her dark eyes sliding over me in cool consideration. She was perfect in every way—flawless complexion, hair glossy and straight, her assets displayed with a confidence I would never be able to match. Beside her, Drake stood in smoldering sensuality (his natural state), all hard lines and rugged planes and extremely droolworthy masculinity.

And then there was me, the third person in the tableau. I knew exactly what Drake and the woman were seeing—a hot, sweaty woman in her early thirties dressed in a loose T-shirt and worn jeans, hair coming loose from the scrunchie used in an attempt to tame wild curls, without so much as a single eyelash having seen the benefit of cosmetics.

It was no good. I couldn't compete. I was outclassed and I knew it, but I still had my dignity—what was left of it after my underwear was spread out along the front of the Keleti station ten minutes after my arrival. Raising my chin, I marched forward to Drake, firmly squelching the cheers of delight that several unmentionable parts of my body were sending up.

"I believe those are mine," I told him, holding out my hand for the underwear.

Heat flared deep in his emerald eyes, but I looked down at his hand, refusing to be drawn into that trap. I knew well the power of his desire.

"You have excellent taste in undergarments," he said, his voice a little rough around the edges as he placed the item in my hand. "Victoria's Secret?"

"No," I said, allowing my eyes to meet his for a moment. I swear a tiny little wisp of smoke curled out of one of his nostrils. "Naughty Nellie's House of Knickers. Portland, Oregon. Thank you. Good-bye."

He inclined his head as I spun around, ignoring the disdainful arched brows of the woman and marching back to where Jim sat next to my ravaged suitcase. The taxi rank was empty, the elderly couple evidently having snagged a taxi while I was retrieving my undies.

"Don't say it," I warned Jim as I squatted next to the suitcase, transferring to it my collected lingerie and the amulet. A taxi pulled up beside me as I double-checked the zipper, wondering what the street gypsies had done with the evidently useless lock I'd used to secure the bag. "Just don't say it, OK?"

"Me? I'm not saying anything."

I waited. I'd lived with Jim for a little over a month now. It was virtually impossible for the demon to let something as mortifyingly embarrassing as having my underwear scattered on my former lover go without comment.

"But if I was going to say something, it would be something along the lines of 'Smooth move, Ex-Lax!'"

The limo passed us with a gentle, expensive purr of its

engine, the tinted windows thankfully keeping the sight of Drake's no doubt politely amused face from my view.

I didn't have to see him to know he was looking at me, though. I could feel it. There was just something about being the object of a dragon's regard that left the hair on the back of my neck standing on end.

2

"No talking in the taxi," I reminded Jim in an undertone as I pulled a Hungarian phrase book out of my bag's side pocket, riffling through the book until I came to the section on transportation. I leaned down next to the open taxi window to tell the driver where I wanted to go. "Let's see . . . Where is the post office, please. Where is the bus station, please. Where is an Internet café, please. Oh, for heaven's sake, you'd think it would have a simple 'Please take me to the blah-blah hotel,' but no, that would be just way too convenient."

"I do not know of a Hotel Blah-Blah, but perhaps it is new?" the taxi driver asked in accented English. *French*-accented English.

Both my book and my jaw dropped as I peered into the recesses of the cab. The driver was a dark-haired man of middling age with a friendly smile that delighted me down to my toenails. "Rene! What—you're—but this is—you were in Paris—"

"You da man," Jim drawled, shoving me out of the way so it could put its paws on the door and stick its nose into the taxi, giving Rene a couple of good swipes with its tongue. "Thank god you're here. She's falling to pieces, and we've only been in the country a couple of hours."

"Jim! It is a pleasure to see you again. Thank you for the postcard from the Oregon coast. I didn't know you could write."

Jim shot me a nasty look. "I can't, not after one of my toes went missing. I dictated and Aisling wrote for me."

I shook my head in an attempt to clear it as Rene leaned out through the window to reach back and open the door of the taxi. "This doesn't make sense. You're a Paris taxi driver. This is Budapest. The two aren't even remotely close. Something here does not compute."

Jim leaped into the car. I stood on the sidewalk clutching my luggage, the phrase book fluttering at my feet. Rene grinned, got out of the taxi, and gently pried my fingers off the handle of the suitcase before taking it to the trunk. "My cousin Bela, he is a taxi driver most discreet here in Budapest. But his stone of kidneys erupted, causing him much pain, so he is unable to drive for the next two weeks. I am here to fill in for him."

"Fill in?" I asked, grabbing my phrase book and allowing him to shoo me into the car. Jim had its head out the far window, great big ropes of drool thankfully dribbling outside rather than down its chest, as they usually did. "Wait a minute. Didn't you say that you and your family take a vacation during the month of August? Why are you spending your vacation time working?"

Rene grinned at me as he slid into the driver's seat, carefully buckling the seat belt. I hurried to do the same. I'd ridden with Rene and knew that there was nothing he loved more than driving through cities in a manner that left passengers flung around the interior of the car if they weren't strapped in. "*Hein,* my wife and the little ones are in Normandy. It is hot there, Aisling, very hot. And the children, they will have sand rashes and sunburns and stomachs upset from too much ice cream and candy, and my wife will be without her wits trying to control them. Me, I prefer Budapest and tourists to that horror."

I slumped back against the hot faux-leather upholstery as Rene eased us into the busy traffic. "Well, I'm profoundly grateful that you're here. I've had a hell of a day."

"Ahem," Jim said, pulling its head in the window to give me a glare.

"Sorry. Heck of a day. First there were thieves trying to steal the item I'm couriering, and then   "

"Drake's in Budapest," Jim told Rene before sticking its head back out the window. "She had a meltdown seeing him with another babe."

I pinched the thick fur of Jim's haunch as Rene sucked in his breath. "Drake? The wyvern of the green dragons?"

"One and the same, and I did *not* have a meltdown." I gnawed my lower lip for a couple of seconds, absently admiring the lovely architecture in the row of historic white stone buildings we were passing. "You don't happen to know why he's here, do you, Rene? It's kind of an odd twist of fate that he, you, and Jim and I are all here at the same time."

Rene's eyes met mine for a moment in his rearview mirror. He gave one of his effortless but expressive French shrugs. "You never know with fate, *hein*? Perhaps it is trying to tell you something. For you and your mate to be in the same city after you left him most cruelly—"

"He's not my mate. I'm his," I said sourly, watching the

city slide past us. This was only my second time abroad, and part of me was utterly thrilled at being in such a beautiful city. We passed historic buildings, small leafy green squares surrounded by the ubiquitous black wrought-iron fences, streets filled with stores and shoppers, a couple of pedestrian arcades, and more churches than you could shake a stick at. It was all lovely, and I made a mental note to try to squeeze into my busy schedule a little time to see the sights. "And I didn't leave Drake cruelly. I explained to him why being a wyvern's mate didn't fit in with my plans. Just for the record, he didn't even try to stop me. Nor did he call me and beg me to come back to him. Not that I wanted to, but just in case you were wondering, he didn't. So fate can just go take a flying leap where that whole issue is concerned."

Rene's brown eyes flashed in the mirror again.

"He didn't even e-mail me," I groused, feeling ashamed even as the words left my lips. I had had four long weeks to come to grips with the fact that life evidently had ideas for me that I wasn't ready to accept, one of which was that I'd been born the mate of a wyvern, the head of one of the four dragon septs. The other was a talent I was more willing to allow into my life—assuming I could find someone to mentor me in learning Guardian skills.

"You want a little cheese with that whine?" Jim pulled its head in long enough to ask.

"Rene is a friend. I'm allowed to complain a little to a friend. You are a furry demon. Put your head back out the window and don't get any bugs up your nose because I don't have the money or time to take you to the vet."

"See what I mean?" Jim asked Rene. "Meltdown."

"What hotel am I taking you to?" Rene asked quickly. He'd been around Jim, too. He knew just how much the demon dog could get on my nerves.

"The Thermal Hotel Danu. It's on Margaret Island. It's supposed to be a big conference hotel with all sorts of bennies."

"Bennies?"

"Benefits. Services. Amenities. You know, stuff like world-class masseuses, parkland surrounding the hotel with walking and jogging paths, saunas, thermal baths, and something the hotel brochure called an amusement bath. I can't wait to see what that is."

"Ah. I know the Hotel Danu. It is very expensive, very chic." One of Rene's eyebrows rose as his reflection looked at me. I yelped and pointed out the front window. The taxi swerved to avoid colliding with another car, throwing Jim onto my lap before the vehicle settled down. "It is not like you to stay in such a place, yes?"

Only Rene could take a near head-on collision with such bland disregard. I twitched with the effect of the adrenaline pumping into my body at the close call, taking deep breaths to calm my pounding heart. "No, it's not like me, but yes, I'm staying there. I'm here for a conference that's being held at the hotel, and they had special rates. It's taken most of my savings to pay for the conference, but I figured it's worth it. When I found out the conference was going to be held in the same city where I'm supposed to deliver the amulet, I decided it was too good an opportunity to miss."

"You see?" Rene nodded. "You listen to fate. That is good. I did not realize that you knew goddamn."

I mentally shook my head. I couldn't possibly have heard him correctly. "I beg your pardon?"

"Goddamn. The conference. You are here for the conference of Guardians, Oracles, Diviners—"

"—Theurgists, and Mages," I finished with him, wondering how he knew about the conference. Like me, Rene had been a newcomer to the Otherworld, becoming involved with it via my attempts to extricate myself from a nasty murder rap. "Yes, that's it. GODTAM. Gotcha. How did *you* hear about it?"

"I am not so sheltered as you think," he answered with a great air of mystery. "It is good that you are listening to your heart about being a Guardian. It is what you are meant to be, yes? But you mentioned an object? You are still the courier most faithful for your uncle?"

"Yeah. Something has to pay the bills—not to mention my ex's alimony. Uncle Damian is giving me another chance to prove that I can transport a priceless object without having it stolen by a certain green-eyed dragon in hunk form. It doesn't have any gold on it, so it should be safe enough from him. How familiar are you with Budapest? The guy I'm supposed to deliver the amulet to is a hermit. He doesn't have any fixed address, but supposedly he hangs around the city parks."

"A hermit?" Rene shook his head, then leaned on the horn when a bicycle courier dashed out in front of him. "I do not know about a hermit, but there are many parks in Budapest. Margaret Island is itself a park botanical. Jim will enjoy the Rose Garden, I think."

"Jim has no trouble finding enjoyment wherever it goes. I'm not worried about Jim. I'm worried about how Uncle Damian expects me to find a hermit whose whereabouts no one knows. All I have to go on is an address at which the hermit is supposed to pick up mail, but who knows if it's still valid?"

"Do not worry. I am here. We did most well in Paris, yes? We will conquer this hermit, too."

I smiled at Rene's reflection. "Yeah, we did work together well, didn't we? I'm very grateful you're here. Are you taking private passengers? I managed to talk my uncle into giving me a tiny little expense account for travel and such. I'm going to need someone to drive me around to all the parks in the area."

"Because walking would be, like, so healthy," Jim said, glancing toward me for a minute.

"I get enough exercise taking you out for the gazillion walkies you seem to feel necessary each day," I pointed out. "Besides, unlike some four-legged demons I could mention, Rene is smart, insightful, and most importantly, willing to help. I'd welcome any assistance he wants to offer in finding the hermit."

Jim made a sour face. "Look, you knew when you summoned me that I'd been kicked out of Abaddon and didn't have any powers. Don't come whining to me about how I can't tap into the dark powers to do your bidding."

I opened my mouth to protest that I'd not known any such thing but bit back the words. Bickering with Jim always left me frustrated and resentful, two things I had hoped to banish from my life when I closed the relationship door on Drake.

Drake. Dammit, why did he have to reappear in my life, just when I was trying to get a good solid grip on it?

"Here is the Thermal Hotel Danu," Rene said, interrupting my murky thoughts. The taxi swept around a grand curved drive to pull up in front of an astonishingly modern hotel. After the drive through the historic area of town, I was surprised to find this hotel looking more like an office building in Portland. It was white stone (no surprise there—many of the buildings in Budapest seemed to be made of white stone) and glass, layered into stripes that rose at least twelve stories high, but it was surrounded by the most gorgeous gardens I had ever seen. I followed Jim as the demon leaped out of the taxi, and stood looking out across a narrow parking lot to a long expanse of lush green lawn and flower beds brilliant with reds, yellows, deep blues, and at least a hundred shades of green.

"Wow! I could get used to this!"

"Gotta pee!" Jim said as it shambled toward a nearby shrub.

"Not on any flowers," I yelled after it, then turned to grab my luggage. "Oh, god, Rene, I'm sorry about the taxi. Are there any car washes nearby?"

Rene came around the taxi and stared in surprise at the long ropes of partially dried Newfie drool that were plastered along the side of the car and the window.

"I should have realized when I didn't have to mop Jim up on the ride here where all that slobber was going. How much will it cost to have that cleaned off?"

"Eh . . . it is of no account."

"You sure?" Due to the pileup of conference-goers and tourists arriving before us, Rene had pulled in about sixty feet down the long reception area. We walked around the back of the taxi to the sidewalk, Rene pausing long enough to grab my suitcase from the trunk. I headed for the hotel lobby, stopping when I saw that sitting smack-dab in front of the hotel was a long black limousine. "Crap!"

Rene looked over to where Jim was circling a laurel bush. "No, he is just making much peepee."

"No, not Jim. That." I pointed to the limo. "It would just be my luck that Drake and his bit o' hussy chose this hotel to stay at. I wonder if I can get a room anywhere else?"

"Are you so afraid of the dragon, then?" Rene asked, his head tipped to the side as he considered me. I smoothed down my T-shirt with a self-conscious gesture.

"Afraid? No. Terrified is more like it—terrified that he's going to seduce me again and I won't have the willpower to refuse. How much do I owe you? Dog slobber cleanup included?"

"Thirteen euros. I will help you with your luggage."

Suspicious, I glanced at Rene's face, but there was nothing but polite interest displayed. "You've never offered to carry my bag before. You just want to see if Drake's hanging around the lobby, don't you? You want to see if I'm going to make a fool of myself over him again, don't you? It's not bad enough that my underwear attacked the man in front of half of Budapest. Oh, no. Now you're secretly hoping for an encore. You ought to be ashamed of yourself, Rene! You're as bad as Jim!"

He grinned and took my arm, gently pushing me down the sidewalk toward the hotel's entrance. "I do not understand what you say about your underwear attacking Drake, but I will admit that to me it is most curious that you and he fight your mutual attraction. Despite this, I have no wish to see you make a fool of yourself."

Mollified, I allowed him to escort me to the entrance, pausing long enough for Jim to catch up to us.

"Behave," I warned it, grabbing its leash and giving it a look to let it know I meant business. "And yes, that's an order."

The demon rolled its eyes. "The hotel is full of denizens of the Otherworld and you're worried about something as mundane as a demon?"

"Shh! You know as well as I do that citizens of the Otherworld do not like to stand out and be noticeable. Besides, there are other people staying here. Sane ones who don't need a Demon 101 course. You will remember at all times that this is a nice, normal hotel, with nice, normal"—

A woman with a long blond braid wheeled a crate past us stamped LIVE IMPS: HANDLE WITH CAUTION.

—"people," I sighed.

Rene snickered.

The lobby of the Thermal Hotel Danu was done in shades of peach, rust, and cream, a combination that sounds ghastly but that was pulled off here with an elegance that left me wishing I had changed into something a bit more sophisticated before we entered. Rene whistled in admiration as he followed us. I started across the huge lobby, admiring the ambiance and praying that Jim behaved itself when we were in public. We had gotten off to a bad start, but with luck nothing else embarrassing would strike me in public.

A short blond man with a fuzzy upper lip strolled by as I was passing a clutch of peach-colored chairs grouped in a conversation nook, pausing just long enough to send me a bland look before he continued past. "You will trip and fall."

"Huh?" I asked, peering backward at the man as he headed out the front door. "Rene, did you hear that man? He said I would—"

Jim stopped suddenly in front of me. I tripped. I fell. With a loud squawk that seemed to echo to every corner of the elegant lobby.

"My back! My liver! My spleen! You've killed me!" Jim wailed from where it lay beneath me.

"You're a demon. You can't be killed. And shut up! Someone will hear you," I hissed, mortified to the tips of my toes as I tried to gather my sprawled limbs. People all over the lobby stopped chatting, mingling, sipping cool drinks, checking in, and doing all the various other things people did in fancy hotel lobbies, and turned en masse to look at where Jim and I lay in a tangled heap.

A hand came into view, offering assistance. I grabbed it, allowing Rene to help me to my feet.

As I stood, I realized the hand didn't belong to Rene.

Jim looked up at the hand. "Drake, would you tell my demon lord that while it's true I can't be killed, this extremely handsome form can be damaged, and she's probably broken every rib in my body? Man, someone needs to drop a few pounds, and I can tell you one thing—it ain't me!"

3

I gritted my teeth both at the sight of Drake's amused green eyes and at Jim's demon lord reference. I hated when it called me that. Technically the title was true, because Jim had been cast out of its previous lord's legions when I summoned it (thus binding the demon to me until I could figure out how to release it), but I resented being called a demon lord. Everyone knew demon lords were pure evil.

Whereas I was merely clumsy. Or cursed. Or probably both.

"Mate, your demon wishes me to inform you—"

I raised my hand to stop Drake. "Point one, I'm not your mate. Point two . . . er . . . OK, there is no point two. So, thank you for helping me up, oh stranger who parades around with gorgeous women who evidently shop at the Madonna Pointy Breast Bustier Boutique. Now you may be on your merry little way and leave us mortals to go about our lives without the addition of an annoying, fire-breathing lizard in a human suit."

Drake leaned forward, his eyes going dark with emotion. "You have never seen me breathe fire, mate. You might enjoy it."

Heat swept through me at his words, a familiar heat that flared into the inferno that was his dragon's fire. I fought it for a few seconds, knowing that if I didn't accept it, it would consume me where I stood, leaving nothing but a few charred ashes to mark what I had been. Smoke began to rise from my hair as Drake's fire flashed through me, setting every cell in my body alight. My mind screamed a warning that I was seconds away from total combustion and death, Drake's glittering eyes holding mine as I fought his heat, fought the connection we had, fought the fact that despite my wishes to the contrary I was one of the rare people who were able to withstand the test of a true wyvern's mate. With a growl of futility against the inevitable, I opened the door in my mind that allowed me access to newly discovered powers, embracing the dragon flame as it consumed and renewed me, a fiery rebirth that I reveled in for a few seconds before turning it back on Drake.

I wanted to say something witty and caustic to prove to Drake that nothing he did or said mattered to me, but all I did was pant a little at the effect of channeling so much of his heat. Triumph glowed in his eyes for a moment before he banked his fire. Without another word to me, he turned and strolled back to where the VIP and her gang of three were waiting impatiently.

"I am *so* over my head with him," I moaned softly to myself, unable to keep from watching Drake's derrière as he walked away. Say what you will about dragons (and I had a number of things I wanted to say), they really knew how to move when they chose to appear in human form.

"Yes, yes, you are. Don't you think she is, Rene?"

"Very much, yes. He looks at her, she looks at him, and foof! Sparks, they fly. Look, her hair is still on fire."

I stopped ogling Drake and slapped a few errant curls that were smoldering with the aftereffects of my run-in with dragon boy. "All right, enough of the wiseass comments. The show's over. It was just a little fire exchange, nothing more. Nothing to get excited over. Now perhaps I can get on with things. Important things. Like life without you-know-who."

Pál and István, two redheaded men who were part of Drake's sept (and served as his bodyguards), stood watching impassively as Drake returned to the Asian woman's side. Pál lifted his hand toward me in friendly greeting. István glowered, first at me, then at Jim.

"Looks like István hasn't forgiven you for almost neutering him," Jim commented.

"That was an accident and you know it. Besides, I've sworn never to play darts again, so he has nothing to be surly about." I gritted out a smile at both men, gave Pál a little wave in return, and ignoring the stares and whispered comments from everyone in the lobby, made my way to the front desk.

"Here is my cousin Bela's mobile number." When I was finished checking in, Rene pressed into my hand a postcard with a phone number scrawled across the back. "You will call me when you are ready to find the hermit, yes? I do not like to think of what trouble will find you if you were to go off on your own. Did you learn any language for this trip?"

"Language? Oh, Hungarian. Yeah. There was this guy I ran into in a chat room when I was online looking up information on the hotel, and he gave me a couple of phrases to say. Let's see . . . uh . . . *szeretnelek latni ruha nelkul*."

Rene's eyes widened as he choked. "What . . . eh . . . what is it you think you just said?"

I frowned. "What do you mean what do I *think* I said? I said, 'It's a lovely day out.'"

He shook his head. Jim snickered.

I thinned my lips at them both. "Well, I'm sorry, my pronunciation is probably a little off. I'm new to this learning foreign languages thing, as you both very well know. What did I say wrong?"

Jim licked its leg with strange absorption. A faint smile tugged at the corners of Rene's lips. "This once, your pronunciation was good. Not excellent, as is mine, but good enough to be understood."

"Oh," I said, pleased by his praise. Rene had tried to teach me some useful French a month ago (useful if you want to say things like "I have frogs in my bidet") and previously had only scathing things to say about my pronunciation. Clearly French was not going to be my forte, but Hungarian was obviously another thing altogether. Maybe I'd turn out to be a linguist after all. "So what was wrong with what I said?"

He stopped fighting the smile as Jim put a paw over its eyes and groaned. "To me, you say, 'I would like to see you naked.'"

"No!" I gasped, mentally damning the man in the chat room. "That poop! And I went to the trouble of learning all the stuff he gave me. Dammit!"

Rene shook his head as he laughed, giving my hand a sympathetic squeeze. "You will be sure to call me? I do not want to think of you walking around Budapest telling people you like to see them naked. You call if you need a driver. Or if you need help with others. You remember I am much good behind your back."

I gave him a hug. "Yes, thank you, you are wonderful at watching my back, and I very much appreciate all your help. It's getting too late today to find the hermit, but what say we make an appointment for tomorrow?"

We agreed upon a time, and with a final grin, Rene toddled off, his hands in his pockets as he whistled a jaunty tune, looking utterly normal in a world that I was fast realizing was anything but.

"Come on, you hairy hound from"—Jim raised an eyebrow at me—"Abaddon. Let's go get ourselves spiffed up, and we'll see what's going on with all the Diviners and Theurgists and Guardians."

"You do that really well," Jim said as I dragged the suitcase over to an elevator, checking the plastic key card for the room number.

"Do what? Twelve-fifteen. Drat. I hate rooms above the third floor."

"Ignore the fact that the second you saw Drake, you stood *en pointe* faster than an Irish setter spotting a pheasant."

I glared at it. "I am not a dog, and I resent you comparing me to one. You're the one with the dog fetish, not me. I'll thank you to remember that I'm perfectly happy being a human."

"No, you're not a dog, but you *are* changing the subject."

"So observant, my little demon." I patted Jim on the head as the elevator doors closed.

"Do you really think you can just ignore him? It didn't

work when you were on the other side of the world, Aisling. Now you two are in the same city—the same hotel. And the second you see him you're all but drooling on the man."

"Demon, I order thee to keep thy trap zipped until I tell thee otherwise."

Jim glared at me, unable to violate a direct order. I hated having to resort to such harsh measures, but I was having a hard enough time getting my brain to stop running around like a deranged Chihuahua to tolerate Jim poking at something I just couldn't deal with at the moment.

"I am a professional," I told the empty hallway as I dragged my suitcase down the long, opulent passage, Jim walking silently behind me. "I have seen the worst and triumphed over it. I can do this."

I didn't release Jim from its bondage of silence until I had taken a fast shower, changed into a gauze peasant skirt and matching blouse that I thought looked exotically pretty, wrapped a colorful scarf around my hair in an attempt to look totally and completely different from the crazed woman who had fallen in the lobby, and gathered my new organizer.

"You're to be on your best behavior," I warned Jim on the ride down to the conference level of the hotel. "No peeing on anything unless I say you can. No gender checks by sniffing anyone's pertinent body parts. No wisecracks about me in relation to men named Drake. You got all that?"

Jim's lips curled, but its great black furry head gave a curt nod of agreement.

"Good. You may speak now."

"I hate it when you do that," it burst out, eyes bulging a little with the strain of having kept its comments to itself. "Not even Amayon used to make us be silent!"

"Don't tell tales about your former demon master. Ah, I think this is where we're supposed to be." We exited the elevator to walk through a busy reception area. Over a wall of doors a huge banner hung, reading (in French, English, and what I assumed was Hungarian) 238TH INTERNATIONAL CONFERENCE OF GODTAM. Although the conference wasn't due to start for another hour—with the official kickoff banquet—there were a number of people in business attire milling around, some sitting on the scattered benches and chairs, others in small clutches talking quietly with one another. A latte stand in the corner of the room did brisk business. "Wow. Our first conference. Maybe I should have worn my brown suit? Do I look dressy enough to you? This is kind of exciting, huh?"

"Yes, no, yes, and it would be downright thrilling if you were to feed me," Jim answered, watching an attractive couple wander past bearing paper latte cups and elaborate pastries bristling with almonds.

"The dinner will start in an hour or so. You will kindly remember that I had to pay for you to attend the meal and not embarrass me by demanding horsemeat or something ghastly like that."

"You sure know how to take the fun out of life," Jim snorted as we joined a short line before a skirted table manned by several individuals all wearing badges with a nine-pointed symbol.

Although I knew from experience that most of the citizens of the Otherworld looked perfectly normal—the dragons' slightly elongated pupils being the only physical sign that they weren't human—I still half expected to see something out of the ordinary, some indication that we had stepped out of the real world and into something cloaked in mystery and magic.

"Name?"

I pulled my mind from its wanderings to attend to the registration woman. "Aisling Grey."

"Ashling?"

"That's right." I spelled my name for her. "It's Irish."

"Denomination?"

"Huh? Well, my mother is Catholic, but my father was Presbyterian. I'm kind of neither."

The woman gave me an annoyed look. "Are you a Diviner, Theurgist, Guardian, Oracle, or Mage?"

"Oh, *that* sort of denomination. Guardian. Kind of. Really more like Guardian lite."

"Less filling, half the fat," Jim quipped.

The woman ignored both of us as she pulled a box of envelopes toward her.

"And there should also be a registration for my . . . um . . . demon. Its name is Effrijim."

Jim nosed the box. "I hope it just says 'Jim' on the name tag. I don't want anyone to think I'm a sissy."

"A demon?" She gave Jim a cold look before flicking through the thick envelopes, finally extracting two. She handed me clip-on name badges for both of us, as well as a thick packet of material. I clipped my badge to a ruffle on my peasant blouse, then attached Jim's to its collar. "Demons are expected to be kept under control at all times and are not to be left unattended. If you do leave your demon without supervision, it will be trapped in limbo and returned to its demon lord at your expense. The main convention hall and ballroom have been warded and spelled so that you cannot conduct dark magic within their confines. The meeting rooms are unprotected, however. Do you understand and accept these terms?"

Jim started to tell the woman that *I* was its demon lord, but I interrupted it before it could blather that news to everyone. "Sure. No problem. I'm not really hip with dark magic. I'm just here to find a Guardian mentor."

The woman tapped a few keys on the laptop computer sitting next to the registration materials, and a printer at the end of the table hummed to life. She pulled a piece of what looked like parchment from it, sliding it toward me along with an old-fashioned nib pen.

"Kind of an odd mixture of high-tech and quasi-medieval, huh?" I commented, waving at the printed parchment with the pen.

She just looked pointedly at the paper.

In the upper corner of the sheet was my name, written in a beautiful, ornate calligraphic font. In the center was drawn the same elaborate nine-pointed star that the conference workers wore. I looked closer at the pen and realized that it wasn't a pen at all. It was a lance, the sort diabetics use to get a drop of blood for testing. "Uh—"

"You must seal the agreement in blood," the woman said in an annoyed, put-upon voice. "Failure to do so will result in ejection from the conference."

"Heaven forbid," I murmured as I jabbed my thumb with the lance. "Where do you want it?"

"In the nonagram." I blinked. She sighed. "A nonagram is a nine-pointed star. It is the symbol of studied achievement, which is part of the motto of the GOD-TAM."

Without further ado I pressed the bead of blood into the center of the star. The parchment must have had some magic worked on it, because the second my blood touched it, I was overtaken by the sensation of silken cords wrapping around and around me.

"What—was that—?" I rubbed my arms. Despite the fact that I could see there was nothing on me other than my clothing, the feeling of the bonds remained.

"You are now bound by the covenant of the GOD-TAM," the registration woman intoned in a bored voice. "Welcome to the conference, and blessed be. Next!"

"Oh. Does my demon need to be bound as well?"

"Demons cannot be bound in such a manner. You are responsible for its behavior. NEXT!"

Jim and I passed through the doors into the main conference area, following a group of men in expensive, well-tailored suits.

"Mages," Jim said in an undertone, its eyes on the men.

"Really? How can you tell?"

"Their shoes. Mages go in for Italian footwear. So do dragons, but those guys don't smell like dragons."

I slid a curious glance down to Jim, walking at my side. "Just what exactly do dragons smell like?"

It lifted a furry black lip in a sneer. "You ought to know, you've spent enough time with your nose buried in Drake's—"

"Jim!" I shrieked.

"—neck."

I pinched the thick skin on its back. "Just forget I asked, OK? Shall we mingle?"

"Oh, yeah. Are those hors d'oeuvres for everyone? I'm gonna get me some before I starve to death." Jim shimmied toward a waiter wandering through the gathering crowd offering a tray of tall champagne flutes and another with tiny canapés.

"Save room for dinner!" I called after the demon, then stood looking around at everyone in their suits and chic outfits, feeling very out of place, very bumpkin visiting polished town cousins.

"Hullo. You're a Guardian, too? Is this your first time?"

I turned at the friendly singsong voice. A tall blond woman wearing a slinky black dress smiled at me. She looked like a Barbie doll come to life, a Scandinavian Barbie doll, if her accent was anything to go by. "Yes, to both questions, although the first one is kind of iffy. I'm Aisling. I'm actually here looking for a mentor."

"Really?" She eyed me from crown to toes, walking a circle around me to get a better look. I wished I had put on my brown power suit. It might not be a sexy little black dress, but at least I looked professional in it. "I have been thinking it time to take on an apprentice. We might suit. I am Moa. I am from Berge, Sweden. You have completed the ritual?"

"Ritual?" I bit my lip. "I've done a couple of rituals. I summoned a demon, and later I almost summoned a demon lord—"

"No." She waved away my paranormal résumé with an elegant scarlet-tipped hand. "The ritual. The test that

all apprentices must pass in order to begin formal training. You have *not* passed it?"

Oh, great. There was a test I had to pass just to sign up
to be an apprentice? Why did no one ever tell me these
things? "No, I haven't passed it. I didn't know anything
about it until you mentioned it. Is it difficult? How long
will it take? I don't have a lot of time to spend studying.
Is there a cheat sheet I can buy somewhere?"

Her lips pursed as she pulled out a thin gold notebook,
flipping through the pages until she came to one she
liked. "I have time tomorrow after the panel on troll re-
habilitation but before the demon-tormenting workshop.
Shall we make an appointment to meet then? I will discuss with you the ritual and my requirements in an apprentice."

"Great," I said, watching as she extracted a gold pen
from the notebook and made a note. "Maybe we can sit
together at the demon-tormenting thing."

She gave me a blinding smile. "Yes, it is always nice
to have an acquaintance at torture workshops. Be sure to
bring a plastic raincoat. Until tomorrow, Aisling."

"Thanks. I look forward to it."

She headed off toward the Mages in expensive suits,
leaving me standing by myself, feeling even more at sea
than I had in the last month.

But at least I had an appointment with a potential mentor! At last things were looking up.

4

By the time the evening was over, I'd been stabbed, propositioned more times than I could count, and had my amulet stolen.

And that was before the real action started.

"Hello, I am Tiffany. You're a Guardian, aren't you? Here is my card. I am a professional virgin. You will please let me know if you have any need of my services." The pretty blond woman who sat next to me at the large round table smiled an aggressive smile full of teeth and passed business cards out to everyone at the table, laying one in front of Jim's plate. "Is that your demon? How large it is! I knew a Guardian once who had a pet demon, but it killed her one night when she was cooking a lobster. The demon tossed her into the pot of boiling water. It was very sad. I wept pearly tears of sorrow."

I stared at her for a moment before turning my gaze to my other side, where Jim sat, and gave the demon a good glare.

Its eyebrows rose. "Hey, don't look at me, I don't even *like* lobster."

"Who is new? This is my fifth GODTAM conference," Tiffany chirped happily, giving us all another blast of her toothpaste-commercial-white smile. "Oooh, fruit cups! I love the fruit cups. Fruit is the flower of our souls, don't you think?"

There were eight of us at the round table, one of about two hundred tables that filled the huge conference ballroom. We were sitting along the left edge of the room, near enough to the podium that we could see the speakers but out of the main crush in the center of the room.

"I am Monish Lakshmanan, and this is Tej, my apprentice. I am a part-time oracle." The speaker was a small, dark-haired man with lovely large brown eyes. He spoke English with great precision, biting off each word as if he was afraid it was going to escape from him. Next to him was a friendly-looking young man of about eighteen, dressed in a faded T-shirt and a sports jacket that was probably two sizes too small for him. He smiled at us all as his mentor continued, "We are from Bangalore. That is in India."

"Oracles! Part-time ones at that!" A woman on the other side of Jim, with big moussed 1980s hair, snorted in an Ozarky twang, digging her elbow into the rabbity man next to her. "Honey, you haven't seen an oracle till you meet my Hank. That's Hank O'Hallahan. You've heard of him, of course. We were on *Jerry Springer*. Show 'em what you can do, Hank."

Hank, wearing a slightly hunted look, sat up straight as everyone at the table looked at him. One hand automatically tugged at his tie until it was a bit askew. "Oh. Uh. Here? You think here, Marvabelle? Is that a . . . uh . . . good idea? Someone might overhear. There are those book people who are interested in my thoughts, you remember."

A suspicious look stole over his wife's face as she narrowed her eyes at the rest of us. "You're right, muffin. You shouldn't show them your stuff, not right out here where anyone could steal your wonderful deep oracle thoughts and sell them to publishers. You just never know about people."

Silence descended at our table with a thud. I stared at the atrocious Marvabelle, surprised and outraged on behalf of everyone she'd just insulted. Before I could inform her that I doubted anyone would be interested in stealing Hank's oracular thoughts, the eighth person at the table, a middle-aged black woman with bright red glasses and a dramatic white streak down the middle of her ebony hair, spoke. "Hullo. My name is Nora Charles—no relationship to the fictional character, I assure you—and I live in London. I'm a Guardian, and this is my fifth conference. I have a dog as well," she added, smiling at Jim. "His name is Paco. He's a Chihuahua, but he's not a demon."

"I see you're still blind as a bat," Marvabelle said, making a grimace that no doubt passed as her version of a smile. "Just jokin', honey. You know me."

"Yes," Nora said in a very neutral tone of voice that spoke volumes.

"You know each other?" I couldn't help but ask, glancing from the rather garishly made-up Marvabelle to the quiet Nora.

"I was a Guardian, too, years and years ago, when I was young and foolish," Marvabelle said, cutting across Nora's response. "Nora and I studied under the same mentor for a year. But I gave it up when I married Hank.

Oracles are just so much more important than Guardians, you know."

"And you?" Monish looked at Jim and me, thankfully ending the embarrassed silence that had followed Marvabelle's verbal slap in the face.

I tried my best to look poised and not at all like the sort of woman who falls down in hotel lobbies. "Oh. Hi, everyone, it's a pleasure to meet you all. I'm Aisling, and this is Jim, my demon. This is our first conference, and as you might have guessed, I'm a Guardian. Kind of. Not quite, but I hope to be. I think. It depends on whether I find a mentor or not."

Five sets of eyes opened wide, then hurriedly looked away from me. The sixth, Nora's, watched me with a faint frown wrinkling her brow. "You are not yet a fully trained Guardian?" Her eyes slid over to Jim. "But you have a demon."

"Yeah, but Jim is kind of a mistake."

The demon sniffled in mock sadness. "You mean that you and Daddy didn't plan to have me? Oh, the pain! Oh, the heartache!"

I pinched its paw. "When I say mistake, I mean—" My hands waved around in an inarticulate sort of manner. The rest of the table watched me with silent avidity, waiting expectantly. I gave up trying to come up with a lucid explanation of just how I'd come to summon Jim. There was no way I could explain without taking up the rest of the evening. "Well, I guess *mistake* is as good a word as any. No, I'm not a trained Guardian. I'm here hoping to find someone who'll be willing to teach me all the ins and outs of the job. I don't suppose you're looking for an apprentice?"

"As it happens, I am," she said, her gaze dropping to the bowl of chilled fruit that a waiter had set before her.

"Ah." She looked less than thrilled with the idea of me. Then again, she might just be shy. "Perhaps we can talk later?"

The waiter placed a bowl on Jim's plate, then slid one in front of me. Nora murmured something about setting up an appointment.

I heaved a mental sigh over her lack of enthusiasm and shook out a napkin to tuck into Jim's collar.

"I believe we can start. Everyone else is eating," Tiffany said, flicking a long blond corkscrew curl over her shoulder, suddenly freezing into a pose with pouting lips and arched neck. I was just about to ask her if she was all right when a flash went off behind me.

A photographer skulked over to another table.

"That was Shy Eyes," Tiffany said to me, her soft European accent giving an odd but pleasing lilt to the words.

"I beg your pardon?"

"Shy Eyes. It is one of my fabulous looks. I have many of them. In addition to being a professional virgin, I am a model very much successful. I do it because being a professional virgin doesn't take up much of my time, and you know, the world would be much happier if everyone used their time to smile. I like to share my smile with people everywhere. It is a duty when you are as beautiful as me, do you not think?"

"Uh . . . sure." I picked up my spoon, stirring the fruit and wondering why weird people always seemed to sit next to me. Then again, I was the one with a demonic Newfie. . . . Oh, lord, *I* had become one of the weird people!

On the far side of the table, a man passed behind Monish and Tej on his way to his own table, pausing to look me in the eye and say, "You will spill fruit juice on your breasts."

The spoonful of chopped fruit and fizzy citrusy dressing that I was in the process of piloting to my mouth splattered down my front.

"What the—dammit!" I swore, throwing down the spoon and grabbing the thick linen napkin to mop up the big wet globules of fruit that plastered the thin gauze of my peasant blouse to my left breast. "Who the *hell* is that man, and why is he doing this to me?"

"Oh, tsk," Tiffany said, making a sad little face as I dipped one corner of my now sticky napkin into my water glass. She actually said the word *tsk*. "Maybe your demon could lick it off for you?"

"Yeah," Jim said with a leer on its canine lips. "It seems such a shame to waste good soul flowers like that."

"You move your tongue one inch toward my breasts, and I swear I'll get a grapefruit knife and saw off your—"

"Sheesh, I was just offering to be helpful. Some people!" Jim turned its attention back to its own fruit cup, one massive black paw holding down the flared bottom of the sorbet dish.

"That gentleman is Paolo di Stephano," Monish said. "He is a Diviner most extraordinary. He also works with me for the committee."

"Ha! Diviner. Or so he *claims*," Marvabelle added with a sniff, patting her husband's hand. "Hank could be a Diviner if he wanted. But I told him no, his talents would be wasted doin' simple divinations. His gift is much more profound than that."

Spoons clinked on glass as everyone slurped down the fruit. I finished cleaning off my blouse, trying desperately to shift the sodden material so that the wet spot wasn't quite so obvious. Mentally, I cursed my decision to wear the sheerest and most elegant of my bras under the peasant top. It did nothing to disguise my breast beneath the almost transparent wet gauze. "Bully for Hank," I murmured, jerking my blouse to the side so the wet spot was more or less under my arm. The silence that resulted made me very aware that I had once again put my foot in my mouth. I offered a smile to a tight-lipped Marvabelle. "Sorry. I didn't mean that to sound as obnoxious as it did. To be honest, I don't quite have a grip on this whole Diviner/oracle thing. Can you explain the difference to me?"

"An oracle is one who provides counsel upon petition of the person seeking advice," she answered in a stiff voice, carefully spooning up her fruit without spilling a drop. "Oracles guide our lives with their sage wisdom. Diviners are nothin' more than charlatans. Mind readers and their ilk."

Jim, finished with licking out its dish of fruit, leaned its head on my shoulder and stared at my uneaten portion.

"Much as I would hate to disagree with the gracious lady," Monish said in his soft Indian accent, "Diviners are not mere charlatans or mind readers. They are known best for their ability to see into the immediate future. Many, such as Paolo, feel obligated to tell those around them of any mishaps they foresee."

A soft voice spoke in my ear. "You gonna eat that fruit, nipple girl?"

I looked down. My blouse had untwisted itself, my

breast all but bared beneath the wet material. "Son of a—"
I jerked the scarf off my hair and wrapped it around my
neck so that the ends hung down over my exposed breast,
shoving my dish over to Jim's plate so the demon could
eat the fruit. "I appreciate the fact that this Paolo guy
feels it's his duty to tell me when I'm about to trip or spill
food, but I can't help but feel that it is his warnings that
are causing the events."

"Schrödinger's cat," Nora said, nodding her head. We
all stared at her. "Quantum physics, you know. A man
named Erwin Schrödinger proposed a mental experiment
involving a sealed box containing a cat, a bottle of poisonous gas, and a radioactive mineral. The mineral is
such that it has a fifty-fifty chance of decaying during the
time the cat is sealed in the box, and if it does so, it will
release the gas and that will kill the cat."

"Poor kitty," Tiffany said, her brow wrinkled in a
scowl. "I don't believe in testing being conducted on animals, even mental testing. It is wrong. It does not make
for happy thoughts."

"Schrödinger . . . I think I've heard of him," I said
slowly, digging through my memories to the summer I
was madly infatuated with a physics professor and took
classes that made absolutely no sense to me. "Didn't the
experiment have something to do with observation of
the cat determining whether it was alive or dead? Oh, I
see what you're getting at—by Paolo telling me what
he sees in my future, he influences it?"

Nora nodded, her dark eyes glinting behind the lenses
of her bright red glasses. "Exactly. Just like Schrödinger's
cat, until Paolo speaks, the future exists in many states,
but as soon as he tells you the future, it becomes real."

"Cheap parlor trick," Marvabelle said, her expression sour. "Oracles offer much more profound guidance than simply predictin' someone's clumsiness. Oracles offer words to influence a lifetime."

"Really?" I looked at Hank. He didn't look much along the lines of a lifetime-influencing man. He looked like an uncomfortable, slightly sweating bald man with a sizeable beer belly. "So how do you do the oracle thing? Does stuff just come to you, or do people seek your advice, or what?"

Hank opened his mouth to speak, but his wife spoke before he could. "Hank is from the classical school of oracles," she said, with a pointed look at Monish. "First, he communes with the god and goddess of all bein'. Then he lights a special blend of herbs that allows his mind and soul to merge into a higher plain. At that point, he is tappin' into the wisdom of the Ancients, and he is open to questions from those seekin' his advice."

"I bet I can tell you just what sort of herbs he lights, too," Jim said sotto voce.

I stifled a snicker, careful to keep it soundless. I might not think too much of Marvabelle's boasts, but I was new to this society, and it behooved me to mind my p's and q's.

We discussed the various ways oracles consulted their sources of wisdom, and then the conversation turned to upcoming workshops and events of the conference. By the time the banquet was over, my head was spinning with thoughts of water altars, Argentinean *curanderismo,* ten signs that your significant other is a soul stealer (I could have used that advice before I married my ex-husband), and of course, the demon-tormenting workshops—so popular that three separate sessions were planned.

"Tell me you're not going to *any* of them," Jim demanded as I walked him out to the side lawn, which I'd been told was the area reserved for dogs to do their thing.

"Oh, I don't know. I think they sound interesting. I might pick up some techniques to keep you in line."

"Yeah, like you need to learn any more ways to make my life a living Abaddon?"

He stopped next to a large laurel bush. I moved over to a small wooden bench almost obscured by a rowdy group of azaleas and breathed deeply of the night air. It was scented with the perfume of midsummer flowers—tall gladiolas, delicately colored roses, early-blooming mums, and beautifully waving beds of poppies in almost every color. The dog walk was a long, narrow stretch of grass that was bordered on three sides by a woodland copse, the tall fir trees casting long shadows that sent inky fingers across the grass.

"This really is a gorgeous city—it has exquisite gardens," I said, allowing myself to drink in the beauty of the surroundings. Despite the big hotel and conference complex a few hundred yards behind us, it felt as if we were totally alone in a little piece of paradise.

"Hello, remember me?" Jim asked, a pointed look on its face. "You can still see me!"

"What? Oh. Sorry."

I turned around, giving the demon my back so it could do what it had to do without a witness. Jim didn't mind that I had to clean up after it performed its outdoor activities, but experience had proven that privacy was necessary to the act. Since I didn't want to spend all night out here waiting for the demon to take care of business, I strolled down the lawn toward the firs. The sun was a burnt orange ball half disappeared behind the distant hills, but it didn't seem to lessen the heat of the day very much. The shade of the dense clutch of trees looked cool and inviting.

From behind the nearest tree, a shadow separated from the copse. Before I could suck in a startled breath, a familiar figure lunged toward me. The street thief who had tried to rip me off at the train station slammed his fist into my shoulder, sending me flying backward into another tree. He jerked at my belt, half pulling me forward onto him.

"Hey!" I yelled, suddenly realizing what was happening. I had tied the amulet in its soft leather pouch to my belt in order to keep it safe with me, in case anyone had thoughts of searching my hotel room while I was out. (It had happened in the past.) "Stop it! Help! Jim!"

The young man snarled something as he pulled at the amulet, but I had tied it with a couple of sailor's knots, guaranteed to withstand even the most nimble pickpocket's fingers.

"I'm busy here, Aisling!" Jim's voice drifted down the lawn as I struggled with my assailant. The man grunted when I stomped his foot, retaliating by slamming his elbow into my jaw so that I reeled backwards.

"Effrijim, I command thee to stop thy pooping and help thy master right this frigging second!" I yelled, my fingers clawing the man's hands as he fought to release my belt.

"Fires of Abaddon, Aisling, don't ever do that to me

again. It's bad for my prostate or something—hey, who's that?"

"Get him," I snarled as the man spat an oath at me in Hungarian. Before I could clarify to Jim just how I wanted the demon to attack—one of the trials of being in command of a demon was that you had to give it very specific orders—a glint of silver flashed in the man's hands.

He had a knife. One that would laugh scornfully at my intricate sailor's knots, damn him. I tried to remember everything I'd learned in my self-defense classes about disarming a man with a knife, but before I could put it into practice the man slammed his forearm against my neck, pinning me to the tree. I reached up to poke my fingers in his eyes just as his knife swung forward in an arc intended to sever the leather straps binding the pouch to my belt.

I screamed as the knife slashed through the thin gauze and reached my tender flesh.

Jim yelled something in Latin and lunged at the man, but even as I struggled to disarm him, he cut the thongs to the pouch and bounded away, a quicksilver shadow in the woods.

I slumped to the ground, cradling my arm.

"Are you all right?" Jim asked. "How bad are you hurt? Should I go after him?"

"Yes," I answered, rocking with the sharp, burning pain that snaked up my arm.

"Really?" Jim looked into the dark woods. "You want me to chase him? Uh . . . he's got a knife, Aisling."

A voice shouted behind Jim.

"Yeah? He also has my amulet, and Uncle Damian

isn't going to forgive and forget if I lose another priceless object. Demon, I order thee to—"

A man loomed up behind him, immediately crouching down next to me. "You are injured? I smell blood. Allow me to see. I am a healer."

"You can smell blood?" I asked, momentarily disoriented by the man who bent over my arm. All thoughts of the amulet evaporated as he lifted his head and his silver eyes laughed into mine.

"Yes, I can. It is not a bad injury. I believe no muscles or tendons were severed—"

"You're a dragon," I interrupted, noticing the slightly elongated pupils. His skin was a warm caramel color, his long hair pulled back in a ponytail, but it was his eyes that held my attention. Bright silver, like illuminated mercury, they glinted through the darkening shadows, exotically tilted, full of secrets and mysteries.

"Yes, I am. How perspicacious of you. I am Gabriel Tauhou. I have the honor of being the wyvern of the silver dragons. And you"—he brushed aside a ruffle of my blouse, exposing the brand on my collarbone that Drake had left the month before—"you are a wyvern's mate."

"Just what we need—another wyvern," Jim drawled, sitting down next to me, giving Gabriel a piercing glare. "Look, she's been hurt, OK? Why don't you get on with the healer thing and stop flirting with her? She's got enough to deal with without you, too."

As much pain as I was in, I had to admit Jim's protective stance warmed my heart a little bit.

Gabriel's finger traced the circle pattern of Drake's brand. "This is the symbol of the wyvern of the green dragons. You are Drake Vireo's mate?"

"Not necessarily," I started to say, wanting to refute anything to do with the handsome, arrogant man who had the tendency to literally haunt my dreams when he was so inclined.

Gabriel's blinding smile stopped me. "Ah, good. You are versed in dragon lore. Then you know that a wyvern's mate is subject to the laws of *lusus naturae*."

"Huh?"

"*Lusus naturae*. It is Latin for 'whim of nature.'" His fingers caressed my jaw as he pushed a curl off my face. "It simply means that a wyvern may challenge another for the right to a mate."

"You have got to be kidding!" I gasped, my brain grinding to a halt at the idea of what it was he was saying.

Jim heaved an exaggerated sigh. "Oh, great, now you're going to be into threesomes. I can't wait to tell Drake about *that*!"

5

"The amulet!" I shouted, glaring at Jim before I pushed my way out of Gabriel's near embrace.

"You have lost an amulet?" he asked, looking around at the flower beds and the lawn.

"No, the man who stabbed me stole it."

"Ah, I see. It is valuable?"

I opened my mouth to say it was priceless but remembered in time how dragons reacted to any form of treasure. They were hoarders, acquiring treasure to be hidden away in their lairs, and even if the amulet had no gold— which acted more or less like the dragon version of catnip—it was still a very valuable piece.

"It's valuable to me," I said, choosing my words carefully. "I'm a courier, and I'm supposed to deliver it to someone here in Budapest. I have to get it back."

"Sit," he ordered, pushing me back to the ground from which I had struggled to get to my feet. "I will find this amulet for you."

"But how—?" I knew from the experience of the previous month that each of the four dragon septs had special skills for which it was known. Drake and the members of his sept were master thieves, while the blue dragons, headed by a veritable god of a man named Fiat Blu, were trackers extraordinaire. But Gabriel had said he was a healer—

"The one who attacked you has your blood on him. I will find him. But first I will attend to your wound." Gabriel lifted my arm and bent his head over it. For a second I felt an abnormal fear that he was going to bite me, but it wasn't his teeth that touched my skin.

His mouth, lips, and tongue caressed the bleeding gash. I sucked in my breath at the intimate feel of his mouth on my flesh, part of me disgusted by the thought of what he was doing, another part, a dark, secret part, strangely intrigued. His breath was hot on my arm, and for an instant I thought it was dragon fire I felt licking along my skin—but that couldn't be right. Drake was the only dragon whose fire I could feel.

Gabriel looked up from my arm, a tiny bead of my blood in the corner of his mouth. His tongue flicked out to suck it into his mouth, his eyes smiling at me as he leaped to his feet and quickly scented the air. Then he was off with the grace of a very male, very sexy gazelle.

"Holy cow," I said, my breath made uneven by the experience of his type of healing.

"I'm going to tell Drake that you have a new boyfriend," Jim said, watching me with unreadable dark eyes. "One who likes to suck owies. I'm a demon and even *I* think that's just gross."

I looked down at my arm. The long cut was still red, but it had closed and stopped bleeding, as if there was something in Gabriel's saliva that promoted healing. "You say anything to Drake at all, and I swear we'll go to the neutering clinic. Have you ever heard of a dragon who can heal?"

"Sure, dragon spit is well known for its healing properties." I glanced up at Jim, puzzled by the sarcastic tone in its voice. "*Not!* Dragons aren't healers, Aisling. They take, they don't give. You know that."

"Well, this dragon has something going for him, because not only is the pain gone but the cut is closed. Come on. Maybe you can track the guy who cut me. Or Gabriel. I need that amulet back, and as much as I appreciate Gabriel's first-aid skills, I don't trust him where treasure is concerned."

We ran through the copse of trees, emerging on the other side to find ourselves in a rock garden filled with exotic plants and a little waterfall that splashed prettily down a mossy cliff.

"Oh, man, now I gotta pee," Jim complained as we ran by the waterfall to the stretch of lawn beyond it.

"You do not. It's just a psychological thing. Do you smell either Gabriel or the guy who did the slash and dash?"

"What do I look like, a bloodhound? I'm a Newfoundland! We're water dogs. We don't do the tracking thing!"

We ran up to the outer edges of a church ruin. Beyond it was an open-air theater. I stopped next to a marble plaque marking the site of an ancient convent, clutching it for a moment as I caught my breath. Jim panted beside me, its tongue hanging a good six inches out of its mouth.

"This is ridiculous. This island is something like a mile and a half long and who knows how wide. We'll never be able to find them if you can't track them."

"I'm not the only one around here who can do something. You're the one who wants to be a Guardian. So do your thing. Look around you."

I opened my mouth to snap out a nasty comment but closed it without saying anything. Jim was right (dammit!). One of the abilities I had discovered the month before was that I could see things not apparent to the visible eye by opening myself up to my environment, allowing what a very wise woman in Paris had called "the possibilities" to become clear to me. "Why does everyone in the Otherworld seem to have a quantum physics degree?" I grumbled as I straightened up, closing my eyes and trying to calm my distraught mind so I could really see the world around me.

"What do you see?" Jim asked as I opened the door in my mind that allowed my mental sight to see reality.

Jim backed away from me as I stood next to the wall bearing the plaque. Beyond Jim the ruins of the convent shimmered in the night, the walls stretching and yawning as if they were alive. Before my bewildered sight, the convent came to life, the broken walls slowly rebuilding themselves, dark figures moving gracefully down paved pathways, a bell tolling somberly in the distance.

"Aisling? Do you see Gabriel or that mugger?"

"Uh . . ." Two of the dark figures glided toward me, their heads covered by white coifs. "No. Not Gabriel. I think I'm seeing a memory or something of the convent."

"Ghosts? Cool. Where? Oh, yeah, the two over by the well, do you mean?"

I turned my mental vision on Jim. "What do you mean, 'the two over by the well'? You can see ghosts? Why didn't you tell me that?"

Jim shrugged. "You never asked."

I sighed and turned to look beyond the convent ruins, my mind's eye scanning the gardens and tiny forest that curved around the south end of the convent.

"Ash? The grass is on fire."

"Really badly?" I asked without looking down. One of the side effects of using my mental sight was that I pulled some of Drake's dragon fire as a form of power. Unfortunately I didn't have the control he had, and it tended to get away from me.

"Not bad. Just a ring around you. But it's a good thing those two nuns next to you are already dead or they'd be barbecue."

I spun around. Two ghostly nuns stood right behind me, their faces eerily semitransparent ovals in the dark of the evening. As I stared in horror, one of them stretched a beseeching white hand toward me. "Criminy! Why didn't you tell me they were right—ow!"

"You're standing in the middle of the fire," Jim said helpfully.

I jumped out of the four-inch-thick barrier of fire and stomped my foot in the cool grass to put out the flames that licked the toes of my shoes. "Dammit, these are new! Why didn't you tell me they were there?"

"I thought you knew."

I eyed the two see-through nuns a bit nervously. I'd never seen a ghost before. What if they went all ghoulish and crawling with maggots on me? "Do you think they're here just to say hi? Or are they like sentinels or something, trying to keep me away from the ruins? Ghosts aren't evil, are they?"

"Who knows, maybe, and what planet are you living on? Ghosts are ghosts, nothing more."

"Oh, thank you. That's a fat lot of help. What do you think they want?"

Jim looked at the ghosts. Their images wavered in the heat of the fire. "Dunno. You could ask them."

"Ask them? You mean they'll talk to me? But I'm a Guardian. Almost. Can Guardians talk to ghosts, too?"

"You can talk to whoever you want to if you know how," Jim said with a disinterested sniff. "They probably want you to do something for them so they can find their rest. That's the usual modus operandi of ghosts. You going to take care of that fire?"

"I don't have time for ghosts," I said, wringing my hands, stopping myself when I realized what I was doing. Only Gothic romance heroines wrung their hands. I was a modern, proficient, professional woman, one whose life had no room for hand-wringing. "I have to get that stupid amulet back. Then I have to find the hermit and figure out what this horrible ritual is that I have to pass in order to find a mentor, not to mention finding said mentor, figuring out just what the devil Drake is doing here and who that woman is who slinks around like she has snake hips, as well as why she gets all touchy-feely with Drake."

Jim snickered.

"I'm sorry," I told the two ghosts. I pulled out the planner notebook from my purse and showed them the entries for the next few days. "I just don't have room for ghost problems in my schedule. But if you like, I can mention you to some of the other GODTAM people, and perhaps one of them would come out here and take care of whatever it is you need taken care of."

The ghosts shimmered sadly, regret and sorrow seeming to leak out of them and wrap around me.

"Look," I said, pointing to the notebook. "No time, see? Busy Aisling."

A woeful dirge drifted on the upper reaches of the evening breeze.

"Maybe they don't speak English?" I said to Jim before turning back to the ghosts, dredging through my memory for the appropriate phrase. "*Köszönjük, hogy nem dohányzik.*"

Jim began coughing. The nuns shimmered some more, a bit aggressively this time.

"Well, sheesh," I said, closing my notebook and tucking it away in my purse. "I'm sorry if my apology—"

"You said, and I quote, 'Thank you for not smoking.' "

"—if my request that they . . . er . . . not smoke didn't go down well, but I—I—oh, hell!"

"Abaddon."

"Abaddon! Right. I'll pencil you in for Saturday morning, right after breakfast. I was going to get an herbal massage, but I'll come here instead. Is that copacetic with you guys?"

The ghosts' figures wavered for a moment as if they were considering it, then they slowly dissolved into the night.

"I'll take that as a yes," I grumbled as I turned to face the gardens and stretch of woodland that ran down the island, my mental vision seeing only shadows of the things not touched by the Otherworld. A flash of silver slipped through the trees, resolving itself into the figure of a man walking toward us. It had to be Gabriel. "There he is. Does he look like he has the amulet?"

"You're the one with super-vision, not me. You going to let the place burn down or what?"

"Oh." My vision returned to normal as I glanced back at the ring of fire that was burning merrily. As had happened before when I used my Guardian abilities to see, a pang of regret whispered through me, leaving me mourning the fact that the world looked so much drearier and mundane in reality. "Put it out for me, would you, Jim? I'm going to go see if Gabriel got my amulet back."

"Put it out?" Jim asked, its voice rising as I loped off toward the distant figure. "Just how do you expect me to do that without a fire extinguisher?"

"Pee on it," I yelled over my shoulder.

The last sight I had of the demon was its lifting a back leg and hopping around the fire. Considering the amount of watering Jim did on bushes whenever I took it on walkies, I knew it would have no difficulty in putting out a small fire.

"I realized as soon as I saw you coming toward me that I don't know your name," Gabriel said as I ran up to him.

"It's Aisling. Did you find the guy who stabbed me? Did you get my amulet back?"

Gabriel made a courtly bow, white teeth flashing against the darkness of his skin as he smiled at me. We had met near a stone path that cut across the island, a streetlamp flooding the ground with a pool of yellow sodium light. Even with that dim illumination, I could see the flash of molten silver in his eyes as he held out his hand to me. "It is my extreme pleasure to meet you, Aisling the mate."

"You found it!" I yelled, relief filling me as I snatched

the crystal amulet from his hand. Overjoyed, I threw my arms around him, pressing a kiss to his cheek in gratitude. "Thank you so much! Did you have any trouble with the guy? Who is he? Did you beat him to a pulp? Thank you, thank you, thank you!"

He chuckled as I hugged him again. Then he stepped away. "I had no trouble tracking the man, as he carried the scent of your blood. I'm afraid I had little time to question him about his actions, feeling you would prefer a return of your amulet to an interview with the attacker. He had two young companions waiting for him at a dock on the Pest side, so, alas, I was not able to beat him to a pulp."

"Three thieves? The one who stabbed me was the same guy who tried to steal the amulet at the train station."

"Due to the high number of tourists, this area is a target of thieves. No doubt they followed you to the hotel and have been waiting for another chance to rob you," Gabriel said, gesturing toward the amulet. "It might be safer if you wore it beneath your clothing, rather than carrying it."

"Yeah, but how did they know I was here?"

Gabriel shrugged. "It wouldn't be difficult for them to follow you if they thought you were worth their effort."

That didn't seem very likely, but then again, how likely was it that someone would randomly pick me out to stab?

"Regardless of why they picked on me, I owe you more than I can say."

"Indeed," he said, with a sudden flash in his bright silver eyes. I wondered at it for a moment but let it go in favor of more important concerns.

"I hope they didn't give you any trouble." I ran my eyes over him quickly, worried that he might have been injured as a result of his chivalrous act. As a dragon, he was more or less immortal, but even a wyvern could be killed. It just wasn't easy.

"Nothing I am unused to," Gabriel said, laughter rich in his voice.

"I can't tell you how much I appreciate this," I said, looking at the crystal amulet. "My uncle would kill me if I lost another one."

"You have lost an amulet before?"

He walked with me as I started toward the ruined convent where I had left Jim. "Not an amulet, no. Drake stole an aquamanile that I was transporting last month. A gold aquamanile."

"Gold," he said, an avaricious light glowing in his eyes. I swear he all but licked his lips at the word. He paused, putting his hand on my arm to stop me so I faced him, his chin tilting up as he scented the air. "Ah, I thought so. You are wearing gold."

"Just a tiny bit," I said, pulling away from him. I slipped the amulet's chain over my head, tucking the crystal down beneath my peasant blouse so it rested next to the tiny green jade pendant that hung between my breasts. "It's a jade talisman given to me as protection against dragons. It has tiny little itty-bitty gold touches on it, that's all. Drake himself said it wasn't valuable or worth his time."

"I do not necessarily share Drake's opinions," Gabriel said, his hand on my arm again as he halted me.

"Oh, for heaven's sake—here! See? Just a jade dragon. Minuscule amounts of gold. Happy now?"

The dimples that had been hinted at in the slight indentations in his cheeks flared to life as he grinned at me. "I would not take it even if it was made of solid gold, Aisling. It is yours. I am not a thief."

"You wouldn't?" I didn't want to come right out and say I didn't believe him, but I had some experience with dragons. Gold was irresistible to them.

"No. Did I not just return to you a most valuable piece of what looks to be fifteenth-century jewelry? I am not a thief like your current wyvern. I am a healer, first and foremost. I am interested only in benefiting mankind—and womankind."

Healer? Uh-huh. Charmer, that's what he was—full of charm and suave sexuality that I could feel even though I was not man-shopping. Or dragon-shopping, for that matter. Subtlety was obviously not his forte. Like I didn't notice that "current wyvern" he'd thrown in his reference to Drake? "Valuable?" My voice was a bit squeaky. I cleared it, licking my lips nervously. "What makes you think the amulet is valuable?"

He gently pushed me forward, leaving his hand resting on the small of my back. It wasn't an unpleasant feeling, but I was very aware of his nearness. I couldn't help but wonder if he was trying to put a move on me, or if he was just one of those touchy-feely sorts of people who like to maintain physical contact. Or maybe he felt all manly and protective because there were amulet thieves lurking behind every tree?

Or better yet, maybe my feminine allure was just too

much for him, and he was smitten with my many charms.
I fluttered my eyelashes as I peeked up at him.

"You are employed to transport an object to a man in
a different country. There is much expense involved in
such an act. Thus, the object itself must be worth a great
deal of money."

Then again, he could just be keeping me within arm's
distance so he could snatch the amulet and run.

I felt a little fudging was necessary. I would *not* lose
another antiquity to a dragon. "That would make sense if
the only reason I was here was to deliver the amulet, but
I'm here to attend the GODTAM conference. I told my
uncle I'd bring the amulet so he wouldn't have to go to
the expense of shipping it." Not the truth, but not quite a
flat-out lie, either, so it didn't really count.

I hoped.

"Ah. I see." We reached the edge of the hotel's property, the side garden that was set aside for dogs' use. Beyond a low bank of rhododendrons, Jim sat chatting to
the Swedish Moa. I was grateful the demon hadn't gone
off on its own, since I had no idea how I was supposed to
retrieve it from the limbo it would find itself in if one of
the GODTAM officials found it alone. "I knew you were
a Guardian, of course, but I had forgotten about the conference. Yes, you are here for it."

"Yup." I stopped and gave Gabriel what I hoped was a
friendly—but not too friendly—smile. "That's why I'm
here. Why are you here, if you don't mind my asking? I
kind of gathered from Drake that you wyverns don't get
along too well, so I'm a bit surprised to see you staying
in the same hotel he is at."

The faint smile that lingered on Gabriel's lips faded as he gave me a quizzical look. "I am here for the summit."

"The summit?" As far as I knew, dragons had nothing to do with the GODTAM conference. I'd checked into that before I registered, wanting to avoid the very situation in which I now found myself—in close proximity to Drake. "What summit is that?"

He was silent for a moment before finally saying, "I am surprised Drake has not mentioned it to you. The wyverns of all four septs are meeting here for a peace summit. Drake arranged it. We are attempting to reach an accord so that the conflicts between the septs will cease. Drake and I are not the only two wyverns here—Fiat Blu and Lung Tik Chuan Ren are also here."

"I know Fiat," I said slowly, my glance sliding over to the hotel. A vague suspicion was forming in the back of my beleaguered brain. "But I don't know the fourth wyvern. He must be with the group of Asian people Drake met earlier."

"He? No. Chuan Ren is a woman." Gabriel flicked an amused glance my way. "A lovely woman—lovely but very deadly. She is the wyvern of the red dragons. You have heard of them, of course."

I shook my head, pieces of the puzzle falling into place, a spike of happiness overlaying the questions surrounding Drake's appearance. I squelched the happy thought that the only reason he was escorting the Chinese woman was because she was a fellow wyvern and reminded myself that it was nothing to me what the dragons did.

"He has not spoken to you of her?" Gabriel made a

half shrug. "Then I will leave it to him to detail her history."

"I didn't know things were really dicey between you guys," I said, one eye on Jim. A couple of people with small dogs were at the near end of the garden, but no one was close enough to hear my conversation with Gabriel. "I hope the accord goes well. Drake isn't really forthcoming with a lot of information, but to be honest, I haven't asked him about much. And as for me being his mate—well, he hasn't quite accepted the fact that I turned down the position."

"Excellent," he said, clapping his hands together in a gesture of pleasure. "Then it will be that much easier to challenge him."

I shook my head. "Not if you mean to challenge him for me. I understand that you said there's some sort of Latin rule that says you can claim another wyvern's mate, but this girl isn't into dragon-swapping. So thanks but no thanks, if you were thinking along those lines, not that I'm saying you were, because we just met, but if you were, I'm not. So don't. OK?"

He laughed again, and I smiled in response. I had met only one other wyvern, but Gabriel felt different to me. He didn't feel powerful like Drake and Fiat did. His presence was warm, but not overwhelming like Drake's or coolly menacing like Fiat's. "You are charming. I look forward to seeing you at the summit."

He bowed again and was off down the lawn before I could protest that he wouldn't be seeing me again, at least not at any dragon function. Moa stood as I strolled up to them, greeting her politely. The last thing I needed was to look like a raving idiot to a potential mentor.

"Your demon was telling me that you are a wyvern's mate as well as a Guardian," she answered in response to my comment about the lovely evening. She looked me over again, a slight frown between her brows. "Guardian apprenticeship is long and detailed. It is not something to be done in the spare time. A dragon's mate might have the ability to focus on her training, but a wyvern's mate has many more demands on her time."

I glared at Jim for a moment before turning my attention to Moa. "My demon is a bit confused. Drake is confused. In fact, a lot of people are confused, including, I regret to say, me at times. But I can assure you that I will throw myself wholeheartedly into my Guardian training, and the dragons will not be an issue."

"Really?" She tipped her head to the side, the long blond hair sliding like a curtain of silver. "But the dragons are having their summit here."

"That's just a coincidence—"

She interrupted me before I could finish. "It is being said by all that the summit was moved to this hotel from one in Paris because you, the mate of the green dragon wyvern, wished to attend the conference. Everyone knows the importance of the role of a wyvern's mate in negotiation, so for you to deny such gives me grave concern about your fitness as an apprentice." She shook her head, saying before she drifted off toward the hotel, "I must give long thought to your candidacy."

"But—but—" I called out after her, sputtering to a stop when it was evident my protests would serve no purpose. My fingers curled into fists as I glared at the innocent hotel. So Drake, who lived in Paris part of the year, had the summit moved to the very hotel that was hosting the GODTAM convention, did he? And he never once bothered to contact me or tell me that he was going to show up here, obviously expecting that I'd fall victim to his sexy self and do whatever he wanted without saying so much as boo in return? Ha! I marched forward, my jaw set as indignation roiled righteously within me. "Jim? I want you to go out and find me a big, long lance. I'm in the slaying mood, and I know just who I'm going to Saint George."

"You know, that term has a sexual connotation"— I gave the demon a look—"Right. Not important. Shutting up now."

I hoisted my purse over my shoulder as I shoved open the door to the hotel. I was armed and ready for battle. Now all I needed was for my foe to show his head and allow me to lop it off with a few well-chosen words.

6

One hundred and thirteen.

"There's just nothing so amusing as a really ticked-off Guardian wannabe in dragon-slaying mode when there're no dragons around to oblige her."

I snarled something obscene to Jim as I turned and paced past the demon for the one hundred and fourteenth time.

"You're going to wear a trench in the carpet. Why don't you take a load off for a few minutes, and I'll pace for you?"

One hundred and fifteen.

"Man, I didn't know you could make that face. Do you know that one of Amayon's higher demons looks just like that? Only without the flames shooting out the ears."

"Ack!" I stopped pacing long enough to feel my ears, realized Jim was exaggerating, shot it another glare that should have stripped every last hair off its furry body, and resumed pacing. One hundred and sixteen.

"Just thought a little levity would help the long, long hours pass until Drake comes back from his date with that Chinese babe."

A growl welled up within me, but I squelched it

along with the spurt of jealousy. I was not jealous of the
red wyvern. I was vaguely, mildly interested, that's all.
"It wasn't a date. It was a dinner, a business dinner.
With a bunch of other people—Drake's men and the red
dragons. You can't date when everyone has bodyguards
up to their armpits. One seventeen."

"You know, you should consider switching to decaf.
All this nervous energy can't be good for your—oh, boy."

I spun around, my heart leaping at the hope that Drake
had returned, but it was a blond vision of godliness rather
than a brunette one that swanked his way across the lobby
of the Thermal Hotel Danu toward the small, out-of-the-
way corner where Jim sat and I paced.

Fiat Blu, so gorgeous he'd make a *GQ* cover model
look as if he'd been covered in hideous boils in compari-
son, paused on his way to the elevator.

"What is it about the dragon septs that they all take
their colors so seriously?" I asked Jim, crossing my arms
over my chest as Fiat waved his two blue-suited bullyboys
toward the elevator before making a beeline for me. The
man himself was dressed in a midnight blue shirt embroidered with an opulent pattern of gold, open almost to his
navel, and black linen pants that probably cost more than
my entire travel wardrobe. "Would it destroy the whole
social structure of the septs if Fiat wore something red and
Drake stopped wearing those beautiful Italian green raw-
silk shirts?"

Jim lay down and put a big furry paw over its eyes.
"Dragons tend to be very literal, if you haven't noticed."

"I had," I said, then summoned up a polite smile for
Fiat as he stopped before me, making one of those bows
all the dragon boys seemed to know how to pull off with-

out looking like a hammy actor. "Hi, Fiat. Fancy meeting you here."

He took my hand in his, pressing a kiss to my knuckles, his fingers oddly cool around mine. Jim had told me once that the blue dragons' element was air, which left them feeling cooler to the touch than the other dragons. "Aisling, it is my extreme pleasure to see you again. Might I hope you have changed your mind about that rude Drake and have decided to join your considerable talents with mine? You know I would welcome such a union."

Like the other wyverns, Fiat had a beautiful voice, his with a mesmerizing Italian cadence. I remembered just in time that one of Fiat's skills was in mind reading and quickly imagined myself in a thick-walled tower with shutters clamped tightly shut. Fiat's smile turned a little brittle as I closed him out of my mind. "Are you offering to fight Drake for me, Fiat? You going to challenge him *draco et draco*?"

He froze for a moment, then touched a cool finger to the mark on my collarbone. "I do not seek a mate, Aisling. What I am offering requires less commitment on your part, which, I believe, is something you find attractive. Join with me, and I will see to it that all your desires are fulfilled."

I gave him a wry smile. "You know, that would sound a whole lot more impressive if your nose wasn't twitching like mad at the gold on my dragon talisman. It's not me you want, Fiat—it's what I represent. So thanks, but I'm going to pass on your generous offer."

His eyes, a dark blue, glittered at me as he tried to push his way through my mental barriers. Menace, always an undertone of emotion around Fiat, swept off him and over me like I was a marshmallow trying to stop a steamroller. "You would be wise to think most strenuously about your decision to ally yourself with Drake, *cara.* I have much power. In the days to come I will grow stronger, and I would hate for you to find yourself on the wrong side of that which cannot be avoided."

"Hyperbole and mystic aggrandizement, you mean?"

His eyes narrowed slightly as I smiled a perky smile at him. "Your levity in moments of seriousness is known to me. I accept that you do not believe that of which I have spoken. Yet. I can only hope that you accept the truth in time, lest you, too, be destroyed in the coming battle."

"I thought you guys were here to discuss a peace accord," I said, a little shiver running down my back at the darkness within his eyes.

"Peace is a foolish hope held by your mate. He is blind to the truth, but he, too, will learn how dangerous it is to underestimate me. I wish you a pleasant evening, Aisling . . . and hope it will not be the last of its kind."

I rubbed my arms as Fiat moved off to rejoin his men, more disturbed by his vague threats and innuendos than I wanted to admit. "I'm going to have to tell Drake what he said about a battle."

"Drake?" Jim asked, sitting up to give my hand a reassuring snuffle. I patted the demon's head. "The same Drake that only a few minutes ago you were muttering about decapitating and disemboweling? *That* Drake?"

"Just because I want to kill him doesn't mean I want to see him destroyed."

Jim just looked at me.

"Oh, right, yes, I know." I answered the look with a wave of my hand. "That doesn't make any sense. Stop picking on me. I'm tired, and I'm going to bed. That last double-shot latte didn't do me any good."

The lobby was empty as we made our way up to the room on the twelfth floor. In fact, we didn't see anyone but a couple of maids skittering around bringing extra pillows and towels and such. I knew from speaking with the people I'd met at dinner that the bar in the basement of the hotel was the place to go to meet and greet, but the jet lag had caught up with me, and even though it was early evening, I decided to hunt Guardian mentors tomorrow, when I wasn't babbling like an idiot and clearly out of control of my emotions.

"If Drake thinks he's going to come to me in a dream tonight, he's insane," I remarked to Jim as I crawled into the double bed. "I'm wearing the dragon talisman. That ought to keep him at bay."

Jim snorted on the bed of blankets I'd made it next to the open window. "Like that's worked in the past."

"I haven't been this pissed before," I answered, clutching both the dragon talisman and the amulet, which two attempted thefts had left me deciding was safer around my neck where no one knew where it was. "He'd just better watch out. I'm not in a mood where I want *any* man in my bed, especially a sexed-up stud."

I woke up two hours later to find a man in my bed, murmuring sexed-up studly sweet nothings in my ear.

"Dammit, Drake, you just can't take no for an answer, can you?" I mumbled groggily as I struggled to extricate myself from both the sheets that had twisted around my legs and the embrace of the man who leaned over me. I was about to punch him where I knew it would really hurt when something filtered through my sleepy anger. This man didn't smell right. I knew Drake's part woodsy, part spicy scent, and this wasn't it. Which meant . . . "Jiiiiiiii-iim! Rape! Help! Demon, I command thee to attack this man and rip his balls right off and—"

"That's not a man, Aisling."

Jim's voice, also sleepy, came from the other side of the bed. The man rolled off me as I freed a hand and clicked on the bedside lamp. I looked at him. He was a stranger, a nice-looking man with auburn hair and a cleft in his chin, but still, a stranger. A naked stranger. A naked, aroused stranger. In bed with me.

The man smiled as he stretched. All of him.

"Uh . . . Jim, I may not have been around a lot, but I know a naked man when I see one, and I'm seeing one. Just who the hel . . . Abaddon are you, and what the devil do you think you're doing here?" The last question was addressed to the naked man. His smile wasn't the only thing that got bigger as I clutched the sheet to my chest and scooted over to the edge of the bed, wishing like the dickens that international security regulations hadn't required me to leave my pepper spray at home.

"My name is Piotr. I am here to pleasure you."

I stared at the man. "I beg your pardon?"

"I am here to pleasure you. I will bring you many delights if you allow me."

Oh, great. I had a Slavic gigolo in my bed. I glanced at the clock. It was only 11:14 P.M. Could this day possibly get any worse?

"Don't believe it, Aisling. That's not a man. Doesn't smell like one."

I made a tentative sniff in Piotr's direction. Jim was right. He didn't smell like any man I'd ever met. He smelled smoky, as if he'd been standing around a bonfire. "Look, I don't know you, and I don't want you in my bed, and I certainly don't want you giving me any delights, so why don't you just get the many expletives deleted out of here and don't ever come back!"

Piotr drew a finger down my uninjured arm. "I will bring you the most erotic pleasure you have ever known, Aisling."

I jumped out of the bed, taking the sheet with me. "Right. That's it. You have three seconds to get the *hell* out of here, and then I'm calling hotel security. One!"

Piotr stood up slowly, allowing me to get a good long look at his attributes. Which, I had to admit, were worth admiring.

"Two!"

He smiled again and spread his hands wide in a gesture of obedience. "If you wish for me, all you need do is call."

I wrapped the sheet more securely around me, marched over to the door, and flung it open. "Three!" I shouted as I pointed out the door.

Piotr was gone.

I stood openmouthed by the door for a few seconds, then closed both before spinning around to face Jim. "Where'd he go?"

It made a thoughtful face. "Disappeared in a puff of smoke."

"He *what*?"

"Disappeared in a puff of smoke. You know, kind of like that Barbara Eden babe on *I Dream of Jeannie*, only without the blond wig and wiggle hips."

I didn't believe Jim. Men—naked, aroused men— didn't just appear and disappear in a cloud of smoke. I searched the room, examining the side of the hotel immediately outside my open window (no ledge and a twelve-floor drop to the glass ceiling of one of the thermal pools) before finally conceding that maybe Jim was right after all.

"OK, so what sort of creature appears and disappears on smoke?" I asked the demon as we settled down in our respective beds.

"Lots. You're not asking the right question."

I peered over the edge of the bed to where Jim was flaked out on its blankies. "You know, you could just volunteer the information for once. I could do with a lot less aggravation in my life right now."

"I told you before, that's against the demon–demon lord rules. You have to ask the right question in order for me to answer."

I sighed and lay back down on the bed, irritably readjusting the sheets so they weren't twisted around me. Although my nightwear was not heavy—a pair of thin cotton sleeping shorts and tank top—I was hot and sweaty lying in bed, the air-conditioning unit having been deemed earlier in the evening more or less worthless. There was more of a breeze coming in from the open window than I had with the AC cranked up high. "I hate demon rules. You know that, right?"

"Yup."

"Good. So. What sort of a being shows up naked and wanting to play bed games and later disappears without a sign?"

"Would that be a male or a female being?"

I slapped both hands on the bed. "For heaven's sake, Jim—"

"Incubus or succubus, depending on the gender. Incubi are men, succubi are women. Unless you're gay, and then they're vice versa. I think. I'm not too sure. I haven't had a chat with a succubus in a long time, so I'm not hip with where they all are on the alternative-lifestyle issues."

"Incubus?" I sat up and stared at the demon. "Incubus? The . . . the . . ." My hands waved wildly as I tried to think of a description of an incubus.

"The nudie boy toy spirits who come to women in the night and want to jump their bones? Yes. That sort of incubus."

"But they aren't real!" I sputtered, finally able to articulate again. "They're just a myth, aren't they?"

Jim shot me a knowing look. "Kind of like dragons and ghosts?"

I slumped against the headboard. "Good point. Incubus. I've never seen one before. It wasn't quite what I expected. He looked perfectly normal, and he certainly felt real."

"He was real, at least in that form he was. Incubi are dream lovers. They can turn to smoke, entering a room through the tiniest crack, then take a more substantial form. I've heard that some of them, the really old ones, can carry their mortal lovers away with them. A couple hundred years ago in the north of Italy, there was a rumor going around that women were being spirited off on clouds of dense smoke, never to be seen again."

"Good lord! What on earth did this one want with *me*?"

Jim sniggered.

"Get your mind out of the gutter. I know what he wanted. He almost put my eye out with his manly bits. I meant why me? I've never had an incubus visit me before. Do they hang around hotels and stuff?"

"Not that I know of."

"Huh." I mused on the question of why a spirit bent on engaging in sexual relations would pay me a visit, toyed with the idea that I was suddenly irresistible to men, but sadly discounted that theory. No one but the male wyverns seemed to find me anything but barely interesting, and that was because I evidently had some sort of genetic wyvern mate marker that made me look like hot stuff to them.

Some of them. Mostly just Drake. Although Gabriel seemed to like me . . .

Despite the jet lag, it took me an hour to fall asleep again, even with the bedside lamp on to keep the monsters away. To my surprise, Drake didn't visit me in my dreams, as I had half hoped, half feared he would, but I did have one of the most erotic dreams of my life. It started with *my* dream version of Drake licking my ankles, slowly working his way up my legs to my thighs. Just as he gently parted my legs, I woke up.

To find it wasn't a dream after all.

"Gawk!" I squealed, the sight of a man's blond head lounging around my crotch area more than enough to leave me momentarily without the power of coherent speech. "Wha'? Get off!"

"I am Gregory. I will bring you—"

I brought both knees up and kicked the man as hard as I could in his noogies. He grunted and rolled off the side of the bed, clutching his privates. I jumped to my feet right there on the bed and screamed at Jim, the bed springs squeaking as I did a little dance of fury. "Incubus! Incubus! Incubus! Jim, I command you to wake up!"

"Who can sleep with all that yelling and squeaking going on? It's an incubus, Aisling, not a mouse. It's not going to crawl up your leg."

"That's what you think! Kill it! Or disperse it! Or whatever you did to make the other one go away."

Jim sighed and shambled over to where the incubus was struggling to sit up. "Look, buddy, you might as well leave. She's got a boyfriend already, and given the way they were making the whole house shake the last time they got it on, I'd say you don't stand a chance with her."

"But I am most talented," the blond night spirit protested in a heavy German accent. "I am the stallion extraordinary in bed."

I beat him on the head with one of my pillows. "Go away! And don't come back!"

"You do not want me? You do not crave my body? This is unheard of! This cannot be!"

"Believe it, stallion boy," Jim said. "She's tough when she wants to be, so if I were you, I'd take a hike."

"A knife!" I yelled, still brandishing my pillow. "Jim, I command you to get me a gelding knife. If this guy wants to be a stallion—"

He dissolved in a flurry of white smoke even before I could finish the sentence.

"Ha! Victorious again!"

"Yeah," Jim drawled while I remade the bed and fluffed up my pillows. "Aisling, two; sexy, naked men who just want to give her the pleasure of a lifetime with no commitment, zero."

"Yeah, but . . . but . . . "

Jim cocked an eyebrow. I gave up and plopped down on the bed. "You're right. I'm crazy."

I woke up two hours later to find the third incubus sucking on my earlobe.

"Hello," he said, with a roguish grin. "I am Teodore, and I'm here—"

"Right, that's it," I snarled, shoving him aside as I grabbed my silk bathrobe, pulling it on and tying the belt so tightly it almost cut off circulation to my lower half. "Come on, Jim."

"Come on? Come on where?" Jim sat up, shaking itself as it blinked at the incubus, who now rolled around striking seductive poses on my bed. "Another one? Geez, girl, what perfume are you using?"

I snatched up my purse, throwing open the door. "We're going someplace where I can get some sleep without being molested. Demon, follow me."

Jim trailed me as I marched to the elevator, out to the thankfully empty lobby, across to the night clerk, waited while I asked my question and paid a large bribe to get an employee to break the hotel's rule regarding guest information, padded after me as I went back to the elevator, all without saying a word. I rapped hard on the door to the suite on the fifth floor.

A tousle-headed Pál opened it up, blinking sleepily at me.

"Morning," I said, pushing past him to enter the suite. "Which room is Drake's?"

He blinked a couple more times, then pointed to the left.

"Thanks. Jim, you can sleep out here, on the couch.

Don't pee on anything. Don't eat anything that isn't offered to you first. Don't hump István's leg. Good night."

I marched over to Drake's bedroom, pausing to look back at Pál, who still stood by the open door. "Uh . . . he *is* alone, isn't he?"

Pál nodded.

"Good." Head high, I swept open the door, entering Drake's room with enough noise to alert him to my presence.

"Hello," I told him when he clicked on the light. I ignored the rush of heat that swept through me at the sight of a sleepy, naked Drake, forcing myself to not stare at his bare chest, more than a little grateful for the blankets covering his lower parts. "I'm sleeping with you tonight. Just sleeping. No sex. No touching. Not even a kiss. My room is infested with incubi."

He watched me silently as I tossed my silk bathrobe onto a tapestry armchair before sliding under the blankets on the bed (his air conditioner, I noticed, was working extremely well). I lay as close to the edge of the bed as I could to avoid touching him, clutching the blankets over my chest as I closed my eyes, trying like mad to ignore his heat.

"Incubi?" he finally said, his voice all but rubbing along my skin.

The mattress dipped. I opened my eyes to find a dark-haired man leering suggestively at me. "I am Jacob."

"Look behind you," I told him.

"Eh?" His head swiveled as he looked back to see Drake propped up on one elbow. "Blet!"

He disappeared without another word. I cocked a questioning eyebrow at Drake.

"Incubi," he agreed, nodding.

7

"So, assuming I pass this ritual that no one wants to talk about, and you like the looks of my application, what happens then? I assume we'd have to live fairly close together? At least in the same country?"

Rose the Guardian nodded. "The traditional method of Guardian training is for the apprentice to live with the mentor, studying the various aspects of the dark powers and assisting with minor jobs until the mentor feels the apprentice is skilled enough to maintain a portal on her own."

"That would be a portal to Hell, right? Not, say, a portal to Cleveland?"

Rose nodded again. She was slight, dark-haired, and hailed from the Virgin Islands. Thus far my Guardian appointments had been with women from Chicago, Marseilles, and Istanbul. Out of the four, the Virgin Islands sounded like an idyllic place to learn to put the lid on the portal between the real world and the dark side of the Otherworld. "Once I evaluate your application, and those of the others who are seeking a mentor, I will let you know if we need to schedule a further interview. I admit that the fact you have the ability to summon and bind to you an unattached demon raises you significantly in my estimation, but I am concerned about the fact that you are also a wyvern's mate."

I waved a negligent hand. "Don't let it worry you. It's not an issue."

"Ah. Good. Well, I have your room number, so if I have any further questions, I will be in contact. Good afternoon."

"Thanks, and same to you."

I waited until Rose left the tiny café situated on a wide, shady verandah on the south side of the hotel before dropping my weary head onto my hands.

A cold, moist object pressed against my ankle.

"You may speak, Jim," I answered the unspoken request, my voice muffled against the cool marble tabletop.

"Did you *have* to command me to shut my yap in front of the Guardian? You couldn't have put it nicer? You couldn't have wrapped it up in that hokey medieval-speak you like to use whenever you're bossing me around? I may be a demon, Aisling, but I do have feelings!"

"Aisling, you like more drink? Food, maybe?"

"No, thank you, Zaccheo. I'm just peachy keen." I didn't look up to see the hopeful face of the waiter responsible for serving patrons on the verandah. Zaccheo had been hovering around me ever since I'd sat down to keep my Guardian appointments, rather like an annoying, if friendly, pimply eighteen-year-old gawky bee.

"You like me to wait here until you need something?"

"No, thank you. I'm just fine."

"I be just over there if you need me. You call if you want something, yes?"

"Yes," I told the tabletop. "Absolutely. The very second a desire comes to mind, I'll let you know."

"Good. You call. I be over there, by the door. You call."

Zaccheo shuffled away.

"You could have asked him for another couple of sandwiches. This fabulous form of mine needs a lot of food, and that diet you've put me on is going to make it waste away to nothing."

I peered out through my fingers to where Jim was flaked out in the shade beside a bowl of water and an empty bowl that had previously held a chopped-up chicken sandwich. "The vet said you are twenty pounds over the standard for Newfies. No extra snacks, remember? And I'm sorry about hurting your feelings, but do you have to tell everyone that Drake thinks I'm his mate? Every single Guardian has been enthusiastic about me until you pipe up and mention that. I have two more appointments with potential mentors, and I'm telling you right here and now that I forbid you—*forbid* you—to mention to them that I'm a wyvern's mate!"

"You are a wyvern's mate? A *wyvern's* mate?"

My head shot up off my hands like it was one of those early NASA rockets. The kind that didn't explode a few feet off the launch pad. On the other side of the round café table stood the tall black woman I'd met at the banquet the night before, a businesslike attaché case in her hand, wearing a beautifully patterned African print dress. "Oh. Nora. Hi. Um . . . the wyvern thing . . . it's not a certainty, not really. That is a really pretty dress. Are those zebras? I love batiks. There's just something about handmade cloth that really rings my chimes."

She stared expressionless for a moment at me, then her face broke into a smile as she chuckled. Setting her attaché on an adjacent chair, she settled in the one Rose had vacated a few moments before. "Yes, they are zebras, and I quite agree about batiks. You are not very good at changing subjects, are you?"

I groaned and closed my eyes for a moment. Five Guardians down, and Moa left—and she had already expressed her dubiousness about my ability to be an apprentice. Crap.

"Aisling? Are you well? You look tired."

Jim snorted. "She should. What with all the naked guys hopping in and out of her bed all night—"

"Jim!" I yelled.

"Not to mention running to Drake for a little late-night nooky. The poor thing didn't get any rest last night." I poured one of the three pitchers of half-melted ice water that sat on my table onto Jim's head. It yelped in surprise. "Hey!"

I pointed out to the open lawn beyond the verandah. "Go smell the flowers."

Jim got to its feet slowly, water running off its dense black coat. "You're not supposed to leave me unattended, remember? If someone catches me, they'll bind me to limbo until you can fetch me back."

"I'll take that chance. Go. Walk. Smell. No peeing on anything pretty. And if you have to do anything else, just hold it until Nora and I are done talking."

Jim's furry face was sullen. "Is that—"

"Yes, it's an order." I waited until the demon was gone to turn back to Nora. She was making notes on a little pad with a ballpoint that had teeth marks on the non-writing end. I smiled at that. I had a tendency to absentmindedly chew on pens myself when I was trying to write something. "I'm sorry about that. Jim is a little irreverent, but underneath, it's really a good demon."

Her eyebrows raised high above the red frames of her glasses, the lenses of which had reacted to the bright sunlight and turned dark. "It is a *good* demon?"

"Yeah. I know that's kind of an oxymoron, but the truth is, Jim was cast out of its demon lord's legions. I don't know all the circumstances, but I think it was because Jim's heart wasn't as dark as those of the other demons."

"Demons do not have hearts," she pointed out.

"You want more water, Aisling? You need more water, yes? I saw you use the water I bring you earlier. It is good. Here is more water. I bring it just for you." Zaccheo materialized at my elbow with a tray full of pitchers of ice water. He set them on the table, his eyes, which I can only describe as moony, watching me besottedly the entire time.

"Thanks, Zaccheo. I think five pitchers is my limit."

"Water is good. Very good for the womens. My mother, she tells me this. Very good for their peepees, yes? Makes no trouble there. I go now. You talk. You drink water."

He zipped off to his serving station, a happy smile on his face. I glanced at Nora. "He's very attentive."

"Yes, I can see that. And evidently well trained by his mother to anticipate a woman's need of water to avoid urinary tract infections. Commendable, that."

I made a half shrug. There was no way I could explain why Zaccheo seemed to be so enamored of me, so I didn't even try. "I suppose you want to know about this wyvern thing."

She accepted the glass of ice water I poured, absent-mindedly plucking out a slice of lemon and squeezing it into the water. "Yes, but to be honest, I'm more interested in hearing about the naked men hopping in and out of your bed all night long."

"OK," I said, placing both palms down on the table to lean forward, "let me just say right here and now that I had nothing to do with that, nothing at all. They were incubi, and they were definitely not invited. Jim makes it sound like there was a whole battalion of them, but there wasn't."

"No? How many were there?"

Even through the darkened lenses of her glasses I could see the amusement in her eyes.

"Er . . . six. No, seven. But the last one got a little confused, and he ended up making a play for Drake."

"Ah. Drake. That would be Drake Vireo, the green wyvern, the dragon whose mate you say you are not?"

"Yes, that's him."

Her lips pursed a little as she made another note on her notepad. I resisted the urge to crane my neck to see what it was she was writing. "I see. And yet, despite this, you did spend the night with him?"

I bristled. Just a little bit. "I realize you have to ask all sorts of personal questions about me in order to judge compatibility and all that, but I draw the line at discussing my personal relationships. Since you don't know me well enough to know that Drake is not a factor in my life, I'll make an exception this once. Yes, I spent the night in Drake's bed, but nothing happened there, nothing nate-ish, nothing intimate. We're just acquaintances, Drake and I. That's all."

"I wouldn't say that," a smooth, silky voice spoke behind me mere nanoseconds before warm fingers caressed the back of my bare neck. Drake pulled out the chair next to me and sat down, his movements smoothly elegant, hinting of controlled power. His fingers remained clasped around the back of my neck, stirring little wisps of heat that streaked through me, touching off any number of banked fires. "Surely mere acquaintances do not fall asleep clasped in each other's arms?"

I shrugged his hand off my neck, giving him a good glare. How dare he come along and mess up my chances with Nora? "You know full well I was so tired and groggy I fell asleep a few minutes after that last incubus left. That's what you said this morning—that and that slanderous bit about me snoring, which is so patently untrue, I laugh at it. Ha ha."

"You did snore," he said mendaciously, cocking an eyebrow at Zaccheo. The waiter came running, giving me plaintive looks before Drake gave him an order for a Bloody Mary and sent him on his way.

"I am not the one who left scorch marks on the sheets," I pointed out, then quickly explained when Nora's eyebrows rose in shock again. "Unlike silent me, Drake *does* snore, and things tend to get a little fiery. Trust me—you never want to sleep facing him, or you'll end up with your eyebrows singed."

"Thank you for that advice," Nora said, her voice choked. My heart fell at the sound of it. Clearly she was marking me off the list of apprentice candidates.

Damn Drake and his manly-lipped blabbermouth!

"The only time I breathe fire when I sleep is when my mate is with me," the annoying man said, giving me a sultry look. I thinned my lips at him before I remembered that Nora was watching. I turned a smile on her—not that it would do me any good. My first full day at the conference, and already I had run through five—no six, counting Moa—potential mentors. At the rate I was going, I'd be through all of the attending Guardians before the final awards ceremony.

"I'm sure you have some questions for me. That is, assuming you're willing to overlook certain aspects of my life that would seem to prohibit a serious apprenticeship." I gave the certain aspect in question a quelling look. He simmered at me.

"Actually"—Nora eyed Drake in a thoughtful manner—"I don't think you being a wyvern's mate is prohibitive at all."

I almost choked on the piece of ice I was crunching. "You don't? But all the other Guardians—Nora, I'll be frank. The other Guardians all more or less washed their respective hands of me the minute they learned about Drake." I cast a glance at him. "Not that there's anything going on there to be worried about."

"Do you challenge me, mate?" he asked, not touching me with anything but his gaze, but oh, baby, that was enough. I shivered under the heated look he was giving me and dragged my reluctant eyes to Nora. "You have not yet paid the price for failing your last challenge."

I ignored Drake. Sometimes it helped. Usually it didn't.

"I believe you must be an extraordinary woman to be a Guardian, a wyvern's mate, and a demon lord," Nora said briskly, putting her notepad in her case and standing up.

"What?" I blinked at her stupidly for a moment, then stood as well, shaking the hand she offered me. "Wait a second. I'm confused. You don't think the whole mate thing is an issue, but you're leaving? We're not going to have an interview? Don't you want me to fill out an application form like the other Guardians?"

"No," she said, turning to give her hand to Drake. He rose in a graceful movement, soberly taking her hand.

"Aisling is indeed a woman of many talents," he said, "but her priority lies with my sept. She is and will always be my mate. Because of that, I do not approve her seeking to apprentice herself to another."

"Hey!" I said, startled and angry at the same time. How dare he!

"I understand," Nora said. That's all. She just said she understood, and she walked away.

Fury like nothing I'd known since—well, since the last time Drake annoyed me—rose with its brothers irritation and vengeance.

Mindful of the audience of other conference attendees who were taking their midmorning break on the verandah, I didn't light into him right then and there. No, I reminded myself that I was a professional amongst my peers, or people I hoped would be my peers once I had the appropriate training, and professionals do not create scenes in public.

"You are *so* going to get it when no one can see me rip a strip off you," I hissed, grabbing my purse and conference program from the table.

"Have I told you how arousing I find it when you threaten me?"

I kept my voice low and as mean as I could make it. "Then you're going to love the descriptions of how I'm going to decapitate you if you ever again embarrass me that way. You do not approve me seeking a mentor, Drake? Just who the devil do you think you are? I told you last month that I wasn't going to be your mate. You let me walk away without a single word of protest, if you recall. So don't give me this domineering crap now, because I'm not going to stand for it."

He grabbed my arm as I pushed my way past him, swinging me around to face him. His hand on my bare arm sent little frissons of heat throughout my body, frissons I steadfastly ignored. I had made my choice, and by god, I was going to stick to it, no matter how much his gorgeous green eyes seemed to sear my soul.

"I did not explain the situation to you last night because you were exhausted and needed sleep, and you slipped away this morning before I could inform you of your duties, but if you insist on having the discussion in public, I will oblige you. I allowed you to leave last month because you were still confused about your new role."

"Allowed?" I gasped, struggling to keep my voice low. A few people sitting nearby glanced over at us, but no one else seemed to notice. My throat ached with the need to yell at Drake, while my body warred with my mind over whether or not it would be a good idea to throw myself in his arms and kiss the fire right out of him. My mind won the battle, but my body had its revenge—unable to resist the temptation, I pushed back an

errant lock of his dark hair from where it had fallen over his brow. "You did not allow me to do anything, you scaly-skinned lizard. We had a little fling, it didn't work out, I left. End of story. There was no *allowing* going on anywhere."

"You are my mate."

"So you say."

A tiny little wisp of smoke curled out of his nostril, always a sign that I was pushing his notoriously short temper. "You came to me of your own accord last night."

"Only because I was being plagued by naked men, and you're big enough and bad enough to scare them off."

"You want me."

That last was said in a low, sexy growl that set my whole body vibrating. I thought about denying his statement, but I knew if I did, he'd consider it a challenge and feel obliged to prove he could arouse me with just a look.

"Yeah, I do. But you want me, too, so we're even Steven."

"I need you."

My mind ground to a halt at his words. I had a horrible suspicion that my mouth hung open a little, too, but I was too stunned by his admission to worry about that. "What?"

"You are my mate and an important member of my sept. I need you. The summit cannot continue without your participation."

"Me? What on earth do I have to do with anything dragonish?"

"Mates bear an important part in our society. If something was to happen to me, it would be you who would control the sept. It is tradition that mates are involved in all important decisions."

"But I don't know anything about you guys! I wouldn't know what to do at an important summit."

"You sit next to me and answer any questions asked of you. That is all. It will not be difficult. I will conduct the actual negotiations. Your role as mate is primarily one of showing assent and support for my proposals."

I shook my head, more to clear it than to negate what he was saying. "Drake, I appreciate the fact that you think I have a role to play with your clan, but we've talked about this. It's not going to happen."

"If you do not help me, the dragons will war, and although our peace has been tentative, a full war is something that has not happened for seven hundred years. The last time it happened, the mortal world suffered most grievously."

"How?" I asked, unable to keep myself from asking.

"Plague. As a result of the last dragon war, a plague struck Europe and twenty-five million people died. Do you wish to risk such an atrocity recurring?" I stared deep into his emerald eyes to determine the slightest sign of deception or ulterior motive. His eyes were unshadowed by anything but sadness. "Lunch is at two in the atrium. Wear something green."

The black plague. He had to be talking about the black plague, which struck Europe in the mid-fourteenth century and decimated almost half the population . . . *wear something green*? Drake walked away without waiting for me to answer. I ground my teeth, biting back all the things I wanted to say as I stormed into the hotel, swearing this was the very last time Drake would have the opportunity to manipulate me. Damn his finessing self, pushing me into doing his wishes by giving me a choice between two evils.

I could bring down a plague upon the world, or I could have lunch with a few bossy dragons. When put that way, it didn't seem like such a momentous choice to make.

I just hate it when I'm wrong about things like that . . .

8

"You forgot about me!"

"I did not. I just got a little busy."

"You forgot me and you left me. Two strikes, Aisling."

"I was held up, that's all."

Jim shot me an accusatory glare as we waited outside the hotel for Rene. "You said you were waiting for your appointment with Moa. How busy can you be just hanging around the lobby?"

"For your information, I was trying to deal with some non-Otherworld businessman staying here who wouldn't take no for an answer. He all but ripped down the door to our room when I tried to escape. I had to call security."

Jim rolled its big eyes. "Oh, right. Like I'm going to believe that?"

"It's true! I was accosted! Hit on! By some guy in a nice suit, and no, he wasn't old or insane—at least, he wasn't old."

"Ha!"

"Moa never showed up, either," I said, kicking irritably at a pebble on the pavement. "You'd think she would at least have left me a message on the message board, but no, she just left me waiting for her in the lobby, fending off randy businessmen."

"A likely story. You forgot me, pure and simple, leaving me to the nonexistent mercies of that butch Guardian who sent me into limbo." Jim's body shook. "It was horrible, a ghastly nightmare of nothingness, just me and a couple of late-night talk show hosts floating around with nothing to do but listen to them name-drop. Don't ever do that to me again."

"I don't know why *you're* complaining. They fined *me* a hundred euros for your containment. Do you see Rene's taxi?" I stood up from the wooden bench alongside the lobby doors and peered down the curved drive that ended at the front of the hotel. It was the only place cars were allowed on the whole of Margaret Island, and thus far Rene was ten minutes late.

"No. But fruit girl is at six o'clock and coming on strong."

I turned to smile at Tiffany as she greeted us. "Hello, Aisling and Jim. That is a very pretty dress, Aisling. I had one just like it when I was going through my Romany stage, although I quickly outgrew it when I realized that all those ruffles and flounces made my hips look positively huge. Why is Jim wearing a towel around his neck?"

I smoothed my hands down my lightweight gauze ruffly, beflounced broomstick skirt, wondering if Tiffany was being catty or if my hips did, in fact, look so massive she had to give me a gentle pointer. One glance at her white denim miniskirt and matching halter top left me believing the latter. She didn't look catty—she looked fashionable. "Jim managed to leave the last of its drool cloths in limbo, so now it has to wear a towel. Do you think if I belted this blouse instead of tucking it into the skirt it would be more flattering in the hip region?"

"Warning, warning! Do not mention her butt! Whatever you do, do not mention her butt!"

Both Tiffany and I ignored Jim. Her head tipped to the side, her long blond ponytail swinging gently behind her. "It might help a little bit. What are you doing here?"

I yanked the sleeveless gauze blouse out of my skirt and used the silk scarf that I'd been wearing to confine my hair as a belt instead. "We're waiting on a friend who drives a taxi. We're going into the city because I have to deliver something to someone."

"Oooh, a drive! I love to go for drives. I love to see people, and share smiles, and feel the warm glowing goodness that always follows me."

She waited, expectant.

My lips curved into a bit of a forced smile. I didn't want to be downright rude to Tiffany, but I really didn't relish the thought of being confined with her chirpy brand of self-centered altruism, either. "Er . . . we'd love to have you come with us, Tiffany, but the truth is, I don't know where to find the person I'm looking for, so the trip is bound to take at least a few hours. I'm sure you'd be bored, not to mention you'd miss the lunch banquet and some of the afternoon's workshops."

She clapped her hands together happily. "A long ride! That is even better, because then there are so many more people to see and share smiles and happiness with! We will be like butterflies flitting from person to person, bringing joy wherever we go. Thank you for the kind invitation to join you, Aisling. I do not mind in the least missing either lunch or a few workshops, and I do not have any appointments until the moon comes up later tonight."

"Uh—"

A car had pulled up while we were speaking, disgorging a couple of occupants, the driver coming around to pull luggage from the rear of the car while the man and woman went into the hotel. The driver, a handsome man with a brown goatee, turned to walk past us. Instead, the bags fell from his hands as he flung himself at me, wrapping his arms around my legs and saying something in fervent Hungarian into my pelvis.

"What the—hey! Get off me!" I tried to step backwards out of the man's embrace, but he just clung tighter to me, speaking in between the kisses he was pressing into my stomach.

"How very curious," Tiffany said, eyeing the man doubtfully. She pulled a mirror from her purse and checked herself. "Most unexplained. This man, he says he wishes to have many sex acts with you."

I grabbed the man's ears and tried to push him off me. He just made kissy lips at me, his arms locked around the back of my legs. "Well, he's not getting any! You! Go away! No sex! Bad man! Leave me alone or I'll deck you! Crap, he doesn't seem to understand. Tiffany, you must speak Hungarian if you understood what he said?"

"Yes, my mother was from a small town near the Romanian border," she said, still primping as she frowned slightly into the mirror. "It does not make sense at all. Here am I, all sunshine and beauty and glorious Summer Eyes, and yet the man, he kisses her belly and not mine. My belly is very smooth and nice."

"Look, this isn't a—hey, hey, hey! No squeezing cheek, buster! This isn't a contest, Tiffany. Nor do I want this man's attentions. Would you please tell him to go away and leave me alone?"

She rattled off something to the man. He answered her as he shook his head, releasing one arm around my legs in order to grab my wrist and begin placing wet, smacking kisses along my hand.

Tiffany shrugged. "He says he will give you many fine babies. He says he will spend every waking moment making many sex acts with you. It is obvious to me that he is without his brains. I am a virgin. I have much charm and attractiveness, and my smile is very happy. It is impossible that he should desire you over me unless he is without his brains."

"No babies," I shrieked, pulling ruthlessly on his hair. "No sex acts! Jim, dammit, help me!"

"What do you want me to do, bite him?" Jim asked, sitting next to the bench, watching the scene with amusement glittering in its eyes.

"Yes, thank you, if it wouldn't be too much trouble," I snarled, pounding the man's head with my free arm.

Rene pulled up on the other side of the lust-crazed madman's car, his lips pursing in a silent whistle when he saw us.

"Right, that's it. No more miss nice guy." I brought the knee of my free leg up into the crazy man's jaw, his head snapping back with an audible grunt of pain. He fell backwards when I lunged sideways, but he didn't completely release me, one hand grabbing frantically for my ankle. I threw myself toward the taxi, trying desperately to shake him off. Tiffany had already entered the car, with

Jim right behind her. Rene leaned out the window as I staggered toward the taxi, the mad driver doing a commando crawl after me, refusing to release my ankle.

"You are having some difficulty, yes?" Rene asked.

"Difficulty? I don't know what you mean," I answered, whirling around to stomp my sandal down hard on the man's wrist. He screeched and let go of my ankle, sobbing into the pavement as I jumped into the taxi. "Nothing out of the ordinary as far as my life goes. Drive, please, Rene, before he stops crying about his hand."

Rene cocked his head for a moment as he listened to the man blubber, then shifted gears and pulled out. "He was sobbing most harshly about your rejection of him, Aisling, not because you stepped on his arm. Who is he?"

I tightened the strap on my ankle that the madman had loosened. "I have no idea. He jumped me for no reason. I've never met him before. As far as I know, he's just a taxi driver."

"One without his brains," Tiffany added, putting away her mirror and gifting Rene with a dazzling smile. "I am Tiffany. I am a professional virgin. If you were to choose between kissing Aisling's belly and mine, you would choose mine, would you not? My belly is very smooth and white."

Rene's glance flickered from Tiffany to me in the mirror. "A professional virgin?"

Her smile brightened until it almost blinded me. "Yes. I am very happy to meet you and bring you the joy of my beauty. You are friend to Aisling and Jim the demon?"

"Rene is a very good friend," I answered, since Rene seemed to be a bit stunned by Tiffany's statement regarding her occupation. I should have known better, though.

Anyone who took Jim's existence in stride after only a few moments was not a man who balked at meeting a professional virgin.

"I believe that if I were to make a choice, I would have to choose Aisling's belly to kiss, but that is only because she is my *bon ami, hein*? If she was not, then I would choose your belly above all others."

Tiffany seemed to accept that, sitting back against the seat, looking around with pleasure. Jim sat with its head hanging out the window, as usual. "Where is it we are going to on this long and pleasant drive?"

I met Rene's gaze in the mirror and mentally shrugged. It looked like I was saddled with a virgin while I hermit-hunted. "I'm going to a shop on the Andrássy út. It's the last address my uncle had for the hermit. Supposedly, he picks up his mail there, but Uncle Damian's last letter two weeks ago warning of my arrival went unanswered."

"A hermit? You seek a hermit?" Tiffany smiled brightly as I nodded. "This is excellent! Virgins, as you know, are most helpful when it comes to hermits."

"Really?" I said, unable to keep from asking. "I thought it was unicorns that couldn't resist a virgin."

"Unicorns, hermits, sprites—both water and forest—and werefolk of all forms. You will find that employing a professional virgin will increase your Guardian productivity many times. It will give you quite the cachet amongst other Guardians, as well."

"Employ? No, I—"

"My rates are quite reasonable," Tiffany continued, just as if I hadn't spoken. "I have many good testimonies and, of course, my portfolio, which has splendid pictures of me in many happy poses. You will be most pleased with my excellent services."

"But I don't have a budget for a virgin," I protested, my mind squirreling desperately for a way to extract myself from her clutches. "I couldn't possibly afford your services, as wonderful as I'm sure they are."

"Perhaps your uncle will allow you one if you explain to him the situation," Rene offered as we drove through the city toward a popular street in the center.

I groaned. "Not you, too, Rene."

He smiled at me in the mirror. "It seems to me that you cannot have too much help, *hein*?"

"That's a matter of opinion—"

Jim pulled in its head long enough to shoot me a weary look. "Give it up, Ash. You need help, and Tiffany here is offering it. You'd be a fool to turn her down because you're a tightwad."

"I am *not* a tight—"

"Jim speaks correctly," Rene interrupted with a nod. "You need help. Me, I am the driver *très bon, très extraordinaire*, but I am not knowing Budapest as well as Paris. So if this young lady of the smooth white belly offers to help you find the lost hermit, you should not spurn up your nose at her."

"Turn your nose up," I corrected him, giving in with a little reluctance and a whole lot of misgivings. I knew when I was bested, and to be honest, both Jim and Rene had a point. I didn't know the city at all, and if Tiffany really did have some sort of hermit-attracting powers, she would come in handy. "All right, you can help, but I can't pay you more than a hundred and fifty bucks. That was supposed to be my mad money, but I guess nothing defines mad quite so much as buying a professional virgin."

"It is acceptable," Tiffany said, doing her little happy hand-clapping thing. "Now, let us plan how to find this hermit. He will be in the nearby forests, yes? A cave, perhaps? There are many caves in Hungary, many around the city."

"I don't know exactly where he is," I answered. "My uncle seemed to think he'd be camping out in a forest or something like that, but who knows with hermits? Uncle Damian said this guy was a bit flighty, not wanting to give his real name or any identifying information. And he paid in gold. Not gold ingots or anything like that—he paid in gold coins stamped with some strange symbols. I didn't have time to look them up, but they seemed very strange, not at all like the sorts of things I've seen in theurgical books."

"Do not worry. We will find this hermit," Rene said, gaily blowing his horn and flipping off a discourteous driver. "It is a challenge, and we are *par excellence* when it comes to challenges, are we not?"

I thought of the last challenge I'd issued—to Drake, of all people—and its subsequent outcome. Although I had intended for him to beat me, I had hoped that he'd recognize my generous act in saving face for him and eliminate the punishment I was due by his sept, but he hadn't. Back home in Oregon the fact that his entire clan had a say in how I was to be punished for failing the challenge hadn't worried me, but it was another matter now that I was here, about to be mixed up in dragon politics.

As much as my frugal nature resented being put in a position where I had to hire Tiffany, I admitted two hours later that she had been a very useful translator. I had planned on pressing Rene into that position, since my skills with the language were obviously faulty, but it turned out that he was needed to keep Jim in line while Tiffany and I went on a wild-goose chase that led us from the Pest side (west of the Danube) to the Buda side of the city, finally ending in a tiny, dusty antique shop.

"Well, that was an utter waste of two hours," I said as we emerged from the dark shop. I wiped a few cobwebs off my arm where it had brushed against a faded, battered trunk. "We're no better off than when we started."

"That is not true. We have spread much joy. I have smiled at seventeen people. And you know that the hermit is definitely in a park outside the limits of the city."

"A fact that would be more helpful if there weren't gazillions of parks around Budapest," I groused, then immediately felt bad. It wasn't Tiffany's fault that the hermit was evidently so paranoid he shuffled his mail through six different points, all of which knew only the next forwarding address. "I'm sorry, Tiffany. My bad mood is no reflection on you. You were a great help translating for me. It would have taken a lot longer without you."

She looked pleased as we walked down the busy street toward a car park Rene had found hidden behind an office building that still bore on its walls the shadows of communist slogans that had been ripped off during Hungary's bloodless revolution. We had seen many such buildings during our unintentional tour of the city, taking us from stately, ornately decorated buildings that counted time by the century to modern, brightly lit shops whose neon lights promised everything from discos to Internet access.

"I am very good with people. It is my eyes. They see kindness within, and it spills out to light their lives with happy thoughts. Now you have seen how I do it, you, too, must share your happiness with others."

Rene was a block away, walking toward us with Jim on a leash beside him, the ubiquitous white plastic bag tied to the leash signaling to all that we were in full compliance with the rules regarding dogs and their leavings. Evidently Jim had finally convinced Rene to take it for a quick walkie. Tiffany and I stopped next to Rene's car, Tiffany careful to avoid touching the hot metal of the vehicle. I leaned against it, my arms crossed, as I thought about my options. "Fiat's offer notwithstanding, assuming I had the money, which I don't, I could hire one of his men to do a little hermit tracking for me, but I'm fairly certain they'd need a scent or something to follow, so that's out."

Tiffany murmured something noncommittal.

I chewed on my lower lip as the heat of the car swirled up and around me, bathing me in a pleasant sensation of warm comfort. "I don't know anything about the red dragons, other than that they're clearly clotheshorses, but Gabriel . . . hmmm. He might help me find the hermit if I asked him."

"You would ask another for assistance when you have me?" Tiffany stopped buffing a fingernail to give me an outraged look.

"You said your skills would be in drawing the hermit out from where he was hiding once we found the general location," I pointed out. "Unless you want to walk every square inch of every park outside the city, I'm going to need more help. And if there's one thing I've learned from my time with Drake, it's that dragons can be very resourceful when they want to be."

She sniffed and looked away. "Why do you not ask this Drake person to help you? Jim says he is a wyvern and you are his mate, which means he must do as you ask."

I had a good long mental giggle over the thought of Drake doing as I asked, sobering when I realized that his earlier maneuvering might actually benefit me as much as him. "You know, you just may have something there, Tiff. Drake is going to owe me after this lunch—oh, crap, the lunch! What time is it? Is it anywhere near two?"

"Any."

"Huh?" What on earth was her problem? Tiffany was giving me a thin-lipped look that left her shy happy eyes expressing a whole lot of pointed discontent.

"Any. My name, it is Tiff*any*. Mama named me for the very elegant shop that sells jewelry in New York, New York."

"Oh. Sorry."

She nodded primly and glanced at her wrist. "It is ten minutes after two o'clock."

"Crap, crap, and double crap. Rene! We have to go! Right now!"

I did an agitated little dance as Rene and Jim hurried toward us, mentally writing the apology I'd make to Drake when I arrived back at the hotel, late, not dressed in green, and sweaty from driving all around the city in a non-air-conditioned car.

Sometimes it seemed like life was really against me.

9

As I feared, the dragons' lunch was well under way when Jim and I arrived at the atrium at the back of the hotel, overlooking the muddy brown (never blue, I found out from Tiffany) Danube River.

"Hi. Sorry I'm late," I said breathlessly as I stopped in front of the large round table that dominated the small restaurant. Fronds of tall, spiky palms waved gracefully as Jim and I rushed past them to the two empty seats next to Drake. "Traffic was horrible. There's been no . . . uh . . . plague talk or anything, has there?"

The men at the table rose, leaving the Chinese woman the only one seated. Drake waved an elegant hand at them, saying, "You are acquainted with Fiat and his men."

I murmured a polite hello, first making sure my mental guards were up to keep Fiat out of my head.

"The man to the left of Renaldo is Gabriel Tauhou, the wyvern of the silver dragons. Accompanying him are Tipene and Maata."

I realized as the two silver dragon bodyguards bowed that the taller of the two, the one named Maata, was a woman. All three dragons had beautiful coffee-colored skin, short glossy black hair, and astonishingly bright gray eyes, but hefty as Tipene was, Maata had a glint to her eyes that made me think she was the more dangerous of the two.

"Nice to meet you. Hi again, Gabriel."

"Hi . . . again?" Drake asked, his jaw tightening as he swung around to pin me back with an emerald-eyed glare. "You know Gabriel?"

"Aisling and I met last night," Gabriel said with a slight smile. His eyes, however, danced merrily, which made me think he was enjoying teasing Drake. "She was in some difficulty, and I was happy to be of service to her."

"He sucked her arm," Jim said, climbing onto one of the free chairs. "There was tongue everywhere. It was a horrible thing to see."

Drake's fire—usually carefully banked—roared to life within him as I shot Jim a fulminating glare before turning back to the irate dragon next to me. "It's not like the demon is making it sound."

"Did you know that you only call me 'the demon' when you're pissed at me?"

I ignored Jim's attempt to bait me. Drake didn't have a terribly passive temper, and if I wanted to avoid horrible repercussions to the world as I knew it, I'd have to keep him calm so he didn't trigger a modern plague epidemic.

"Someone stole the amulet I'm supposed to deliver, and my arm got knifed in the process. Gabriel stopped the bleeding, then got my amulet back. That's all there was to it."

"She was not hurt seriously," Gabriel added. "Otherwise I would, as is my duty, have taken her into protective custody."

I almost groaned, instead thinning my lips at Gabriel and sending him a look that demanded he cease and desist.

Drake stiffened beside me, his voice as smooth and cold as Italian marble as he said, "Aisling is my mate. Do you wish to challenge me for her, Tauhou?"

Silence fell in the atrium, broken only by the faint chirping of birds in a huge aviary that spanned one wall. Evidently the dragons had reserved the entire restaurant, because there were no other patrons, not even a waitperson in sight. My breath stopped for a moment while I joined everyone else to watch Gabriel. Then I remembered that I was there under protest and wasn't the wimpy, weak sort of woman who allowed other people to make decisions about her life.

"If anyone is going to challenge for me, it's going to be me," I said, somewhat irrationally. "Now, can we stop this pissing contest and get on with things? There's a poltergeist seminar I'd like to attend in an hour."

Drake didn't move as I tried to tug him down into his chair. His eyes remained locked on Gabriel. The latter smiled even brighter as he glanced toward me, making a slight gesture of surrender.

"I do not challenge you for your mate, Vireo." I don't know if everyone breathed a sigh of relief at Gabriel's words, but I sure did. Until he went and ruined it. *"Yet."*

Drake made him a formal bow. "I await your pleasure."

"Oh, for heaven's sake. Can we stop with the

manly . . . er . . . dragonly posturing, please? No one is challenging anyone."

"Someone already has," István muttered under his breath, shooting me a look that could pierce cement.

Drake evidently saw reason (at last) because he gestured toward the rest of the dragons. "Beyond Maata is Shing and Sying, elite guards of Lung Tik Chuan Ren, the wyvern of the red dragons. Her mate is Li."

Li gave me a tight-lipped smile, turning solicitously toward his wyvern. Chuan Ren wore a scarlet dress so heavily embroidered with gold, pearls, hematite, and jade that it must have weighed a ton. The front laced up to the bottom of her breastbone, leaving most of her chest exposed, her nipples just barely hidden by the wide red ribbon lacing. It was sexy, scandalous, and deliberately worn to be as provocative as possible, and I knew the minute her assessing gaze passed over my rumpled, sweat-stained gauze skirt and blouse that she dismissed me as being not worth her consideration.

"Your name, it is a man's?" she asked in nearly unaccented English.

"No, my name, it is Irish. But very female." I rustled up a polite smile before sitting in the chair Drake held for me, reminding myself that all I had to do was sit and nod and just make it through the lunch without Fiat throwing a monkey wrench in the peace talks, or the dragons starting a plague on humankind, or Jim embarrassing me any further. Three little things, that's all I had to do. Four if you counted getting Drake aside long enough to warn him that Fiat was up to no good.

Drake snapped his fingers, and out of a dense clutch of palms a waiter in black appeared, hurrying toward me with two plates of salad in his hands. He paused before Jim, giving the demon a curious glance, but at a word from Drake he placed the salad carefully on the table before turning to me.

Endive, arugula, and escarole scattered everywhere as the waiter suddenly flung the plate down and threw himself on me, his mouth pressed against my neck, his hands caressing me.

"Um," I said. Every single person at the table was staring at me, eyebrows raised at the sight of a waiter slurping away on my neck while groping my nearby available body parts. I scooped a few bits of greens back onto the salad plate and lifted my fork. "So, how are the negotiations going?"

Drake cocked a glossy black eyebrow, his voice dry as he asked, "Is there something you wish to share with us, mate?"

"Share?" I asked, my voice cracking as between kisses the waiter murmured soft words into my collarbone, his hands sweeping upward to my breasts. I plucked them off and put them back on my waist. "I haven't the slightest idea what you mean. Oh, him?" I laughed a gay little laugh. Or I tried to—what came out was more than a little tinged with hysteria. "You mean this man glued to my front? Think nothing of it. I believe my great and overwhelming charm is overcoming men, and helpless against me, they—"

I stopped. I had to. Not even in my wildest, most unrealistic dreams did I believe that it was plain old Aisling Grey who had men suddenly powerless with lust. Something supernatural was going on, and I finally had the sense to admit it.

Drake said something in Hungarian that had the waiter lifting his head from my neck, but the rest of him was still pressed tightly against me. He shook his head and refused to leave me. Drake insisted. I sat helpless, embarrassed as hell, mentally going over everything I had done since arriving in Hungary to figure out what it was that was making me irresistible.

"Never mess with a dragon's mate," Jim warned the waiter seconds before Drake's fire flashed in his eyes. The waiter let go of me then, flinging himself from me to run screaming from the room.

"I didn't know you could set people's hair on fire with just a look," I told Drake.

He shrugged. "You never asked. Now let us see what it is that is causing such trouble." His long fingers were warm on my collarbone as he plucked out the chain holding the dragon talisman. Immediately, twelve pairs of eyes lit up.

"No!" I said firmly, giving each and every dragon present a quelling look. "It has hardly any gold on it, and it's not valuable, and it's mine, you all got that? Mine! No one takes it!"

Chuan Ren looked closely at it for a moment before brushing it away with her scarlet and gold-tipped fingernails. "It is the Qing dynasty. Very poor quality."

"The talisman is not what is causing your difficulties," Drake said, his fingers dipping down under my blouse.

"Hey!" I said, momentarily scandalized before his hand emerged with the amulet. I wasn't fooled, though. His fingers had done a little extra touching while down in the Valley o' Breasts.

He pulled the thin chain bearing the amulet over my

head, holding the piece up to catch the sunlight that streaked in through the palm leaves, the amber and white crystal gleaming brightly as he turned it. "What do the markings say?"

"I have no idea. My uncle thought they were Etruscan. The provenance says the piece came from an Italian collector of Pompeian artifacts, so it might well be—kind of a side interest, I guess."

"Allow me to see it," Fiat said, reaching for the amulet.

"No!" I shouted, leaning forward to snatch the crystal out of Drake's hand. Fiat's eyes narrowed at me, his nostrils flaring with anger over my apparent rudeness.

"I'm sorry, but no one gets to touch this. It's not mine to share. It belongs to someone else, and until I deliver it I'm responsible for its safekeeping."

"Aisling, Fiat has asked to see the amulet, not steal it from you." Drake's voice was low and persuasive, but I wasn't going to allow it to seduce me into handing over the amulet.

"I might be able to translate the markings for you," Fiat added, his lips stretched into a tight smile that didn't match the coldness in his eyes. "I have some experience with ancient languages of Italy."

"Thank you. That's very kind. I'll be sure to tell the buyer of your generous offer."

"Aisling," Drake said in my ear, his voice as soft and caressing as the fingers that stroked the back of my neck. "You are being impolite. This summit is a time for the septs to put away their differences and work toward common understanding. Your distrust of Fiat will unmake all the work we have done so far."

I smiled at everyone, a great big smile, while hissing awkwardly through my teeth at Drake, "Just how stupid do you think I am? Once Fiat gets his hands on the amulet, I'll never see it again."

"He would not dare take it from you." Drake's breath was hot on my ear, sending little skittles of fire down my neck to shiver down my back.

My voice rose in indignation. The occupants of the table watched with fascinated interest as I pushed Drake away and pulled the amulet over my head, tucking it back down into my shirt before crossing my arms over my chest. "Oh, he wouldn't, huh? Just like you wouldn't steal my aquamanile and refuse to give it back?"

His fingers paused for a moment, then slid down my back in a gentle caress that did nothing to reassure me. "That is different."

"Really? How is it different?"

"You gave me the aquamanile. You said you trusted only me to keep it and the other Tools of Bael."

"I didn't give it to you. You took it. You *stole* it from me! I just let you keep it. There's a difference."

"I grow weary of this," Chuan Ren said, pushing her plate back. "Your mate shows much disrespect, Drake. Punish her, give Fiat the crystal, and let us get on with more important matters."

I bristled at her demand. "Now, just wait a second, sister—"

She rose up out of her chair, her eyes huge with outrage. "I am not your sister—"

"Mate, I must insist—"

"You want that salad, Ash? This diet is going to be the death of me—"

All hell broke loose at that point. Literally. It wasn't just the babble of voices as everyone at the table started talking at once, the indignant demands from Fiat and his boys that I hand over the amulet, or the screeching of Chuan Ren that signaled the opening of the portal to Hell. No, it was the sudden appearance in the middle of the table of a man in hot-pink fishnet stockings, matching leather corset, and turquoise feather tutu that let everyone know that something was seriously wrong.

"Fires of Abaddon, Ilarax, what are you wearing? Don't tell me you've gone transvestite!" Drake pulled me away as Jim put its front paws on the table and snuffled the demon's nearest leg. "Aw, damn, it's true. You've gone girly."

"What the—"

"Don't say it," Drake growled, clamping a hand over my mouth as he pulled me backwards to the relative safety of a pillar framed with palms. "Never say that word in the presence of an open portal."

"Guardian!" Chuan Ran shouted, pointing her finger at me. "Close this portal immediately!"

The demon in drag squawked, its voice shattering the water glasses on the table. From a shimmering area at its feet, dozens of tiny little pink and turquoise creatures burst forth, scampering over the table, leaping onto the chairs and the floor with tiny little eek-eek yips.

"Man, he's gone and tinted his imps to match his costume." Jim jumped off the table, shaking its head as it walked toward us. "Now that's the sign of a demon needing some serious therapy time."

"Imps?" I said. "You mean they're real? They're not some sort of weirdo Otherworld joke?"

"Do they look like a joke?" Drake asked, shaking a turquoise imp off from where it was gnawing on his shoelace. When the little creature made like it was going to return to his shoe, Drake narrowed his eyes and allowed a little smoke to trickle out of his nose. The imp squeaked in horror and ran to join a few of its brethren in an attempt to push a crystal glass off a nearby table.

"Do you want the honest answer, or the thoughtful and erudite one that I as a future Guardian would give? Jim! What in heaven's name are you doing?"

Jim's head whipped around to look at me, two tiny turquoise feet twitching between its lips. Jim gulped, ran its tongue around its lips, and blinked innocently. "What?"

"Bad demon! You're on a diet, and besides, it's not nice to eat imps! They're kind of cute even if they are a bit troublesome—" Three pink imps succeeded in knocking a water goblet over, dancing a happy little victory dance around the soggy tablecloth. One of them stopped in front of me, turned around, and bent over until its pointy little chin touched its knees. "Oh my god, did that little monster just moon me?"

"You were saying?" Jim asked, sucking its teeth.

"Guardian!" Chuan Ren bellowed. Two of her men were struggling with the demon, but it was clear to see that against the minion of Hell the dragons didn't have a lot of power. "Close the portal. Now!"

Drake gave me a little shove forward. "Perhaps it would be best if you do as she asks, Aisling. The imps are harmless, but who knows what will follow the demon?"

I looked at him as if he had imps dancing on his head.

"What? You're kidding, right? You don't actually expect me to close that portal?"

"That's going to stain," Jim said as one of Fiat's men stomped on an imp that was running toward him with a cocktail fork clutched in three of its four arms, scraping the turquoise smear off onto the ceramic pot holding a nearby palm.

"I realize you do not have much experience as a Guardian—" Drake started to say.

I interrupted him. "None. Try none. Other than summoning Jim and dealing with that demon lord last month, my experience with portals to you-know-where is exactly nil."

"*A fene egye meg,*" Drake muttered.

"You can say that again, not that I know what you said, but the way you said it leads me to believe that you've captured my feelings in a few succinct words."

"It means 'damn it.' I thought you were being modest when you told me about your lack of skills," Drake said hurriedly, turning to bark out a few orders to Pál and István before turning the others. "We will have to locate a Guardian quickly. Chuan Ren, you must keep the demon from leaving this room. Subdue it if you can, but at all costs it must be kept from leaving. Fiat, your men must stand guard at the portal to ensure nothing else enters. Gabriel and I will gather the imps before they do any real damage. Pál and István will find a Guardian."

"What do you want me to do?" I asked as Drake's men ran past, out to the hotel proper. The look they gave me spoke volumes, and none of it was overly flattering.

"Stay out of the way," Drake answered, grabbing a

tablecloth and throwing it on a fire a small herd of imps had started using lunch menus.

I felt lower than a snake's belly, helpless, a waste of oxygen standing there while the dragons handled the imps and demons and who knew what else that might spew forth from the portal.

"Dammit, I'm a Guardian!" I told Jim. "I'm a professional! I have power!"

"Uh-huh. And Ilarax there is going to take the title of studmuffin of the year."

"I do have power. I have lots of power, oodles of it floating around me. How many people do you know who can harness a dragon's fire? I just need to focus. If I do that, perhaps I can slam the portal shut until one of Drake's guys shows up with an experienced Guardian."

The demon, which had been engaging in a fairly impressive display of martial arts with two of Chuan Ren's bodyguards, leaped back onto the table and started chanting a familiar spell. It was summoning other demons. Chuan Ren threw herself at it, knocking it down onto the table, but despite its femmy getup, it was strong. She went flying across the room with a shriek that was almost as painful on the ears as the demon's.

If I didn't stop the demon, it would summon up its demon lord's horde. And *that* could only be bad news. "Come on, Jim," I said, mentally girding my loins as I strode forward. "We have a portal to close."

"What? Are you insane? You don't know the first thing about closing portals!" Jim stared at me in openmouthed horror as I pushed past it and marched to the table. The demon Ilarax, which had resumed its invocation, spun around and glared at me as I approached.

"That's right, but you do. Quickly, what do I have to do to shove your colorful friend back through the portal?"

"Ilarax is no friend of mine. He's in Magoth's legions, and that, let me tell you, is one badass demon lord. You don't want to mess with one of his demons."

"I don't care if it's a member of the Supreme Court. I just want to know how to shove it back," I said through my teeth, trying to maintain my smile as Ilarax stomped its way across the table to stand in front of me, its hands on its befeathered tutu hips. Three imps marched behind the demon, their arms (they each had four) on their tiny little hips in a very bizarre parody as they eek-eeked aggressively at me.

"You need the twelve words," Jim answered, hiding behind me, its big furry head peeking around my thighs to look at the demon.

"Guardian! You do not have the strength to hold me!" Ilarax snarled in a high-pitched voice. "To try is folly. Bow down unto the power of Ilarax and acknowledge me as your master!"

"Twelve words? Not the twelve words that are different for each demon? Not the twelve friggin' words that no one but the demon knows? Not *those* twelve words, Jim?"

"Yup, those are the ones."

One of Chuan Ren's men pulled himself up from the floor, wiping blood out of his eyes as he snarled something that sounded really nasty. A knife flashed in his hand as he attacked the demon, but it fell impotently when the demon twisted the dragon's arm into an unnatural position, the horrible crunching, popping sound making my stomach turn over.

"You sure you're up to this?" Jim whispered.

The dragon guard screamed as the demon threw him through one of the glass walls.

"Sure I'm sure. It's just a demon, right? I can handle that."

Li, the red wyvern's mate, leaped up from where he was trying to revive Chuan Ren and ran screaming toward the demon. Without even looking at the dragon, the demon lashed a leg out and caught Li full in the belly. He slammed into a wall, sliding down it like a limp sack of potatoes.

Jim raised its eyebrows. Drake and Gabriel's men were engaged in putting out the fire, which had quickly spread along the wooden paneling on the near wall. Fiat and his guys were beating back the wave of imps as they emerged from the portal, but even with the three of them stomping and squashing as fast as they could, the little turquoise and pink creatures were getting away from them, quickly wreaking havoc.

I turned back to eye the demon. It was standing with its back to me, its arms waving as it continued the words of summoning.

"Right. Force is out. Martial arts is out. It's just me and my brain against the demon."

Jim groaned. "We're doomed."

I ignored my furry demon, a little tickle of an idea coming to mind as I snatched up the knife that one of the red dragons had dropped. There was only one thing to do.

Five minutes later Nora raced into the atrium, Pál on her heels. She skidded to a stop at the sight of me sitting on the now-subdued demon, my hand buried in its tutu. "I came as quickly as I could. The dragon said it was an emergency—are you holding a *knife* to that demon's genitalia?"

"Yep," I answered, pressing the tip of the steak knife into the demon's tender flesh. Its shriek was muffled by Jim lying across its head, but it still had enough power to cause an ice sculpture bearing caviar to crack and fall to the floor in a nasty mess. Around us, order was slowly being returned to the room. Ilarax's limbs, tied with linen napkins to the table legs, twitched as I allowed the knife to slide a little bit into its skin. "Knock off the sonic screaming or they're going to be calling you Sally."

"Ash, honey, I don't think that's going to serve as much of a threat in this instance," Jim said.

I looked down at the demon's bizarre outfit. "Oh. You may be right. Still, it surrendered rather than allowing me to hurt its noogies, which says something about it."

"But—but—" Nora looked around the room before pushing her glasses up and leaning forward to speak quietly. "Demons cannot be hurt, Aisling."

"I know, but the form they take can be destroyed. That's what made me think of a way to control this demon other than wards or the twelve words. The dragons tried to beat it up, but they didn't get very far because they didn't use their brains."

"Their brains?" Nora parroted, looking more than a little confused.

"I like to think that I take an alternate path to a solution," I said with a tiny bit of pride. "One of the things I've learned is that tackling a problem head-on isn't always the way to triumph over it. In this case, I knew there was no way I'd be able to beat the demon when it was physically stronger than me, so I decided to go for its weak point."

She looked at the demon's groin.

I nodded. "It's pretty obvious that it has masculinity issues, which means it values its manly bits. A little flick of the knife in the demonic happy zone and voilà! Instant compliance."

Nora shook her head, a slight smile on her face. "I don't believe I've ever seen anyone control a demon using only the threat of emasculation. It is unprecedented. It is . . . a quite odd method of control."

"Aisling is a very unique woman," Drake said as he walked by holding a smoking, quivering tablecloth full of imps. "It is one of her many charms."

I grinned at him.

His eyes simmered with annoyance. "It is also one of her most irritating traits. I will dispose of these imps. If you could send the demon back and close the portal, Guardian, we will ascertain the extent of our injuries and hopefully be able to continue with our summit."

Nora looked at me as Drake strode off, followed by István, Pál, and two of Fiat's men, all of whom also held imp-filled tablecloths. The red dragons had taken the brunt of the damage, but they were all conscious, bloody but unbowed, receiving medical care from Gabriel and his crew. "I am beginning to think that perhaps you are not so much in need of a mentor as you are a scorekeeper," she said cryptically, then set about sending the demon back where it came from and closing the portal.

I pondered her words the entire time she was busy, but couldn't come to any conclusion other than that she obviously thought I was a bad risk apprentice-wise.

Welcome to the club, an inner voice giggled.

10

The remainder of the dragon lunch was anticlimactic. It's hard to top a demon suddenly opening a portal to Hell right there in the middle of the table, and luckily for my peace of mind, no one tried. Nora was swift and efficient as she set about first dispersing the demon, then closing the portal, although as she left, she pointed out the portal wasn't eliminated, just closed.

"As I'm sure Aisling knows," she said with an odd look at me as she tucked away her copy of the *Grimoire of Magus Turiel,* a sixteenth-century book of conjurations, invocations, and general "how to get rid of a pesky demon" guidelines. I had a copy of the grimoire at home but hadn't thought to bring it with me since I assumed the conference was going to be nothing but lectures. "A portal can be destroyed only by a Guardian of great power. This one is merely closed. It can be reopened should a demon possessing the necessary strength desire it."

"Yeah," I said, nodding my head like mad at Drake in an attempt to look like I knew what she was talking about. "What she said. It's just closed. So don't be messing around with it."

He gave me a long look. "It was not my presence that

summoned the demon and caused it to open the portal in the first place."

I bristled at the implication in his words. "What, you're saying I did? Drake, I did *not* summon a demon. That involves drawing a circle of ash and salt and saying the invocation. I'd know if I did that, thank you very much, and I didn't!" Turning to Nora, my hands spread in supplication, I asked her, "There's no other way to summon a demon, right? You have to say the words and do the circle thing?"

"That is the most common way to summon a servant of a dark lord," she agreed, "but not the only way."

Drake tugged on one of the two chains around my neck, pulling the amulet up to wave it before my eyes. "This is why the demon opened the portal before you. It was drawn by the power in the amulet, power that was enhanced and amplified by your abilities. I suspect it is also what is making mortal men apparently unable to resist the lure of your charms."

I snatched the amulet back and tucked it away, irrationally stung by the knowledge that he had to be right. Ever since I'd put the blasted thing on in order to keep it from being stolen, men—non-Otherworld men—had been on me like flies on imp droppings. I didn't want them slobbering on me, and I knew almost from the beginning that it had to be something other than me that was attracting them, but to be told that to your face by a man so incredibly handsome he made your internal organs want to jump for joy whenever he was near did no little damage to my ego. "Well, of course it's the amulet. No one said it was me doing all that."

He leaned forward, briefly brushing his lips against

mine, letting just a little flicker of his dragon fire leap to me. I embraced it, played with it, allowing it to coil around me as he said softly, "I find you utterly irresistible, Aisling."

"That's just the amulet talking," I answered, reluctantly sending his fire back to him before stepping back, away from him. There were definite limits I had when it came to Drake, and standing so close to him that I could smell that wonderfully spicy scent that was uniquely his own was way over the line of what I could deal with.

His eyes glittered with heat. "Shall we test that theory tonight?"

"No," I said quickly, stiffening my knees and backing away even farther, giving Nora a bright "Will not be having sex with a wyvern tonight because I'm dedicated to being a Guardian" smile. "Absolutely not. It's completely and utterly out of the question."

Drake just smiled. A slow, sensual, thoroughly wicked smile. One that pretty much told me my goose wasn't just cooked, it was roasted over an open fire.

I sat more or less mute for the remainder of the lunch while the four wyverns were sidetracked from the big negotiations to hash out a territorial dispute that was evidently a roadblock to a formal peace declaration. Since my input on that was not required, I mentally lectured myself while I ate *csirkemell bazsalikommal és fekete olivabogyóval* (chicken breast with basil and an olive tapenade), which was one of the most delicious dishes I'd ever tasted, and pointed out to myself that a renewal of relations with Drake was not on my list of tasks to be accomplished before the conference was over. He might be sexy as hell, he might clang my chains like no other man—or dragon—but he was a complication I didn't need in my life.

Why is it good intentions are always the first thing to go?

An hour later I checked the message board used by some of the almost two thousand conference attendees to post messages, but didn't see anything addressed to me.

"Do you think Moa is sick or something?" I asked Jim, pulling the demon aside so we weren't in the direct flow of traffic. That hour's workshops had just let out, and the halls of the convention center were suddenly filled with Mages, oracles, Guardians, and all the assorted other denizens of the Otherworld as they made a beeline for the bathrooms, checked their conference programs to decide which workshop they'd go to next, or simply stood in small groups chatting. I had asked around as soon as Drake released me from lunch duties, but no one had seen Moa since the evening before, when she and Jim and I had talked in the dog garden. "She's so professional, it doesn't seem terribly like her to miss our appointment or change it without first leaving me word."

"Maybe she's just trying to avoid you," Jim suggested, eyeing a plate containing a half-eaten sandwich that had been carelessly tossed onto a table bearing bottles of water. "Maybe you're a social pariah. Maybe word has gotten out to all Guardian mentors that you've got a badass demon in handsome dog form and a dragon who practically makes you drool when you look at him."

"I don't drool when I look at Drake." Jim cocked an eyebrow at me. "I don't! I was just hungry, and that chicken smelled yummy. And thank you for the lovely vote of confidence, but I don't believe Moa is trying to hide from me. If she changed her mind about meeting with me, she'd tell me. I think. Maybe I'll try the front desk and see if she left word for me there."

It wasn't until I had the bright idea of trying the room number that she'd mentioned earlier that the truth struck me: There was something about Europe—or rather, me *in* a European country—that was damned. Cursed. Bad to the bone, baby.

"What's going on?" Jim and I stopped about twenty feet away from the door to what I assumed was Moa's room. A small crowd of hotel maids, a couple of conference attendees, and police officials blocked the hallway.

The person in front of me turned. It was Marvabelle, drat my luck. "Why, if it isn't Ashley. Hank, look. It's Ashley and that talkin' dawg of hers."

Hank gave me a weak smile before hurriedly stepping out of the way to allow two men bearing a stretcher to pass.

"Is someone hurt?" A horrible feeling filled the pit of my belly, wrestling with the chicken and tapenade and crunchy Chinese noodles that had been served with lunch. "It's not Moa, is it?"

Marvabelle gave me an odd look. "Now, fancy you knowin' that. Hank, fancy her knowin' that."

"Oh, god," I said, fighting a bout of nausea as the men bearing the stretcher reappeared. A heavy black wool blanket was draped over the person on the stretcher, not in a keep-away-shock sort of way, but in a covered-head-to-toe way. "She's dead, isn't she? Moa's dead."

"Yes, she is. Killed, they say, by person or persons unknown." Marvabelle looked me up and down, her eyes glistening with an unholy delight. The sight of it added to my already nervous state. Someone had killed Moa? Lovely, elegant Moa? I looked around at the now scattering crowd of people, the maids standing together in a tight clutch, speaking almost soundlessly, the police disappearing back into the hotel room. The few remaining GODTAMers drifted past me. Who on earth could want to kill Moa?

Marvabelle's nasal voice pierced my horrified musings. "It's said that a woman and a big black dog were the last to see the Guardian alive."

My mouth, which I admit has a tendency to hang open when people more or less accuse me of being an accessory to murder, if not the murderer herself, did, in fact, gape slightly for the passing of a few seconds while I stared in disbelief at Marvabelle.

"The police will detain you for several hours in a small, windowless room. You will receive a sliver there," a man said as he strolled past.

"Oh, no, not you again," I growled, glaring at the back of the head of the blond Diviner named Paolo. I would have followed him and asked him just what it was he had against me, but at that moment a policewoman stepped from the hotel room and glanced toward where we stood.

"The police are going to detain you for several hours— is that what that man said?" Marvabelle asked at the top of her lungs, shooting a triumphant glance toward the policewoman. "Could that be because they realize that you, Aisling Grey, were the very last livin' soul to see that poor Guardian alive? What is it they say about the last person to see a person before they are killed, Hank?"

The policewoman pulled out a notebook and riffled

through the pages before snapping it shut and starting toward us.

Hank had the grace to look ashamed as he sidled past me. "Come along, Ma. There's that panel on water scrying you wanted to see."

"I'm sure it is somethin' about the last person to see a murder victim bein' the likeliest person to have killed them," Marvabelle said as Hank led her away.

Despite the policewoman bearing down on us, I felt obligated to set Marvabelle straight on a few things. "Look, I've been a murder suspect before, so it's nothing new and exciting. Been there, done that, figured out who the real killer was." Jim's cold nose nudged my hand. I turned to face the policewoman. "Um. Hi. I expect you'd like to talk to me, huh?"

"You are Aisling Grey? You will please to come with me. We are wishing to question you about the death of the woman named Moa Haraldsson."

I'll say this for Paolo—his interpersonal skills might not ever enchant me, but he's damned uncanny when it comes to predicting my immediate future.

By the time the police released Jim and me (the former having been ordered into silence, since I was not up to explaining to non-Otherworldians just how I came to have a wisecracking Newfie), a pale moon shone weakly in the night sky.

"I am so hungry, I could eat a skrat," Jim complained as we emerged from the depths of the police station. Worn out by the five hours of questioning, I stopped on the steps outside, sucking the tiny puncture wound on my thumb. Jim slid a glance at me. "How's the finger?"

"Fine now that Detective Lakatos finally trusted me

with a needle so I could dig the sliver out." I stopped sucking my thumb and looked around, my stomach growling audibly. "I'm hungry, too. Since we've long since missed the dinner banquet, I suppose we could stop at a fast-food place before going back to the hotel. What's a skrat?"

"House spirit. Looks like a wet chicken. You'd think that Detective Lakatos could have fed us."

I shrugged and started down the stairs. "I didn't expect food, but a cup of coffee or tea might have been nice."

Jim snickered as I hesitated on the sidewalk, unsure of which way I'd stand the best chance of finding a taxi. "Maybe she didn't offer anything because she was Lakatos intolerant. Lactose. Detective Lakatos. Get it? Ha! I kill me sometimes."

"If only," I said at the same moment a long black limo purred to a stop beside me. A tinted window slid downward with a soft electric hum.

"Would you, by any chance, be looking for a ride?" Drake asked.

I made a little face at him. "Why am I not surprised to see you?"

He smiled as the door nearest me clicked open. Inside I could see that Drake was not alone—Gabriel grinned at me from where he sat, next to a haughty Chuan Ren. "Perhaps you know it is because I would never leave my mate in a position of vulnerability? Then again, if you did not persist in following this foolish course of action, you would not have found yourself in such an untenable position."

I froze outside the limo. "Being a Guardian isn't foolish, Drake. You're the only one who has a problem with it. And you know full well that I had nothing to do with Moa's death—"

He waved away my protest. "We will discuss it at a later time."

"No, we will not. There is nothing to discuss." I gave him my best squinty eyes to let him know I meant what I said.

He wasn't at all impressed. "Come. Join us. We are going to Klub Fekete Halál. You will enjoy yourself."

"Is that a nightclub?" I asked, following Jim into the limo, doubling over into an unattractive crouch as I looked for an empty seat. Pretty much everyone but Fiat and his boys was in the limo, leaving little space for one gigantic Newfie and me. Pál, sitting next to Drake, shifted over a couple of inches. "I'll go with you, but you have to promise to feed us. We haven't had anything to eat since lunch. Um. There doesn't seem to be much space. Maybe I should sit on the floor with Jim—"

Drake stopped my waffling by pulling me half onto his lap, the remainder of me squished up against Pál. I thanked my stars that it was him and not István, who was at that very moment glaring at me, and arranged my arms and legs so that I was not draped quite so much across Drake.

"The police were not abusive to you, were they?" Gabriel asked, leaning forward to scan me for signs of police brutality. "They held you a long time for just a questioning."

"No rubber hoses or hot lights, if that's what you mean, although they weren't exactly hospitable. The reason it took so long was the seven male policemen that fell victim to the amulet."

Gabriel looked amused. "Fell victim? Did they . . . ah . . . "

"Throw themselves at my feet?" I nodded. "And not just metaphorically, either. By the time the policewoman who had me brought in got there, things had pretty much reached critical mass. Most of the policemen in the station were trying to get an orgy going, while the policewomen stood around and made what I assumed were snarky comments. Not that I blame them. The men were acting like dogs."

"But they were under the influence of the amulet, and thus they were not responsible," Gabriel argued, laughter lighting his gray eyes.

"Mmm." I rubbed the tip of my still sore thumb. "It ended up all right. The policewoman who spoke English got through with the hotel people and interviewed me, then let us go."

"Good. I worried on your behalf," Gabriel said, sitting back with a dazzling smile.

"You have injured yourself, mate?" Drake's voice, hot with innuendo and desire, swept over me as he examined my thumb.

"Yeah. But it's really that pest Paolo's fault—he predicted it just before the cops took me away. I'm really going to have to have a talk with him the next time I see him."

A wicked light entered Drake's eyes, one that had the parts of me that had never seen the light of day standing up and getting ready to party. "Would you like me to kiss it for you?"

"Hoo," I said on a breath, too tired, hungry, and exhausted to fight the attraction that always flared between us. My brain made a last-ditch attempt to point out that allowing Drake's lips near any part of my body was a bad idea, but I'd simply been through too much to fight him any more.

Luckily for my good intentions, the presence of others kept him from doing more than merely caressing the pad of my thumb with his lips. And tongue.

I don't suppose I need to mention that by the time the limo pulled up outside a tall glass-and-metal building in a chic area of town, I was a mere puddle of want and need laced with great huge dollops of desire.

Here's a little tip for those of you seeking entrance at hip nightclubs: Go with dragons. No doorman in the world will stand in their way. The line that snaked around the block outside the club meant nothing to the dragons, and who was I to complain? I walked next to Drake, his hand warm on my back as we strolled past the waiting crowd as if they weren't even there. I tried to adopt the elegant, powerful movement that was Drake's natural walk, but stopped when Jim asked in a loud voice if I had to use the bathroom.

The doorman took one look at Drake (black silk shirt, black leather pants), Chuan Ren (floor-length glittery dress, split to either hip, stilettos that could put an eye out at five paces), and Gabriel (dark khaki pants, silver net transparent shirt bearing elaborate designs in pale green) and almost swooned with joy. He couldn't get the door open fast enough, waving the rest of the dragon entourage in, including Jim, without blinking an eye. The music from the dance floor swept out and caught us up in its lithe grip, pulling us into a smoky high-ceilinged hall filled with the standard dance club metal pillars, crisscrossed by girders laden with pulsing laser lights arcing above and through the mass of humanity that covered every square inch of the floor.

"Would you like to dance?" Drake asked, his breath skittering down my spine, sinking deep into my blood.

"No, we'd like to eat. As in now." Jim didn't wait for me to answer. It just marched off in a very determined manner to find a table.

I grimaced, then gave Drake half a smile. "Jim's a bit testy because it missed its dinner."

"And you?" he asked, his hands sliding up my arms, his head tipped toward mine so I could see straight into his beautiful forest eyes. Heat shimmered between us. "Are you testy as well?"

I gasped, looking around nervously, as his dragon fire flickered out to lick my skin. Although we stood on the fringe of the dance floor, the club really was packed. Most of the floor space was taken up by a dense collection of people who bounced, swayed, and twirled in time to the low, pulsing music, but along the outer edges small round red tables and chairs had been scattered. Most of those were claimed, too.

"Drake, you can't. Not here. Not where someone might notice that you're not exactly human."

"Aisling, this club is owned by a nymph. No one will think anything of us being here." The heat of his desire and need rippled around me, teasing me, touching me just long enough to awaken the fire that Drake had started in me, which never seemed to go entirely cold.

"Oh. Well, if that's the case—" I threw myself on him. Drake rocked backwards with the force of my body slamming into his, every last shred of my good intentions shriveled and blown away on a wind of arousal that left me breathless even as I sucked the air right out of his mouth. His fire roared to life around us, through us, a shared flame that I not only embraced but celebrated. His mouth and hands were hard on me, softening as I relaxed against him, knowing he loved to dominate and finding little to complain about when I let him have his way. The touch of his tongue on mine drove my temperature even higher, his mouth a heady banquet of sensations that left my head spinning, my body tight and aching, and my soul burning bright alongside his in an erotic conflagration.

It wasn't until the overhead fire sprinklers turned on that I realized that what I had assumed was only an emotion shared between us had materialized physically. I pulled my mouth from Drake's and glanced up at the sprinkler, then around in surprise. We stood alone, the dancers and music having stopped, everyone giving us a wide berth. And we were on fire. No, that's not quite accurate—we were the fire. Flames leaped up around us, as if we were standing in the middle of a bonfire.

"Drake," I said, my eyes getting big as I watched flames lick down my arms to him. "I'm on fire."

He nuzzled my neck. "I burn for you, as well, mate."

I blew experimentally on the fire burning merrily on my shoulder. I couldn't feel anything other than the power of his dragon fire, but it was extremely unnerving to see my body fully engulfed in flames. "No, I mean I'm really on fire. Big yellow and red flamey things on my arms." I stepped backwards, out of his embrace, looking down at myself. "And my legs. Both of them. They're burning, Drake. So are yours."

A woman in a spangled white and gold miniskirt pushed her way through the watching crowd.

"Is this normal? I've felt your dragon fire before, but it's never actually done the barbecue thing on us. Why am I not screaming in agony? Why doesn't it hurt?"

"It is a sign of your passion, of the passion we share, a manifestation of your true nature. My fire cannot hurt you so long as you accept it," Drake answered before turning to greet the miniskirt. "Flavia, how lovely you look this evening."

The woman stopped next to me, hands on her hips as she glared up at him. She was a good foot and a half shorter than Drake, but her steely glare packed a wallop that had me backed up a couple of steps until Drake grabbed my arm and pulled me up close to him. "Drake Vireo! I might have known it was you causing all this trouble. Look what you've done to my dance floor!"

I looked down, slapping at the flames creeping up my thighs. The floor had a sooty, singed look where we had been standing.

"Do you have any idea how expensive it is to refinish this floor? I insist that you stop showing off this instant."

Drake bowed and reclaimed his fire, the flames around us dying into nothing. "Naturally I will pay for any damage my mate has caused."

"Excuse me?" I poked him in the chest. "I'm not Torchy the Dragon. You are! Don't go blaming your lack of fire control on me."

The nymph named Flavia turned on me, giving me a furious look. "And you—what sort of a Guardian are you who would endanger the lives of others? You are supposed to protect people, not be so selfish that your own needs come before the good of others. You disgust me! I spit on you!"

And she did, she spat right at my feet. Luckily I moved aside before it could hit me. "But—but—it was *his* fire—I didn't do anything other than kiss him—"

Her eyes narrowed. Her nostrils flared. Her lips curled in scorn. "You are the mate, it is you who triggers his fire. You will never again do so in my club or I will ban you from the premises forever!"

My jaw worked soundlessly a couple of times before I turned to Drake and tried to glare the hair right off his head. "Don't you want to say something? Don't you want to explain that it was you who started this, not me? Don't you want to take the responsibility for anything you do?"

He pursed his lips thoughtfully. "What will you give me if I do?"

"Argh!"

Drake pulled me away at that point, which was a good thing because I was about ready to throttle him. Everything had a price with him. Every time I needed his help, it was only available if I had something to trade for it. The man was entirely untrustworthy, unreliable, and thoroughly maddening. What had I been thinking to allow myself back into a position of intimacy with him?

I fumed all the way to the table Jim had claimed. The red dragons were in the quickly re-forming mob on the dance floor, but Gabriel and one of his guards sat next to Jim, drinking and watching the crowd.

"That was a dirty trick, lighting me up and making a scene, then letting me take the rap for it without one single, solitary word of explanation," I muttered to Drake as he held out a chair for me. I leaned into him so the others couldn't hear. "I swear, Drake, this time we're really through. It's over. There is no passion. There is no touching, no kissing, no more of that mind-meltingly-fabulous sex, and no dragon fire. It's over. You got that?"

Drake just smiled, his fire still visible in his eyes.

I growled to myself and slumped back in the chair, hungry, tired, and angry at my own stupidity. Well, twice burned, well learned—or however that phrase went. This time I was serious. This time it was truly over.

11

Drake came to me in a dream. He'd done it before, using some tenuous psychic connection between us to parade his seductive self around in my dreams, turning them into erotic experiences that left me jerking awake with my heart racing, my skin sweaty, the taste of him still on my tongue.

Not to mention other places.

I knew the moment I dipped my toe into the warm water that I was having a dream, one of Drake's dreams, the kind that would end up with me more confused than ever.

"This isn't going to work," I said aloud, my voice echoing slightly, the rustle of my clothing as it fell to the floor the only other sound. I stood on the steps leading down into a big square pool of water, scented and warmed so it lapped around my toes like a lover's tongue. Surrounding me were classical white columns, the walls of the room—if there were any—hidden in shadows, the floor of black-and-white marble cool against the soles of my feet. Lining three sides of the pool were statues of couples locked in intimate embraces. I couldn't see into the shadows beyond the statues, but I knew Drake was there. I could smell him. I could feel him. He was everywhere. I stepped into the water, shivering a little when it touched my sensitized skin. "You can't just waltz into my mind and seduce me in a dream world because I've rejected you in reality. I will not play this game again."

I sank deeper into the waiting embrace of the water, swimming out to the middle of the pool, a thousand little touches lapping against my skin, arousing me.

"Drake, I know you're there. I don't have these sorts of dreams on my own. You're the only one who makes me feel this way, so you might as well stop hiding and show yourself."

Beyond the edge of my vision, something moved. Something large. A breeze whirled around me, accompanied by the sound of what could only be very large wings. I turned, treading water, trying to see into the darkness. From the corner of my eye a sinuous green object caressed a marble column, sliding like a snake into the darkness when my head whipped around to look at it. Deep in the shadows a darker shape rose, a long, thin neck arching back along a powerful body before twisting itself deeper into the darkness. "I'm not seeing this. It's just a dream. I'm not about to be ravished by a really gigantic four-legged scaly lizard with sexy eyes. Your eyes are still green when you're in dragon form, aren't they, Drake?"

"Perhaps someday you will find out the answer yourself," a voice answered. It was Drake's voice, but it wasn't—this voice was deeper, with more resonance, a voice that seemed to fill the room.

I shivered again in the water, aroused by his nearness despite my intentions to resist him. "Let me see you.

You've never let me see your dragon form. Come out here and let me see you. Let me see what you really look like."

The shadows moved, shifted, seemed to part as if they were as tangible as a curtain. From the depths strode a man, long-legged, broad of chest, hips narrow and powerful. He was also stark naked, a fact I didn't miss, nor did I neglect looking at the part of him that was leading the way. I've always thought the sight of a fully aroused man walking was a bit comical—the engorged bits of flesh bobbing with the rhythm of the walk—but Drake didn't walk. He glided. His muscles rippled in a beautiful symphony of power as he approached, his hands relaxed at his sides, the long, thick muscles of his thighs capturing my gaze. I loved Drake's legs. I loved the strength in them, the ability they had to move with all the grace and power of a very large panther.

He stopped at the edge of the pool, arrogantly male, watching me with unreadable eyes as I lazily swam toward him. As I approached, an image arose in my mind of his hands skimming me, touching me in all sorts of sensitive places, stirring me until I couldn't catch my breath. "I'd tell you you're beautiful, but you already know that, don't you? You know how much I like to look at you. You know I want to touch you, and taste you, and feel you burning deep inside me. You know all that, and yet you know you can never have me except in this dreamscape."

With a swift, graceful move he dived into the water. It was about nipple-high on him, allowing him to walk slowly to where I was still languidly treading water. "This is your dream, Aisling. You summoned me to it."

My eyes widened in surprise. In the past, Drake had come to me in dreams, always initiating them himself, and it had only been with practice that I had learned how to end them despite his wishes to the contrary. But I had never called him to me in a dream—I didn't think I knew how. "Is this some sort of a trick? Something to make me even more confused than before? I didn't summon you, Drake. I want you out of my life."

"You want what I represent out of your life, but if you truly wished me gone, then you would not have called me to you tonight."

I swam around him, a need building within me to touch him, to have him touch me, but I knew what would happen if I did. We'd have wild, fiery dragon sex, and I'd end up torn with indecision. I hated being indecisive. I liked my life in control. "And just what, Mr. Smarty Pants, do you think you represent in my life?"

"The future," he answered, standing still in the water, the tiny waves of my wake caressing the wonderfully warm flesh of his back and chest. I wanted to be those waves.

"Ha," I said, putting as much scorn as I could into the word. I swam a complete circle around him and stopped to face him, just a scant foot separating us. "I'm not afraid of the future. I'm a professional. I am in control. I am—"

"Mine," he growled, his hand a blur as it snared me, jerking me forward until I was pressed tightly against his chest. "You tease me purposely, Aisling. You tell me you don't want me, but you tempt me shamelessly, offering yourself in body but not in mind. Make the decision, mate. Make it now. Accept me, or not, but do not torment me any longer."

It was strange, but in the dream world his fire didn't touch me. The heat of his body sank into me everywhere our skin touched, but his fire was missing. "Where does your fire go when you dream?" I asked, unable to keep from sliding my hand up his arm to the lovely muscles of his shoulders. There must have been oil in the water, too, because his skin was as slick as the finest satin, smooth and enticing. Even the curly dark hairs on his chest rubbing against my tight, sensitive nipples were soft and silky.

He just looked at me, his eyes bright with emotion, so filled with need that it almost hurt to look at him.

Almost.

I sighed. "All right, I admit that maybe my mind isn't quite as clear as I'd like it to be when it comes to a relationship with you, but I'd like to point out that I am not the one who moved an important peace summit just on the hopes of getting lucky."

One eyebrow rose in a silent objection.

"Don't you give me that look! You can't possibly deny the fact that you came after me."

His eyes were deep and dark and infinitely beautiful. "I don't wish to deny it. I have explained to you that as my mate you have a role in the summit. Since I knew you would be attending this conference, I rearranged my life to accommodate you."

When he put it like that, it took all the fun out of being annoyed.

I sighed again, aware that he was still waiting for me to give him an answer. "The truth is, I don't want to make a decision, because you want something from me I can't give. You want all of me, you want me forever at your side, forgoing my own life to be a part of yours. I can't do that. I *won't* do that. I have a life of my own to lead, and even though I'm willing to admit that there's something between us"—

He growled deep in his chest, the arm that was banded around my back sliding lower to pull my hips against his. I wiggled a tiny little wiggle to let him know I appreciated his anticipation.

—"neither of us is of a particularly accommodating nature, and the bottom line is that I'm not going to give up being a Guardian. If you are willing to try to work out some sort of an agreement that will allow me to study whatever it is apprentices study, and working together whenever possible, well, then, I'm your girl. But if you can't see your way clear to working out a compromise, then there's no hope for us."

Drake was silent for a few moments, the muscles in his jaw working. I thought he was going to refuse outright, but he surprised me. "I am here to negotiate a peaceful settlement of hostilities between the septs. I want the same with you. Therefore, I will agree to do whatever it takes to achieve that goal."

"You will? Really?" I goggled at him, hope glowing warmly in my heart, while in my less ethereal girly parts, outright celebration was the order of the day. "You won't fight me anymore on this? No more snarky comments about being a Guardian? No more saying things to potential mentors that might ruin my chances with them? If they ask, you'll say you support my decision?"

He inclined his head in acquiescence. "I will not say

anything to a mentor that could be interpreted as being anything but wholly behind your plans."

"Oh," I said—less than brilliant, I admit, but to be honest, I was overwhelmed. I'd never thought Drake would come around, never thought he'd be willing to compromise. He was such an inflexible man, I couldn't help but grin at him as I slid my other hand up his arm, tangling my fingers in his hair. "See? Giving me what I want didn't hurt very much, now did it?"

His eyes burned bright, and his hands were hard on my bottom as he rubbed against me. "You have yet to ask what it is I want from this agreement, mate."

"I think I can guess," I answered, sucking his earlobe into my mouth, nipping it just hard enough to get his attention. "You want someone to attend the peace summit with you. You want someone to pour when you have other wyverns over for tea. You want to make steamy, sensual, passionate love to me three times each and every night."

Both of his eyebrows went up. "Three times?"

I kissed the tip of his nose. "You're immortal. You can't die of a heart attack. Three is good."

"There is more to being a mate than pouring tea, Aisling." His voice rumbled around and through me as I kissed a line along his jaw. "To be a wyvern's mate is to be bound for all time to the sept. You must take an oath to never turn your back on the green dragons. If you are called on for help, you cannot refuse. To do so would mean death. This is not something to be taken lightly."

I nipped his chin, smiling into his so serious face. "That seems a fair trade. I get to have you at my beck and call, and now and again I watch the kids when you're busy."

"Aisling—" he said, his voice filled with reproach.

I stopped the words by sliding my fingers across his lips. "I'm sorry. I don't mean to be flip. It's just that I'm happy. Can we do this oath now, or is there some sort of special oath at the clan ceremony?"

"We can do it now." His lips compressed for a moment before the corners of his mouth relaxed. "But you must be certain. The oath will be binding."

"OK." I cleared my throat and thought for a long moment about what I was going to do. It was a big step, a major step, one of those life-altering steps that always seem to come about without the least hint, but the time had come to stop running from what the fates kept throwing in my path. Drake was meant to be a part of my life. Either I could spend my lifetime fighting us both, or I could accept the compromise. "I, Aisling Grey, Guardian, swear upon my soul to fulfill my duties as your mate. I swear to uphold the well-being and happiness of the sept of the green dragons. I swear that whatever help is mine to give shall be given wholeheartedly, of my own free will."

My heart beat madly with the realization of what I was doing. I was binding myself to one man, for eternity, wyverns' mates being immortal. Somehow it seemed fitting that at this most important moment in my life I should be naked, held tight against the warm flesh of the man who filled my heart and soul with something so profound I couldn't bear to examine it closely.

"I, Drake Vireo, wyvern of the green dragons, accept and acknowledge your fealty. You will forever hence be known as my mate, and as such will receive all protection, honor, and respect due you."

His voice echoed in the empty room. I waited until the last of the bass echo faded away, then licked my lips. "That's it?"

He nodded.

"There's nothing else? Nothing else that we say or do?"

"What did you expect?"

"I don't know." I looked downward, although I was pressed so tightly to him, there was little beyond my breasts squashed into his chest to see. "I guess I thought that maybe there would be something like a bolt of lightning going through me or that I'd feel something, you know, *big*."

One eyebrow cocked. I giggled. "No, not that. I feel that. And I refuse to pander to your male ego by discussing size. I meant with the whole mate thing. Does it take a while to go into effect?"

He walked forward, toward the steps at the far end of the pool. "The oath was binding the moment it was completed. You are my mate, Aisling. Now and forever."

"Ah." He bent to scoop me up, carrying me up the marble steps. "So, what do we do now?"

He grinned then, his eyes filled with desire and heat and a need so intense it made my skin prickly. My body rubbed sinuously against the warm flesh of his torso as he headed into the shadows, where a bed magically appeared, and he set me down in the center of it with care.

"Now you wake up."

12

Jim lifted its heavy head and blinked sleepily at me as I leaped out of bed and ran for the door. "What burr got under your bustle?"

"Don't ask stupid questions. Just come with me!"

The demon slowly got to its feet, stretching with a loud groan. "I don't smell an incubus, so what's the big deal—ow! That's my ear you're pinching!"

"It's going to be your former ear if you don't get a move on." I dragged Jim toward the open door, snatching up the plastic key card before hurrying out of the room.

"I was sleeping! I can't go from flat-out sleep to racing around like a lunatic like some people I can name," Jim said grumpily as I all but dragged it down the hallway to the elevators. "Don't tell me, let me guess— you've had another nocturnal visit from the Studly Dragon?"

I slid Jim a curious glance. "How do you know about my dreams with Drake?"

Jim snorted. "How could I *not* know? I shared a room with you back in Paris, if you recall. For a couple of nights before you and he got it on, there was a whole lot of, 'Oh, yes, Drake, yes, yes!' and 'Take me, you dragon studmuffin, take me hard and fast!' going on. It was all I could do to get a couple of hours' sleep before you'd start with the moaning and thrashing."

"I never once said, 'Take me, you dragon studmuffin!' That's a lie, pure and simple. Hey! I thought you weren't supposed to be able to lie to me when I asked you a question." I punched the elevator button, struggling to keep from doing an impatient little dance. How long did it take elevators in this country to move?

Jim yawned. "It wasn't a lie, it was an exaggeration. Nothing in the Big Demon Book o' Rules says I can't exaggerate now and again."

"Hrmph." I pushed the button a couple more times, trying to hurry the elevator along.

"Oh, yeah, that's going to do some good. Everyone knows an elevator doesn't shift into second until you really lean on the call button."

I pressed it another fifteen times, giving Jim a triumphant smile when the green light lit above the door. "Ha! See? It does too work—oh, sorry. Didn't mean to step on your foot."

Jim waited until the door had closed on the man whose toes I had inadvertently tromped on before saying, "It's gotta be Drake sending you sexy dreams. Why else would you run around the hotel in nothing but a T-shirt, trampling innocent tourists in your lust to get to your boy toy?"

"He's not a boy, and this is a perfectly decent sleep shirt, so shuteth thy moutheth upeth, demon."

By the time I pounded on the door of Drake's suite, my desperation to reach him and throw myself into his strong, manly arms had been doused a little by the cold glare of reality as seen by the artificial light of two a.m. What if I had manufactured that whole dream on my own? What if I had attributed to Drake things he'd never agree to? What if it was all wishful thinking, my mind's version of a happy little fantasy wherein everything in my life worked out the way I wanted it?

Drake had the door open before my hand fell. "You were much quicker than I anticipated, *kincsem.*"

His eyes were smoldering with a familiar look, one that went straight to my blood and set it boiling. It was all the answer I needed—obviously he had been a participant in the dream, which meant that he really had agreed to my terms, and that meant— "Hoobah!" I shouted as I leaped on him, wrapping my arms and legs around him.

He chuckled a sexy chuckle in my ear as he started for the door to his room, calling over his shoulder, "Jim, close the door, would you?"

Jim's face bore a canine version of disgruntlement as it turned from nosing the door closed. "Oh, sure, you two just go off to Boink-Land. I'll stay out here, then, shall I? Alone? Without my blankie? With no water bowl? With no one to talk to and nothing to do but listen to the bed squeaking all night lon—"

"You're not naked," I said as Drake slammed his bedroom door shut on Jim's plaint. I was almost giggling into his neck, I was so happy. Of their own volition, my fingers crept across the opening of the blue and green satin robe Drake was wearing, sliding beneath the cool material to find the hot flesh of his pectoral muscles. "I liked you better when you were naked."

"I like you liking me naked." Drake's voice, always sensual, took on a new level of eroticism as he stopped next to the big bed that claimed most of the space in the room, allowing me to slide down his body until my feet were on the floor. I glanced at the rumpled sheets, then back at Drake, smiling a smile I hadn't known was in my repertoire.

"You were sleeping? Since I know you don't like to sleep wearing anything, I guess that means that under this very nice robe there's nothing but a really hunky dragon."

My hand slid down to the carelessly tied belt, tugging it loose.

"You're wrong about me not liking to wear anything while I sleep," he answered, his breath sucking in as I slid my hand down the lovely warm planes of his chest to his belly. Drake had what I thought of as a B-grade amount of body hair—not so much that he looked like a Darwinian throwback, but enough to make me appreciate the differences between his body and mine. His chest was moderately haired, but what I loved was the little tail of dark hair that led from the bottom of his breastbone to his groin. My fingers followed the silky path down to where he was already hard and hot.

"Really?" I breathed into his mouth, flicking my tongue along the length of his lower lip. I adored Drake's lower lip. It was full, sensual, with a curve to it that never failed to make my innards melt. "What exactly do you like to wear to bed?"

"You," he growled, tossing me onto the bed and following so quickly behind that I didn't have time for anything more than a happy squeak before his mouth claimed mine.

Wyverns, I had occasion to note, were naturally dominant individuals. I suppose that made sense—arrogance, an innate belief in your own talent, and a healthy ego had to be attributes that were needed to rule an entire sept of dragons (also naturally arrogant), but my experience with Drake led me to believe that the wyverns, male and female, were also extremely comfortable in their skins. Even if it was not their original skin.

"You have my express permission to wear me as often as you like," I said on a gasp, Drake's mouth having released mine to move to a very sensitive spot on my neck, just behind my ear. Little shivers of delight zipped up and down my body, but it wasn't enough. I wanted more.

I shoved the robe off his shoulders. His teeth nipped my neck as he shrugged out of the robe, his hands returning to claim my breasts. I wrapped one leg around his, digging my fingers into the smooth muscle of his behind. "Drake?"

"Mmm?" His mouth moved to my collarbone, pausing over the mark he had branded a month before, the warm heat of his tongue swirling over it sending a sharp bolt of desire zinging through me.

"That dream—I have to know for sure. You did agree to what I asked, right? I didn't just imagine that?"

"You didn't imagine it," he answered, pressing a line of wet, hot kisses across my chest. I shivered as he approached my breast, my aching nipples about ready to implode, they were so tight. "You swore fealty to me. I formally accepted you as my mate. We are now bound together."

My hands slid up his back as his head moved lower, avoiding my breasts, which were heaving themselves about in a wanton display intended on capturing his attention. "And . . . and . . . the other? You agreed to support me in my Guardian training? You won't interfere with that?"

His tongue flicked my belly button, then he exhaled— fire. My stomach contracted as the flames licked my skin for a few seconds, heating but not burning, seeming to sink straight down into the pool of dormant heat that lay deep within me.

And suddenly there didn't seem to be enough air in the room to breathe.

"Good god, Drake," I gasped, struggling to get air back into my lungs as he looked up, a half smile on his delicious lips. "Next time you want to roast me, warn me, will you? That almost brought me straight up off the bed!"

"Almost, hmm?" Every single atom in my body froze as he gave me a speculative glance, then parted my legs, draping one leg over his shoulder. "We can't have an almost. Let me see if I can do better."

"Drake!" I shrieked as his hands spread up my thighs, heading for party central. "You can't! You'll burn me!"

"No, mate. You'll burn *for* me," he said moments before he lowered his mouth to me.

I tried to muffle the shriek that rose in my throat, not wanting to alert everyone in the hotel that I was about to have the wildest oral sex experience of my life, but the touch of his tongue on all my sensitive parts was too much for me. He licked, he swirled, he sucked . . . then his teeth joined the fun and gently tugged on tugable parts, his fingers doing an equally erotic dance in the surrounding scenery.

An oddly disconnected voice moaned nonstop as wave after wave of exquisite tension wound me tighter and tighter, my body tense and hard and trembling with an indefinable need that I knew to the depths of my soul only he could fill.

And still he tormented me. Four separate times my body arched up, on the very edge of an orgasm to end all orgasms, and each time he sensed my nearness and changed the angle of his attack, his mouth caressing a different spot until I was shaking with frustration, ecstasy, and so many other emotions I couldn't begin to name them.

"Drake!" I sobbed, my fingers tangled in his hair, trying to pull him closer, demanding that he allow me the completion I was going to die if I didn't get. "If you have any mercy in your soul—finish!"

Heat seared into me, scorching, sizzling, singeing, and all sorts of other s-words that my brain was too overwhelmed to think of. Dragon fire burned a hot brand deep into my womb, arcing through my body like lightning until I exploded in an endless flame of ecstasy. I don't know if I actually went up in a fireball of Drake's fire or not, but I can say this: When I returned to consciousness and gathered enough wits to make sure my body was still whole and not desiccated and charbroiled, there was an Aisling-shaped outline burnt into the sheet.

I blinked in bemusement at Drake. He was lying on his belly, his chin resting on my pelvic bone, an extremely smug, thoroughly masculine smile on his face.

"I told you that you'd like it when I breathed fire," he said.

"Just as soon as I recover use of my limbs, you are going to pay for that smile," I told him. "Do you happen to have one of those heart attack kits handy? I think I'm going to need defiberilizaton or whatever it is they do to get people's hearts going again. At the very least, my brain is going to need shocking to get it functioning."

He laughed, pressing a kiss into my belly before crawling up my body. "That is how dragons mate, Aisling. You will get used to it with time."

"Glorioski, I hope not!" I pushed him onto his back, summoning enough strength to roll over and plop myself on top of him. "And what do you mean that's how dragons mate? You didn't do that the first time we made love. You said we had to do it the dragon way then, because you were claiming me. Not that I had any complaints, mind you, but I would have remembered this."

"You had not agreed to be my mate then," he answered, heat simmering in his eyes. He winced as my thigh brushed his erection. "Now it is different. Now you are truly mine. I can take you in many ways which will be new to you."

"Really? New is good. I look forward to being fully indoctrinated into hot, steamy dragon sex," I purred, sliding my hand down to boldly caress him, smiling as he sucked in air when I wrapped my fingers around the hard length of his arousal, wallowing in the flickers of desire that were visible in his eyes. "Did you know that when you're aroused, your pupils get dragonier? They get longer and thinner until they are little slits of black in a beautiful sea of emerald."

He groaned as I bent my head down to capture a pert little brown nipple that peeked through his chest hair. "You have no idea what you do to me, do you, mate?"

"Oh, I have an idea," I said, reaching lower to gently scrape my fingernails first along his balls, then up the

long length of his penis. His hips bucked upward, forcing
him back through my hands. I looked down his body, enjoying every little bit of it, from the lovely bulgy bits of
his chest to the flat belly, and lower, to the thick ropes of
muscles along his thighs. "You really are beautiful,
Drake. You take my breath away—you're just that gorgeous. I'm actually salivating looking at you. When you
took this form, was it something you planned, or did you
just think human and this is what resulted?"

His hips bucked again, thrusting up off the bed as I
began to stroke him, quickly finding a rhythm that had
him clutching handfuls of the scorched bedspread. "I
don't—I can't—you're going to make me—Christ's
bones, woman! Don't stop!"

I grinned my special wicked grin at the look of furious
disbelief on his face as I released him in order to swing
my leg over his hips. I paused long enough to take the
very tip of him into my mouth, taking a moment to swirl
my tongue along the sensitive underside.

Drake began to yell. In Hungarian.

That was all I needed. With one last loving flick of my
tongue, I slid up his body, positioning him so that when I
sank slowly down upon him, we both gasped in delight.
He was so hard, so hot, almost as hot as his fire as he bur-
rowed deeper into me, my flesh clinging to his as I sank
down his full length, tightening every muscle I had
around him.

His back arched off the bed.

"Let me see the dragon in you, Drake," I whispered
against his lips, claiming his mouth as he'd done to mine
so often, my tongue dancing an enticing tango around his

as my hips moved. "Let me see the real you. Let go of yourself."

A tremor rippled down his body as I moved up and down on him, riding him slowly at first, but driven to a greater speed both by my own need and by the passion that filled his eyes. Beneath my legs the skin of his belly shimmered, blurring for a moment as it shifted from tanned skin to yellowish-green scales, then back to skin, so fast I almost didn't catch the change. His fingernails lengthened into long blue claws, wickedly sharp, digging almost painfully into my hips as he urged me on faster and faster.

"Aisling!" he cried, his eyes opening wide as his climax claimed him, and for a moment, for the space between seconds, he shifted, changed from man to dragon, and I was filled with an emotion unlike anything I'd ever known. It was power, it was rapture, it was ecstasy and fear and joy, all rolled together and merged into something totally new. He caught my shout of exultation in his mouth as the strength of my own orgasm drove him to peak a second time.

Hours later, when Jim stood outside our door and started singing at the top of its lungs in a very off-key voice in order to convince me to take it out for its morning walk, I looked up from where I was plastered against Drake's body.

"That was, hands down, the most erotic night of my life. I feel like I ran a marathon. My body is weak, my brain is numb, and my girl parts are still smoking. Is it going to be like this every time, or were you just starting things off with a bang, so to speak?"

The very edges of his lips curled. "You are mated to a dragon, *kincsem*. You will have a bang every night."

I glanced up to see if he meant the double entendre, but his eyes were closed.

His lips curled even more, though.

He meant it.

13

"What do you mean, I could have a bun in the oven? Drake is a dragon! I'm a human! That's a cross-species thing!"

Jim sauntered over from where it had been watering a small laurel shrub, one eyebrow lifted in delicate scorn. "You *were* a human. Now you're a dragon's mate, signed, sealed, and spent-all-night-making-little-dragons."

I stared at the demon, my mind screaming in horror. I had nothing against kids per se, but I wasn't ready to have them yet. Not to mention that I wasn't sure I wanted to have them with Drake. Not only did he not seem terribly paternal, I wasn't ready to be mom to a dragon. "But— but—it's got to be physically impossible! Last month, when Drake and I . . . I asked him about condoms, and he said that pregnancy was impossible between us, and that he didn't have any nasty dragon or human diseases, and since I don't either, we . . . No. You're wrong. You have to be wrong."

Jim shrugged, and sat to scratch behind its collar. "You agreed to be his mate last night. You swore fealty. He accepted you. That makes you officially a dragon's mate.

You're immortal, no longer human. You're kind of human plus, if you get my drift."

"That doesn't mean that suddenly Drake has super sperm that can leap a building in a single bound."

The big demon stood up again and shook itself before nodding toward the front of the hotel. Rene had pulled up, right on time, and was standing chatting with Tiffany. I tied on its drool cloth and followed after it. "A discussion of Drake's swimmers is going well over the border into Too Much Information Land. Just how do you think dragons reproduce, anyway?"

"I assumed they mated with female dragons, and then, I don't know, the females laid eggs or something."

Jim shook its head, muttering something about getting with the times, but the damage had been done. I tried to remember just what Drake had said the first time we made love, but I couldn't recall the exact details. I made a mental note to question him about it before he laid claw on me again, then slapped a smile on my face to greet Rene and Tiffany.

"—and I said to him, 'Josef, you might be an oracle, but that doesn't mean you know everything. I was born to be a virgin. It is a very high calling, and a most important position. Where would all the witches and sorcerers be without blood of a virgin?' And do you know what he said to me? He said, 'I might not know everything, but I know enough to recognize an ice princess when I see one.' Wasn't that thoughtful of him? He thinks I am like a princess. One made of ice. I like ice. It is pretty and shines nicely. Good morning, Aisling. Good morning, demon. I was just telling Rene the lovely compliment I had this morning."

"Yes, we heard. Ice princess. That's really . . . uh . . . nice. Morning, Rene. Are you both ready to do a little hermit hunting?"

Rene opened the back door to the cab. Tiffany swept inside with a regal smile. "I am most anxious to help you, Aisling. I feel it in my bones that today we shall be triumphant." He squinted at me as I started toward the back of the car. "Something is different about you today, yes? You look . . . how is it said, like the cat who has eaten all the milk? Have you done something? Something important?"

Jim barked a short laugh. I ignored the demon and tried to look a little less like a woman who had spent most of the night being pleasured to the very tips of her toenails and more like one who was professional, determined, and every inch reliable. "It's 'cat who's licked up all the cream,' and nothing has happened, nothing at all. Nothing important."

Rene tipped his head as he eyed me even more carefully. "There is something different, Aisling. I know I am not mistaken."

My hand went to the chains around my neck. Thus far Rene hadn't shown any signs of caving under the influence of the dratted amulet, but at last its magic had worked its way through his normally placid temperament. My heart sank. I was counting on Rene to help me, but if he started acting like all the other lovesick mortals, I'd have to keep away from him.

"Honestly, there's nothing. Now, if you're ready, we can head out to the first park. I figure if we split up, we'll cover more ground, so I cut up maps I bummed from the concierge. Each one of us will take a section of the park and search for the hermit. Then we'll rendezvous and report our progress."

Rene still wore a puzzled look as I got into the car, followed by Jim. The demon stepped on my foot while climbing over me to claim the window next to the jump seat.

"Whoops. Sorry, Mama."

"Stop it," I hissed, making mean eyes at Jim.

"What was that?" Rene asked, sliding behind the steering wheel.

"Nothing. Ignore Jim. It's just being a smart-ass."

"Better than being a dumb-ass," Jim intoned, its head out the window.

"But not as good as an ice princess," Tiffany pointed out, smiling at her reflection in the rearview mirror.

I heaved a mental sigh. It was going to be a long, long day.

We found the hermit shortly after noon, sharing a pond in the Budakeszi Wildlife Park with a couple of fallow deer. Jim had been fretting because I insisted on searching one last park before we had to call it quits and return to the hotel. I had two more apprentice interviews, and I'd promised Drake I would attend a clan function with him that evening. It was my first time to formally meet his dragons, and I was more than a little nervous about the whole thing.

"But this is a wildlife park," Jim protested, its furry lips curled as it glanced around the parking lot. I passed out maps to the park. "It's big. And I don't see any handy food stands."

"We'll search as much of it as we can now. If we can't cover the whole thing, we'll come back this afternoon, after we get something to eat and I meet with the Guardians," I promised. "Jim, you search the area surrounding the big-game enclosures and the wildlife feeding points. I doubt a hermit would be there, but we shouldn't overlook any potential hiding spot. Tiffany, if you could take the Z trail and check out the beech forest, that would be helpful. Rene, do you mind doing the open woodland? I think I can handle both the pine and the oak forests. We'll meet at the owl enclosure next to the main entrance in an hour, OK?"

Everyone agreed, and we scattered, Jim's grousing following me as I headed off to the deepest part of the park. There were a couple of trails that wound through the acreage of the park, taking the visitor through a number of environments, the surroundings changing from deciduous trees to marshland to alpine forest. It was gorgeous, and I only wished I had more time to appreciate the flora and abundant fauna. As it was, I was about to head back to the entrance when I spied a little glimmer of water through the dense oak trees. I left the trail and carefully picked my way through the undergrowth to a little pond.

A small long-necked, white-spotted deer about Jim's height lifted its head from the pond, gazing at me with big, liquid eyes that showed no fear. I've always liked deer, but this one was so elegant, so beautiful in its purity, it took my breath away.

"Oh," I said softly, freezing so as not to startle the deer. It blinked impossibly long eyelashes while it considered me for a moment or two, then turned and slowly made its way around the perimeter of the pond.

A man's voice spoke Hungarian behind me as soon as the deer disappeared into the growth. I spun around, a strangled little scream emerging from my throat. "Lord above, you scared me!"

The man was clad in what I thought of as ranger clothing—khaki pants and shirt, a kerchief knotted around his neck—and his hands rested easily on his hips. Surprise lit his dark eyes for a moment, then changed to amusement as he grinned. "You are American? You are tourist?"

"Yes to both," I said, looking back toward where the deer had disappeared. "Did you see that little deer?"

"*Dámborjú.*"

"I beg your pardon?"

"It is a *dámborjú*. A female. Her name is Draga."

"Dragon?" I asked, for one moment wondering if the dragon population in Budapest was unusually high. But a closer look at this man's eyes ruled out that idea—his pupils were normal circles, not the elongated ovals that marked dragons' eyes.

"Draga. It means"—his hands swept out wide while he searched for the word—"darling."

"Very appropriate," I said, glancing around the pond. There wasn't much else to be seen but shrubs, trees, and a couple of yellow ducklings floating with their mother at the far end of the pond. "I hate to sound nosy, but do you come here often? To this park, that is, not just this pond?"

He nodded. "Very often."

"Oh, good. You just might be able to help me, if you don't mind. I'm looking for a man who might hang out a lot around the park, and I wonder if you've seen him."

"Hang out?" The man half turned, gesturing for me to go before him, back toward the hiking path.

"Camp, maybe. Or live in an abandoned ranger's hut

or something. His name is György Berto, and he's probably pretty shy around people, so I wouldn't be surprised if he stays away from contact with the public—"

The man started laughing even before I finished the sentence. I pushed past a laurel bush and glanced back at him. He smiled. "I am György."

I stopped. "You are? You're a hermit?" He didn't look like a hermit. His hair was short, he didn't have a long, scraggly beard or dirty, unkempt fingernails, and his clothing, while unexceptional, was reasonably clean considering he lived in a wildlife park. Not only that, he hadn't shied away when he came upon me.

"Hermit—that is an interesting name. I prefer *erdölakó*, a woodlander."

"Woodsman?" I asked, relieved. Given György's paranoia regarding mail, I had assumed he was one of those people who had retreated entirely from society, a modern-day Howard Hughes, but without the money. György looked perfectly normal. He was obviously just a man who favored spending time in the peace of the woods. "Well, I'm very happy to have found you. I've been looking for a couple of days, and the people who hold your mail had no idea when you would be coming by to pick it up."

He brushed that away with a flick of his hands, the sunlight filtering through the trees and dappling his chest and arms. "The summer, it is so crowded in the city, you know? Tourists everywhere with their constant talking, constant moving around. They do not sit and appreciate the beauty of their surroundings. It is too noisy, too busy there now. I will go into the city when the leaves start to change to red and gold. Not before."

"I know what you mean about noisy and busy, but I've always felt that to be part of the charm of a big city, although I admit I really like staying on Margaret Island. It's so peaceful, a wonderful oasis of beauty smack-dab in the middle of the city." I pulled the chain bearing the hermit's amulet from beneath my blouse, happiness filling me at the thought of being rid of the annoying thing. "I'm from Damian Carson Antiquities. I have the amulet you bought. I'm sorry I've been wearing it, but people kept trying to steal—"

"Aisling? AISLING? Ais—oh, there you. You must come quickly. Your demon, it is having a fit of the most large sort!" Tiffany ran toward me, her lovely face shadowed with concern. She paused to give György a smile (shy) and bat her eyelashes (not so shy) before turning back to me. "You must hurry! The demon, it is on the ground, writhing about, with much froth coming from its mouth. I think maybe it is dying."

"Oh, god," I swore, taking off at a run. I glanced back, yelling over my shoulder to György, "I'll be back as soon as I can. Sorry about this!"

I don't know if he heard me. He was too busy staring at Tiffany, a stunned expression on his face, his hands hanging limp at his sides as he looked at her, just looked at her without saying a word, without even noticing that I had run off. Tiffany, for her part, gave him an extremely coy glance before turning to race lightly after me.

That he noticed.

"Where is Jim?" I asked Tiffany as she caught up to me. We reached a spot in the path where it split, one direction leading to the other side of the park, the other heading toward the main entrance.

"By the feeding area. I searched the beech forest and was returning to find you, when I heard much barking of a large dog. It is beautiful here, is it not? There are many wildflowers. They make me smile. I was wishing more people would come to share the smiles and the wildflowers when I heard the barking. Although I would have preferred to continue thinking about the flowers, I thought perhaps it was Jim who was making the noise, and that he might have found the hermit. But it was not the hermit he found."

"No, the hermit is the man we just left. Don't worry, I'm sure he won't disappear. We'll find him after I see what's going on with Jim."

"That man was the hermit?" Tiffany asked easily, an insight that sent a little zing of annoyance through me. There I was sweating and panting like Jim after the one time I'd made him run with me on the beach, and she wasn't even looking hot. "Are you sure? He did not seem like a hermit to me."

"Nor me, but he says he's György Berto. I haven't checked his identification yet, but I don't see any reason for someone to lie about being him. He didn't seem to know who I was, or even that the amulet was on its way to be delivered. Which way?"

She pointed to the right. We ran down a narrow, lesser-used path around the far perimeter of a fenced area. Beyond it, in a bed of ferns growing in the shadow of an ancient oak tree, lay Jim, groaning and gagging. Rene was squatting next to the big black shape, out of range of the demon's vomiting but close enough to put his hand on Jim's back.

Rene looked up when we approached. "*Bon*. I had

hoped when I saw Tiffany racing away that she would find you."

"All right, Jim," I said, stopping behind it, crossing my arms as I looked down to where it lay groaning. "What is it this time? You're so faint with hunger that you can't stand up anymore? You want me to carry you to the nearest McDonald's, right? You're—"

Jim's back arched as the demon in dog form vomited violently.

Tiffany made little mewling noises, both of her hands over her mouth.

My irritation at what I had assumed was Jim putting on an act quickly turned into horror. The demon wasn't playacting; it was having a severe reaction to something. Ignoring the slimy results of the dry heaves now racking the demon's body, I knelt down and put my hands on Jim's head. "Oh, my god, what is it? What happened?"

Jim's body shook. I stroked the big black head, using the drool cloth to wipe away the long tendrils of saliva that hung from its flews. "I—I—food. Was hungry. Over there."

Rene turned to look at the feeding station. A partially spread bale of hay sat next to a couple of long wooden troughs holding what I assumed was fodder for the deer and other hoofed animals.

"You ate something from the animals' feeding station?" I asked as Rene hurried around the enclosure to enter it. "What did you eat? Jim?"

The demon's eyes rolled back in its head as its body convulsed again. I swore, looking around for help, for a handy vet to miraculously appear and offer his services.

Miracles, I have had occasion to note, seldom happen when you want them.

"Tiffany, can you take Jim's back legs?" I asked, sliding my arms around the demon's big chest. "If Rene carries its middle, I think we can get it back to the entrance. There's got to be a vet who serves the park. Maybe he can help Jim."

Rene met us as Tiffany and I staggered around the fence. He stuffed a bulging handkerchief into his pocket as he wrapped his arms around Jim's sagging middle. "I took a little bit of everything. It is food for the deer, but it could be poisonous, yes?"

"I have no idea," I grunted, Jim's heavy weight pulling painfully on my back and shoulders. I had to keep blinking back tears that pricked behind my eyes, tears that I knew were ridiculous. Demons can't die. The form they take can be destroyed, but they themselves can't die. I didn't know quite exactly what they did if life was extinguished from their temporary body, but I suspected it wasn't anything pleasant. More to the point, I knew Jim loved its body. It had chosen a Newfie above all other forms because it thought them the most handsome of all sentient beings. While most demons chose a human form to appear in—humans being the most powerful of all the mortal world—Jim chose to become a dog, and I would be damned before I let that big, shaggy, lovable body be lost.

By the time we made it to the entrance, even Tiffany was red-faced and puffing a little. We set Jim down on a bench while I ran to the entrance booth, Tiffany alongside me to act as translator.

"Is there a vet here?" I asked, waving my hand toward

the bench where Jim lay unconscious, Rene hovering protectively next to it. "My dog accidentally ate some of the deer food, and it's sick, very, very, sick. Can someone help us?"

Tiffany translated quickly to the woman taking money from visitors. The woman looked alarmed, craning her head to peer around me to see Jim, but I knew from the way she shook her head that her answer wasn't a good one. I spun around, scanning the area, praying for some sort of miracle even while I knew there was none.

Tiffany lightly touched my arm. "The woman, she says the vet comes to visit only on special days."

My stomach lurched. A couple of tears escaped my eyes to roll down my cheeks. I bit my lip, trying to push back the horrible knowledge that Jim's body was dying. I had to do something. I was its demon lord, for heaven's sake—it was my responsibility. I had summoned it, and although I had inadvertently bound it to me, it was my duty to look after the big hairy lug.

"Then we're just going to have to go find the nearest vet," I snarled, running back to Rene. We lifted the demon between us, hauling it out to the parking lot. Tiffany, who had returned to consult with the woman behind the entrance kiosk, ran past us to the car, opening the back door and helping us put Jim in.

"There is a veterinarian a few kilometers down the road," she said, sliding into the front seat next to Rene. "I will direct you."

Jim's head lolled senselessly on my lap as Rene drove. I gave up fighting the tears, stroking the demon's head, holding back sobs that made my throat ache. Crying wouldn't help Jim. Only a miracle, the miracle that had not materialized in the wildlife park, could help the demon now.

An hour later we emerged from the loud and somewhat antiquated confines of the animal health clinic mentioned to Tiffany by the wildlife park attendant. Despite the heat of the day, I felt cold, both inside and out. I rubbed my bare arms as we walked slowly to Rene's cousin's taxi.

"The demon Jim, he will be all right now," Rene said with mock cheerfulness that I knew was intended to impart reassurance. "The doctor said that would be so, *hein?*"

"I guess," I answered, not willing to burst Rene's bubble in case he really did believe Jim was out of trouble. What the vet had said, duly translated by Tiffany, and later Rene when Tiffany couldn't stand the animal surgery area, was that the vet thought Jim had ingested a toxic plant or berry, but wouldn't know until they analyzed the results of the stomach pumping. Rene turned over the handful of grain and plant matter he had culled from the deer trough. I stood silent, watching Jim's still unconscious form, my hand on its neck. Beneath the fur, the demon's heart beat slowly. I closed my eyes and opened myself up, trying to touch its spirit, but there was nothing there for me to hold.

"Is it over?" Tiffany asked, white-faced, clutching her hands as she stood next to the taxi. "The demon Jim, it is . . . "

"Resting," I answered when her voice trailed off. I blinked back a couple more tears, this time of gratitude that Tiffany would be so concerned about a demon she'd just met. "The doctor thinks they got all the toxins out, but he said Jim would be out of it until tomorrow morning."

"That is very good," she said, taking my hand in hers for a moment. "Resting is very good for animals, is it not? The demon, it will recover its strength, and be back by your side to bring joy and happiness to everyone it meets."

I almost choked on the thought of Jim bringing joy and happiness to anyone, but smiled and said nothing, sitting in the back of the taxi, allowing Tiffany's terminally optimistic chatter to wash over me as we drove back into town.

It was only when Rene dropped us off at the hotel that I remembered I hadn't delivered the amulet to György the hermit.

14

The lunch banquet had just ended when Tiffany and I walked into the hotel lobby. She murmured something about needing to spend some time in the sun perfecting her tan.

"A day without the sun is like a day without a smile shared with everyone you see, and that is a tragedy, don't you think? I will practice my ice princess smile while I am on the verandah. Do you wish to join me?" she said, eyeing my pale, freckled arms.

"No, thanks. I've got appointments this afternoon, and besides, I burn easily. My smile will just have to be shared from the confines of a pasty, tanless body. Thanks for all your help today, Tiffany. I really appreciate it."

She patted me on the shoulder. "Did I not tell you that I would be of great use to you? Now you know the power of a professional virgin."

"It is an awesome thing to behold," I agreed, without one single quiver of my lips, which I thought was awfully darn good of me. Tiffany tripped off to her room. I checked the conference message board quickly in case either of the two Guardians with whom I had arranged interviews had begged off, but there was nothing for me.

As I approached the elevators, a familiar man passed me, pausing to say, "You will—"

"Stop it right there!" I yelled, interrupting Paolo the Diviner before he could cause any more trouble for me. People in the area turned to look at us. I lowered the volume of my voice, but kept my tone as mean as I could. "I have no idea why you've decided to become my personal voice of doom, but I would appreciate it if you would stop telling me that I'm going to trip, or spill stuff on myself, or be arrested, or any of the thousand other disasters I'm sure you behold in my future, because frankly, I don't want to know. OK?"

Paolo looked offended. His nostrils flared. He backed up a step, looking down his long nose at me, his lips pressed together tightly.

"I'm sorry to be so brusque," I said, realizing I had insulted him. "And I want you to know that I appreciate your concern for my well-being"—a little white lie never hurt anyone—"but I will take my chances with life on my own."

He said nothing, just raised a supercilious eyebrow at me.

"Thank you," I said, figuring that he might leave me alone if I thanked him for his effort. "Uh . . . have a nice day."

Paolo continued to stare silently at me as I made a little good-bye wave and walked toward the elevator.

I got in it with three other people, all chatting about the delicious lunch served at the banquet. Paolo continued to stand like a statue, staring at me with cold, dark eyes.

The doors started to close, I heaved a mental sigh of relief that I had escaped his dire prognostications.

"—face one who wishes you gone," Paolo finished, triumph flashing across his face as the elevator doors closed with a soft swoosh.

"Like *that's* some sort of news flash," I muttered, smiling a toothy smile when the woman next to me cast a questioning glance at me.

It was odd walking down the long hotel hallway without Jim at my side. Since I had summoned the demon, just a little more than a month before, we hadn't been parted for longer than a few hours. Yes, it was a demon, and yes, it wasn't technically alive, but smart mouth, nagging tendencies, and demands for frequent feeding and walks notwithstanding, it was also my friend. I missed the big hairy galoot.

"My room is going to seem awfully empty without Jim taking up all the space," I said softly to myself as I slid the plastic key card into the slot on my door, opening the door with plans of a quick shower before I ran downstairs to meet with the two Guardians. "Hell's bells! Not again!"

The room was indeed emptier without Jim—extremely empty. Of all my possessions, that is. Everything of mine was gone—my suitcases, my clothing, Jim's paraphernalia, everything! It was as if someone had come in and wiped the room clean of me.

I turned on my heel and started for the front desk, growling to myself about what I was going to say to the police. "How dare they confiscate my things! It was bad enough in Paris when they took my stuff, but at least they mailed everything back to me a couple of weeks later. This time, I'm going to get pushy. I'll go straight to the U.S. Embassy and demand that they—hi, István."

Drake's red-haired bodyguard gave me a stiff bow, his muddied hazel eyes as hard as stone. István had never really forgiven me for a slight accident that resulted in him being mistaken by me for a dartboard. I couldn't blame him for being a bit testy over that, although I had apologized profusely at the time. No permanent damage had been done, but István hadn't seemed to be able to move on. "I am sent to bring you."

I glanced at my watch. "It's only a little after one. Drake said the green dragon party wasn't until seven."

István looked like a bodyguard. Both he and Pál were as tall as Drake, but where Drake was elegant and exuded a sense of coiled power held in check, István was blocky and thick-muscled, looking more like a cross between a bodybuilder and a linebacker. His heavy brows remained in a straight line as he glared at me. "You come. The wyvern commands."

"Oh, he commands me?" I was in no mood to go head-to-head with Drake, not when I had a police department to tackle, two Guardians to meet and sway with my perfectness for an apprenticeship, and a vast amount of worrying to do about Jim. Suddenly it seemed like too much for me, so rather than get prickly and tell István just where Drake could stuff his command, I nodded wearily and followed him silently to the elevator, saying nothing until he pushed open the door to the green dragon's suite.

Right there in the middle of the living room was a blanket folded into a dog bed, Jim's traveling foldable water bowl sitting next to it, along with the demon's extra drool bibs, its brush, spare leash, and the couple of copies of *People* that Jim insisted I buy to keep it from being bored.

I burst into tears.

István looked at me like I was covered in boils. Pál emerged from a room and hurried over, his face twisted in concern. "Aisling, what is wrong? Are you in pain? Has someone harmed you? Drake is not here, but I can call him—"

"No, it's OK," I sniffled, pulling a few tissues from the box he offered. "It's just been kind of a long day."

He looked at a clock sitting on a nearby gateleg table. "It is just an hour past midday."

"I know." I blew my nose as discreetly as I could. "That's what worries me. What did Drake want, and why do you have Jim's things? Do you have mine as well?"

Pál nodded, gesturing toward the double doors that led to the master bedroom. "Drake said that now you had accepted him as wyvern, you would be living with us."

István muttered something under his breath before throwing himself down in a nearby chair. I ignored him. I'd have to make my peace with him at some point, but I was too tired to struggle with him now.

"Drake was being presumptuous, but I'll take that up with him. At least now I don't have to battle the police on top of everything else." I started to turn toward the room, but Pál reached out a hand as if he was going to stop me, then snatched it back quickly. I gave him a curious look. "Did you want something?"

He glanced nervously at István, who promptly grabbed a Hungarian magazine and started reading it. "It is just that you seem . . . sad."

"I am sad. Jim is in a vet clinic on the outskirts of town. It ate something poisonous and almost destroyed its body. I'm very worried."

"But even if it does need to take a new form, the demon will be the same," Pál said helpfully.

I nodded, then shook my head, then ran my fingers through my hair. My activities with Drake the night before hadn't left us time for much sleep, and with everything else going on, my brain was starting to feel a bit ragged around the edges. "I know, but it won't be Jim. I'm going to take a shower, then I have to leave for a bit. If you see Drake, tell him . . ." I struggled to think of something that wasn't too snarky but would let Drake know I didn't appreciate him taking the high hand with me. "Tell him I'll talk to him about this tonight."

István said something I didn't understand. I cocked a questioning eyebrow at Pál. Not only was he friendlier than István, his English was as good as mine.

Pál looked uncomfortable and didn't meet my eyes. "He said that there would be much talking tonight."

István snorted. I decided to ignore him, feeling a shower and possibly a quick nap would do more for me than figuring out a surly bodyguard.

My first appointment went off without any disasters striking me—Paolo didn't stop by to give me another warning, Drake didn't show up to go bossy on me, and Jim wasn't there to say inappropriate things at the very worst moment.

Despite all that, it was a complete failure.

"I will make a note of your phone number," Fiona the Scottish Guardian said, giving me a look that pretty much said she'd rather consort with a demon lord than ever give me a jingle. "As I said at the beginning of the interview, I have many applicants hoping to gain an apprenticeship with me, so the competition is naturally very intense."

"Understood. And thank you for considering me. It sounds like your program of training is very comprehensive." I drew a line through her name on my mental list of potential mentors. The only good thing that had come out of this interview was a nugget of information regarding the ritual examination that all would-be apprentices must pass in order to be formally accepted. I stood and shook hands with Fiona, waiting until she left before looking at the name on the back of a business card she'd handed me.

"Marvabelle O'Hallahan" was written in Fiona's neat script.

My heart sank. I was contemplating just how horrible this ritual could be with Marvabelle in charge (my imagination is way too good for my peace of mind) when a shadow moved over the card.

"Disaster follows your every footstep."

I looked up, the card crumpling in my hand as I glared at the back of the man who walked away from me. I shook my fist at him. "Yeah, and its name is Paolo! Leave me alone, will you?"

"Are you still beset with admirers?" a soft, English-accented voice asked.

I smiled at Nora and waved her to a chair. Fiona had opted to meet me on the shady side of the verandah, a favorite spot for all the conference attendees, if the number of tables filled to capacity was any sign to go by. "Hi, Nora. Are you looking for a place to sit? I have an appointment in a few minutes, but you're welcome to share my table."

She nudged a chair out with her foot, carefully balancing a tall glass of iced tea and a plate of fresh fruit. "Thank you. I missed lunch and didn't think I could go until dinner without eating. Where is Jim?"

I explained briefly what had happened at the park.

"I'm so sorry to hear that. Poor Jim. But if the vet is positive he got all the poison out, I am sure Jim's resilience will help the body recover quickly. You might be able to destroy a demon's physical form, but they are heartier than a mortal being."

My stomach growled loudly as she speared a piece of melon. "Sorry," I said, trying not to look like I was starving. I had fallen asleep on Drake's bed—now, I guess, also my bed—after my shower, and I only barely made it to the appointment with Fiona without being late. There hadn't been any time to rustle up something for lunch.

"You're welcome to some," she offered, pushing her plate toward me.

"Thanks, but that's not necessary." I looked at my watch, chewed my lip in thought for a second, then turned around and looked at the doorway leading into the hotel. Zaccheo stood next to the wall, a pitcher of water clutched in his hands, his body tense and quivering slightly in anticipation as if he was waiting at the starting line of a race. I smiled at him and he shot over to me, almost knocking down an elderly couple in his haste.

"You want water?" he asked, holding the pitcher as if it was made of precious gems. "You want more water?"

"No," I said, speaking slowly but firmly. The only way I'd managed to have a conversation with Fiona without him drowning me in ice water was to forbid him to approach me until I signaled I wanted something. He had remained against the wall, ignoring other patrons as he stood poised to race to my side at the merest flick of my finger. "I have to leave in five minutes, but I missed lunch and I'm hungry. Do you think you can find something quickly—"

He was off before I finished the sentence, ice water splashing everywhere as he raced into the hotel.

I turned back to Nora. "You know, I could get used to this amulet."

"Amulet?"

"It's a delivery I have to make." She just looked at me as she ate her fruit, the sunlight glinting off her glasses. I started to explain, but a crash behind me heralded the return of Zaccheo. He skidded to a stop at the table, bumping it hard enough that I grabbed for my water glass and Nora's iced tea to keep them from being knocked over.

"Here is bread and soup and fish and very fine meats and cheese," Zaccheo said, unloading his armful of plates onto the tiny table. "You eat these, yes?"

I looked at the food mounded before me. It looked like he had raided the kitchen's store of conference food, grabbing an uncut baguette, a huge round party plate of cheeses, a similarly large plate of rolled cold cuts bedecked with parsley and olives, and a bowl of a thick, spicy soup. "I will eat one of these. I don't have enough time—or stomach capacity—for all of it."

His face fell.

"I promise that I'll come back and eat more another time," I said, feeling guilty that the amulet could play him so cruelly. "But right now I'll just have this delicious-looking soup. All right?"

His Adam's apple bobbed as he swallowed back his

sorrow, but he removed all the extra plates without making me feel any worse.

"How is your search for a mentor going?" Nora asked once the table was cleared and she could put her plate of fruit down again.

"If I say abysmally, would that make you feel sorry enough for me that you'd take me on?" I asked, only half joking.

She smiled and shook her head, chewing a couple of grapes before answering. "It would not. I never make appointments based on pity."

I stifled a sigh with a spoonful of chilled curried seafood soup. "Are you having a good time here? Get lots of applicants for the apprentice spot?"

"I'm having a very nice time. The workshops are very interesting, but I will admit, I'm more intrigued with the non-official events."

"The sightseeing stuff? I wish I had time to take part in some of them. I really want to see the castle, but what with everything going on, I just don't seem to have time. Although I can recommend the Budakeszi Wildlife Park. So long as you don't eat the deer food. Drat, I have to run. It's nice seeing you again, Nora. Good luck with your apprentice hunt."

"The same to you," she called as I gathered my things and dashed off, stopping only long enough to stuff euros in Zaccheo's hands before running through the inner restaurant to the lobby of the hotel.

I had arranged to meet Theodora Del Arco, a Guardian from Belize, there before we proceeded to her room for the interview. Theodora, a short, elegant woman with waist-length black hair that made me green with envy, told me she preferred a neutral environment to interview applicants, claiming that only in a room that had been cleansed of the imprints of others could she truly judge a person's qualifications.

Ten minutes after our appointment time I asked at the front desk if Theodora had left a message for me. She hadn't. I tried calling her room. There was no answer.

It was the faintest niggle of worry that sent me to the elevators, a niggle that grew steadily in my mind as I walked down the hallway on the seventeenth floor, scanning the room numbers for the one Theodora had mentioned she was in.

"This is ridiculous," I told myself as I turned a corner and headed down another corridor. "What happened to Moa was a fluke. It had nothing to do with me. She died in her sleep, that's what the policewoman said she thought happened. Her heart gave out while she was sleeping, and she died. It was nothing to do with the fact that I've been the one to find bodies before—"

I stopped as I turned another corner. The hallway was filled with people speaking in shocked, hushed voices. A maid's cart had been shoved to the side, a woman in a hotel uniform sitting on a chair in the corner, two of her coworkers crouched around her, offering sympathetic pats on her shoulders while she sobbed into the white hand towel clutched to her mouth. A man in a police uniform stood guard in a doorway, not saying anything to the handful of people gathered, many of whom wore conference badges.

I closed my eyes for a second, then opened them again to count the doors. Yup. It was Theodora's. Sick with fear, I turned, intending to leave before anyone spotted me, only to come face-to-face with a woman who grinned at me with wicked delight.

"Why, Hank, look who's here. It's that Guardian woman. The one the police arrested before, when that other Guardian was killed." Marvabelle's voice scraped along my skin with all the gentleness of poison-tipped barbed wire. "Fancy her being here, too. Right on the scene where yet another Guardian was discovered killed. How very *coincidental*."

I summoned a weak smile. There really wasn't much else I could do.

15

"This is becoming repetitive," Drake said as I emerged from the local police station.

I squinted at where he leaned against the limo, the sun low in the sky behind him, blinding me so that all I could see was his silhouette. "Tell me about it. You're not the one who keeps getting hauled in by the police."

He held the door to the car open for me. I climbed in, relieved to see we were the only occupants in the rear. Pál and István were in the front seat, Pál giving me a cheery smile before turning to face the front.

"Aisling, I like to think of myself as tolerant, but I must remind you that you now bear a certain responsibility for the welfare of the sept, and thus I would appreciate it if you could pass the day without attracting the attention of the police."

I leaned back against the soft leather, closing my eyes and wishing for a tiny little moment that I could roll back time to just before I had agreed to courier an aquamanile to Paris. I would never have been involved in the murders there, never have summoned Jim, never have discovered that I was born to be a Guardian, and never have met Drake.

Little flickers of flame teased my fingertips. I opened my eyes, expecting to see Drake kissing them, but he wasn't.

My fingernails were on fire.

I glared at him. "Now what?"

He tried to look innocent, but we both knew he wasn't. "It is a manifestation," he said, picking up my hand and sucking the tip of each finger to extinguish the flames.

"A manifestation?" I pulled my hand from his, not because I wanted him to stop sucking my fingers, but because my body started up its usual clamor to jump him. "Of what, exactly?"

"My fire. It sometimes happens in new mates. You will learn to control it in time, or so I am told."

"You haven't had a mate before, have you?" I asked, allowing him to pull me close to his side. He smelled good. He felt better. "Jim said that dragons mate for life. So that means you've never had a mate, right? You're new to all this, too?"

"I am familiar with the ways of the dragons," he said, handily avoiding answering my question. Drake was a master at that. "I know what passes between a wyvern and his mate."

"Uh-huh." I wasn't convinced, but I let it pass. "Aren't you going to ask me what the police said?"

"They requested an interview with you because your name was in the Guardian's appointment book. They asked you about your relationship with her. They inquired as to the last time you had seen her. And they confiscated your passport and informed you to not leave the country without first consulting with them."

I pushed myself away from his warm body to stare at

him. "Don't tell me—you've suddenly developed Fiat's psychic abilities?"

He looked disgusted. "A green dragon is above the antics of such a lesser being."

"Mmm." I rubbed my forehead, almost too tired to think. "I'd just like to know what's going on. The detective I spoke with said preliminary reports showed Theodora also died in her sleep—a weak heart was said to be the cause. But that makes two Guardians dying just a couple of days apart, a situation that stretches the boundaries of coincidence. Any ideas about what could be happening here?"

Drake shrugged. "I have been consumed by our negotiations. I have not had time to play detective."

"Do you think there's something to play detective about?" I asked.

"I have no idea. It doesn't seem likely that two Guardians should die so quickly, but it seems less likely that their deaths were anything but natural."

I wasn't at all convinced, but since there was little I could do, I let it go and changed the subject. I curled up against him again, welcoming his heat as it sank into my flesh. "Fiat isn't to be trusted, Drake. I meant to tell you this earlier, but what with everything going on, I forgot. He's not at all committed to this peace accord you're trying to hammer out. He spoke to me a few days ago about some battle he's anticipating. It sounded like he meant a battle for supremacy over all the dragon septs." I turned my head and looked up at him. His gaze was steady, no real anger or even surprise visible in his eyes. "You're not concerned about this?"

One eyebrow slowly rose. "About Fiat? No. It is not he who concerns me."

"But he's clearly planning something underhanded, Drake. He's a baddie, in case you haven't noticed. He's going to throw a monkey wrench in the negotiations, if he hasn't already." I stopped for a moment, prodding my tired mind into thinking. "How did things go today, speaking of that?"

"We move forward—slowly."

"Oh. Good. But I'd be a lot happier if you took Fiat's threat a little more seriously. He's bad business, Drake."

"I appreciate your concern, *kincsem*. It is unnecessary, but it pleases me that you put the welfare of the sept before your own concerns."

I didn't say anything to that. It was just better if I didn't admit that for a good portion of the day I hadn't thought of the green dragons at all. I looked down at my fingernails. They looked perfectly normal, not at all like the sort of fingernails that might spontaneously burst into dragon fire. "What does *kincsem* mean?"

" 'My treasure.' "

A warm spurt of pleasure mingled with a tiny dash of irritation. I looked up at Drake, admiring his manly profile for a moment or two. "Trust a dragon to use the word *treasure* as a love name."

He said nothing, just sat there, one arm around me, the other hand resting on his thigh. I looked at his hand. I looked at his thigh. My mind came up with a number of interesting scenarios for investigating the latter. I ignored them. "I want one for you."

"One what?"

"A love name. 'Drake' doesn't lend itself to nicknames. I want a seductive foreign word I can whisper in your ear to make you go wild with passion. What's 'dragon' in Hungarian?"

" 'Dragon.' "

"Poop."

Drake's lips curled into a smile. "Do you wish for me to translate that, too?"

I dug my elbow into his side. "Pass. Give me a sexy Hungarian love name."

He thought for a moment. *"Draga."*

" 'Dragon' is too mundane." He went stiff at that. "I meant the word, not you guys. Besides, I already call you 'dragon.' I want something fun. Something mushy."

He relaxed, his arm tightening around me. "I did not say 'dragon,' I said *draga.*"

"Oh! I know that word—it means 'darling'!" I glanced up at him. He was smiling. "What sort of a darling? I know that smirk, Drake. It means there's something you're not telling me. Does *draga* mean hot, sexy studmuffin darling? Manly fleshed, well-endowed darling? Darling man who makes me slobber great big puddles of drool whenever I see him?"

His lips brushed mine. "No, although you may certainly endow the word with those meanings if you desire. In this instance, *draga* also means expensive."

"Ha!" I laughed. "That's certainly applicable. OK, *draga* it is."

"For your use, *dragam* is the correct form of the word. It means 'my darling.' "

"Gotcha. Um. Drake?"

"Yes?"

"Do you suddenly not find me attractive?"

He turned to look at me at that, his eyes wide with surprise. "What are you talking about?"

I bit my lip, wondering if the lack of sleep was making me wonky. "It's just that usually when you kiss me, I end up a big puddle of jellified Aisling. That last kiss was kind of . . . anticlimactic. I wondered if maybe that now we were officially mated and all if suddenly the zip had gone out of our relationship. Last night was fun, but the man who gave me that little peck is definitely not the same one who had my body erupting in flames. Literally."

"You think I do not desire you?"

"Well—"

"You think that because I have what I want, I no longer am interested in a physical relationship?"

"That kiss—"

He turned so he could grip me with both hands, his eyes darkening to a deep forest green. "You think that this was all about the chase?"

Lord, I'm a fool sometimes. Still, I felt obligated to point out the obvious. "You're a predatory kind of guy, Drake. I bet you liked the chase."

"I did. But I like the yielding better."

I looked into his eyes, wanting to believe him but suddenly feeling very vulnerable. He sighed a gusty sigh, sliding his hand down my arm until he captured my hand, dragging it over to his groin.

"Tell me I do not desire you."

A blush heated my cheeks. Beneath the soft linen of his pants, he was hard. Fully aroused. *For me.* "I'm sorry. Clearly, I'm at a loss with this mate stuff. I apologize."

He accepted my apology with a graceful nod of his head,

releasing me to sit back against the seat. I gave his happy parts a little pat, then slid my hand over to rest on his thigh. It was a possessive move, but it felt good.

"Aisling?"

"Mmm?" My mind, always willing to indulge in Drake-centered fantasies, went off on a wild tangent involving that pool of warm water that had been featured in my dragon dream.

"I did not kiss you as I would have liked because it is not proper. We are in public." His voice was gruff and oddly stiff. It took a minute to sink in through the lustful fantasies that were developing with startling clarity.

"What?" I asked, twisting out of his embrace to look at him. "Since when have you ever let a little thing like innocent bystanders stop you from kissing me?"

"That was before," he answered, trying to pull me back against his side. I slapped his hands off my arms. "You had not accepted me then. It is not proper for a wyvern to treat his mate in such a manner. It is disrespectful."

I blinked a couple of times, hoping it would clear up my confusion. It didn't help. "So all those times you grabbed me and sucked the tongue right out of my head in front of everyone, great big huge crowds of people, *strangers*, you didn't give a damn about respecting me?"

Drake pursed his lips. His eyes took on a wary glint.

I poked him in the chest. "Well?"

Heat flickered in his eyes. He jerked me back against him, holding me tight with an iron-hewn arm. "There is no way I can answer that question without making you angry with me. I choose not to answer it."

I dug my elbow into his side until he released me. He

must have been expecting me to jump to the other seat, because he looked surprised when I lunged for him, straddling his legs, clasping his head in my hands. "Some rules are meant to be broken, *dragam*, and this is one of them."

I kissed him aggressively. I clutched his hair and tugged until he gave me what I wanted, opening his mouth to me, his dragon fire racing through me, leaping back and forth between us until I thought we'd set the limo on fire.

He allowed me to dominate him for a few minutes, my hands sliding from his head to his chest as I sent my tongue forth on a search-and-explore mission. But when I reached down to yank his belt open, he decided he'd had enough.

"You defy sept laws?" he growled into my mouth, pinning me against the side of the limo, his body hard against me.

"No. I just want to drive you wild for a change. Come here, dragon, and let me feel your fire."

We both still had our clothes on when the limo stopped at the hotel, although Drake's hand was beneath my blouse, his finger teasing my breast while I had both hands on his rear end, trying to pull him closer to the part of me that was all but sending up flares in order to attract his attention.

Neither one of us noticed that the car had stopped. We did notice, however, when Pál, unable to see into the limo through the tinted windows, opened the door and we spilled out onto the pavement.

"Oomph," I grunted when Drake landed on top of me, knocking the breath out of me and causing me to bite his tongue. A pair of shoes stopped beside my head. Drake heaved himself off me, touching his mouth and pulling away a finger red with blood.

"You will be seen in an inappropriate state by many people." The dispassionate voice drifted down to me.

"Dammit," I snarled, grabbing Drake's arm to haul myself to my feet. "That's it. I've had it with you! You are *so* on my list! Come back here, you coward!"

Drake stopped me from going after the deranged Diviner. "Aisling, do not. You will just embarrass yourself."

"I don't care. He's deliberately tormenting me, and it's going to stop now," I said, fighting the restraining arm he'd wrapped around me for a second, then realized that indeed, the people who'd been sitting outside the hotel were all watching us avidly. I stopped struggling, straightened my shirt, and tried to look like I hadn't just been indulging in a makeout session. "Sorry about your tongue. How bad is it? Let me see."

He refused to stick out his tongue so I could determine how badly I'd bitten him, ushering me into the hotel instead, ignoring all the titters and giggles from the people who'd seen our memorable arrival.

The people at the front desk acted like I was some sort of Typhoid Mary. "Hi, I'm Aisling Grey, and I was wondering—"

"I am very well aware of who you are, madam," a starchy man with graying hair and a shiny navy blue suit said. He looked unhappy, angry even. I searched my mind for reasons the hotel staff would be angry at me and came up blank. "It is good you stopped here. It will save me the trouble of visiting you. The management of the

Thermal Hotel Danu wishes to respectfully suggest that you seek lodgings in another hotel."

I goggled at the man. He wanted me to leave? "I beg your pardon? If this is about the spot on the carpet, I can promise you it wasn't my dog. That spot was there when we first got to the room—"

"The management's objection to your presence is not due to a spot on the carpet," the man said, speaking carefully, as if he had a mouthful of marbles and was afraid of swallowing one of them.

"But—why?"

"It has been drawn to the management's attention that you have been personally involved in the two recent tragedies that have blighted the good name of the Thermal Hotel Danu. This hotel has been in this location for one hundred and twenty-seven years. We would like to remain for one hundred and twenty-seven more, and I highly doubt that will be possible if customers continue to drop dead while in the hotel. It is for the good of the hotel that we request that you seek lodgings elsewhere."

"You can't possibly believe I had anything to do with the deaths of those two women? I barely knew them!"

The man tidied an already tidy penholder. "You have, I believe, been detained not once but twice by officials regarding the deaths?"

"Yes, but that was just routine questioning—"

"Nonetheless, the staff are beginning to talk. They say you are the angel of death. They say that all those people whom you meet with end up dead. Such things are foolishness, naturally, but the fact remains that you are connected to the deaths. We wish to avoid any more, thus we politely but adamantly request that you remove yourself and your belongings from the hotel. We realize that you must be allowed access to the premises during the hours of the GODTAM conference, but beyond that, we ask that you locate yourself elsewhere."

"Is there a problem?"

I straightened up as Drake's voice rolled around me. I debated handling the situation myself, explaining to the hotel man that despite a couple of odd coincidences, I had nothing to do with the Guardians' deaths, but decided that one of the perks of having a boyfriend who was arrogant, bossy, and rich was leaving such petty details to him.

"This guy is trying to throw me out of the hotel," I said, and gave Drake a questioning look.

"Is he?" Drake's eyes considered me carefully.

"Yes, he is." I waited for a moment, but Drake didn't do anything but look at me expectantly. I prodded him. "Aren't you going to do something about it?"

"That depends. What will you give me to help you?"

My jaw dropped. "What? I'm your mate—you can't ask me that anymore!"

"It seems to me I just did."

"Drake!"

Laughter lit his eyes. He was teasing me, the great big lizard. I almost pinched him, I was so irritated.

Drake turned to the hotel man, the amusement in his eyes quickly changing into something a whole lot less pleasant. I thought the guy was going to swallow his tongue. His whole body panicked, his hands suddenly trembling as they clutched the penholder while he stammered out an excuse.

"Mr. Vireo, I had no idea this lady was connected with you. She has been involved in two recent deaths—"

"The lady is my fiancée," Drake said smoothly, but beneath his velvet voice menace hung heavily in the air. The man's fingers spasmed, dropping the penholder. "She is therefore under my protection. You will accord her every respect you do me. Is that understood?"

"Yes, sir. Of course, sir. But the bodies . . . "

"Do not concern me. I trust she will not be bothered further."

"Of course not, sir. My felicitations to you both. The hotel is delighted to have Miss Grey continue her stay with us."

Drake gave the man another dragon-eyed look, then gave me a gentle shove toward the bank of elevators.

"Fiancée?" I asked him through my teeth, trying to hold on to my tight smile in case anyone was looking at us. "I don't remember agreeing to marry you."

"It is the closest mortal equivalent to being a mate," he answered.

"Oh, I suppose so. And thanks for bailing me out there, although I could have done with a little less teasing. Why didn't you tell the man that I didn't have anything to do with the murders? He probably thinks you're covering up for me."

He stopped in front of the elevator that Pál and István were holding for him. "Are you coming with me to the room?"

I glanced at my watch. "Damn, the wildlife park will be closed in twenty minutes. I had hoped I could run back out there and give György his amulet, but there's not enough time right now. I want to call the vet's office and then try to make it to at least one workshop. And then there's the evening dinner. I've had to miss so much of the conference, I'd like to try to socialize and meet a few more Guardians."

"Do not forget our appointment later," he said, stepping into the elevator.

"Right. Seven. How fancy is this shindig?"

"Fancy?" His gaze burned green. "I would suggest that you wear something . . . washable."

The elevator doors closed on my confused "Huh?"

It was only when I had the lobby phone in my hand that I realized he had never answered my question about why he didn't tell the man at reception that I wasn't involved with the murders.

Drake, I found out later, didn't lie unless he felt it was absolutely necessary.

16

Two hours after I hung up the phone to the vet's office, relieved to hear that Jim had regained consciousness and, although groggy, seemed to have suffered no permanent effects of its misadventures, I almost wept at the sight of a familiar—and more to the point, friendly—face.

"Nora, thank heavens for you. Um. That is, unless you don't want to sit with me?"

Nora looked at me sitting all by my lonesome at the big round table in a ballroom that was packed solid with GODTAM participants. "Why wouldn't I want to sit with you?"

I tipped my head to indicate the nearby tables. They were all full. "Word has gotten around. Evidently I have become some sort of a social pariah."

"Ah. Because of the Guardian deaths, you mean?" she asked as she pulled out a chair and sat. I was so pathetically grateful that I wasn't going to have to sit by myself for dinner, I didn't even flinch when she mentioned me and the deaths in the same breath.

"Yes. Not that I had anything to do with them. You've heard what everyone is saying, I'm sure. No one's accused me of outright murder, but they're saying that I'm cursed, that Guardians who make an appointment with me stand a chance of dying in their sleep, just like Moa and Theodora."

Her eyes were dark, all-seeing behind the garish red glasses. "I have not died in my sleep, and I had an appointment with you."

"You're one of the lucky ones," I said grumpily, then immediately apologized. "I'm sorry. I didn't mean to be rude, but things just seemed to have gone to hell in a handbasket for me lately. Most of it. Some is good. But a lot has been difficult."

"You're new to this world," she said, nodding her understanding. "It can be overwhelming at first, but you're struggling against what is, rather than accepting it. You should meditate, be at one with who you are, and with your new vision of the world. It will help you cope."

"I think it's going to take a whole lot more than a little meditation to fix my life, but I'll try. Oh, no, not the gruesome twosome!" I ducked my head and pretended fascinated interest in a loose thread on the cuff of my sleeve.

"What? Oh."

Nora's polite interest as she looked behind her shamed me. I might feel that because she had written me off her list of potential apprentices I didn't have to maintain a dignified appearance with her, but it didn't mean I had to let her see the catty side of me.

"Sorry," I said quietly, a fake smile of welcome plastered on my lips. "I'm just tired. I didn't mean to say that. They're nice." In a horrible, cruel sort of way.

"Well! All alone, are we?" Marvabelle asked in a voice loud enough to guarantee attention would be drawn to us.

I held on to my smile, biting back the urge to tell her it was too late, everyone already knew that I was there. They had to know—people avoided me like I was a plague-bearing, oozing-sored leper. With an STD. "Hank, just look who's here—it's that Ashley who keeps gettin' herself arrested. And Nora! You two wouldn't be"—her pale gray eyes took on a sly cast—"workin' together, would you?"

"I wish we were, but I'm afraid Nora has had a lot of better-qualified applicants for the spot of apprentice," I said politely, sharing my smile with the ever-silent Hank as he sat down next to Nora.

"Is that so? Well, I just hope that she counts her blessin's that your meeting went off without her endin' up dead like all the others." Marvabelle picked up her napkin and waved it toward a waiter. I braced myself, hoping against hope that our table had one of the local Otherworld denizens who had been drafted into service. I'd been told earlier, by a chatty Mage, that the conference folk tried to fill the ranks of meal servers with people who would not be startled to see demons sitting amongst all the other guests. Luck, for once, was with me. The waiter didn't so much as bat an eyelash at me. I waited until Marvabelle demanded water from the waiter (he hadn't bothered to bring water when it was just me sitting here) before inquiring politely of Hank how he was enjoying the conference.

"We're having a great time, aren't we, Mother?" he answered, opening his mouth to say more, but his wife wasn't one to sit around and let someone else have the limelight.

"Yes, we are, for the most part. The conference people

might have picked a nicer-quality hotel," she said with an irritated sniff. "Hank and I are used to the best hotels, naturally. And the prices they charge for a simple sandwich! Scandalous! But the workshops are good—some of them—although they don't really have enough addressin' the needs of oracles. So much of what they offer is geared for Diviners, too, and you and I both know they're just not the same thing. The two panels I was on were standin' room only, of course. There were many people who came up afterwards to tell me how much they appreciated my plan to license all Otherworld practitioners. It's to keep the riffraff out," she said to Nora, with a meaningful look my way. "As it is now, anyone can call themselves a Guardian without havin' any form of trainin'."

"Oh, speaking of that," I said, determined not to let her bait me into responding, "I was told that you're the person to talk to about undergoing the ritual to officially be recognized as an apprentice."

Her smile, which had never left her lips, brightened significantly. A little shiver of worry rippled down my back. "Ye-es," she drawled. "I am, but I had no idea that you hadn't undergone the ritual. They shouldn't have allowed you to register for the conference. Only accepted apprentices are entitled to approach mentors. I shall have to report this oversight to the appropriate officials, naturally. They will no doubt ask you to leave the conference."

Oh, great. Kicked out of a hotel and a conference, all in one day. My star certainly was rising.

"There's no need to do that," Nora said thoughtfully. "If you allow Aisling to undergo the ritual tonight, she will be officially recognized and can enjoy the rest of the conference."

"Aw, what a shame—I'm busy tonight," Marvabelle replied, her shark-toothed smile getting even sharkier as she turned it on me. "In fact, I'm busy the whole rest of the conference!"

"That's not a problem," Nora said quickly, stopping me from grinding my teeth. Her face was placid, but there was a little spark in her eyes that told me she didn't appreciate Marvabelle's attitude any more than I did. "I will oversee the ritual. I can rearrange my appointments this evening to accommodate Aisling."

Marvabelle's smile faded. "Only people with special trainin' can do that. You know that as well as I do."

Nora pulled the snowy white linen napkin from her water glass as the waiter approached with a pitcher. "I am a class three mentor now, Marvabelle. I've had a lot of training since the days when we both studied under the same mentor. I can train, evaluate, and administer proxy tests as required." She looked at me. "I can be free at nine tonight, if that is good with you."

I flashed her a look of pure appreciation. She might not think I was apprentice material, but she was obviously a woman of honor. "I wish I could take you up on it, but I have a dragon thing I have to go to later, and I doubt if it will be over by then."

Marvabelle wasn't going to stand for anyone doing her out of a chance to get rid of me. "I'm afraid that if Ashley here doesn't pass the ritual tonight, I'll have to report her to the committee. You know the rules as well as I do, Guardian. She'll have to go if she's not recognized."

"Would eleven-thirty work for you?" Nora asked, ignoring Marvabelle's near-gloating.

"I'll make it work," I answered, making a mental note to explain to Drake that I had to leave the green dragon party no later than eleven. "Thank you, Nora. I really appreciate you going to all this trouble on my behalf."

She murmured something about it being an interesting experience.

We managed to pass the remainder of the meal in polite conversation even though Marvabelle baited me as often as she could. I, hoping there might be a chance Nora would overlook the poor impression I'd made on her and still consider me as an apprentice, was on my very best behavior.

Hank contributed little to the conversation, confining himself to opening his mouth only to shovel a forkful of food into it. Whenever Nora and I tried to draw him out, Marvabelle would answer for him, drowning out any reply he might make. He didn't seem to be upset or even bothered by her, so I assumed he was so downtrodden that he didn't even notice anymore.

Dinner ended, the evening's speakers did their thing, and a number of awards were given out to outstanding Mages, Theurgists, Guardians, and so on. I hadn't the slightest idea what the awards of excellence were for, but I applauded with the rest of the audience. Nora scooted over to sit next to me, softly giving me a brief résumé on each winner, and by the end of the banquet I felt a little more as if I was getting a handle on the whole Otherworld thing.

That feeling withered into a dusty little ball and blew

away with the arrival of the Otherworld police force—in the form of Monish and my friend the happy Diviner.

"Aisling, it is with much regret that I must act in my official capacity as L'au-delà officer of the watch and speak with you regarding the deaths of two Guardians," Monish said as everyone in the ballroom gathered up their things to leave. "If you have a short amount of time now, we can conduct the necessary interview."

Marvabelle snickered. Monish's chocolate-brown eyes flickered to her before returning to me.

"Oh," I said, feeling less than brilliant. "You're the watch? That's like police?"

Monish nodded and gestured toward a silent (but smug-looking) Paolo. "There are seven of us. Paolo and I were asked to take this detail since we had met you earlier. The L'au-delà committee felt it was to your benefit to be questioned by someone you knew."

"That was nice of them," I said, suddenly nervous. I hadn't done anything wrong, and heaven knew I'd been grilled by the real police for hours concerning my relationship with both Guardians, but the worst the police could do was detain me. I had a feeling the immortal version of the police had a lot worse things they could do. "Sure, we can talk now, although I'd appreciate it if you can keep it as short as possible. I have an important function to go to in a little less than an hour."

Under Nora's watchful—and Marvabelle's anticipatorily gleeful—eyes, the two men escorted me to a small meeting room off the main conference hall. I was half expecting Paolo to trot forth some comment about my threat to take care of him earlier, but he said nothing about that. In fact, he said nothing to me at all, merely nodding

whenever Monish explained something or made a pertinent point. It was a bit of a letdown, to be honest. I figured he would hit me with at least one "You will find
yourself in deep, deep trouble" prediction.

Not that I believed I wasn't already in that state.

"You must first allow me to give you a warning, what
is called a statement of obligation," Monish said as soon
as he seated me at one end of one side of the long table.
Paolo and he sat across from me, both men opening black
leather portfolios. I tried hard not to peek at what they
had there. "Simply stated, it says that you recognize the
authority of the L'au-delà watch and you place yourself
under our jurisdiction. Whatever punishment is deemed
appropriate by the watch will be duly carried out with
your full acceptance."

"Punishment?" I said, clearing my throat when my
voice came out husky and strained. "What sort of punishment? And why am I going to be punished? I haven't
done anything wrong. I didn't have anything to do with
the two Guardians' deaths—"

Monish held up a hand to stop me. "I did not say you
will be punished. I said merely that if that action is
deemed necessary by the watch and the committee, you
will agree to abide by such a decision."

I took a deep breath. "And what if I don't agree to recognize the authority of you or the committee?"

Monish's hands rested flat on the table. Paolo looked
bored. "Then you will be ejected from the L'au-delà. You
will not be allowed to participate with any members of
the society, nor will be you recognized as a Guardian."

"Ah." I gnawed on my lower lip, thinking it over.
Surely there must be some non-official Guardians? Peo-

ple had recognized me as one from the time I first set foot in the Otherworld sphere, and I hadn't know anything about the society. Perhaps if I went my own way, I would be left in peace.

"Removal from the L'au-delà is a serious matter, Aisling. It means that all the society will be closed to you. You will receive no training, no help, have no recourse to information if you choose to not recognize its authority. I urge you to think carefully before you decide to take such an irreversible and devastating course of action." Monish's face was carefully impassive, but I paid heed to the warning in his soft, lilting voice.

It looked like I had no choice in the matter at all. Either I could recognize the Otherworld leadership and play by their rules, or I wouldn't be allowed to play at all. I could always say no and just go off to be Drake's mate, but I wouldn't be happy doing that. I wanted to be a Guardian. I wanted to be valued for myself, because I had value and skills and importance of my own, not just because my chromosomes meshed well with Drake's.

I swallowed back my worry and no little amount of fear and nodded. "All right. I recognize your authority."

Monish relaxed into the soft leather chair, a tiny smile flickering across his lips before he became serious again. "Good. Regarding the two Guardians, you will please explain what your meetings with them consisted of and how you came about selecting them as potential mentors."

The next twenty minutes were spent going over the same ground I'd covered with the Budapest police—how I came to be at the conference (although the BP police had no idea about the true scope of the conference, viewing us more or less as harmless crackpots), why I was searching for a mentor, and what had led me to talk to Moa and Theodora. By the time Paolo had fetched coffee for all three of us, my throat was dry, but I was fairly relaxed and confident. This was nothing worse than the grilling I'd undergone with the police.

That thought evaporated quickly.

"Very well. Your information matches what you told the police," Monish said as I took a sip of the coffee Paolo set before me. I thanked him, but he didn't say anything, just resumed his seat next to Monish, his pen in hand as he made occasional notes. "Now we come to the point of this meeting."

"The point?" I asked, surprised. "I assumed the point was finding out how I had met the Guardians. You can't imagine I have anything to do with their deaths! The police inspector said the preliminary examinations showed that the women died in their sleep."

Monish inclined his head. "That is so, but we in the L'au-delà are better qualified than the mortal police to judge the origins of questionable deaths. The two Guardians did, indeed, die in their sleep, but we believe they were murdered."

I stared at him, half believing he was joking with me. He wasn't, of course. His face was all seriousness.

"Murdered? Are you sure? How? By who?"

"That is what we have asked you here for," Monish said, setting his pen down and lacing his fingers together on top of his portfolio. "It has come to the attention of the L'au-delà committee that you were a suspect in two recent murders in Paris."

A horrible, dreadful feeling of déjà vu crept over me. It couldn't happen again, could it?

"Because of that, and because of your involvement with the two Guardians who were killed, the committee views you with extreme suspicion. I do not believe you are responsible for the Guardians' murders"—

I relaxed into an ungraceful slump.

—"but I believe you had something to do with them, even if it is a connection you yourself do not yet recognize."

"But—but—"

The horrible feeling swelled. It *was* happening again! Dammit, it couldn't! I wouldn't let it!

"The committee has recommended a course of action that I hesitate to take."

The loathing in his voice pulled me out of a temporary wallow in self-pity to take note of what he was saying. "What course is that?" I asked, dreading the answer.

Paolo and he exchanged glances. Meaningful glances. "I believe that information is not relevant. Know simply that it would be most . . . unpleasant."

Oh, great. He was talking about supernatural torture. The head of the Otherworld's government wanted to torture me because of what had happened in Paris.

"That thing in Paris—it was just a coincidence." I started to explain, but Monish wouldn't let me finish.

"I have read the report filed by the wiccan Amelie Merllain. I am familiar with the happenings of that time. But you must understand my position, Aisling. The committee members are calling for your head. They believe that you have an uncontrolled power that with or without your knowledge was used in conjunction with the Guardians' deaths. They want me to take you into custody and . . ." His gaze shifted to Paolo for a second or two before returning to me. At the implication of some-thing so awful, I went from merely being sick to my stomach to sheer, unadulterated terror. "I have obtained their agreement to refrain from committing you to such a regrettable course of action by promising them that you would, under the authority of the watch, identify the mur-derers of both Guardians."

My heart dropped down to my feet, joining my stom-ach. "But, Monish, I'm not a detective! I don't know the first thing about finding murderers! And I don't have any uncontrolled powers! Well, all right, I'm not terribly in control of the power I do have, but it's not a big power. And it couldn't kill anyone. I wouldn't know how to even go about making someone sick, let alone kill them. In-tentionally or otherwise. I'm just a Guardian wannabe, pure and simple."

"You are also a wyvern's mate," Monish pointed out. Paolo nodded.

"Yeah, but—"

"A portal was opened and a demon came forth before you during a lunch."

"The dragons—"

"And it has not escaped notice that mortal men seem to be, if you will forgive the impertinence, unduly at-tracted to you."

"That's the amulet," I interrupted quickly, pulling the amulet's chain up so they could see it. "I was supposed to give it to its owner today, but my demon got sick and I had to take it to the vet."

"The fact that you are also a demon lord is an added concern to the committee," Monish said softly.

I slumped even further into my chair. "It's just the one

demon. I don't know why they insist that binding one little, insignificant demon to you makes you a demon lord."

"It is not everyone who has sufficient power to control even a little, insignificant demon."

I wanted to melt into the floor. It was no use to try to protest my innocence. The damned committee I had just agreed to recognize had set me up for a fall, and they weren't going to be happy until I tumbled into their grasp.

"There is a positive side to this, you know," Monish said, chivalrously refraining from gloating over my acquiescence.

I looked up at him, heartsick, soul-sick, entire-rotten-life-sick. "No, there's not."

"Yes, there is," he said, and for the first time that evening he smiled. "You solved the murder of a very influential member of the Paris L'au-delà. Surely it will present no difficulty for you to use your powers to identify the murderer of two simple Guardians."

17

My meeting with Monish didn't end on that ridiculous note, thankfully. Instead, once he sensed he had emotionally beaten me into numbness and compliance, he shared with me all the information the Otherworld watch had gleaned thus far.

It wasn't much, just background material on the two women and the fact that they had both been discovered dead in their beds by maids who had let themselves into the rooms to clean. Neither woman had any signs of trauma, wounds, or obvious cause of death.

Detailed examination showed one similarity between them: They had both recently engaged in sex.

"Well . . . they were both pretty and, according to your records, single. It's not surprising they kicked up their heels a little," I said, flicking through the two files Monish had handed me. Most of it was in French, which I did not read, but he translated parts he felt were pertinent. I avoided the autopsy pictures he'd somehow managed to get a hold of.

Monish looked vaguely embarrassed. "When I said there was a link between the two women, I did not mean that the fact that they had both engaged in sexual relations was it. That alone would not be sufficient evidence of a connection." His eyes did a subtle little dance. "I suspect that many people attending the conference have spent their evenings in such a fashion."

I slapped an innocent look on my face. "Mmm."

The light in his eyes died as he continued, "What ties the deaths of the two women together is the manner of their . . . er . . . relations."

"Manner?" I asked, my forehead wrinkling as I tried to read between the lines. "You mean they were into something kinky? Bondage? That sort of thing?"

A faint blush stole over Paolo's cheeks. I watched it, intrigued, more than a little amazed that the man who had taken to plaguing me could blush over the mention of a little kinky sex.

"No. It was not the type of their sexual relations that I find curious."

I blinked a couple of times and waited for Monish to finish.

"It was the amount."

"Amount?"

His skin was too dark to see if he blushed or not, but his gaze did drop to his notes. "Each Guardian had evidently participated in several sexual acts the evening and morning of her death. The best estimate, based on the physical evidence left behind, is that each of them participated twelve times."

"TWELVE TIMES?" I yelped, my eyes all but bugging out of my head. "You're joking, aren't you? Twelve times? That's impossible! I mean, twice is pushing it, and three times makes you sore, but twelve times is just downright impossible! Even if they wanted to, where on earth are you going to find a guy who can . . . you know . . . twelve times? Wait—the physical evidence—was that male or female evidence?"

Monish looked extremely uncomfortable. "Male. Even allowing for variations in quantity, the best-guess estimate is twelve incidents."

"Holy cats," I said, crossing my legs in sympathy for the two women. "So in other words, what you're saying is that they were sexed to death."

"It is believed that the stress of so much intense physical activity is responsible for their deaths."

I dragged my mind away from what sort of man had the ability to ejaculate twelve times in the span of a night and moved to what was uppermost in my mind. "You're leaving out something important."

Both men nodded. "Your mind is as quick as I knew it would be, given the Paris reports," Monish said. "One of the watch acquired a sample of evidence from both bodies. It matches."

I shook my head, not to dispute what he was saying, but because I just didn't believe it. "What man can go at it twelve times with a woman, killing her but leaving him just fine and dandy, and then repeat the whole process with another woman the next night?"

"One who is not mortal," Monish said. He plucked the file from my hands and began to gather up his things.

"That pretty much goes without saying. What I don't understand is how you can show this to your committee and they can think I have something to do with the deaths. Surely I lack the obvious equipment."

His eyebrows rose at my flip tone. "They do not believe you directly caused the deaths of the Guardians,

Aisling, but they do very much believe that the killer was either summoned by you or drawn to your proximity involuntarily."

I started to protest my innocence, but the memory of the night I had been swarmed by incubi flitted through my mind. I hadn't summoned them, yet they appeared. I couldn't help but wonder what an incubus's stamina was like—that, and whether or not they left physical traces of themselves.

"We're just going to have to agree to disagree on that point," I said. "What exactly do you expect *me* to do? You guys are investigating this, so I don't see where I come in."

"You have powers that the watch does not. You have the ability to see things that are hidden from us. We will continue to investigate the murders as best we can, but we are limited in scope. That is why the committee agreed to not pursue their course of action with you— they recognize that although you have the power to raise the being that killed the Guardian, if you are innocent, you also have the power to discover the source and identity of that being." He paused, sending me a hard, unbending look. "If you wish to have a future in the L'au-delà, Aisling, I urge you to use every means possible to locate the murderer. Quickly. The committee is not known for their patience."

The two men stood, and after wishing me well and giving me a cell phone number where he could be contacted at any time of the day, Monish left, Paolo trailing after him.

The door to the conference room closed with an almost silent *shush.*

I sat alone, fingering the amulet, wondering just how the hell I was supposed to find a sex fiend murderer when I couldn't even do something as simple as deliver an old piece of crystal or find a mentor without running into trouble.

At least Paolo hadn't divined anything horrible for me in the near future. At least he hadn't—

I turned at the sound of the door clicking open. Paolo stuck his head in. "You will befriend a pigeon while contemplating plunging to your death."

"I've got something important to tell you," I told Drake as I rushed past Pál, who was holding the door open for me. I'd forgotten to take the room key he'd left for me earlier.

Drake, clad in an absolutely mouthwatering long green tunic that shimmered with a faint gold pattern every time he moved, cocked a glossy black eyebrow at me and silently looked at the clock.

"It's just now seven, so you can stop giving me that annoying male 'waiting for a woman who's always late' look."

"I said we needed to leave at seven." Drake's lips pursed ever so slightly as he let his gaze wander down me.

"Yes, I'm going to change, but what I have to tell you is important."

"You say green dragons not important?" István asked in a belligerent tone. He moved to stand beside Drake. Both Pál and István were dressed similarly to Drake, in long forest green tunics and matching pants, but the material on their clothes was different, minus the faint, elusive gold pattern in the cloth of Drake's.

"No, I don't mean that. All I'm saying is—oh, all right! I'll go change and tell you in the car."

I had brought one formal dress along with me for the ending banquet, which the GODTAM registration packet had said was black tie. My dress was a simple black matte floor-length sheath, nothing terribly fancy but of sturdy travel material. It was *not* the dress I found laid out on the bed along with a pair of stiletto heels that I knew just by looking at them would probably cripple at least three toes on each foot.

I thought at first the dress was black, but closer inspection revealed it to be a dark, dark green-black. Even draped over the bed, the lines of it made my mouth water. A simple, elegant ballerina bodice flowed down into a long, sweeping chiffon formal-length skirt, the bodice heavy with an intricate beaded vine embroidery. The tiny little beads swept serpentine paths down the skirt, causing the whole thing to glitter and sparkle with a thousand little green lights as I held it in my hands.

I had to give Drake credit—the man knew how to pick clothes.

When I emerged from the bedroom, he didn't even comment on the fact that I was now twenty-four minutes late. He just rose slowly from an armchair, his head tipped to one side as he looked me over. A long finger tapped his lips for a moment, then he drew a little circle in the air.

"Turn." Obediently, I did my best to mimic a model's graceful turn. Drake nodded. "Yes. I was correct in the choice of that gown. Come. The sept awaits."

"Hey!" I said, dropping my arms from my model spin. "Less congratulating yourself on your fashion sense and more complimenting me would be a good thing right now."

"I should not have to compliment you. You are my mate. You will always look the part."

"Yeah, but it would be nice if you could break down and tell me that I look nice in this admittedly gorgeous dress you found."

István snickered. Drake gave me an impassive look. "Wyverns treat their mates with respect at all times. They do not give effusive praise."

"You remember that rule that says you can't kiss me in public? That's not the only one that's going to be changed," I said as I gathered up my evening bag and the thin black silk wrap I'd brought.

Pál grinned as he and István went out the door. Drake stood by the open door, waiting for me. As I neared him, he wrapped an arm around me and pulled me close. "*Kincsem*, do you know what I would do if we did not have to leave tonight?"

"Compliment me? Fork your tongue and kiss me the way I deserve to be kissed?"

His breath was hot on my ear, his lips even hotter as he pressed a wet, steaming kiss licked with fire to the spot behind my ear that never failed to make me shiver. "No. I would press you against the wall, slide that expensive dress up, part your soft, delectable thighs, and plunge deep inside you."

My entire body quivered as a result of his heated words. I had to lick my lips in order to get them to work, and I noticed with dismay that my voice cracked when I spoke. "I bet if we tried we could work that into our schedules."

Drake chuckled, his eyes leaving me in no doubt that although his wyvernly code of honor might forbid him from pursuing those activities that my body ached to pursue, he would satisfy both our desires later.

I glanced at him as we went downstairs. "I love the dress, not that you were in any doubt of it, I'm sure, but I thought you said to wear something washable?"

"I changed my mind. I like you in this better."

"So do I. Where is this party being held?" I asked once we had settled into the limo. István and Pál were up front again, leaving Drake and me in sole possession of the back. "And is it far enough away that I can molest you before we get there?"

"I thought you had something important to tell me," he said, his arm solid where it rested next to me.

"I do, but I think if I put my mind to it I can fit in both telling you about the important stuff and kissing you until your dragon eyes cross."

He didn't laugh, as I thought he would. He didn't even give me the patented Drake sexy look. He just stroked my arm and remained silent.

"Drake?" I touched his leg. "I've been selfish, haven't I? I'm sorry I haven't asked you about your day. How did the negotiations go?"

"They are at an impasse for the moment, but I hope things will move forward again tomorrow."

"Ah. I hope so, too." I fell silent, waiting to see if he would say more, but Drake at his most relaxed was never a chatty soul, and now, with the weighty concerns of dragon politics, he was even less verbose. But things had changed. He had me now. While I might be no great shakes at being a mate, at least I could listen, giving him an opportunity to vent if he needed it. "We've had kind of a rocky beginning, Drake, but I want you to know that I'm here for you if you want to talk about things. Is there something that's bothering you?"

He looked downright nervous, his eyes shuttered, his jaw as tense as the fingers that gripped my arm. "I suppose it would be best if you were prepared."

"Prepared for what?" Why was I suddenly suspicious? Why did I have a feeling that something was coming up that Drake didn't want to tell me about, something to do with me? Something unpleasant. "Just what exactly is this party we're going to?"

"I wouldn't particularly call the gathering a party," Drake said, evading the question just as he always did, but I haven't tangled with demons and doppelgangers and assorted other strange beings without learning a thing or two, especially about a certain dragon and the way he liked to dodge giving answers.

I plopped myself onto his lap (carefully, so as to avoid unduly wrinkling the gorgeous dress) and pushed him back so he couldn't escape looking at me. "Right, let's have it. What's going on? You said we were going to a green dragon function. You said it was to introduce me to the sept."

"I said you would be introduced to the members of the sept in residence in this area. And so you will be." His eyes didn't blink once as I peered into them. With Drake, the usual signs that someone was lying were useless. What was, however, a dead giveaway was the way his pupils reacted. Whenever he was at his most dragonish, his most evasive, his pupils got very, very narrow. At that moment, his eyes looked like they were set with clear emeralds. They had almost no visible pupil.

"And?" I poked him in the shoulder to let him know I wasn't going to be satisfied with half an answer.

He sighed, his fingers digging into my hips as if to hold me down. "Do you recall last month when you challenged me for control of the sept?"

"That's not something I'm likely to forget."

"Nor I. According to the terms of the challenge, if I lost, I had to turn myself in to the police for murders I did not commit."

"Right. But you didn't lose, because I knew you didn't murder the Venediger and Mme Deauxville."

"Which means you did lose the challenge."

I frowned. His pupils were still thin vertical lines. Why wasn't he relaxing? "I planned it that way, if you remember."

His breath ruffled little tendrils of hair that escaped the couple of jeweled combs with which I'd pinned it. "Aisling, part of the terms of the challenge was that if you lost, you would be subject to punishment meted out by the sept."

Oh, crap. I'd forgotten all about that.

"Punishment?" I asked for the second time that night. Only this time I was much, much more worried. The dragons took their oaths very seriously. "I remember. But I kind of thought that since I'm now officially your mate, that whole punishment thing would be forgotten."

"It isn't," he said dryly.

"I guess not. So that's what's going on tonight? You're

taking me to be punished by your sept? The people who obey every single command you give them?"

"I seldom issue commands, mate."

I scooted off his lap, sure not only that whatever it was that was planned for the evening was *not* going to be fun but that Drake would do nothing to stop it.

"You know, just when I think things are just about as horrible as they can get, something like a dragon gang punishment happens. OK. I'm resigned. I made the challenge, I accepted the terms, even though I'd like to remind you that I set the whole thing up so you would be cleared and the real murderer revealed. How am I going to be punished?"

He shrugged, taking my hand.

I tried to pull it back. "I don't want you holding my hand."

"I know you don't." He didn't release my hand, though. He just stroked my fingers until they uncurled against his.

"I don't want to be punished, Drake. Punishment is never fun, and right now I have an awful lot of non-fun stuff on my plate. Is there any way you can order your dragons to not punish me?"

"Yes."

I looked at him, hope burgeoning within me.

"But I won't."

Hope fled. I wished I could go with it.

He turned to face me, my hand caught between his. "Understand me, Aisling—I could command my sept to disregard the punishment due you, but to do so would undermine my leadership. It would leave me open to another challenge, a serious challenge from a dragon who wished to take control of the sept. Such a challenge would divide the green dragons and result in much suffering for everyone before it was resolved. As much as I dislike the thought of you receiving punishment, I will not sacrifice the welfare of my clan for this."

"I understand," I said, more than a little bit surprised because I really did understand. Although I doubted Drake about many things, I never once questioned that he put himself second to the welfare of his sept. He was a born leader, and even in human form, he wore the mantle of responsibility well. I accepted that when I accepted him—but that didn't make it rankle any less. "You didn't answer my question about how I'm to be punished."

"I cannot. No, don't look daggers at me. I am not being evasive. It is not me who decides your punishment—that is left up to a convocation drawn for that purpose. Members of my sept have flown in from many countries to consider the type and extent of your punishment."

"Convocation? They've *flown* in?" I had a horrible feeling my mouth was hanging open. "People have flown here to discuss me? Good god, Drake! This doesn't sound like a simple failed-a-challenge punishment. This sounds serious."

His thumb stroked a circle on my bare arm. "It is serious. I told you that last month, when you challenged me."

"You didn't say I was likely to die over it!"

"You will not die. At least . . . no. You will not. For all intents and purposes, you are immortal now, Aisling. Your body can withstand much more abuse than when it was mortal."

Abuse? Good lord!

"Your reassurance technique totally sucks," I said, jerking away from him, scooting over to sit in the corner, my arms crossed over my chest. "Just don't tell me any more. You're *not* making me feel any better."

Drake didn't try to follow me, or soothe me, or tell me that whatever inventive punishment his sept had come up with wouldn't actually kill me. He just sat there and looked out the window, as if it didn't matter to him in the least that he was taking me to a group of people whose sole purpose was figuring out ways to punish my newly immortal self. What if the immortal thing hadn't had time to take effect yet? What if they went to whip me, or use red-hot pokers, or any of the other Savaronella-esque Inquisition tortures that suddenly popped into my mind with startlingly clear detail? What if I hadn't been an official mate long enough for my body to convert wholly to one that could withstand dragon punishment?

Might serve him right if I did die. Jim had told me once that dragons mate for life, which meant that if for some reason I died, Drake would end up grieving himself into the grave, too. I peeked at him from under my eyelashes. He might irritate me with his arrogance and unbending nature, and he might drive me nuts with all the rules and laws of the dragons, but I didn't want him to die. I wasn't willing to admit to being head over heels in love with him—that seemed like such an uncomfortable thing—but I certainly wasn't uncaring. There was a lot of emotion tied up with Drake—I just didn't want to look at it too closely, lest something happen.

Something like I get tortured to death. Gah!

Fortunately for my sanity, I didn't have long to wait before we arrived at our destination. I glanced at the bright blue-and-purple neon sign above the door and turned to Drake. "You must have paid Flavia for her floor."

He gestured toward the door. A doorman held it open, Pál and István flanking either side. I licked my lips, nerves making my stomach turn somersaults. "Do we have to do this in public? It can't be good for the negotiations if Gabriel and Fiat and Chuan Ren see me being humiliated in front of everyone."

"This is a matter for the green dragons, not the other septs. No one is present but members of this clan."

"Oh. Good. I think. Although come to think of it, maybe we should call them all up and see how they feel about me being destroyed—"

Drake didn't lay a finger on me, he just gave me another slitty-irised look.

I stopped stalling and marched past him, pausing long enough to say, "I am not going to forget this, Drake Vireo. Assuming I survive, I'm going to remember this for a very . . . long . . . time."

I swept into the club with my head held high, clutching the ragged tatters of my pride, telling myself that although I wanted to be furious with Drake, I really had put myself in this situation. That didn't mean I couldn't glare at him a lot, though, which I did. At every possible moment. He didn't try to avoid my glares, either. He just stood watching me, impassive as the group of fifty or so people, all dressed to the nines, held a court. I was offered a chair. I refused it, figuring the pain of my feet stuffed into unaccustomed stilettos might possibly distract me from the red-hot pokers.

As if.

Other than István and Pál, I didn't recognize a single person there. They looked just as human as Drake and his bodyguards, but I wasn't fooled, not when I found out who was leading the team to pick a punishment.

István smiled for the first time since I had left Paris.

18

"What's he saying now?" I leaned to the side and asked Drake, who was sitting in a huge thronelike chair. István had been pontificating for ten minutes, periodically gesturing toward me, the dragons in the audience nodding their heads at whatever he said. My one last wild hope that the members of the sept—those whose noogies hadn't almost been pierced by my lack of skill in throwing a dart—might take pity on their leader's new mate by ensuring she wouldn't die a cruel death.

"You don't want to know."

"Why? Does it involve some horrible torture?" Of course it did. This was István we were talking about.

"No. He's telling them how uncontrolled you are and how you left last month swearing to have nothing to do with me or the green dragons."

I shifted my glare to István. "Do I get to a chance to speak before they decide on the punishment?"

"You may speak, but the punishment has already been decided."

"Well, that's hardly fair!" I glared even harder at the back of István's head. He was really going to town now, emoting like a soap opera actor.

"This is not about being fair, mate. It is a punishment."

"A few more minutes of István soliloquizing up there, and they'll lynch me before I can be punished," I muttered. I thought I heard Drake laugh, but when I looked, he was as stone-faced as ever, the fingers tapping restlessly on the arm of his chair the only sign that he wasn't as unconcerned as he wanted me to believe.

István wrapped up whatever it was he was saying, sweeping his arm toward me in a grand gesture. The audience looked stunned for a moment, then erupted into cheers. I locked my knees and fought like mad to keep from screaming and running from the room. I would not shame myself that way.

As my gaze moved along the front row of dragons cheering István, I made a vow that no matter what they did to me, no matter how horribly they tortured me, I would not scream. I would not beg, or plead, or grovel. I was a Guardian, dammit. I was a demon lord. I was a friggin' wyvern's mate. I would face their punishment with dignity. I would not give them the satisfaction of seeing that I was terrified.

"I've changed my mind," I yelled a scant half hour later, clutching myself against the cold wind as I looked below at the tiny winking lights of cars passing beneath me. My dress whipped around my legs, snapping audibly. Although the summer evening was warm, the wind coming off the river definitely wasn't. "I'm fully prepared to scream my fool head off if that's what it takes to get me off of here!"

"I'm sorry, mate. It was the decision of the sept." Drake looked at me from the safe confines of the three-man bucket held aloft by the hydraulic crane arm of the aerial lift truck parked below. "I am sure you will have no difficulty finding a way down."

"Damn right I won't. My way down is you rescuing me!"

He shook his head, his hair ruffling in the same wind that snatched his words away almost before they reached me. "It is forbidden, *kincsem*. This is your punishment. It is for you alone to bear."

"Goddamn it, Drake!" I yelled as he flipped a lever in the big white metal bucket. "You can't leave me here! There's no way down!"

The bucket hummed to life, slowly pulling back from the edge of the stone platform upon which I was perched. "Be careful of the dress, Aisling. The emeralds sewn onto it are worth more than two hundred thousand dollars."

"Be careful of the dress?" I screamed, unable to believe what I was hearing. "*Be careful of the dress?* You dirty, rotten—" I stopped, looking down at the beautiful beaded embroidery of the gown, gently touching one of the faceted beads. "These are *real* emeralds?"

"Of course," he shouted back, the bucket starting to lower. His eyes glittered brighter than the emeralds. "You are my mate. I would not put you in costume jewelry."

I braced myself into the wind and leaned as far forward as I could without falling off the arch standing over the Buda side of the famous Chain Bridge. "If you don't get me off this damned bridge, you're not going to *have* a mate!"

He just blew me a kiss, the long hydraulic arm slowly folding down onto the body of the aerial lift truck below.

"Goddamn it, Drake, I take the point! I won't challenge you again! I've been punished enough . . . oh, hell."

He was gone. I watched as a tiny little itty-bitty speck that I knew was Drake climbed out of the bucket and got into the truck along with an István-shaped speck. Then the truck left, driving across the bridge, leaving me completely alone.

"On the top of a frigging bridge!" I yelled to the night sky. I thought seriously about crying but decided that wouldn't do anything other than leave me with a stuffy nose. I walked the length of the tall, flat-topped arch, one of two that marked either end of the bridge that crossed the Danube connecting Buda to Pest, careful not to get too close to the edge. The way the wind was gusting, I stood a chance of being blown right off the top.

"All right, Aisling, get a grip. You're a professional. You have powers. So let's think about how to use them to get you off this bridge." I paced back and forth the length of the arch, scanning every word of conversation I'd had since arriving in Paris and finding out about the whole other world that had existed alongside the one I'd known my entire life. Had anyone mentioned anything to do with flying? Even levitation skills would be helpful at this point. I peered carefully over the edge of the arch, wondering if I had enough belief in my own powers to just step off the edge.

Cars rushed by beneath me, tiny as little toys.

"That's a big no," I said, whimpering just a little as I collapsed in a miserable ball of Aisling, still clutching my evening bag and my black silk scarf. I looked at the latter closely for a moment, then swiveled around to look at the long cables that arced downward from the arch to the

Buda shore. Maybe I could James Bond my way down the cable if I draped the scarf over it, clinging to the ends as my body careened down it to safety—

Careened. What an ugly word that was.

"That's it. I've clearly gone insane," I announced aloud. No one disputed that, which only made me feel worse. I searched my bag to see if there was anything there to help me, maybe a magic wishing ring, or a genie or two, or even a cell phone so I could call a helicopter, but there was nothing other than my lipstick, a tiny vial of perfume, and the pitiful remains of my mad money. I didn't even have my passport, so when the officials finally recovered my vulture-pecked, bleached bones from the top of this bridge, they wouldn't know who I was.

I spent some time railing against Drake, István, dragons in general, and pretty much everyone who had ever given me grief, but once I was finished running down the list, I was left to contemplate the situation with a less heated mind.

A pigeon fluttered to the edge of the arch, strutting toward me with a jerky little head bob. Damn that Paolo and his predictions!

"So. I'm to befriend you. I don't suppose you'd care to summon the king of eagles to rescue an old friend like me?" I asked the pigeon. It pecked aimlessly at the cold stone. "No, I didn't think so. All right, Pidge. Time to get serious. Let's use our brain. I'm Drake's mate. If I die, he dies. Which means he wouldn't tolerate his people putting me in a situation where I was going to die. Thus, there has to be a solution to this problem."

I sucked my lower lip, watching the pigeon as it wandered around the top of the arch, looking for tiny insects.

"If only I could fly like you. But I can't. I don't remember hearing anything about Guardians being able to fly. There must be some beings who can fly, though. Let's see . . . ghosts float. I bet they could fly. But they're insubstantial, so even if I could summon a ghost to me, and it agreed to float me off of here, there's no way it could. What I need is someone who can float like a ghost, but turn solid enough to hold me . . . holy cats!"

The pigeon's wings flapped madly as I yelled. I yanked up the chain and showed it the amulet.

"Incubi, Pidge, incubi! That's the answer. They've shown up every night, why not tonight? All I have to do is summon one. Um. The question is how."

I racked my brain to think of anything helpful that Jim had said about the incubi, but the only thing I remembered was women being carried away on a cloud of smoke. "They're dream lovers. And they appeared to me when I was in bed, asleep or very sleepy. This is a less than ideal bed, but it'll have to do."

Have you ever tried to fall asleep on the top of an arched bridge a hundred and fifty feet above dense traffic and a river after your lover has abandoned you? It's not easy. I finally figured out that sleep wasn't necessary (or likely), but a calm, quiet mind was. Fifteen minutes after I told my plan to my pigeon friend (now huddled into a fluffy pigeon ball at my feet), I carefully hiked up the chiffon skirt of my gown and assumed the lotus position.

Ten minutes after that, I discovered I had to go to the bathroom.

Luckily, two minutes after *that* revelation, my mind was cleared and quiet enough, focused on nothing, as my old yoga instructor used to demand, that an incubus showed up.

One moment I was sitting with my eyes closed, humming softly to myself, holding the mental image of a door made of alabaster in a snowstorm, and the next a warm, woodsy breath was touching my ear.

Slowly, so as not to scare away the incubus, I turned my head. A familiar dark-haired man was kissing my bare shoulder.

"Hi, Jacob," I said softly.

His head snapped up, his eyes opening wide as he jerked backward. I grabbed hold of his arm to keep him from going over the edge of the arch. "You! It is you! The one with the dragon—"

"Yes, but he's not here. I'm all alone," I said, keeping my voice low and what I hoped was seductive. He tried to pull away from me, but I used both hands to hold on to him as I batted my lashes. "All alone. Just little old me. By myself. And I'm *terribly* lonely."

He stopped trying to pull away, looking around the top of the arch suspiciously. "The dragon is not here?"

"No." I gave an insouciant little shrug. "He's abandoned me for the night. I'm so glad to see you, Jacob. I had hoped you would come."

"You did?" he asked, watching in surprise as I traced a finger down his bare arm. He was naked, but all I cared about was that his arms were strong enough to hold me while he got me the hell off the bridge.

"Yes. I'm in a bit of a bind, though. I'm stuck up here—the dragons put me here as punishment—but I'd much rather be in bed, where it's comfortable."

He frowned. "A bed is more comfortable," he agreed after looking around. "This is not comfortable."

"No. And not conducive at all to romance."

His eyes swiveled from the pigeon to me. I could see him weighing the possibilities in his mind. I leaned forward and blew a little breath on his lips. "I would be ever so grateful to the man—incubus—who got me down off here. *Very* grateful."

The frown cleared as his eyes lit with the same lusty look that had been present in the eyes of all the other incubi. He nodded. "I will give you pleasure, lady."

"I know you would. If we were on the ground, I know that you could give me great pleasure."

"For many hours," he added, his shoulders thrown back as he puffed out his chest. "I am a virile lover."

"I can see that," I said, sliding my hand down his chest, avoiding looking at any parts that might be rampant. Well, all right, I peeked, but only for a second, and just for curiosity's sake. "Why don't you get me off of here, and then we can discuss just how virile a lover you are?"

He frowned again as he looked down at the traffic on the bridge. "It will be necessary for me to carry you."

"Yes," I answered, sucking in my cheeks and trying to look weightless.

He nodded and held out his arms. "I can do that."

I sent up a fervent prayer of thanks as I scooted over to him, leaning into his chest.

"I must change form now, but fear not, beauteous one. I will clasp you most firmly."

"All righaiiiiieee!" I clamped my lips shut tight as the man holding me in his arms suddenly dissolved into a thick gray smoke, seemingly bodiless, but then I was lifted from the cold stone of the arch, the smoke surrounding me, wrapping me in warm, dry tendrils. I bit my lip until I tasted blood to keep from shrieking as the cars and water and buildings drifted by beneath me, my brain finally taking the preventive measure of ordering my eyes tightly shut until it was over.

I can't honestly say how long it took for Jacob to get me off that bridge. All I know is that time seemed to hold its breath, seconds slowed until it seemed they had stopped altogether. Then the smoke embracing me slithered away, and I found myself standing in the garden outside the hotel, staring with blinking, disbelieving eyes at the bright lights and soft music streaming out of the restaurant that overlooked the garden.

"Now we will go to your room, and I will pleasure you a thousand times before the sun rises," a thick voice said behind me. I spun around, so grateful that I actually hugged Jacob, pressing a kiss to his cheek before releasing him.

"Thank you. Thank you, thank you, thank you. I can't believe it worked! I can't believe you got me off that horrible bridge! Boy, do I owe you. I can't tell you how much I appreciate that. Whenever I need an incubus, you're going to be the one I call, I guarantee you that."

He looked inordinately pleased. "It was nothing. I have much more impressive skills . . . in bed."

"Ah." I stepped back, aware that I was standing in full view of the restaurant windows with a naked incubus. One who, indeed, looked fully prepared to fulfill his promise. "About that—you know, I'm . . . um . . . thinking that my trauma about the bridge was so great, that I couldn't really appreciate any of your wonderful love-making talents tonight. But if you don't mind"—with a glance over my shoulder at a small group of people who emerged from the restaurant, I gently pushed Jacob toward a tall hedge that would provide a bit of privacy—"I'd like to ask you some questions."

"Questions?" He looked at me sullenly. "You question my ability to give you pleasure? I am almost six hundred years old, lady. I have pleasured thousands of women in that time. Hundreds of thousands!"

"I'm sure you have," I said softly, shoving him a bit farther along the hedge.

"I am a lover extraordinaire! No matter how debauched your tastes, I will satisfy you."

"Yes, yes, I'm sure you would."

"Flogging, bondage, fetishes—I have experience in all methods."

"Just so, but the thing is, I don't want to question you about your technique. I want to ask you about the number of times you can do it in a night."

He stared at me, his mouth slightly ajar.

"That thousand times you mentioned a minute ago—is there a limit to the times you can make love in one night, or are you pretty much the Energizer Bunny?"

"The what?"

"Limitless?"

He looked taken aback for a moment, then he puffed out his chest again, his chin up, his eyes blazing. "I am an incubus of the House of Balint. We are the oldest and most virile line in all of Eastern Europe. My loins can provide you with as much pleasure as you can survive."

"Ah, but how much would it take to kill someone, I

wonder?" I asked, one piece of the puzzle sliding into place.

"A dozen times, perhaps less, depending on the strength of your heart," Jacob answered matter-of-factly. "Of course, that matters not if you are immortal."

I looked up from where I was contemplating the hedge, startled by what he said. "Guardians aren't immortal."

"No, they are not. Come, lovely one. Let us find your bed, and I will put your mind at rest as to the power to be found in my manhood."

"Just a second. I have another question. You said you are from the House of Balint. Are all incubi from specific houses?"

"Yes. It is a family designation, you understand."

"And are they regional? That is, do all the incubi who work this area belong to the same house?"

"Yes," he said, tugging me toward the hotel.

"So you know all the others who hang out around here?"

He stopped tugging and gave me an outraged look. "You will want no other after you have had me!"

I held up my hand. "I'm certain I won't. I just wanted to know if you know everyone in this area."

"They are family, brothers in the House of Balint. I know them. But none are such a good lover as me."

I eluded his grasp. "You wouldn't happen to know if one of your brothers had been to the hotel the last couple of nights . . . er . . . visiting Guardians?"

"Many of my brothers have pleasured women here," he said, grabbing me around the waist like he was going to pick me up and carry me.

"Lately?" I asked, trying to squirm out of his grasp without much luck.

"Yes, recently. The last few nights. Many have summoned us, just as you summoned me. Come, my adorable one, and allow me to worship you as you deserve to be worshiped."

"Names," I squawked. "Do you have their names?"

He let go of me, putting his hands on his naked hips as he glared. "I begin to think it is not me you desire at all. I begin to think you question me about another of my house."

"It's not that. I'm just interested in who has been visiting Guardians during the last few nights. If you could give me their names, I'd be very grateful."

He thought about it for a minute, then suddenly he scooped me up in his arms and started walking—buck naked—toward the hotel. "No. You have heard tales from these other women about their dream lovers, and you think that only they can satisfy you. But I tell you I am better than them. I will make you forget all about them."

"Oh, look, there's Drake! My dragon!"

Jacob stopped dead, but still held me.

"Uh-oh. I think he's seen us. And he looks angry. Is that fire coming out of his nose? The last incubus he caught with me—ooof!" I hit the ground hard. Jacob, without waiting to see Drake (which was a good thing, since he wasn't there), dissolved into smoke and disappeared into the night.

I got painfully to my feet, carefully brushing grass off my gorgeous dress before limping into the hotel. A quick stop by the front desk to get a room key, an elevator ride to the seventh floor, and before you could say "Ricky Ricardo" I was throwing open the doors to Drake's suite.

Drake, István, and Pál all looked up from where they were sitting.

I stared at each one of them, letting them see everything they'd put me through before slamming the door behind me with a particularly meaningful "Honey, I'm home!"

19

"Aisling, I am not lying. I do not lie."

"Oh, I like that!"

"When have I lied to you?"

"Just three seconds ago when you told me you knew I would get off that damned bridge."

"*Kincsem—*"

I jerked away from where Drake was trying to grab me, marching past him with a glare so fulminating that it literally started a fire on the bureau behind him. "Don't you dare *kincsem* me!"

Drake absently slapped the fire out, watching as I paced back and forth between the bed and the wall.

"How could you do it, Drake? How could you park me on top of that bridge and just go blithely on your way?"

"I told you, mate. I knew you would find a way down. If nothing else, you could have dived into the river."

"And broken every bone in my body."

"No." He looked thoughtful for a moment. "Perhaps one or two, but I am sure that would be the most damage."

I hitched my glare up another notch. The curtains burst into flame.

Drake sighed as he looked at them. "You must learn to control my fire, Aisling. I know you are angry at me for allowing the punishment to be carried out, but I assure you that it was by far the least objectionable of all the punishments suggested."

I growled something physically impossible, snatched a tiny fire extinguisher from the wall, and plastered the drapes with white chemical foam. "Oh, right, like I'm supposed to believe that? I could have died up there, Drake."

"But you didn't."

"No, but that's no reflection on you."

"I agree." I toyed for a moment with spraying him, too, but in the end set the extinguisher down and stared at him. His normally expressive eyes were unreadable. "But it is a reflection on you, mate." He stopped me as I made a disgusted noise, about to walk out of the bedroom. Just the feel of his hands on my arms sent little frissons of fire whipping through my body. "Aisling, I knew you would find a way off the bridge. You are smart and resourceful, and you command more power than you can imagine. I knew that you would either start a fire on the bridge, thus summoning aid, or summon a being to rescue you."

Damn. I hadn't thought about starting a fire. I bet that would have brought the fire department out pretty quickly.

"All right," I said, holding on to my anger just a little bit longer despite knowing it was mostly unwarranted. "That excuses you from trying to kill me. But you could have given me a couple of hints on how to get down off there before you went zooming off. You could have reminded me that I can bring up your fire."

His hands slid down my arms, a slight smile playing around his mouth. My anger melted at the sight of it. "You don't need me to rescue you, *kincsem*. You never did."

"That doesn't mean it wouldn't be nice once in a while," I said, relenting. I knew in my heart he was right—he hadn't left me in as dire a situation as I could have found myself. I did possess power, and although I didn't have the confidence he seemed to have in my brain's reasoning abilities, there was a certain satisfaction to be found in the fact that I didn't have to rely on a man to save me. "You're going to have to work very hard tonight to make up for all that time I stood shivering on the top of the bridge."

His hands swept up my exposed back, his dragon fire leaping between us. "I will do my best, mate."

I leaned forward to lick his lips. "I know you—oh, crap!"

The ornate carriage clock on the bureau behind him chimed the half hour.

I gave him a crooked kiss, then gathered up the skirt of my dress and ran for the door to the living room of the suite.

"Aisling? I thought you wanted me to bathe you in fire?"

The room was empty of dragons, but my purse and wrap were sitting on an end table where I'd thrown them before storming into Drake's bedroom to chew him up one side and down the other. I grabbed them, racing for the door. "I have an appointment with Nora. It's the apprentice ritual. It has to be done tonight or else I'll be expelled from the conference. Be back as soon as I can."

I started to close the door, then popped my head back through it to blow a kiss to Drake. "Keep your fire stoked, *dragam*. I'm going to need a lot of warming."

It was only thirty-five after by the time I ran, breathless, into a now dark and empty coffee lounge. Nora was sitting at a table reading by the light of one small floor lamp. She looked up when I started sputtering my apologies.

"There's no need to apologize," she said, tucking a bookmark in the book and closing it carefully. "As long as the ritual is completed by midnight, you will be fine. Are you ready to begin?"

"Yes," I said, trying to catch my breath, calm my beating heart, and focus my mind to whatever task she was going to ask.

"Very well," she said, making a gesture to take in the immediate area. "The first test of the ritual is to locate the five wards that I have drawn. Please point them out to me."

I looked around the room. The coffee lounge was a large alcove off the main lobby, with a long counter bearing a couple of espresso machines, a number of small round tables, and a couch along one wall. I didn't see anything that looked wardish, not that I knew what a ward looked like.

"Um. Wards. Do I get a hint as to what kind of wards?"

She shook her head, her eyes dark and watchful. I frowned as I looked around again, walking the perimeter of the alcove, looking carefully at the tables, chairs, walls, pictures . . . everything. Nothing jumped up and said "Warded!" to me.

Even Nora's body language screamed that I was failing the test. I was going to be kicked out. Before I even had a chance to learn, I was going to be kicked out. It just wasn't fair! I didn't ask for this, it was pushed on me. One minute I was fine and dandy, and the next minute people like Amelie, the shopkeeper in Paris, were telling me I had to look at all the possibilities to see beyond the mortal world.

Hmm. I turned back to the room, my eyes scanning it again. Nothing. But what if I opened that magic door in my head? I closed my eyes and did that, released the power of my mental sight, and suddenly the room burst into glorious color. Reds, greens, deep indigos—all the colors that I had seen before were heightened tenfold, so bright it was almost blinding. And glowing a sparkly gold, five intricate, knotted symbols floated above various objects in the room.

"There's a ward on the big espresso machine, one on the tall palm in the corner, two more on the two windows, and the last one is on the tile at your feet."

"Correct." Relief was visible for a moment in her eyes, but it was gone before I could do more than smile weakly. "Now you will draw the following five wards on any object of your choice: binding, protection, restraint, luck, and forgiveness."

Panic, sharp and hot, filled me at her words. I didn't know how to draw wards! Jim had told me a little about them, saying there were various types used for a number of purposes, but other than that, I had no idea how to go about drawing one. I looked at Nora with my heightened vision, about to admit to her that I hadn't the slightest idea how to draw one ward, let alone five, but something in the aura that glowed around her kept my mouth shut. She was silent. But her eyes flickered to the wards that I had seen scattered around the room, then back to me, just as if she was trying to tell me something.

I grinned and walked over to the palm, tracing the pattern of the ward that hung in front of it onto a nearby lamp.

"The protection ward. Very good," Nora said. I shot her a look of gratitude before continuing to the next ward.

"The luck ward. Well drawn."

The patterns I drew in the air didn't last like Nora's did—I assumed it had something to do with my inexperience—but the symbols burst into sparkly life for a second before dissolving away into nothing. By the time I drew the last one, I was feeling much better. Nora might be bound by the rules of proctoring to avoid helping me outright, but she was obviously taking my unorthodox entrance into her world into consideration as she set the tests. I thanked my stars that she, rather than Marvabelle, had offered to conduct the ritual.

"Excellent," Nora said as I finished and came back to stand before her. There was the usual momentary sense of loss as my vision returned to normal, but it took a lot of energy and concentration to look at the world the pretty way. I could do it for only short amounts of time. "You will now please recite the names of the eight princes of Abaddon."

Now that was something I knew. I hadn't read all those ancient medieval demonology texts for nothing! "In alphabetical order, they are Amayon, Ariton, Asmodeus, Ashtaroth, Bezlebud, Oriens, and Paymon."

"Very good. Now name for me three demons and the demon lords they are bound to."

I almost laughed out loud. "Ilarax is bound to Magoth, Bafamal is bound to Ashtaroth, and . . . er . . . Effrijim is bound to me."

Laughter flashed in her eyes. "That is correct. The last part of the ritual involves you drawing and closing a circle with which you might summon a being."

"That's it?" I asked, a little stunned. "I just need to draw and close a circle? I don't have to summon a demon or anything?"

"No. Applicants to the position of apprentice generally do not have the experience or skill to do something so demanding as to summon a demon."

Well, hell! I could draw a circle with my eyes closed. I knelt carefully on the wood tile floor, accepting the piece of chalk she handed me, drawing a circle about two feet in diameter. I didn't have any blood, ash, or salt to seal the circle (all of which were used for varying purposes), but since it wasn't intended to do anything, I pulled a strand of my hair out and carefully laid it across the point where the circle started and ended. Then I stood and called the four quarters, which had the effect of extending the circle from the mortal world to the Otherworld.

"I guess that's it," I said, as I stood looking at the circle.

"Yes, that is it. And it was very well done, too. I especially liked the peace signs you drew as wards when you called the quarter. A very unique and fascinating touch."

I gnawed my lip, wondering if my improvisation would count against me, but Nora was smiling. She rubbed out the chalk circle with the toe of her shoe and gave my arm a little squeeze. "You needn't look so worried, Aisling. You completed the ritual successfully, and with seven minutes to spare. I will inform the committee tomorrow morning that you have done so. You are free to seek a mentor with the goodwill of the L'au-delà."

"Thank god. I don't think I could stand to be kicked out of one more thing."

She walked with me to the elevators, and I wished with all my heart that I could summon up the nerve to ask her to be my mentor. But I had read the etiquette in the conference packet—it wasn't polite to pressure a potential mentor. There were more apprentices than mentors, and some people ended up waiting years before they found a mentor willing to take them under their wing. Much as I wanted to beg Nora to teach me, I kept my mouth shut and simply thanked her for making time in her schedule to oversee the ritual. "There is one thing I'd like to know," I said while we waited for an elevator. "Why do some people call it L'au-delà and others refer to it as the Otherworld?"

"The words are interchangeable, and it's just personal preference which you choose to call it. L'au-delà is the closest approximation to *Otherworld* to be found in mortal languages. Amongst other things, the words translate to 'beyond,' which I believe is really a better name for the society than 'Otherworld.' It's not an other world . . . it's just a state beyond the mortal one."

"Yeah, I guess that makes sense. I think I'll stick with—oh, hi, Tiffany. Off to virgin?"

She stepped from the elevator clad in a length of translucent silver material draped in toga fashion. It didn't take much of a glance to see that she was naked underneath the material. "Good evening, Aisling. Good evening, Nora. Yes, the Mages have contracted me to conduct cleansing rituals by the light of the goddess. It is said that a drop of blood from a virgin under a full moon will restore a man's virility and a woman's purity, will reclaim a lost soul, and remove even the most stubborn tarnish stain."

"Wow," I said, trying hard not to laugh. "That's some powerful blood you have!"

"Oh, yes, very powerful. Now you see why being a professional virgin is such an important job. Just think of all the people whose lives I am making better with just one tiny little drop of my perfect blood! All those men able to make happy little babies, and women who will be able to be as they once were. It is a gift I share with the many peoples."

"Selfless to the core," I said, giving her a little wave as she headed toward the front door, where a group of men in expensive suits and shiny shoes were waiting for her. "What I'd give to have that sort of belief in your own abilities."

Nora laughed as we got into the elevator. She asked for my floor number, pressing her own, just one floor above Drake's. "I suspect the chastity she must embrace would soon have you wishing for a little less self-confidence."

I slid a curious glance at her, aware that we had just a few seconds before the elevator arrived at Drake's floor. Would I kill any chances I had with her if I asked her what I wanted to know? No. My chances were long since blown. It couldn't possibly hurt. "I realize this is going to sound very invasive and rude, but I have a really good reason for asking. Have you . . . have you ever summoned an incubus?"

Her eyes widened just a little. "That is a very personal question."

I couldn't help it. A faint blush rose under the mildly offended look she was giving me. "I know it is, it's impertinent and nosy, and honestly, Nora, I wouldn't ask it if it didn't have some bearing on something important, but it does, and if you wouldn't mind telling me, I'd really like to know."

"No," she said after a moment's silence. The elevator doors opened on Drake's floor. I hesitated, wanting to ask her more but not wishing to ruin the easy friendship we seemed to have fallen into.

"Do you know of other Guardians who have? Since they arrived here, I mean?" I asked, grabbing the elevator door right where the electronic eye could see my hand. The door bucked in an attempt to close.

She shook her head. "Aisling, I feel I must warn you. To succumb to the lure of an incubus is a very dangerous thing."

"Dangerous? Dangerous how?" The door bucked again. I stepped in front of it. "The ones I've met seem a little pushy, but not dangerous in any way." Unless they wanted to sex you to death, that is.

"They can be dangerous in that women who resort to calling incubi to fulfill their sexual needs quickly lose the taste for mortal men. They can be satisfied only by incubi. They crave only their touch. They do anything to have them, eventually going so far as bartering their souls. That is how an incubi gains in power—he lives off the souls of the women he enslaves."

"Wow. I had no idea—"

She touched my shoulder gently as the door pushed against my back, trying to shove me out of the way. "I tell you only because it's evident you've been spending time with an incubus. I don't want to see you fall into that trap."

How on earth did she know I'd been with an incubus? Was there a sign? Maybe if there was, I could track down other Guardians who might know something. "How did you know I've spent time with an incubus?"

She smiled a sad little smile. "You smell of incubi smoke."

"Oh." That wasn't going to be very helpful. I couldn't go around smelling every woman at the conference. "Thanks for answering my questions. I appreciate it."

I stepped away from the door, allowing it to close.

"Good luck with the investigation," she said just before the doors met.

Why was it that everyone there seemed to know what was going on before I did?

20

The lights were dimmed in the living room of the suite. Jim's blanket sat in forlorn emptiness next to a couch. The doors to István's and Pál's rooms were closed. The door to Drake's room, however, was enticingly open, golden light spilling out, drawing me to it like a moth. I entered and closed the door, frowning at the bed. It had been turned back, but it was empty of dragons. A little splash from the bathroom had me heading that way.

"I would think that a creature that spends so much of its time playing with fire would avoid water," I said as I entered the huge bathroom.

It was done in black stone tile, the walls, floor, and countertops all glistening in ebony beauty. The usual appliances—sinks, toilet, bidet, and a glass-block-encased shower big enough for two—were present, but they were anything but utilitarian. Drake, who I was beginning to suspect was a true romantic at heart, had lit at least two dozen candles and scattered them around the bathroom. The light from them flickered and danced on the warm, moist air, their faint scent mingling with a familiar spicy smell. Dominating the bathroom was the large sunken bath with steps leading up to the edge that had intrigued me the first time I'd seen it. It could probably fit at least ten people into it. Drake lolled around in the water, his dark hair wet and slicked back showing the widow's peak that always made my stomach clench, a book in one hand, a goblet of a familiar dark red liquid in the other.

"Water is the green dragon's element," he answered, setting the book down on the shelf nearest him. "We find comfort in it."

"So that's why you chose to seduce me in that dream pool," I said, strolling over to kiss him. His lips were as hot as the fire that I knew was captured within him, sparks of it showing in his eyes. I eased back, wanting to take it slow, slow enough to make him burn for me the way I did for him. "You taste like dragon's fire."

"The dream was not of my making, Aisling." He handed me the goblet. I took a small sip of the heavily spiced beverage, trying as I always did to identify the various elements before the punch it carried turned into an inferno. There were cloves, and cinnamon, and a dark, heavy wine . . . and fire. Lots of fire. It was a drink dragons preferred, but most mortals were unable to drink it without risking damage. I had quickly taken to it. Drake told me later that the fact I could drink it was one of the signs that indicated I was his mate. "Mmm. Good year. Nicely spicy without setting off the fire sprinklers like that last bottle did."

He said nothing as I handed him back the glass, but I recognized the look in his eyes. My body did, as well, immediately urging me to throw myself into his arms. I turned my back on him and sauntered over to the counter to fetch a sea sponge. "Would you like me to wash your back?"

"I would greatly enjoy whatever you feel in the mood to wash," he said, his eyes glowing bright even in the candlelight. He set the glass down carefully, then draped both arms over the flat ledge around the perimeter of the tub, looking like some exotic, potent sultan waiting to be attended by a harem girl.

"Mmm." The light in the emeralds glittering on my dress couldn't match the desire in his eyes, the very sight of him wet and naked immediately stirring dark, secret parts of my body. My hand slid down the front of the dress, drawing his attention to my breasts, then the curve of my hip. "I wouldn't want to get this lovely dress wet. Perhaps I had better take it off."

"Perhaps you had," he said, and I smiled over the roughness of his voice. With a great deal of wicked intent I set down the sponge and reached behind me with one hand to slowly pull down the zipper. Drake's gaze flickered between my face, my breasts, and the reflection of flesh being exposed in the mirror as the zipper parted.

The two thin, emerald-encrusted straps that held up the bodice slipped down my shoulders as I gave a delicate shrug. Drake's eyes snapped back to my chest as the bodice gaped. "You do the striptease for me?"

"Well, I do have to take the dress off. I suppose if you want to interpret such a mundane action as a striptease . . ." I let my fingers trail across the curve of my breast before giving a little wiggle, the dress immediately sagging down to my waist.

"It is good. You will continue," he ordered, his voice thickening. He was sitting up straight in the tub now, his hands clenching the edge, his lips curved in a soft smile, the lines of his chest and arms hard and tense.

I spread my fingers on either side of my rib cage, sliding them down to where my hips flared out. Two flicks of my fingers and the dress pooled with a soft sigh at my feet.

Drake made a choking noise, his gaze following the dress down to the floor before slowly sweeping upward, lingering for a few breathless moments on my thighs, the very naughty underwear made up of a couple of scraps of satin and a little lace, then up higher to where I was unhooking my black lace strapless bra.

"*Kincsem,* you are the most glorious creature to ever walk this earth," he said as I dropped the bra, his gaze so heated my nipples tightened with just the merest glance. "And you are mine. Every inch of you is mine."

I walked toward him, enjoying the way his eyes turned almost solid green as his pupils narrowed. I swung my leg across his body, my shoe resting next to him on the rim of the tub. "Help me with the buckle?" I said in a pathetic little voice.

He eyed the exposed part of me, vaguely hidden by my underwear, following the line of my leg down to my foot. "Poor mate. Cannot take off her shoes. It is my duty to give you assistance whenever possible."

His warm hand closed around my ankle, his head dipping toward it. His teeth closed around the buckle, the leather giving almost immediately under the pressure. Long, sensitive fingers stroked away the sting, freeing my foot. He threw the shoe behind him, then licked a path down the top of my foot to my toes.

My knees almost gave way at the touch. He lifted his head and held out his hand. "Your other foot?"

I placed my bare foot carefully next to him in the tub,

the warm water lapping at my knee just as sensually as in my dream. My other foot I draped over his shoulder. His hand slid along my calf toward my thigh, trailing little paths of fire. His mouth closed on the top of my foot, his tongue swirling in a way that raised goose bumps up and down my body. He plucked the shoe off my foot, pulling me a little closer so he could flick his tongue on the spot behind my knee.

"And now, I think, we have no need for this."

My leg slid down his arm as he put both hands on my underwear, literally ripping it right off me. The undies drifted softly to land next to a discarded shoe.

"You're absolutely right. We don't need them," I agreed, sinking to my knees, straddling his thighs, my back arching of its own accord to press my breasts against him. His hands were everywhere, sliding up my thighs, fingers spreading to brush oil-slicked water up my rib cage to where my breasts were aching and heavy with need. I leaned forward to kiss him, tasting his fire, tasting him, the two things merging as my tongue did a sensuous tango around his. His fingers found the hard little knots of pain on my breasts, gently rolling, teasing, tormenting my nipples until I was overwhelmed with the need for him to fill me.

"I want to go for a dragon ride tonight," I said, aware but uncaring that my voice was just as husky as his. My hands slid down his chest, my finger following the slick trail of hair down to his belly. His chest heaved as I found him, hidden in water made inky by the black stone of the tub, a groan slipping from his lips as I stroked his length, fascinated by the feel of the softest velvet over a hardness that resembled the stone surrounding us.

"Ride me, mate," he said on another groan, the tendons in his neck standing out as I nipped his neck. He slid forward a little as I sank downward, his fingers finding the very heart of my desire, opening me for his invasion. I let the tip of him enter, then sucked his lower lip into my mouth as his hands moved up my back, around to my breasts.

"Breathe fire for me again, Drake," I said a moment before dropping down on him. The slickness of my desire for him, combined with the oil and water, meant there was little friction to slow his penetration. A little scream of pleasure burbled in my throat as my body clasped him in an unforgiving embrace. Sharp pinpricks of fire touched my hips, where Drake was holding me, urging me upward again. I resisted the need to move, savoring the feel of him deep inside me, touching parts of me that no one had ever touched before.

His tongue twined against mine as my body's demands became too much for me, and I moved on him, his hands and mouth and every touch of his flesh urging me on faster. Flames licked around our joined bodies, but I paid them no heed. My focus was on the man in my arms, on my heart, which beat so loudly it almost drowned out the sultry, heated words he was moaning into my mouth, on the feel of his flesh sliding along mine, burning me more than any mere fire. The tension inside me that had been building since I had stepped into the bathroom wound tighter, faster, harder, deeper until I knew it was about to explode within me. I tightened my muscles around Drake, willing him to find his release at the same moment I found mine. He yelled something, his body jerking beneath me, his hips thrusting up as I moved down. I arched backward, the orgasm sweeping me up before it, the flames of our passion racing through me, to Drake. His body erupted into mine, his shout of exultation joining mine as we burned brighter than the brightest sun.

I didn't notice the flames until I managed to peel myself off where I had collapsed against him, my heart beating a wild tattoo, my lungs struggling to bring much-needed oxygen into my body, while the sound his harsh breathing in my ear as he did the same was strangely comforting. With arms weak and trembling, I pushed myself back, smiling at the look of bemused satedness in his dusky green eyes. A flicker at the perimeter of my sight had me looking around us in surprise.

"Wow. You lit the water on fire."

"No, *kincsem*, it was your passion that did this," he corrected, pulling my boneless body forward to claim another kiss.

One of these days I really was going to have to learn how to control his fire.

". . . which more or less means if I don't do what he asked, the committee is going to decide I'm guilty of the murders, even if they know full well I didn't do them. Have you ever heard anything so ridiculous?"

"No."

I pushed myself back from where I was draped across Drake's chest. We were in bed, my legs having been so useless that he had to carry me there, but I've long maintained that a little he-man attitude is good now and again, especially when it comes to carrying women to bed. "What do you mean, no? No, I couldn't possibly have been responsible for summoning the incubus that killed the two Guardians, or no, you've never in your life heard anything so stupid?"

"No, it is not a ridiculous idea."

His eyes were closed, his voice sleepy, his hands making lazy, drowsy circles on my behind. "You're asleep. You don't know what you're saying." His eyes opened. My fingers curled into his chest hair, tugging on it. "You have to be sleeping, because if you were awake, you'd see how crazy the whole situation is."

He gently untangled my fingers, smoothing them out until my hand lay flat on his chest. "I know you do not wish to admit to the fact, mate, but you do have the power to summon various beings, incubi included."

I stretched across him and pulled the amulet from where it lay with my talisman (I had to remove the latter whenever I made love with Drake, because the smell of the gold distracted him). "This is what summoned them, as you well know."

He shook his head, his eyes closing again. Framed as it was by the whiteness of the pillow, the dark line of his jaw, shadowed with a faint beard, stood out harshly. "The amulet focuses your power, *kincsem,* but it does not heighten it."

I slithered off him and slid both the amulet and my talisman over my head. "I hate to disillusion you, but the only time men throw themselves at my feet, figuratively or literally, is when I'm wearing this amulet. Everyone is wrong. I can't be summoning incubi without even knowing it."

Drake murmured something sleepily. I looked down at his handsome, hard face with fondness. Poor guy, he'd had a hard day. He might not have been abandoned on the top of a bridge and left to fend for himself, but I knew from a brief chat with Pál that Fiat was doing his best to break the negotiations, and Drake was left with the unenviable role of peacemaker. I pressed a gentle kiss to his lips, which curled in a little smile as his arm snaked around to pull me against him. I turned off the light, sinking down into his warmth. Despite my own strenuous day and lack of sleep, I was wide awake.

I mulled over everything Monish had told me about the two women's deaths, thinking over Nora's comments, spending a little time worrying about Jim, praying it wouldn't be so rummy from the treatment that it spoke without knowing it, and finally, wondering how on earth I was going to overcome the stigma of being once again a murder suspect, which I needed to do in order to find a mentor.

I made a few mental notes of things to do the following day: Drake had requested my attendance at an afternoon meeting, there was Jim to get in the morning, the amulet to deliver to György, and oh, yes, the little matter of that dratted murder investigation.

I was just drifting off to sleep, my arms around Drake, his soft snoring as reassuring as the heavy thigh draped over my legs, when a distant pounding jerked me awake again.

Drake was off the bed, stalking toward the door before I could so much as brush the hair out of my eyes and clutch the sheet to my chest. I sat frozen for a moment, wondering if something had gone wrong with the dragons. Then I recognized a voice intermixed with Drake's and his bodyguards'.

I snatched up the nearest piece of clothing, which

turned out to be Drake's satin bathrobe. Cursing softly, I found my sleeping T-shirt, yanked it over my head, and grabbing the bathrobe, ran out to the living room. Drake was standing in the middle of the room, his hands on his naked hips as Pál tried to wrap a blanket around a sobbing Nora. István, also naked but armed with a wicked-looking pistol, glanced at Drake, then closed the door.

"What the hell happened?" I asked as I ran to Nora.

Incoherent and almost hysterical, she was trying to escape Pál. I shoved Drake's bathrobe at him and took the blanket from Pál. Nora's face was bloody and swollen, looking strangely naked without her glasses. Tears streaked her cheeks, while her body was racked by gut-wrenching sobs. I wrapped the blanket around her, aware of the scratches and bite marks visible on her neck and the upper parts of her breasts. She was wearing a simple cotton nightgown, one side of which looked like it had been shredded by a wild animal.

"Shhhh, it's OK, Nora. It's just me," I said, my arms around her as I looked over her shoulder at Drake. He was giving István an order, which resulted in the bodyguard going back to his room, then emerging a few moments later in jeans and shoes, his gun stuck into the front of his belt. István slipped out the door. "No one's going to hurt you here. It's just me and Drake and his men. You're safe here. No one can hurt you."

I managed to get her onto the couch before her legs collapsed. She clung to me, holding me tight enough to leave bruises. I rocked her, stroking her back like I would a sobbing child. Pál finished his call, spoke quietly with Drake, then ran to his room.

Drake squatted at Nora's feet, careful not to touch her. "Nora, the watch is on its way. Who attacked you?"

She shuddered, her sobs slowing. Her left eye was swelling rapidly, a trickle of blood snaking from her eyebrow to her chin. Her upper lip was split and swollen, blood seeping from who knew how many spots on her mouth. Clearly unable to speak, she stared at Drake out of her good eye, her body shaking nonstop.

"Drake, she's too upset to talk."

"If we know who to look for, we might be able to catch him now, Aisling. To wait would mean he could escape."

"I know, but—"

"I can talk," Nora interrupted, her voice a ragged croak. She leaned into me, little ripples of horror still shaking her. "It was an incubus. He was awful. I didn't summon him. He just showed up. And he wouldn't leave me alone. He . . ." The words dried up as she swallowed hard.

Drake glanced at me, and I knew what he was thinking. "Did he rape you?"

I cringed on Nora's behalf at Drake's blunt question, knowing that there was no nice way to ask such a horrible question.

"No. Not in the sense you mean," she said at last, her voice as shaky as the rest of her. "He assaulted me and struck me several times, and I believe would have raped me, but I fought him. He beat me, but I would not let him rape me. I broke his nose. He left me after that. I didn't know where to go, where I could go that he couldn't return and find me, but I thought of you, and . . ." She broke down again, clutching the blanket to her face as she sobbed into it.

"You did the right thing," I said soothingly, taking the cold washcloth and bowl of ice that Pál brought. Drake went to answer the abrupt knock at the door. "It was very smart of you to break his nose. And you don't have to worry—no incubus would dare step a smoky toe in here, not with three dragons and one really pissed-off wyvern's mate."

She tried to smile, but her mouth was too swollen. I murmured platitudes while gently cleaning off as much blood from her face as I could. To my surprise, the man whom Drake let in wasn't Monish but Gabriel. The two consulted for a moment, then Gabriel approached carefully, kneeling before Nora.

"This is Gabriel," I told her. She looked a little wild around the eyes, but nodded when I told her that his sept was known for their healing abilities. "He's very good," I added, showing her the faint line of scar that was all that remained of my knife wound.

"I would be honored to see to your injuries," Gabriel said gently, keeping his hands on his legs, not rushing her. I flashed him a smile of gratitude and shifted a little to give him room.

"No!" Nora said, clutching my arm. "Please . . . I hate to be so foolish, but if you could . . ."

"I'm not going to leave you," I said firmly. "I'll stay here as long as you want me."

She nodded, swallowing hard. Gabriel gave me a warm look, then proceeded to doctor the worst of Nora's wounds. I was relieved to see that he knew other methods of healing than ones involving his tongue. He pulled from the pocket of his shirt a small silver tube containing a clear gel, which he dabbed on the worst of the injuries. The bleeding stopped immediately, and even the swelling of her eye and lip seemed to go down after he spread a light coat of the ointment on them. Nora tolerated his attentions without a sound until he peeled back the blanket to look at her blood-soaked nightgown. Then she started to panic. "No! I don't want . . . I can't . . ."

"I think she would be more comfortable with you applying this," he said softly, handing me a clean square of gauze bandaging that Pál had brought.

Drake was at the door again, this time admitting Monish, who looked heavy-eyed and sleepy.

"Clean around the scratches first, then use the curcain gel."

I did as he ordered, gently dabbing the long, vicious scratches on her chest and breasts, concealing her as best I could from the men. István returned from his mysterious mission, joining the cluster of Monish and the dragons.

"What exactly is curcain gel?" I asked Gabriel quietly, dabbing it onto a long scratch on Nora's arm. It looked as if the man who attacked her had clawed whatever part he could reach.

He leaned close, his mouth almost touching my ear. "Curcain is a healing enzyme found in some plants. It also occurs in the saliva of the silver dragons."

I looked in horror at the smear of colorless gel on my fingers. "This is dragon spit?" I whispered back.

"A highly concentrated form, yes."

I rubbed on a little more, waiting until I was sure Nora was distracted before asking, "Whose? Yours?"

He just smiled, his dimples flashing. I don't know why it made me feel better to know it was his saliva I was rub-

bing all over Nora, but it did. Chalk it up to not wanting
a strange dragon's saliva all over my friend.

"You're going to be just fine," I told Nora, who sat
staring into the distance, clearly trying to distance herself
from everything that was going on. "You're a strong
woman. You have power. You aren't a helpless victim.
You beat the horrible monster."

Her eyes, still liquid with tears, focused on me as I
pulled the remains of her nightgown over her, gently eas-
ing the blanket around her. She nodded, her throat working hard.

"Nora? I must ask you some questions now. You understand I would prefer to let you recover in peace, but if
we are to locate the being that did this, I must know what
happened. Although we cannot be sure of it, since your
attacker did not leave any physical evidence behind, it is
possible that he is the same being who killed the other
Guardians."

Monish's singsong voice was as soft and soothing as
Gabriel's had been, but Nora stiffened as he took a seat in
the chair next to the couch. She made an effort to pull
herself together, though, saying in a low, raw voice that
she would do whatever she could to help.

"Did you see the man? Can you give us any description?"

She shook her head. "It was dark, and my glasses . . .
I don't see well without them. I saw nothing at all of him,
but I know it was a man. He was nude. Large, and very
strong."

"No scars or any physical deformities that you could
feel?"

"No. Nothing."

"You're quite sure it was an incubus that attacked you? It couldn't have been a *zduhacz*? Or a *liderc*?"

She shook her head. "No, I would know a *zduhacz*, and *lidercs* have a different odor to them. This was an incubus. He smelled of smoke."

Monish made a note on a small notebook he'd pulled from his pocket. "Did he give you his name?"

"No. He said nothing. One moment I was sleeping, the next he was on top of me, biting and clawing."

Monish made a sympathetic face. "You did not summon the incubus?"

"No."

"You did not conduct any spells or incantations that might have drawn one?"

"No," Nora said, a faint line between her brows.

"You did not conduct any rituals at all during the evening hours?"

At the word "ritual" I stiffened. Slowly, Nora's head turned until she was looking at me. I licked my suddenly dry lips. "She oversaw the apprentice ritual for me earlier," I said, fear twisting my innards. "But I did nothing that would summon an incubus. Nothing! It was just basic stuff, like drawing wards and things like that. Nothing *dangerous*."

Beyond her, Drake stood watching impassively

"Nora?" Monish's voice was gentle but insistent. "Was there anything that Aisling did that could summon an incubus?"

Her gaze held mine for another few seconds before it dropped to where Monish had covered her hand with his own. "No. There was nothing in the ritual that could have summoned an incubus."

My shoulders slumped with relief. I was about to give her a reassuring hug when she lifted her head and looked at me with eyes that had gone dead with pain. "But it was your name the incubus invoked when he attacked me."

21

"I think this officially has been the longest day in my existence," I told Drake an hour later. "Do you have some sort of mystical dragon power that would allow you to turn back the clock so I could do the whole day over?"

"No. You need to sleep. You have black smudges under your eyes."

His thumb brushed over my cheek in a caress so gentle it almost brought me to my knees. "So do you. Good night."

"Good night. Sleep well, *kincsem*."

I closed the door of the fourth, previously unused, room in Drake's suite and paused to listen. Nora had resisted taking anything to make her sleep, but I said nothing when Gabriel dropped a pale golden powder into the tea Pál had made for her. She needed sleep as much as the rest of us.

The only sound in the room was of Nora's deep breathing. I crept along the edge of her bed to the rollaway the hotel staff had hastily brought up at Drake's demand, using the moonlight to avoid banging my toes or shins into the few pieces of furniture that were scattered around the room.

The bed was cold. And lumpy. I turned on my side, trying to find a comfortable position, mentally grumbling to myself that Drake's bed was never cold or uncomfortable, immediately riddled with guilt for thinking churlish thoughts. It wasn't Nora's fault she had been attacked, and since she was quite sure the incubus had snarled my name at her before he beat her up, it was the least I could do to stay with her through the night.

I fell asleep fingering the amulet, trying to work out the connection between it and the attacks. There had to be one. It had to be acting as a beacon or something, causing me to unconsciously summon a vile, lust-riddled incubus.

Nora was still sleeping very heavily when I dragged myself out of bed. I mumbled a good morning to Pál, who looked less than his usual perky self, and I was a bit surprised when István, who had been scarfing down breakfast, leaped up to open the door to Drake's room.

"What gives?" I asked, too tired and sleep muzzled to phrase the question in politer tones.

He looked surprised. "Is proper."

I frowned up at him. "You've never opened a door for me before. Why are you doing it now?"

"You get off bridge."

I counted to five. "You put me on that damned bridge."

He nodded. "Is good you got off."

"I will never understand you," I told him, then went in to take a shower and get dressed for the day. Drake was up and about as well, having showered and dressed, and apparently just finished shaving with a wickedly sharp-looking straightedge razor.

"How is Nora?"

"Asleep. No nocturnal visitors. Not that I expected any, but there weren't, in case you were going to ask."

Drake caught me as I reached in to turn on the shower, turning me so I faced the lights above the mirror. "You need more sleep, mate. You should go back to bed. Forget your appointments this morning."

I rallied a smile and kissed his now stubbleless chin. "Thanks for the concern, but I can't. Too much to do, especially now."

His brows pulled together as his fingers slid along the chain to the amulet. "I do not like you wearing this."

"That's one of the things I'm going to be taking care of today. What time did you say the afternoon gig is?"

His fingers caressed my lips for a moment. " 'Gig.' You speak English, and yet sometimes I have difficulty understanding you. Four o'clock."

"Gotcha. Good luck with Fiat and the others."

News of the attack on Nora had evidently gotten out. The people I saw in the hallways and conference rooms were quiet and subdued, many of them watching me, some covertly, from the corners of their eyes, others openly. I avoided the buffet setup, grabbing only a cup of coffee and a muffin, scanning the ballroom for the face I wanted to see. I found him in the corner, in consultation with a white-haired middle-aged man in a colorful red suit.

"Good morning, Monish." I set my coffee and muffin at his table, smiling at the third occupant. "I hope you got some sleep."

"Ah, Aisling. I was speaking to Dr. Kostich about you. This is Aisling Grey, sir."

The man rose, bowing over my hand in an old-fashioned

way. "Monish Lakshmanan has informed me of the happenings earlier this morning. He assures me that he has the matter well in hand and that there will be no further attacks on any woman." The man's eyes, a pale blue that reminded me of Easter eggs, narrowed as his hands traced a symbol in the air before me. I realized with horror that whatever he had done had frozen me into a block, leaving me unable to move, unable to blink or draw a breath, stopping even my heart. "I trust he does not speak false, Aisling Grey."

Panic burst through me, a black, deathly sort of panic as I struggled against the spell he had so easily woven around me. My heart fought to beat, my lungs strained in their attempt to breathe, my brain started to die, and still I stood there, a statue, my eyes locked on those of the man in front of me. With an annoyed sound, he waved his hand at me, turning to stride away as I collapsed onto the chair, gasping for air, my heart racing with the sudden release.

"Who the . . . *heck* . . . was that?" I asked between gasps, watching the man as he moved through the ballroom. People seemed to melt away before him, no one standing in his path. "He almost killed me!"

"He is one of the few people who could," Monish said, handing me a glass of water. I drank half of it, my hands shaking. I could still feel the horrible frozen sensation. "He is an archimage, a high priest among the mages. He is also on the committee that rules the L'au-delà."

I shuddered. If that was an example of the sort of thing the committee would do to me, there was no way I was going to go against them. "Why do I get the feeling he doesn't like me?"

Monish shook his head slowly, his eyes solemn. "You have not made a friend there, Aisling."

"Great. Just what I need, someone else after my blood." I took another deep breath, just for the joy of feeling my lungs inflate, and carefully set down the glass of water, pushing away the muffin. I had lost my appetite. "Listen, I've been thinking about what Nora said last night. There's no way I could summon an incubus and not know it. There just isn't. I think someone's using me as a red herring to pull our attention away from what's really important."

"What would that be?" Monish's frown matched my own.

"I don't know. That's the problem. But there has to be something that will connect the two women who died, and now Nora. They were all Guardians—maybe they went to school together, or had the same mentor, or had something else in common."

Monish sighed. "I have looked deep into the pasts of both women who died, Aisling. There was no connection. They did not know each other. They were from different areas of the world. I will question Nora today, but when I spoke to her before, she did not mention knowing them."

"You spoke to Nora about the two Guardians?" Monish was silent, his gaze steady and unrepentant. "Oh. You spoke to her about me."

"I had to determine just how powerful you were," he said, a slight apology in his voice. "No one knew you. It was difficult for me to assess the situation. I had to take Nora into my confidence. She was most helpful."

"She's a nice woman. I'm sure she was," I said softly, then caught sight of my watch. "I'm sorry, I have to run to pick up my demon and then hunt down a hermit. I'm supposed to give him his amulet, but if it has something to do with what's going on . . . "

Monish's eyes dropped to my fingers, fiddling with the amulet's chain. "I am not convinced that it does, but perhaps the owner would allow you to keep it for another day or two."

"I'll ask. He seemed pretty laid-back." I stood and collected my purse. "I have to go for a bit, but I hope you and your men will keep an eye peeled for Nora. Drake promised to leave one of his bodyguards behind until she wakes up, but I'd feel better knowing someone was watching out for her."

He nodded and stood as well, offering me his hand to shake. "It will be done."

"Thanks. I'll be back as soon as I can to try to figure out what's going on."

To my great surprise, a familiar figure was lounging around the lobby as I passed through it on the way to wait for Rene.

"Hi, Gabriel. Seems like forever since I last had a chance to talk to you." I waved at Maata and Tipene, who were sitting in the coffee lounge. They nodded at me.

"Aisling, I had hoped I would see you. Do you have the time to talk with me?" He gestured toward a chair. I glanced out through the big glass doors and didn't see Rene's taxi anywhere on the hotel drive.

"Never could resist a man with dimples," I said lightly, seating myself across from him. "Where have you been? I haven't seen any dragons around the hotel the last two days other than Drake's men."

"The negotiations have been delayed for a few days

while tempers cool. I have been in Germany, seeking enlightenment. I understand Fiat flew home to Paris, but he is expected back. Chuan Ren has remained in residence."

"Hmm, I haven't seen her, but I've been kind of busy. I'm sorry to hear that the negotiations aren't going too well. I'd hate to think it was because of me that things are stalemated."

"You?" Gabriel asked, crossing one elegant leg over the other, his dimples blaring away like mad. I couldn't help but smile in return, despite being fully aware that he was purposely turning on the charm. "Why do you think you are the cause of the problems in the weyr?"

"That depends—what's a weyr?"

A wicked sparkle danced in his silver eyes. "It means a gathering of dragons."

"Ah. In that case, the answer to your question can be summed up in a couple of words: Chuan Ren."

I expected him to laugh, or smile, or at the very least shake his head and reassure me that nothing so absurd was happening, but instead his dimples disappeared as he considered what I said.

"Er . . . aren't you going to tell me that I'm imagining things?" I finally asked, squirming in my seat. "Or over exaggarating my importance to the summit?"

"You *are* important to the summit," he said, his brows pulling down slightly. "And I would tell you what you want to hear if it was true, but I do not think you would appreciate a mate who lies to you."

"I don't, and he doesn't," I answered, wondering what Gabriel was up to. "As for being so important—I'm just a wyvern's mate. I don't see how that could make or break the negotiations. I know Chuan Ren doesn't like me, but surely that's not going to hold things up?"

He avoided my question to ask one of his own (a dragon trait, I'd found). "Drake has told you of the role a mate plays in weyr politics?"

"Yes," I answered, uncomfortable with the feeling that perhaps Drake hadn't told me everything.

Gabriel's hands rested on his leg, his long fingers toying with the dark fabric of his pants. At my words his hand twitched slightly. "Then you have the answer to your question."

Why is it that even when dragons answered a question, it was as cryptic as possible? "You don't have a mate," I pointed out. "Neither does Fiat. Yet that doesn't seem to be harming your ability to negotiate."

"A mate is a rare find," he answered smoothly, his voice rich and warm and alive with unspoken laughter. "Most wyverns are content to wait until they find theirs."

"Most?" I couldn't help but ask. "But not all?"

He leaned forward, his fingers brushing my knee. "Some of us prefer to have some say in our lives. Some of us refuse to allow fate to dictate its terms, and we make our own path."

I watched him for a few seconds, unsure if he was really saying what I thought he was saying. "I don't play mind games with people, Gabriel," I said finally. "I prefer people say what they mean and don't hide behind a bunch of hyperbole. Are you hinting that you intend to challenge Drake for me? Because if you are, I'm telling you right here and now that there's no way you can lure me away from him. I like you, I think you're nice, but at the risk of sounding conceited I would like to point out that you are not my mate—Drake is."

He stood up. A brief smile flickered across his lips, his eyes alight with secret amusement. "For now, perhaps. But who can say what the future holds?"

He left while I was still trying to formulate a smart answer. I spent a few moments going back over what he'd said, looking for an instance when he had come right out and told me he was going to try to steal me from Drake, but I couldn't come up with a single one. Had I read something into his manner that wasn't intended?

"Just one more mystery for me to solve," I groaned to myself as I gathered up my things and exited the lobby.

Tiffany was waiting near a bench outside. "Good morning, Aisling. Is this not a beautiful day? The sun is shining golden showers of happiness and joy down upon the happy faces of all the little flowers."

"Uh . . . very poetic."

She slipped her arm through mine as we waited for Rene, who was just turning onto the hotel property. "You look terrible. There is darkness beneath your eyes, and your skin looks unhealthy, and your hair is as a concubine's."

There's just nothing like a perky virgin to make you feel ancient and unlovely. Not to mention trampish. "I beg your pardon?"

She made a spiky gesture with her free hand. "Sticking out in points."

"Oh. Porcupine. Yeah. Well, it's been a long night."

"Ah," she said, nodding her head sagely. "Yes, the attack on the Guardian Nora. I heard of this. It is said you are summoning the bad spirits to attack the Guardians who reject you."

"What?" I shrieked, pulling away from her. "People are saying that?"

"Yes. Didn't you know?" She looked shocked for a moment, then waved at someone behind me and beamed. "Carlos! Do I not look muy bonita chica in this? Yes? I knew you would like it. That is Carlos," she said, turning back to me. "He enjoys much my look Innocent Eyes."

"As do we all, Tiffany, but if you don't mind, can you tell me where you heard the rumor that I was offing Guardians who turned me down?"

"Offing?"

"Killing. Murdering."

"Offing," she said, testing the word carefully. "It is good to learn new things. You will tell me more words I do not know, and I, in turn, will teach you how to be an ice princess, and if you study hard, I will teach you Shy Eyes."

Rene pulled up halfway down the drive behind a line of vehicles, giving a little toot on the horn. I waved to let him know I saw him. "I'll teach you as much slang as you like, but first, please, who told you about me summoning bad spirits?"

Her head tipped to the side as she considered me. "You have sad eyes. You should smile more and share it with peoples. It will make you happier."

I counted to ten, I really did, but I wasn't any less frustrated by the time I got there. I spoke through clenched teeth, enunciating each word carefully. "Who . . . told . . . you . . . I . . . was . . . killing . . . Guardians?"

"That woman with the silent husband."

"Silent . . . you mean Hank the oracle?"

She nodded.

Marvabelle. I should have known. For some reason, she'd had it in for me since the day Moa's body was discovered.

Rene demanded on the ride out to the vet clinic to be told what it was we had been discussing so seriously, and after receiving a detailed summary of Tiffany's virgin duties the previous evening, I told him the latest of what had happened with Monish, Nora, and the dragons.

"There is much to think over, no?" he asked as he pulled into the clinic parking lot. "But one thing is obvious—you must do all you can to make the incubus attacks stop."

"I wish I could," I said a little forlornly. "I wish I knew what it was that I am supposedly doing that's bringing them up. I just don't see how I can possibly be responsible."

"Maybe it's just a coincidence, *hein*? Maybe it is what you call fate?"

"Fate," I snorted disgustedly, having had my fill of that idea. "What has fate to do with anything?"

"You are here," he said, getting out of the taxi as Tiffany and I slid out of the backseat. His eyes were serious, his face grim.

"You're saying I'm causing these attacks just because I'm here?" I asked, getting more indignant by the moment. First people accuse me of attacking the Guardians, and now Rene was implying I was the Otherworld equivalent of Typhoid Mary? "You're saying it's something like that thing with Paolo—because he says it, it becomes true, thus because I'm here, the incubi are attacking?"

"No," he answered slowly, his voice gentle. "I am thinking that perhaps you are here because you are the only one who can stop what is happening."

My indignation melted away at what he was said. "Oh. I hadn't thought of that."

"I thought you hadn't," he said, turning and giving me a gentle push toward the vet clinic. "Now let us retrieve Jim, and then we will discuss the situation more, yes?"

"Yes. And thank you, Rene, for being so patient with me. I didn't mean to snap at you, but it's been a hell of a last few days."

"You are tired," he said smoothly, walking with us to the clinic's reception area. "And also, you are not French. Allowances must be made."

Jim received a clean bill of health from the vet, a man who lectured me, via Tiffany, about the follies of leaving my dog alone to eat poisonous plants. He held up a bit of greenstuff extracted from the deer food that Rene had scooped up at the feeding station, explaining that it was Chinese yew, a tree that deer loved but that was deadly poisonous to dogs.

I bore his lecture with all due humility, knowing there was no way I could explain the true situation. By the time I had thanked the man profusely for saving Jim's life and paid the hefty bill, I was more than a little anxious to get Jim out of there. The demon had never been one to hold its tongue for long, and I had not had the wits about me when we brought it in the day before to whisper a command of silence in its furry little ear. Since no one looked freaked, I assumed that thus far Jim hadn't said a word, but I knew it was pushing my luck to expect that it could hold out much longer.

And I really didn't want to have to explain why my dog not only randomly ate deer food but also swore like a sailor and was prone to risqué jokes. There was only so much a girl could deal with at any one time.

22

I was right. The second the door to the vet clinic closed, Jim burst into garrulous, if a bit uncontrolled, speech. "Fires of Abaddon, Aisling, could you have left me there any longer? What an awful place! It was a nightmare! It was horrible! They stuck tubes in my front legs and kept shoving thermometers where the sun don't shine, and worst of all, they wouldn't feed me anything but some sort of horrible watery gruel! Isn't that animal cruelty? Isn't that against some sort of international prisoner law? Is the Geneva convention no longer honored? Just look at the spot they stuck the IV in—does it look infected to you?"

I got on my knees right there in the middle of the parking lot and hugged Jim, burying my face in its thick black fur, so happy to see the demon hale and hearty that my eyes went watery. "Dammit, Jim, I'm a Guardian, not a doctor. It's good to see you up and about. We'd thought we'd lost you there for a little bit."

"You know I can't die." Jim's voice was a bit gruff, but I knew it was happy to see us, too, because it gave my neck a surreptitious slurp.

"Yes, but I also know how much you like this furry

form." I gave its ears a rub, smiling when it groaned with pleasure and leaned into my hand. "We have a new rule, demon—no eating food that I don't give you, OK?"

Jim shook, a cloud of black hair falling to the ground. "You'll get no argument from me there. Now, how about a proper breakfast? Something with lots of meat."

I gave the demon one last pat, then escorted it to the car, where Tiffany and Rene were waiting for us. "The vet said only light food for the next day, just to make sure your tummy doesn't get upset. So no meat, but maybe we can find you some plain toast or something light like that. Rene—the wildlife farm."

Rene nodded as he slid in behind the steering wheel. The conversation in the car on the way to the park consisted of Jim trying to persuade me to let it have a full breakfast and Tiffany telling Jim about her adventures in virginity. I bounced between gratitude that Jim was back where it belonged and worry about what on earth could be going on with the incubus attacks and how I was supposed to figure it all out, not to mention stop it.

By the time we arrived at the wildlife park, Jim had picked up enough from Tiffany to give me a hard time. "So! I go away on an overnighter, and you try to kill a couple of innocent Guardians."

"One innocent Guardian, and I didn't try to kill her." Succinctly, I outlined the facts as we walked to the entrance of the park. "You of all people should know that I didn't summon any of the incubi."

"Hmm," Jim said, but it gave me an odd look.

Tiffany practiced her smile on the few people milling around the entrance waiting for the gates to open. "I hope György will be in a better mood this morning. I hope he will not frown at me and say unpleasant things again. It is not good for the purity of your soul to say unpleasant things. Not even the blood of an exquisite virgin such as myself can cleanse that."

"When did he have time to say anything unpleasant to you?" I asked, confused. "You were only with him for a few seconds before we ran off to rescue Jim."

"Wasn't soon enough," Jim muttered darkly.

"No, not then. Later." Tiffany pulled a small mirror from her purse and examined herself critically before smiling at her reflection. "Last night, when he came to the hotel to throw himself at my feet and beg me to let him make much love to me. Do you think I look more like a princess with my hair up or down?"

I only just stopped myself from goggling at her. "What? Last night? When did György meet you last night? Where did he meet you?"

She looked as surprised as I felt. "It was at the hotel, after I returned from the Mage ceremony. He was in my room, waiting for me. He said many things about how incredible my smile was, and how it lit up his heart inside, and how he would devote himself to me and see to it that I had everything I desired if only I would give myself to him."

Well, this was all news to me! Rene and Jim, ahead of us as the gates were unlocked and opened, entered the park. I grabbed Tiffany's arm to hold her back a moment. "Tiffany, why didn't you tell me this morning that György came to your room last night?"

"You didn't ask me who visited my room last night," she answered, giving my cheek a little pat. "You are making the Sad Eyes again. Do not be sad, Aisling. If you were to stand outside the hotel again, I am sure a man would throw himself on your belly and offer to make much loves to you again."

"Thanks for the pep talk. I wish I had known György was at the hotel last night."

"Why?" Tiffany asked, escaping my hold and hurrying to catch up to Jim and Rene, blasting her happy smile to everyone within range.

"Because it's just another strange happening that doesn't seem to be connected to anything, and yet somehow I feel is," I said slowly, following her.

"Maybe it isn't connected," she answered, looking pleased with life. And why shouldn't she be? She was successful at her job, had men fawning at her feet, and had the whitest, brightest smile in human existence. "Maybe it just is."

Jim and Rene set off for the path that led to the area where I had found György. Tiffany and I followed behind at a slightly slower pace, me so I could think and Tiffany so she could pause occasionally and do the smile-share thing. "A coincidence, you mean?" I shook my head. "No, the things that have happened are just too unlikely to be a coincidence."

"That is not what I meant. Perhaps the things that have happened are meant to make you think they are connected with each other, but in reality they aren't. Oh, look, baby ducks! I would so love to have a baby duck! Look, the one at the end is smiling at me!"

Tiffany hurried off to coo over a clutch of ducklings in the children's petting area while I stood thunderstruck as I considered what she had said.

"Aisling? Is something the matter?" Rene and Jim hoved into view as I thought fast and furious.

"Wrong? No. I don't think so. Maybe."

Jim rolled its eyes. "Well, I see you're in as fine a form as ever. Yes, no, maybe. Boy, this place gives me the hinkey. Any place that allows dogs in and keeps poisonous stuff at mouth level is too creepy for me. How far is it to this hermit dude?"

"You were supposed to be on leash." I glanced back. Jim had stopped at the head of the path, looking around nervously. My heart went out to the poor demon. I supposed if I'd almost died at a place, I'd feel a little weird about coming back to it, too. "Would you be happier if you and Rene waited here while I go find György? There're benches over there, by the petting zoo."

Relief was clearly visible in the demon's eyes. "The car is better. The car is comfortable. The bench looks hard."

"Well, if you're sure—"

It was off before I could say anything else, racing back through the entrance toward Rene's cousin's taxi.

"Do you mind?" I asked Rene. "I don't think Jim needs supervising, but it would probably feel better to have you there."

"It is not a problem. We will wait for you at the car."

I gave him a little hug. "Thanks, Rene. You're a peach."

"*Non*, peaches give me the red splotches. I am an apple."

"A big shiny one. I'll be back as soon as I find my hermit. If I'm not back in twenty minutes or so, send Tiffany for me."

I needn't have bothered with the warning. I wasn't three hundred yards down the trail before a familiar man burst out of a stand of beech trees, heading straight for me.

"Guardian! Where is Tiffany? Where did you leave her? You didn't leave her at the entrance, where all the rangers are? They are iniquitous! She is too innocent, too pure for them!"

"Whoa, wait a sec!" I caught the edge of György's shirt as he barreled around me. The path had curved enough that he couldn't see into the clearing at the main entrance, but he clearly was intent on not even stopping to pick up his amulet before he went hunting for Tiffany. That thought had me wrinkling my brow as his momentum caused me to spin around. "How did you know that Tiffany came with us?"

He froze for a second, then he grinned, his hand closing over mine, still clutching his shirt. "She is a friend of yours, is she not? She told me last night what had happened to your dog. I am sorry it was sick, but it is better now, yes?"

"Yes, my dog is better," I said, biting the inside of my cheek. Something was raising the hairs on the back of my neck, but I couldn't figure out what it was. György looked just the same as he had the day before—pleasant, clean, and innocuous, if a little anxious. It was obvious he'd just come from his morning ablutions and breakfast—his hair was partially wet, there was a smidge of drying soap or shaving cream behind his left ear, and the scent of bacon and campfire clung to his shirt. "And yes, Tiffany is my friend, and she's here, petting the ducklings."

He relaxed, actually sighing in relief. "There are only women at the small animal petting area."

"Yeah. Um. You do know that Tiffany is celibate, right? She mentioned that?"

He made a dismissive head bobble. "She said many things last night. You are thinking that I am too old for her, that she is too pure a flower for me to pluck. But you are wrong! She is like no other. She is the rarest of all hothouse flowers, and only I will enjoy the beauty of her petals as she unfurls for me."

My jaw sagged. He wasn't talking about what I thought he was talking about, was he? I decided that Tiffany's unfurled petals were none of my business. The amulet was. I pulled it over my head and held it up. "I'm sorry I had to run out on you yesterday without giving you the amulet, but as Tiffany told you, it was a bit of an emergency. I wondered if I could ask you a few questions about it—"

"Keep it," he said, trying to tug his shirt from my hands.

I clung even tighter, knowing full well that if I let go, he'd be off and running to the petting zoo. *"What?"*

"Keep it. I have no need for it now. Why don't we check on Tiffany? She might wish to see around the rest of the park. I could show her my cavern. She would like it. She would appreciate all the sights of nature."

"I'm sure she would, but about the am—"

He wrestled his shirt from my grip, backing away from me quickly. "It is yours! I absolve you of your charge to deliver it. Let us find Tiffany!" He hared off without even waiting for me to finish my sentence.

"Well, hell," I said, slipping the horrible thing over my head again. "Now what am I supposed to do?"

Go back to the hotel, apparently. György was unhappy when Tiffany opted to return with us rather than staying at the park and allowing him to show her around.

"But I have many things to show you! Many flowers and sweet animals and birds in the trees!" he protested, almost on his knees begging.

I tried to give them a little privacy, but Tiffany was absolutely indifferent to György's obvious infatuation with her.

"The flowers and birds and sweet animals will be here another day," she told him firmly. "I must go with Aisling. She is paying me. I will share my smile with many people. Perhaps later, if you promise not to say the things to me that you said last night, I will share it with you, too."

With that put-down, she left, scattering sunshine hither and yon as she headed for the main gate.

György groaned such a pathetic, love-struck groan that I felt sorry for him. "She is a goddess. No, beyond a goddess, a . . . a . . . what is beyond a goddess?"

"A virgin?" I suggested.

"Yes! She is a virgin, the purest of the pure. There is no other one like her. She must be mine!"

I gave him half a smile, not at all comfortable with the possessive light in his eyes. "You may have a bit of a fight there. Tiffany is awfully set on her course of celibacy. You might say it's her business. Look, I know you've got other things on your mind right now, what with trying to woo Tiffany, but I can't keep your amulet. It's way too expensive, and besides . . . it's just weird."

"Weird?" he asked, moving to the edge of the waist-high brick wall that marked the boundary of the petting zoo. Beyond, through the big black wrought-iron gates, Tiffany was strolling through the parking lot toward Rene's car. His shoulders sagged. "How is it weird? It is a Venus amulet, created by Marsilio Ficino, inscribed with both the third and the fifth pentacles of Venus."

"Ficino? The Ficino who served the Medicis? The man who wrote the *De triplici vita*?"

"The Three Books on Life, yes, that Ficino. The amulet was one created by his hands, but I have no need for it now. Not now that I have found *her*."

He looked with longing out the gate to the parking lot. I paid him little mind, too busy eyeing the amulet, turning it in the bright sunlight until I found, so faintly etched they were almost invisible, two circles topped with a tiny pentagram, scribed with spells along the perimeter and invocations inside. The pentacles of Venus, as described and drawn in an ancient grimoire known as the *Key of Solomon the King*. I'd seen them before in one of my translations of the *Key of Solomon,* but never had I held an object bearing the marks. One pentacle would be enough for a strong love charm, but for an amulet to be scribed with both . . . hooo! No wonder it rendered me nigh onto irresistible to mortal men.

I frowned at a rogue thought, looking at György. Why hadn't he been overcome with passion for me? I'd been wearing the amulet both times, and yet he hadn't blinked twice at me. I slipped it on over my head, holding it in my hand.

"Well, György, I'd better be going." I leaned close to him, invading his personal space. He nodded, his eyes still on Tiffany as she got into Rene's car. "It's been a pleasure meeting you. If you don't mind me borrowing the amulet for another day or so, I'd like to keep it. I'll return it to you later, of course."

He flashed me a look that was mostly distraction. "Yes, yes, that's fine. You keep it. I have no use for it now that I have found the one who shall save me."

I pursed my lips, blowing a little breath on his cheek. He shifted his weight. Away from me.

"I can't do that, but I will gladly borrow it. Say, I have a thought! Why don't you come with us back to the hotel? There are some lovely gardens there, as you probably know. Maybe we could take a little stroll through them? Just you and I? And you could tell me about the sweet birds and plants and stuff?"

"No, no, it is forbidden."

"Huh?"

He turned and gave me another friendly smile. "It is forbidden to the order of hermits to which I belong that we should dally in regions not assigned to us. This park is within my domain. The gardens on Margaret Island are not."

"But you were there last night," I pointed out.

"I did not visit the gardens. I stayed only in the hotel. My clan is strict, but we are allowed to make contact with an outsider once a day."

"Ah."

I took a deep breath, and while his attention was on the front gate, closed my eyes, opening myself up to the environment and all the possibilities that existed therein. Glorious color flooded my mind, the trees beyond the edge of the clearing clad in a million variations of green and brown, swaying in an intricate dance that I suddenly realized was a form of language. The trees bowed and scraped, almost as if they were talking to each other! Fascinating as that was, it wasn't what I had wanted to examine, so with real regret that I couldn't watch the trees, I pulled my mental vision back until György filled my mind. He looked . . . human.

"Damn."

"You said something?" he asked without turning to look at me.

"Nothing important." I examined him from the tips of his scuffed, worn boots to the top of his head. There was nothing about him that looked different from any other mortal man I'd used my super-Guardian vision on. So why was he immune to the charms of the amulet?

"Yes, I totally agree. You are quite right. Who is that in the car with Tiffany?"

"Rene. He's a friend of mine. He's also a taxi driver, and in case you were worried, he's not looking for a little action. She's perfectly safe with him."

He turned to look at me then. I blinked as my vision returned to normal. "I was not worried. It is clear he poses no threat."

"Ah. Good."

There didn't seem to be much else to say, so I told him again I'd be back to give him the amulet in a day or two, then headed off to the car, my mind a whirlwind of thoughts, none of which seemed to make any sense.

23

"What do you know about Venus amulets?" I asked Jim later, after we had checked on Nora. She was up, dressed, and breakfasting with Pál, who, I couldn't help but notice, was being very pleasant. Nora looked like she'd been to war; Gabriel's magic spit had worked wonders, but not enough to hide the fact that she'd been beaten. Her lip and eye weren't swollen any longer, and the cuts had healed to angry red stripes, but there was a bit of tell-tale bruising.

We left her after she swore she just wanted to rest. Pál vowed he would stay there to protect her, which I thought was a bit unnecessary since it was daylight and incubi sought lovers only in the dark of night, but Nora seemed pleased to have his company. She also looked as if she was recovering her usual cheerful spirits, which, in turn, made me feel better.

"They're amulets. Supposedly created in Venus's name. Supposed to make the wearer irresistible to men. Is that what you've got there?"

"Yup. György says it contains both the third and the fifth pentacles of Venus."

Jim whistled. "No wonder guys have been falling all over you."

"Is it enough to summon incubi without my knowing?" I asked as we stepped off the elevator, heading for the side of the hotel where the dog park was located.

"Well, shyeah! Unless you deliberately summoned those ones who showed up in your bed before you and Drake shacked up together."

"No, not that. Could it be powerful enough to bring forth incubi, but not to my bed? You know, kind of"— I made a vague gesture as we went out into the sunny morning—"free-range incubi."

Jim just stared at me.

"What?" I asked it.

"Free-range incubi?"

"Oh, don't be so pedantic. You know what I mean."

"Yeah, I do, but it's only because I'm a superior sort of demon."

"Uh-huh. Answer my question, superior demon."

"I can't." Jim stopped to smell a beautiful bronze rose, its back leg lifting automatically.

"Use it and lose it," I warned. Jim huffed and marched over to a small shrub. "And I gave you a direct order, buster. You have to answer it."

"I can't. And by that I mean I cannot answer the question, not because I don't want to but because I don't know the answer. I don't know the extent of your powers, Aisling. For all I know you could be some sort of walking turbocharged Guardian who can pull beings in without a conscious thought. I'm only your servant. I have no way of knowing what you can and can't do until I see you do it."

"Oh," I said, kicking a tuft of grass as I strolled down the groomed lawn toward the trees where I'd been ambushed my first night in Budapest. "Poop."

"Thank you. I don't mind if I do."

I shook its leash at it. "No, you won't. I don't have a bag, and besides, you had a potty stop earlier. Come on. If you're done watering everything, I have places to go, ghosts to see."

"The nun ghosts? I thought you'd written them off." Jim shambled along behind me as I cut through the cool shade created by a crescent of trees, emerging on the other side to blink in the sunlight.

"I made a promise, and dammit, I always keep my promises. Most of the time. When I can. Which way is the convent?"

"North."

We walked through the gardens I'd seen only by moonlight, now filled with bike riders, picnickers and sunbathers, and children running after dogs, balls, Frisbees, kites, and balloons. Jim stopped to beg for an ice cream cone, but I refused, mindful of the diet the vet had given me. I made a mental note to come back when I could admire the water lilies in the Japanese garden, the gorgeous roses in the rose garden, and the shady bowers of the English garden. By the time we reached the northeast side of the island where the Saint Margaret's Dominican nunnery lay in picturesque ruins, I was so relaxed and filled with the beauty of the island that I had almost forgotten what we were doing there.

Almost.

"Jim. Go stare at that couple."

Jim looked over to where a young man and woman

were evidently checking each other's tonsils with a thoroughness that would do an ear, nose, and throat specialist proud. "Sure. Can I drool, too?"

"You always drool. Just go make them uncomfortable so they'll leave us alone here."

I looked around the stone ruins, finally finding a partially standing stone-and-mortar arch at the rear that looked like a good spot to commune with ghosts. The lovebirds toddled off after Jim sat unmoving, staring at them while long ropes of saliva dribbled from its flews.

I sat on a shady patch of grass, cleared my mind, and opened the door in it to everything that might be.

The nuns were there waiting for me.

"Hi," I said, trying to look confident and in control, as if I talked with spirits all the time. "I'm glad to see you're so prompt. I don't have a lot of time, so if you could be as brief as possible about what it is you want me to do for you, I'd really appreciate it."

Jim flopped down next to me in the shade, panting just a little. "Oh, way to go, Ash. Rush the poor dead nuns."

"Sorry, um, ladies. Go ahead and tell me what you want."

The first nun, the one closest to me, shimmered and looked agitated. I think. It was hard to tell under all that medieval cowling. Her mouth opened, but she didn't speak, not exactly. A dim, breathy rushing sort of noise came out of her mouth, almost like a wind heard at the end of a tunnel. Riding the top of the noise, so faint it was almost impossible to hear, words formed.

"Thread of crime," the first nun said.

The second wafted forward, her image as translucent

as the first. Her hands stretched toward me, entreating me to understand. "Evil in design."

"Um . . . " I said, goose bumps rising on my back and arms. The ghosts didn't have an evil feel about them, nothing that made me feel sick like some demons did, but it was still very creepy to be sitting in the middle of a haunted convent ruin, listening to ghostly howls. "OK. You want me to solve a crime? Get in line. Oops. Sorry. Didn't mean to be flip. Did someone kill you?"

"Cord go round," nun number one said, her image flickering in an ethereal breeze.

"Cord? You were strangled?"

"Soul be bound," the second one intoned, her voice soft, the words spoken on a half moan.

"Right. Your souls are bound here. I understand. Were you both strangled, or just one of you?"

"Call elements fourfold," the first one said, her image fading until there was just barest faint impression of her.

"OK. I can do that. I think," I said in what I hoped was a reassuring voice, totally at a loss. They were strangled nuns, but they wanted me to call the elements? That was usually done only in conjunction with a being of the dark powers—demons and the like. Maybe ghosts were part of the dark world, and no one had bothered to tell me.

"By the fifth the spirit you hold," the second nun said, then she, too, faded into near-nothingness.

"You want me to call a spirit?" I asked, hoping they would clarify the situation without any further rhymes. "You want me to call a demon to wreak vengeance on the person who strangled you?"

The nuns disappeared completely.

"Hey! Well, crap. What was that supposed to be? Jim, what do yoeeeee!"

The first nun appeared suddenly, her white face pushed into mine, her dark, tormented eyes enough to make my soul weep. "Cast your spell, bind him well. Bright as fire glow, deep as water flow."

Before I could blink, she was gone.

"Now that was truly freaky," I said, rubbing my arms and blinking as I opened my eyes up to the normal world. Despite the heat of the day, I was chilled, little shivers of cold making my skin tighten. "What is it about ghosts that they all have to speak in rhyme?"

Jim shrugged. "Revenge, mostly."

I got up, walked over to a beam of sunlight, and sat on a broken bit of stone wall, still shivering even as I soaked up the heat of the sun-warmed stone. "What are you talking about?"

"Revenge. The dead often get a bit testy about things, mostly the fact that they're dead and you're not. If you had to hang around a place for a couple of hundred years, trying to pass along a bit of information, or ask for help, or offer advice, but no one listened to you, you'd get cranky, too. That's why most spirits speak in rhyme. It's their revenge, to make you work in order to understand them."

"Lovely. Like I don't have enough to do without trying to decode ghostly messages to find some four-hundred-year-old strangler."

"I don't think they were asking for your help, Ash," Jim said, snapping at a bee that buzzed past.

"No?" I leaned back against the wall to consider what the nuns had said. "Thread of crime, evil in design. Cord go round, soul be bound. Call elements fourfold, by the fifth the spirit you hold. You know, you may just be on to something there, Jim. It almost sounds like a warning."

"Or a solution to a problem." Jim rolled onto its back, kicking all four legs into the air in an attempt to scratch its back. "You're forgetting the last part. Cast your spell, bind him well. Bright as fire glow, deep as water flow."

"Cast your spell, bind him well. Damn, Jim, I knew there had to be a reason I was saddled with you! You're right, you're absolutely right. That first part is a spell. A binding spell. The nuns were giving me a spell . . . to catch the murdering bastard incubus!"

I stood up, conviction flowing strong. The nuns had given me a tool to catch the incubus—but why?

"Why would they help me find an incubus?"

Jim shrugged. "Why not?"

"For starters, they don't have anything to do with incubi. They're ghost nuns."

"So? Not everything is a big, dark secret, Aisling. Sometimes things just are. If I were you, I'd stop questioning *why* and put my mind to work on *how* to use the information."

"Hmm." I thought about what Jim said. "You have a point. All right, now all I need to do is to arrange for the incubus to pay another call. If I could catch him and bind him, I'd be able to turn him over to Monish and the Otherworld watch, which not only would clear my name but also would prove to any available Guardians who might happen to be lurking around that I would be hot stuff, apprentice-wise. Come on, Jim-Dog."

"Where are we going now? Can I eat, wherever it is?"

the demon asked, watching as I marched off to the south end of the island.

"We're going back to the conference, and if you're a good demon, you can have lunch. Hurry up, lazybones. Lots to do. Things to plan. Incubi to catch."

I was in such high spirits when we arrived back at the hotel, it was a shame that my life pretty much took a turn for the sucky.

Again.

A glance at my appointment book showed a lamentable lack of Guardian appointments (the three Guardians I'd scheduled with had canceled after Nora's attack— falsely attributed to me—was made public), but there were still interesting workshops to attend, a dragon's brain to pick, and Nora to talk to about the plan that I'd mulled over on the walk back to the hotel.

Monish was waiting for me at the door to the conference area.

"Aisling Grey," he said as I came in.

I froze. Names have power, and when someone who knows how to use that power invokes your full name, it leaves you vulnerable. One of the first things I noticed with people in the Otherworld society was that many of them did not tell you their full names. They used only first names. Only those people who were very self-assured gave you their full name without knowing whether or not you could use that against them.

"Hi, Monish," I said carefully.

He crooked his finger at me. I sighed and followed him to the same room in which he'd first interviewed me. "Why do I have a horrible feeling I'm being sent to the principal's office?"

Jim snickered. Monish shot it a look that shut the demon right up. He didn't waste any time before lighting into me, either, barely waiting for me to be seated. "Why did you not tell me that you had summoned an incubus last night?"

I bit the inside of my cheek, figuring the answer everyone else gave me might just work. "You didn't ask me?"

His eyes narrowed.

I took a deep breath and released it slowly, trying to cling to my happy, hopeful feeling. "Sorry. The reason I didn't tell you about Jacob is because I didn't think it was important."

"Jacob?" he asked, his fingers tightening on the chair he stood behind.

"Jacob of the House of Balint, the incubus I summoned."

For a moment I thought Monish's lovely brown eyes were going to pop right out of his head and roll across the table to me. "You know the incubus you summoned?"

"Well, yeah. At least, I didn't know it was going to be him who came when I summoned an incubus, but it turned out to be Jacob, which was good because I don't think any of the others would have been nearly as gullible. Er . . . helpful."

Monish turned into a statue, I swear. A statue that breathed in and out, but still, a statue. "The others?"

"Yeah, the others. The ones that visited me before Jacob. He was one of the last ones before Drake put an end to the STOP HERE AND RAVISH AISLING sign that was evidently above my bed."

"How many incubi did you summon before the

wyvern stopped them?" Monish sounded like he was having a hard time speaking.

"I didn't summon them. They—" The second the words left my mouth, I saw what I had done—reaffirmed my potential guilt in the eyes of the committee. Here I had been disputing their claims that I had the power to summon incubi without knowing it, and what did I do? I gave them my head on a platter. "It's not like it sounds. I have this Venus amulet—"

That made things worse. His eyebrows shot up to the top of his forehead as he eyed the chain visible against my throat. "The amulet you wear is a Venus amulet."

"One inscribed with two pentacles of Venus," Jim said.

I turned on my demon, not that I hadn't done enough damage, but Jim was supposed to be my servant. It wasn't supposed to suggest someone get a nice rope since there was a tree so handy. "Oh, thank you very much. Do you *want* them to kill me?"

"Don't exaggerate. They couldn't kill you. Well, the committee probably *could,* but they'd have a war with Drake on their hands if they did, so the most they'd do is maim you."

"You are *not* helping," I said through my teeth.

Monish released the chair, walking stiffly around the table to face me. I rose from my chair, backing up a couple of steps. "Aisling Grey," he started to say.

"Wait!" I interrupted, holding my hands up. "Don't say it! Look, I know you're about to say something bad, something I don't want you to say, but you've got to listen to me. Yes, I have the Venus amulet. Yes, incubi were summoned to me without my knowledge, but they were

summoned to me, not to anyone else. I don't know why
the one that attacked Nora said my name, but I wasn't
even wearing the amulet last night, so I couldn't have
summoned it. Besides, I wasn't asleep, and the other
times I summoned the incubi I'd been asleep or deep in
meditation. I think there's something going on, something I don't quite understand, but I swear to you it's not
me. I swear it, Monish. I swear on my own soul that I am
not doing this."

He just looked at me, clearly weighing my plea. Just
as clearly he dismissed it, his mouth opening to speak
again.

"NO!" I shrieked, jumping forward to clamp my hand
over his mouth. His eyes got huge at that, but I didn't
have time to regret such a bold action.

"You have to give me time. I have a plan—at least,
I'll have one once I talk to Nora, but I have to have time
to put the plan into action. I promise you I'll find who
killed the Guardians, but you have to give me just a little more time. I know how to trap the incubus, Monish.
I have a binding spell. I know I can hold him once I draw
him in, but I can't do it if you turn me over to Dr. Kostich and his buddies. Please, Monish. I'm not bad. I'm
not killing Guardians. And I'm not summoning a murderous incubus. But I can end it, if you'll just give me
the room to do so."

He pried my hand off his mouth, giving me a good,
long stare before rubbing a hand over his face. "I must be
mad to even consider allowing you freedom in the face of
such overwhelming evidence, but I have consulted the
high spirits about you. They counsel patience."

"Bless the high spirits! And thank you. You won't regret your trust in me."

His eyes grew hard. "You had best make sure I will not. You have until midnight tonight, Aisling."

I did some calculations in my head, sorting out what I'd need to do, whom I needed to talk to, and said, "Two days. Forty-eight hours."

He shook his head. "Twenty-four. That is as much leniency as I can give you, and for that, I will have to spend hours convincing the committee I have not lost my reasoning."

I swallowed back my fear. "Tomorrow night. Give me until tomorrow night. Midnight. Please, Monish. I won't fail you, I swear."

He opened his mouth, then closed it again, turning to open the door. "It is your own destruction that you hold in the balance, Aisling. Be sure that you remember that. You have until tomorrow evening."

"I won't let you down! And thank you!" I called after him as he left the room, then collapsed on the chair behind me.

"You have a plan?" Jim said, coming around to face me. I used its drool bib to wipe its slobbery lips.

"Yup. I have a plan. It hinges on me being able to pull a rabbit out of a hat, so to speak, but all in all, I think it will work."

Jim shook its shaggy head. "We are *so* doomed."

24

"There are times when I think I just can't get a break."

"And then there are times when we know you're cracked."

I pointed to the lawn at the end of the verandah. "Go. Now. Sit. And don't give me that look. You've been fed, watered, walked, and if you're feeling well enough to make smart-ass comments, you're well enough to lie twenty feet away in the shade."

Jim, wise enough to know when it had pushed me beyond the limits of sympathy and understanding for the night it spent in the doggie hospital, lumbered off to lie in the grass. I gave Nora an apologetic smile. "Sorry about that. Both the whining on my part and the demon's comments."

Nora looked after Jim, a thoughtful look on her face. I was pleased to see that a reapplication of Gabriel's fix-it gel (the source of which I did not share with Nora) had healed the abrasions and scratches to the point where they were easily covered by a little judicious application of cosmetics. "That is a very interesting demon you have. It's not like any other I have seen."

"A pain in the butt, you mean?"

"Evil," she corrected, giving me a mild look.

"Oh. Yeah. Jim's not that. I think that's why it was banished from its former demon lord's legions, to be honest. It never really has talked about why it was kicked out, and since it gets kind of embarrassed whenever the subject swings that way, I've let it go."

A variety of emotions mingled in her eyes, but in the end humor won out. "You have a unique relationship, one that you should value. I can't think of another demon that demonstrates such loyalty as Jim does to you."

"Loyalty? Are you kidding? Do you know what it did? It blabbed to Monish that the Venus amulet was inscribed with two pentacles, and while it's true the damage was already done when I slipped up and told Monish about the incubi visiting me before Drake and I did the oath thing, Jim definitely did not help the situation by mentioning just how powerful the amulet was."

"On the contrary," Nora said, leaning back so Zaccheo, with many fervent and poignant looks at me, could clear away the lunch plates. "Jim telling Monish that indicates the demon's belief in you. It knows, as does Monish, that if you were destroyed, it would suffer the same fate. For a demon to present such a damning piece of information—damning at first look, that is—when it knew you were at risk showed that it knew you were innocent. I'm sure you plead most eloquently, Aisling, but I suspect Jim's show of loyalty gave Monish pause for thought and is likely what changed his mind."

"Well, how do you like that?" I said, glancing fondly over to the big black lump stretched out on the lawn. "And here I thought it just liked to see me in hot water."

Nora laughed. "I'm sure it does. It *is* a demon, after all. Just not a terribly effective one, so to speak."

"I see what you mean." We fell quiet for a moment, enjoying the summer breeze as it caressed us, the afternoon air heavy with the scent of jasmine. Around us, people talked and laughed and ate, as many different languages audible as there were voices. Everyone seemed to be having a wonderful conference—but then, they weren't once again cast in the role of murder suspect number one. I hated to ruin such a peaceful moment, but the clock was definitely ticking, and I had a lot to talk over with Nora. "Tiffany said something today that had me thinking, but I'm not sure what to make of my deductions. There is a very wise woman in Paris who, when I was having difficulty seeing the obvious, told me that I wasn't looking at all the possibilities."

"Ah. Yes. That is an important part of being a Guardian, and one of the hardest elements to learn." She hesitated for a moment, her fingers tracing the edge of her iced tea glass. "I feel as if I know you well, Aisling, so I hope you will not take offense if I speak frankly."

"No, of course not." Uh-oh. She looked serious and uncomfortable. That didn't bode well.

"I . . . the truth of the matter is that I am not sure why you are desirous of seeking a mentor. You know much of the things that apprentices do not learn for several years."

"But there's more that I don't know," I pointed out, warmed by her praise despite the fact that I knew she'd definitely wiped me off the candidate list. "I couldn't close that portal that opened during the dragons' lunch. And I don't know a lot of the stuff that the rest of you guys seem to have learned when you cut your teeth. I had no idea that incubi really existed until one of them showed up in my bed!"

"Yes, but you dealt with them well. Almost instinctively, you solved the problem before it became too great. With the incubi, you sought refuge in a place you knew they would not follow. With the demon at the lunch, you had it held hostage before it could harm anyone. I don't doubt that had you had an appropriate grimoire, you could have returned the demon to Abaddon and closed the portal."

"I'm not very good at controlling Drake's fire. And I don't feel like I have a handle on even a tiny fraction of the Guardian stuff. And I don't know how to draw wards."

"All things that will come to you with practice, Aisling. The elements of knowledge are there within you— you simply have not recognized them."

I thought about that for a minute, but decided that was a conversational path that I really didn't wish to go down. "Thank you for the cheerleading, Nora. Given the ineptness you've witnessed, I appreciate it."

She smiled and kindly changed the subject. "What did Tiffany say?"

I gave my lower lip a little nibble as I worked out how best to explain something I didn't fully grasp. "She said that maybe the things that have been happening aren't really connected after all. Maybe they were meant to look like they were, but really weren't."

"Hmm." Nora looked thoughtful. "I see why that made you stop and think."

"Yeah. Monish is ready to swear that Moa and

Theodora, the two Guardians, didn't know each other. He said you told him you'd never met them."

"I hadn't. I saw Moa talking to you that first evening here, but there are some seven thousand registered Guardians worldwide—I know only a very small fraction of that number."

"Right. And yet you three were attacked by the same incubus, and every other Guardian here was left alone. Which means that if there was no connection between the three of you, you were random victims."

She pursed her lips a little as she thought that over. "I see your point, but I don't understand how that is going to help find the incubus."

"Well, I did a little opening-myself-to-the-possibilities exercise before lunch, and what I came up with was this: Imagine you want to kill someone, but you have a connection to the person you want to kill—a former lover or companion or even a master. If you kill that person, everyone is going to know that you have a good motive for doing it, and since you're on the premises, the odds are probably pretty good that Monish and the watch are going to come after you."

"Yeees," she drawled, her confusion evident.

"But now imagine that you're one of a couple of thousand people at a conference, and whammo! Someone dies—someone wholly and completely unconnected with you, someone you randomly picked out because you had never met her. Attention immediately is centered around the victim's past, who she knew, who had appointments with her, etc."

"Ah," she said, enlightenment dawning in her eyes.

"Then a second murder victim is found. Yes, the watch

now has your means of destruction—in this case, they know you're an incubus—but once again there's nothing about the second victim to lead to you."

"The two deaths were committed to make the watch believe there was a connection, but there really wasn't?"

"Exactly. So you strike again. But this time the woman you pick isn't interested in getting her jollies. I know you don't want to think back on this, but can you remember if when you woke up the incubus was already beating you up, or was he . . . well, was he making love to you?"

A faint flush brightened her dark cheeks. "He was attempting to seduce me. I knew at once it must be an incubus because a woman I shared a flat with many years ago was seeing one. She was obsessed with him. He almost consumed her, almost seduced her soul from her, but she realized in time what he was doing and rejected him. She went back home to the States after that, but her will was almost broken. She turned her back on Guardianship, refuted her calling, and devoted herself to a man she met a few weeks later."

"Wow. No wonder you were warning me about dallying with them. But that just proves my point. The incubus who attacked you didn't do so because he had a grudge against you—you were just another cog in his horrible wheel of death."

She frowned at the spoon she'd been using to stir her iced tea. "But then, that means . . ."

"That means that the true victim of the incubus has yet to be identified. The red herrings have been planted to distract the watch. If he kills again, suspicion will no longer be cast on him because the watch will be focusing on finding something to tie the murders together."

"How very clever," she said, her eyes blank. "How very evil."

"Yes." I waited for her to come back from wherever she'd slipped off to before adding, "The problem now is that we don't know who the true victim of the incubus is."

She nodded.

My stomach turned over in sympathy for the pain I was about to cause her. "Nora, this is asking a lot, but I need to trap this incubus tonight. Monish and the committee will have my head and all the rest of me if I don't. I have to ask you—will you help me trap him? I swear you'll be perfectly safe, but I need you to act as—"

"I'll do anything you ask," she said firmly, not even letting me finish.

I searched her face for any signs of discomfort or hesitancy. "Are you sure? It won't be pleasant."

"I want this monster caught. Like your demon, I, too, have faith in you, Aisling."

I smiled, all warm and fuzzy inside, crying just a little because I knew that what was going to happen was not going to be fun for her. Or me, for that matter. "Great. Let me tell you what I want you to do . . . "

"Sorry I'm late. Had a little trouble with a couple of waiters who got into a bit of a squabble over who would open the door for me." I smiled around the table at the dragons present, noting that it was the same oval table that had been used during the disastrous lunch of a few days previous. "Hello, everyone. What did I miss?"

Drake held a chair out for me, waiting until I was

seated before he said, "This meeting is to formally address the complaint made by the blue and red dragons."

"Ah." I folded my hands in my lap and put on my best mediator face. Drake had mentioned the night before that he believed Fiat was secretly working on Chuan Ren in an attempt to divide the septs so that no peace accord could be achieved. If the hostile looks Chuan Ren was shooting at the green dragons were any sign, Fiat had been successful.

"Sfiatatoio del Fuoco Blu, the weyr recognizes you."

Fiat stood up, looking slowly at everyone around the table, his crystal-blue eyes settling on me. A slight mocking smile curved his lips at the same time I felt the touch of his mind. Immediately I slammed down my mental guards, shutting him out from reading my thoughts. "Wyverns, mates, and dragons, the bitter words of the last few days might have given some of you the impression that I find the thought of peace among the four septs repugnant and impossible. I assure you now that nothing is more distant from the truth. The blue dragons wish an accord with their brothers and sisters. Contrary to rumor, we do not desire to see the fragile peace under which we've lived the last few years torn asunder. We are simple in our needs and desires and do not unduly seek any power or glory."

Fiat paused to give everyone the eyeball again. I fought to keep the disbelief from my face. As Drake's consort, I was supposed to be as impartial as the front he presented—no matter what his private thoughts.

"The blue dragons have ever abided by the laws drawn by the weyr, laws that we might not wholly agree with, and might work to change, but always have we honored them. To do less would dishonor not just the weyr but our own names."

The red dragons nodded their agreement. I had a sudden, inexplicable feeling that Fiat was about to drop a bomb.

"As law-abiding members of the weyr, we feel it only right that all laws set by the wyverns be adhered to, rather than just the ones certain dragons find convenient."

Beside me, Drake's arm tightened.

"As you all know, the laws regarding the rights of a wyvern's mate are few but absolute in nature: A mate must be formally recognized by the wyvern and branded such, a mate must be present at negotiations and approve any acts that have bearing on the welfare of his or her sept, and a mate must under no circumstances have initiated or caused any action to the detriment of the sept to which he or she belongs. You would all agree those laws, set down by our forefathers many centuries before, have stood us in good stead?"

Several heads nodded. The ones owned by green dragons were oddly still. A little whip of Drake's fire flicked along my back, causing me to look at him in surprise. Usually his control of his dragon fire was absolute. His eyes were steady, his body language relaxed, but I sensed the feeling in him of tautly held anger. A matching anger rose within me. Fiat's smooth voice and practiced demeanor might fool some of the dragons, but this mate wasn't buying any of it. I just wanted him to get on with it.

"And yet, despite the fact that every wyvern here has sworn an oath to uphold the laws of the weyr, one has violated them." Fiat's head swiveled to look at Drake, his smile so obnoxiously smug, so triumphant I wanted to smack it right off his face. "Drake Vireo, do you deny that your presence here is an abomination to the laws that we all hold sacred?"

"Yes, I deny it," Drake said calmly, his voice as bland as vanilla pudding. "I have done nothing to violate either my oath or the laws of the weyr. If you have proof of either, I demand you present it now, so that I might dispute your claims."

Fiat strolled around the table to where I sat to the right of Drake, Pál flanking my other side. Fiat's cool fingers trailed along the back of my shoulders. Involuntarily, I shivered, jerking forward, away from those cold, cruel fingers. "Is it not true that your mate, Aisling Grey, did call you to a challenge last month, a challenge in which she fought you for control of the sept?"

"Hey!" I said, twisting around to glare at Fiat. "If you have a problem with something I did, you come to me about it. You don't go running to Drake to blame him. Besides, it's none of your concern what he and I did in the privacy of . . . uh . . . Paris."

"Ah, but sweet Aisling, your actions concerning the sept are of a concern to me. They are a concern to all wyverns, as you sit in a position of power within the weyr. And as I have just stated, our laws—with which you seem to be sadly unfamiliar—state that mates are not allowed to conduct actions that could harm the very dragons they represent."

"Aisling was not formally recognized as my mate when she challenged me," Drake said, his voice still smooth but a green fire now visible in his eyes. "Thus, she could not have impact on the sept, and your point is

moot. We have other, more important issues to discuss,
Fiat. Your attempts to cloud the issues have been many,
but I hope that at last we have reached the end of them
and will be spared any further abuse of our valuable
time."

"Yeah," I said, feeling it important to show the other
dragons that I supported Drake. He put a hand over mine
and squeezed it in warning. I took that to mean he'd
rather I kept quiet, and although heaven knew it wasn't in
my nature to abase myself, I figured this was probably as
good a time as any to learn how.

"*Cara,* your devotion is laudable, but alas, rather late
in coming, is it not?"

"You will address me with your comments, Fiat, not
my mate," Drake said, his voice a bass rumble. The heat
in his eyes was growing, as was my concern that something would push him over the edge. I couldn't imagine
what would happen should Fiat and he really lose their
tempers, but I knew instinctively that it would not be a
good thing for anyone concerned.

Fiat inclined his head in acknowledgment, and for
once I was grateful for the chauvinistic tendencies of
most male dragons. "In response to your claim that your
mate was not, in fact, formally recognized by either you
or your sept, I would like to point out that just a day before the challenge, indeed, hours before she called the
challenge, she bore the brand of a mate of the green
wyvern."

I touched the raised design on my collarbone. Drake
had put it there last month, burnt it into my flesh. At the
time I was merely annoyed, figuring it was his way of

marking me, but I hadn't known just what sort of a mark it really was. Now I knew.

"Aisling was new to our world. She had no idea what a challenge entailed when she called it," Drake answered. "She used the challenge as a way to force out the person who was tapping into the dark powers to take over control of the Paris L'au-delà. She had no intention of seriously challenging me for control of the sept."

I nodded my agreement.

"And yet," Fiat said, moving around the table slowly, "if she had succeeded, she would have put the welfare of the sept at risk, since she possessed neither the skill nor the power to control it. Indeed, if she had become wyvern, she would have put the entire weyr at risk, since who knows what trouble she would have started."

Drake's fingers tightened on mine as I bit back a retort. Now was not the time to get uptight over my pride taking a little dinging.

"The point is moot. She lost the challenge, a challenge that I again state she never seriously called. It was nothing more than a ruse to capture a murderer."

Fiat smiled, and my stomach lurched. I was coming to hate that damned smile. Pál rose and silently padded over to the desk at the entrance of the restaurant, pulling from behind the counter a fire extinguisher, which he then carried around behind me. I swiveled in my chair. He flipped a lever and proceeded to put out a small fire burning on a wooden busing station. I turned back to face everyone.

"Sorry," I murmured, knowing full well the fire was a manifestation of my anger. "I'm having a few control issues at the moment, but I'm sure they'll be sorted out soon."

Not one single person there, not even Pál, looked like he believed me.

"You see what sort of havoc might be wreaked if such an inexperienced, uncontrolled mate were to take over as wyvern?" Fiat asked, brushing away the objections Drake started to make. He bowed his head to Drake, saying, "As you know your mate better than I do, I am willing to concede the point that she did not understand the full nature of the challenge when she called it."

Drake didn't relax one little smidgen. Quite the opposite. The feeling of coiled tension in him went up and over the top of my Drake-o-meter.

"However . . ."—Fiat came to a stop behind his own chair, his long fingers caressing the black-and-gold upholstery—"that does not excuse you for responding to the challenge. You accepted her challenge. You . . . I hesitate to use the word *fought,* since a game of darts seems to be a singularly nonviolent way to conduct a challenge—you fulfilled the terms set by Aisling and defeated her."

"She had arranged the terms so that I would be sure to win." Drake shrugged with nonchalance that I knew he was far from feeling. "The challenge was not seriously offered, nor taken by me or my clan. The scenario you offer that she posed a threat to the well-being of my dragons is thus negated."

"It would be but for one thing." Fiat paused, his gaze sweeping the table again. "Your sept conducted a punishment against Aisling just last night. If you and the green dragons did not take her challenge seriously, why was she formally charged and punished?"

Oy. He had a point. Both Drake and I knew that he was

being a little less than honest over the whole challenge thing last month—although it was true I hadn't a clue what I was doing when I called the challenge, he did take it seriously, as did the members of his clan. Hence the punishment. While Drake might have been able to get away with blurring the lines regarding the nature of my challenge, he couldn't escape the fact that his dragons had fulfilled the terms of the challenge.

Before he could respond, Chuan Ren leaped to her feet and pointed to me. "The probity of this summit has been tainted and defiled by Drake's mate. Through her actions he has violated the laws of the weyr and thus has negated the precepts of wyvern. I move that the summit be adjourned until such time as a new wyvern for the green dragons comes forward."

"I second the motion," Fiat said quickly.

Pál leaped up to put out the three fires that suddenly burst up around Fiat. I stood up with him, slapping my hands down on the table, too angry to keep silent any longer. I'd be damned if I'd have everything Drake had worked for fall to pieces just because of something I did. "Look, I appreciate the fact that you two are clearly in cahoots and want to raise God knows what sort of trouble, but you are not using me as an excuse to do it! What I did last month has no reflection whatsoever on Drake! He has worked harder than any of you for this peace, devoted countless hours to keeping everyone happy, jollied you all along just because he feels it's important that you dragons live in peace. So cut him a little slack!"

Drake pulled me back into my chair, giving me a look that let me know he didn't appreciate my attempt to point the finger of guilt where it belonged. "Your motion is illegally presented and thus is not valid. As for Fiat's attempt to hide the truth by slandering my mate—"

"You defend your woman's actions?" Chuan Ren shrieked, her eyes spitting black fire at him. "You would defy the laws of the weyr for her? You are the one who is hiding the truth! This summit is a mockery of truth!"

"I have *nothing* to hide—" Drake started to say, but Fiat jumped in and added his voice for an adjournment. The blue, green, and red dragon bodyguards all leaped to their feet, yelling at each other, casting slurs and insults across the table while their bosses shouted their own abuse. I stayed in my chair, my gaze meeting that of Gabriel. He and his men were the only ones besides me who had remained sitting. His eyes were unreadable, a polite mask on his face. He reached forward to slap out a little flame that had suddenly come to life.

I wanted to curl up and die, I was so sick with despair, feeling for the first time the full weight of my responsibilities to the dragons. What on earth was I going to do to resolve the situation?

After ten more minutes of screaming from almost everyone present, Fiat regained enough control to demand an immediate vote on whether or not the summit would continue. Drake, cornered, had to allow it despite his obvious reticence. Fiat and Chuan Ren voted to scrap the whole thing and start again at a later, unnamed date. Drake insisted that they had made good progress and would continue if they all remained and dedicated themselves to the cause.

"And you, Gabriel Tauhou, what is your desire?" Fiat demanded hotly, his face flushed, his eyes, like the eyes of every dragon present, burning brightly with his fire. "Do you side with the green wyvern, or will you join us?"

I held my breath, unable to keep the pleading from my eyes as I watched Gabriel. He stood slowly, his face troubled as he looked around the table. Please, please let him do what's right, I prayed, hoping that if there was a tie in the vote, Drake might be able to hammer out some sort of an agreement to move forward.

"Like Drake, I have not been blind to the subcurrents of dissatisfaction that have been a part of these negotiations," Gabriel said in his quiet, warm voice, and my heart lightened. "I find your methods in casting aspersions on a fellow wyvern and his mate heinous and abominable to the extreme."

Thank God. He was going to side with Drake. At least the whole thing hadn't been destroyed.

"However, I believe the damage has been done, and no good can come at this time of further negotiations. I vote to continue them at another time, when the situation regarding the green wyvern has been resolved."

My heart fell. I stared numbly at Gabriel, unable to believe he would stab Drake in the back in this manner. The other dragons shouted their triumph, quickly gathering their things and leaving the room until no one was left but Drake, his two bodyguards, and me.

I turned to the man whose life I had just more or less ruined, unable to think of a single damned thing to say to him. He looked at me for a couple of seconds, then stroked my cheek, pulling his finger back to reveal a tear. He examined it carefully for a moment, then brought it to the spot on his collarbone where he bore the same brand

I did, tracing the symbol of the green dragons with my tear.

He left after that, none of us having spoken a single word.

25

"Are you sure this is going to work?" Nora asked in a whisper.

"No. But it's all I could think of, especially since time is running out."

"In more ways than one," Jim intoned from where it lay on its bed.

I cracked open an eye and glared at it. "Look, it's hard enough trying to meditate with you licking your privates and getting up to drink water and scratching all the time, but it's impossible with you making snarky comments. So unless you want me to command you to silence, zip it up."

Jim looked over to where Nora was curled up into a ball on the chair in her hotel room. "Isn't there some sort of Guardian rule about demon abuse?"

"No," Nora said softly, not wanting to break my concentration. "There are no such laws binding Guardians."

I flinched at the word "laws"; it still rubbed a raw spot after the scene that afternoon with the dragons. When I had gone later to talk to Drake about what happened—and to offer my help—he hadn't been in our room. Neither had Pál or István. I hunted down Nora (who was demon-sitting while I did the dragon thing), and despite my best intentions of not saying a word about what had happened, I ended up spilling every last bean. Nora was subdued and grim when I spoke to her about what had happened, which just deepened my conviction that the situation with the dragons was extremely bad.

With an effort, I pushed down both the sick feeling of despair that roiled within me whenever I thought of the events of the afternoon and the worry about how I was to find an unknown murderer who was targeting someone equally unknown, and focused instead on summoning a known entity.

Twenty minutes later a thin eddy of grayish brown smoke trickled into the room from under the doorway, cohering into the familiar form of a brown-haired, brown-eyed naked man.

"Oh, good, focusing on you works! Hi, Jacob," I said as his body became solid.

He jumped back when I stood up, his body immediately becoming hazy.

"No, there's no dragon! You don't have to leave," I said hastily, waving my hands around to indicate the dragon-free environment. "See? Just me, a friend, and my demon."

Jacob's body solidified again as he looked curiously at Nora. "There are two of you."

"Yes, that's Nora. She's a friend of mine. She's also a Guardian."

"Eh," he said, looking disconcerted for a moment. Then back went his shoulders, and out puffed his chest. "I can handle a threesome. I am a most virile and strenuous lover."

I walked over to where I had filched one of the hotel's navy blue terry bathrobes. "I'm sure you could, and I don't doubt that you are, but tempting as that offer is, I'm afraid we're going to have to turn it down. Nora was assaulted last night, and I've had an awful day. Here, why don't you put this on?"

He stared at the bathrobe I held out for him, eyeing it as if it was made up of slugs. "Why do you want me to wear that garment? Is it part of a game? Will it excite you if I do?"

"It'll make both Nora and me a lot more comfortable if you wear it," I answered, shoving it into his hands. To my relief, he donned it, although he didn't tie the belt very tight, so the front part gaped enough to give anyone who cared to look a view of his prime real estate.

"You do not wish for me to make love to you both?" Jacob asked, still clearly confused. He sat down on the edge of the bed. "It is because you have heard stories of this other one? I told you last night, I will make you forget him."

A little shudder went through Nora. I shared her sentiments. "We don't want sex. We just want to talk to you."

His eyes widened in horror. "You do not want me to service you? To pleasure you unlike you have ever been pleasured? To bring you to the highest peaks of ecstasy?"

"No servicing, no pleasure, no peaks, just answers."

He thought for a moment, then he stood up. "I am an incubus of the House of Balint. I have pleasured women for many centuries. I do not answer questions."

I leaned to the side to look around him. "Nora?"

She got to her feet and before Jacob could so much as

blink, she had drawn binding wards surrounding him in the four compass points.

"A ward," she said in an instructing tone of voice as she pointed to one of the wards that glowed blue in the air, "is only as good as the person drawing it. You must have belief in your own powers for the ward to draw with any success. If you doubt yourself, or if you draw a ward you have seldom used, it will be weak and ineffectual."

Jacob, looking around himself in disbelief, tried to move but couldn't, the four wards flaring to life with his attempt. "What is this? What have you done to me?"

"I believe it is because you have little to no experience drawing wards that the ghosts you met earlier gave you a binding spell. They must have known that you would not be able to hold a strong incubus with wards hastily learned. You can see, however, that once you have gained experience with wards, they are a fast and effective means of controlling many beings."

"I do not wish to be controlled! You will release me at once so that I may make love to you."

"Yes, I can see that," I said, ignoring Jacob's outbursts. "I like how the wards glow bright whenever Jacob tries to break them. How long will they last?"

Nora returned to her chair. "As long as I desire."

"Peh!" Jacob exclaimed, and struggled against the wards again. It was hopeless, of course. Nora was no slouch at ward drawing. Eventually Jacob grew tired of yelling demands to be freed, and he slumped down onto the bed again, the wards allowing him a certain range of motion so long as he didn't try to break free. "You wish to play dominate. I will be submissive, although I am best when I am allowed to be virile and manly."

"Question-and-answer time," I said, kneeling before him. "If you play along with us, we'll free you so you can go seduce hundreds more women."

"You really do not wish me to make love to you?" He seemed to be having a hard time accepting that fact.

"That's right. We just want to talk to you."

"Ai," he said, his shoulders drooping as his eyes closed. Slumped there in resignation, he looked like a totally different man. "It is so tiring, this constant love-making. At last I have found someone who does not wish for me to be the stallion."

I stared at Nora in surprise for a moment, then looked back at Jacob. "Wait a second—are you saying you don't want to have sex?"

He nodded, his eyes still closed.

"But . . . you're an incubus. That's what you do. It's your whole reason for being, isn't it?"

"It is," he agreed, then suddenly sat up straight and opened his eyes. "It is my doom! My curse! I do not wish to be the muffin stud, every night fulfilling the endless fantasies of the women who summon me. And always, they summon me, demanding I give them pleasure after pleasure. For centuries I have been cursed to be the foremost lover in my house, but now"—he sighed and slumped down again—"now I just wish to live quietly and raise horses."

"Horses," I said, knowing control of the situation was slipping away from me, but unable to grasp it. "You want to raise horses."

He looked up, his eyes lit with warmth. "Yes. They are magnificent creatures, are they not? They are strong.

They are beautiful. They allow you to ride them, and they never, ever ask to ride you in return."

Jim snorted. I shot it a look, having earlier ordered it to silence when the incubus showed up. "I don't think I'm going to touch that. Moving on—I have a couple of questions for you. First of all, do you know of any incubus at your house who has murdered women he served?"

"No."

I glanced over to Nora. "How do we know if he's telling the truth? I know a demon can't lie when I ask it a direct question, but does that work on an incubus?"

"I don't believe so," she answered slowly.

"I do not lie," Jacob said, his shoulders straightening. "I have no reason to lie to you. You do not wish for me to make love to you. You are my friends."

"That's right, and friends help each other. You said you don't know of someone at your house, but what about other houses?"

He made a halfhearted shrug. "There are no other houses in Budapest."

"OK, but what about incubi who come here from other houses?"

Jacob looked at me with an expression of mild amusement. "Incubi cannot leave the domain held by their houses. The House of Balint holds domain over Budapest and the surrounding area. No other incubus can cross into our territory."

"Really?" My gaze met Nora's for a moment. I rubbed my forehead. Something was niggling at the back of my mind, but I couldn't pin it down. "So that limits us to just the members of your house. How many are there?"

"Twenty-five," he said. "Twelve brothers, twelve sisters, and the morpheus."

"The morpheus? The god?"

"No. It is a title for the head of the house."

"Ah. Well, that's good. That limits the numbers of incubi to just eleven, twelve minus you."

I raised an eyebrow at Nora. She rose and sat next to Jacob on the bed. He looked at her curiously, recoiling as far as the wards would allow when she suddenly leaned into him and pressed her nose against his neck.

"No, it was not him," she said, resuming her seat, her cheeks an ashen parody of their normally warm color.

"Good. Eleven to go. If you don't mind, Jacob, I want you to tell us about all eleven of your brothers. Give us their names, what they look like, and whether or not they have ever expressed any desire to hurt a Guardian."

It took three hours, but at long last I felt like we'd picked Jacob's brain clean of information about his incubus brothers. Unfortunately, we weren't any closer to finding out who was killing the Guardians, nor did I have even an inkling of who might be the murderer's target. There were some three hundred Guardians at the conference—any of them might be the intended victim.

"Thank you for all your help," I said to Jacob after Nora released the wards. "I appreciate it. If you can think of any of your brothers who have been hanging around the hotel the last couple of nights, I'd appreciate you letting either Nora or me know."

He shrugged out of the bathrobe, not the least bit bothered by his nudity. "Many brothers come in the night, but only because they are summoned. Only a few visit during the day."

I froze in the act of taking the bathrobe. "What? What do you mean, during the day? I thought you guys were tied to a sleep or meditative state. You mean you can come out during the day, too?"

"Yes, of course. When we take human form, we are as humans. We are not vampyr, you know," he said, a bit scornfully. "Sunlight does not bother us. Many of my brothers visit hotels such as this during the day, for how else will they know which summons to answer if they have not first seen the women who appeal to them?"

"Oh. I thought you guys had to more or less come when called."

The look he gave me really was scornful. "We are not attendants to be called with the press of a bell. The only one who can come of his own will is the morpheus, but he has shut himself away, shunning contact with mortals."

"Right. Sorry. No slur intended. So you guys can go anywhere you like in daylight. Are you only in human form in daylight? I mean, can you do the smoke thing during the day, too?"

"Of course! Although once we are in human form, we are indistinguishable from a mortal," he said, rolling his eyes just a little. "It would not make sense to be able to change form only at night. Many people sleep during the day, do they not? We provide twenty-four-hour service."

"Just like a good towing company. Huh. Well, thank you again, Jacob. I appreciate you being so cooperative. And about what we talked about—you really should think about breaking free from your house and moving to the country. There's no reason you need to be a stud if your heart isn't in it."

A wistful expression stole over his face before he dissolved into smoke. The smoke snaked out under the door, leaving behind nothing but the faintest smoky residue.

"Towing company, Ash?" Jim, released from its silence by the disappearance of Jacob, shook its head. "Man, I'm so glad I got a really quality Guardian as a demon lord."

"What do you think?" I asked Nora, sitting down on the bed, clutching the bathrobe, which was still warm from Jacob's body.

She was silent for the count of five. "I think we are going to have to wake up a great many Guardians tonight and warn them of the possibility of attack."

"You don't think they're going to be on their guard after the news of your attack this morning?"

"I think it is better to be safe than sorry," she said, her eyes thoughtful. She glanced at me. "What did you think of what the incubus had to say?"

My fingers smoothed over the bathrobe as I mulled over the miscellaneous bits of information that tumbled around in my brain. There didn't seem to be a pattern, anything I could grasp to unravel, nothing tangible to use to figure out the problem. But there was a nagging sense of familiarity, of something someone had said that was important. Damned if I could think of what it was, though. I rubbed my forehead again, then set the bathrobe aside. "I think you're right—we're going to have to wake up a bunch of Guardians. We'd better split up. The sooner we start, the sooner we can get some sleep."

Two hours later I slipped through the door into Drake's bedroom, still stinging from some of the comments received from irate Guardians I'd woken. At least we'd done what we could for the night. Nora asked to sleep in Drake's spare room again, and since I knew it wouldn't be in use, I told her she could, ordering Jim to sleep in the room with her.

Jim acquiesced, muttering something about finally being able to get a decent night's rest without snoring or squeaking bed springs. I wished Nora a quiet night and went off to make whatever amends I could with my fire-breathing dragon.

The room was dark, but the slight rustle of the sheets told me Drake was in bed. I peeled off my clothing, carefully navigating my way around to the side of the bed I'd claimed as mine, sliding beneath the sheets, hoping against all hope that Drake wasn't so wounded by what had happened earlier that he'd snapped my head off.

"You come at last."

His voice was chilly, but at least he was still speaking to me.

"I'm sorry it's so late, but Nora and I felt we had to warn all the Guardians present to be careful." I slid a little closer to his warmth, unsure of whether he wanted me to comfort him, or if he wanted to be left alone. I fervently hoped it was the former, because just the scent of him was making secret parts of me grow damp with desire. "Drake, about this afternoon—I can't begin to tell you how sorry—"

"No," he said, rolling over on top of me, his body hard and aggressive, his mouth stripping the words from my lips. "We will not speak of this tonight. This night belongs to us only, no one else."

Who was I to complain? I slid my hands down his back, kissing him with just as much passion as he was sharing with me. His fire leaped between us, and I almost laughed with the joy of it. This time it was my fingers that trailed fire as I gently scored his back, sucking his tongue when it got bossy with mine. He growled a low, deep growl from the depths of his chest, the sound of which simultaneously raised goose bumps on my flesh and fanned the flames of the fire within me. Without further ado, Drake kneed my restless legs aside, settling himself between my thighs, his mouth a hot brand on mine. I screamed a scream of absolute ecstasy into his mouth as he thrust into me, hard and deep, my breath stripped not only by the fire he breathed into me but also by the feel of him so deeply embedded in me.

Mindless to everything but the pleasure he built within me, I wrapped my legs around his hips and gave him everything I had, matching each one of his thrusts, claiming his breath as he claimed mine, my fingers digging into the heavy muscle of his behind in an attempt to pull him closer, deeper, hotter until my body went up in a blaze of rapture that set even my soul afire as I gave myself to the power of our joining. I shouted Drake's name into his mouth, his eyes glittering so brightly with heat and desire they glowed in the darkness of his room. His hips lunged forward, pistoning his body into mine, the strength of his force so great it triggered another orgasm. It swept over me just as he arched backwards, his weight braced on his hands, his beautiful chest slick with sweat, and just as he climaxed, his body changed, shifted, and for a breathless moment I beheld the long line of glittering green and yellow scales stretched across a muscular, decidedly not-human chest. Heat blossomed deep within me as he came, filling me with his passion and fire com-

bined, searing the little bit of me that wasn't already
alight.

He collapsed onto me, his body warm and wet and
human, and I knew at that moment that we truly were
bound together. It was more than just a physical attraction, more than an emotional engagement. Our souls
were bound together, tied by something I didn't understand, nor was I sure I wanted to.

I nuzzled his damp neck, my hands resting on the
heaving planes of his back as he struggled for breath. A
deep longing came over me, a wish that we could stay
just as we were at that moment, safe, protected, just the
two of us with no outside connections, no commitments
and responsibilities and demands on our time.

But we did have responsibilities and commitments,
both of us, ones that no amount of wishing would make
go away. While I lay there holding Drake in my arms, his
body still joined intimately to mine, the heavy warmth of
him a welcome weight, the familiar little niggle in the
back of my mind obligingly trotted to the fore and let me
take a good long look at it.

I was so startled that I almost shouted aloud.

Drake dragged his head from my shoulder, shifting
slightly to roll onto one elbow in order to peer backwards.

Light from where the door was aflame flickered along
the beautiful, sleek muscles of his arms and chest.

I touched his cheek. He looked back at me, his eyes
still glowing, bathing me in a sea of emerald.

"Life is going to get easier from here on out," I promised him. "I have a plan, two of them, actually, and you
know, I think they might just work."

26

Jim and I walked into the suite the following day to find two workmen removing the blackened door to Drake's bedroom.

I avoided looking at it, just as I ignored the smirk on István's face when he saw me blush. So I had dragon fire control issues! Was that any reason to grin like a baboon? "Where's Drake? I thought he wanted to see me?"

"He is with wyverns. He tries to talk to them again. He is angry at you."

"So what else is new?" Jim asked sotto voce, only not nearly sotto enough. I flicked my finger against its head. "Ow! That's demon abuse!"

"When is he supposed to be back? And I don't know why he's angry. All I did was tell the other wyverns I would resign the post of mate if they would reconsider canceling the negotiations. They all seemed to think it was a good idea, although that rat Fiat said it didn't change anything. But if Chuan Ren and Gabriel swing over to Drake's side, it won't matter."

István shook his head. "You do not know our ways. Drake would never allow."

"He's not going to have a choice in the matter. I know

how much peace means to him, to all of you. If the problem holding everything back is me being his mate, then I will tender my resignation and that will be the end of it." I glanced at the clock on the end table. It was getting late. Due to the fact that I hadn't gotten to bed until a little after three in morning, I'd slept in until almost noon. Now it was a little after two, and although I had walked Jim and spoken briefly to each of the three wyverns, I still had to find Nora. Time was quickly running out. I had less than twelve hours to find a murderer. "Shoot, I have to go. If Drake comes back, tell him I'll be back this afternoon."

"Where you are going?" István asked, his face pulled into a familiar scowl. "Drake will not like you leaving."

"I'm going to find Nora and ask her a couple of questions, then I'm off to buy a few supplies for tonight. Tell Drake I'll be back soon."

"Kiss, kiss," Jim said to István, following me out the door.

"Why do you do that?" I asked as we got into the elevator. "You know István is not happy with you any more than he is with me. Baiting him is one way to ensure he's never going to give you fresh water or take you out for a walk if I'm busy."

"I know," Jim sighed, a faux look of sadness on its hairy face. "But a demon has to have some fun, and you won't let me blight anyone, so tormenting István is pretty much all that's left to me."

We ran Nora to earth a little while later, as she came out of a workshop on subterranean imps, evidently a new breed that was starting to become bothersome. I was glad to see she bore no further signs of the attack, either physically or emotionally, her eyes as warm and serene as ever behind her bright red glasses.

"Got a moment?" I asked as she separated from a group of friends to walk over to where I was sitting.

She glanced at her watch. "Certainly. There is a seminar on ancient Moldavian curses in ten minutes that I would like to attend, but if you need my help, I will be happy to miss it."

"No, this shouldn't take too long. Basically I wanted to ask you about Marvabelle."

Her eyes widened. "Why?"

"You said the first night of the conference that you knew her years ago, that you and she studied together under the same mentor."

"Yes, we did. It was almost twenty years ago."

"Where exactly did your mentor live?"

A slight frown wrinkled her brow. "As a matter of fact, it was here, in Pest. We both studied with Monette Tomas. She was a Guardian married to a Hungarian Mage. They divorced after a few years, and Monette returned to London. I went with her."

"But Marvabelle didn't?"

Her gaze slid from me to her hands. "No, she didn't. She went home to the States shortly before Monette divorced."

That piece of information slid into place, leaving a space next to it that I needed to fill. "I know you're going to think this is really brash of me for asking, but why did Marvabelle decide to quit being a Guardian and go home?"

Her fingers plucked at her linen skirt for a moment, then suddenly her eyes widened as she looked up in horror. "Oh! That could be it. Aisling, how did you know?"

My scalp pricked at the look on her face as another piece of information slid into its waiting spot. "She was the woman you were telling me about the other night, wasn't she? She was the woman who was smitten with an incubus but found out before she'd given her soul to him, right? That was Marvabelle."

She nodded, her face frozen. "You think she's the target."

Cold swept through me. "I think she could be. It makes sense—you were both here, in Budapest. So that means only a local incubus could be the one she was dallying with. And if she rejected him, spurned him—"

"He would want revenge," she said, her voice faint. "But would he go so far as to kill innocent Guardians?"

I made a face. "Is there anything that says an incubus can't be a homicidal maniac?"

"No. In fact, there is much evidence to prove that they often do kill their victims, although usually it is by sucking the life from them over a period of years."

"If I'm right, then all I need to do is use my handy-dandy Venus amulet and summon up every incubus in town until we have the one who was Marvabelle's lover. I don't suppose you know his name?"

She shook his head. "Marvabelle never told me."

"Rats. Well, we'll just have to do this the hard way. You find Marvabelle and ask her to meet us in the executive conference room in . . . oh, say an hour. It shouldn't be in use because everyone will be getting ready for the big dinner tonight. No, better make that two hours. I have to run into town and pick up the things you said I'd need for the binding spell, and given the afternoon traffic, I'll need the extra time. Ask Monish and Paolo to come, too. We'll want them once Marvabelle identifies the incubus."

"Aisling—" Nora frowned. Obviously she wasn't entirely sold on the plan. "Do you really think Marvabelle is the target? What if she isn't?"

I shrugged. "It's the only thing I can think of that fits. We'll just have to hope that I'm right."

We parted a few minutes later, with Nora promising to find Marvabelle and Monish. Jim and I went to a shop recommended by Nora and bought the items she'd listed as being necessary for a binding spell. By the time we returned, I had only half an hour before I was due to summon up a posse of incubi.

Drake's limo was in the driveway as the taxi driver (there hadn't been time to call Rene) dropped Jim and me off. I paid him and peered into one of the limo's open doors. It was empty. "Huh. I wonder if the dragons are leav—hey!"

Drake, István, and Pál marched out of the hotel, all three grim-faced. Drake didn't stop to greet me, he just wrapped an arm around my waist and more or less tossed me into the car.

"What do you think you're doing?" I yelled, jumping out of the car. Drake stood next to the door, giving an instruction to Pál, who took Jim's leash. "That's my demon! Drake, what's going on?"

"I have managed, by means that I will not go into now, to get Gabriel's agreement to participate in one last negotiation session. Gabriel spoke with Chuan Ren. She also grudgingly agreed to meet again, before she leaves. That meeting is tonight, now, at a neutral spot. You will come with me."

"Wait a minute," I said, holding up my hands to stop him before he could throw me into the car again. "Didn't they tell you? I resigned as your mate. I'm no longer officially important to your negotiations."

For the first time since I'd met him, Drake looked at me utterly exasperated. "Aisling, I have told you repeatedly that you were born to be my mate. In addition to that, you swore an oath to me, fealty to the sept. You cannot simply resign. There are only two ways your fealty can be dissolved, neither of which is you simply resigning. I have spoken to all three wyverns, at great cost to me, and they have agreed to drop the protest regarding your challenge. They have accepted you as my mate. Therefore, you will come with me now."

"I can't," I said, my hands on his. "I wish I could, I really do, and I'm delighted that everyone is giving you another chance at hashing out a peace accord, but Drake, you don't need me. I'll just mess it up again. And even if I wanted to, I can't. Remember that little thing about me being handed over to the committee if I don't find the murderer? Well, I have"—I looked at my watch—"exactly five and a half hours to find him, and I can't do that and attend your peace meeting."

Drake made an annoyed gesture, pushing me into the car. Jim was unceremoniously shoved into the front seat, between Pál and István. "That does not matter. Dragons live beyond the rule of the committee. You are under my protection now. No one will harm you."

I struggled to crawl over him, but he shoved me back, slamming the car door. "Drake! Goddamn it, you can't do this! Stop! István, stop!"

The car swept off with a subdued purr. I looked back at

the hotel, cursing under my breath, uniformly damning headstrong dragons, bossy committee members, and murderous incubi. Drake's jaw was tight, his fingers clenched with tension, his eyes burning with a light that I'd never seen before.

I took a deep breath and reminded myself that he had just as much at stake as I did, and therefore I would respect the urgency he felt. "I know how important this is to you. I understand and accept that you want me by your side. I know that as your mate, it is my duty to be there, supporting you. But there are bound to be times when I just can't be with you, and this is one of them. This is important."

"No," he snapped, his eyes brittle with heat. "You do not understand. I have allowed you to pursue your interests because they did not interfere with mine, but that is at an end. You are my mate. My sept is your first priority. All else is secondary."

My jaw dropped for a second, then snapped shut with an audible clink of my teeth. I shoved Drake back from where he'd leaned over to snarl at me, my anger thoroughly roused. "Secondary? My career is secondary?"

"Your career is being my mate."

"Wrong!" I yelled, flinging off the possessive hand he wrapped around my wrist. "My career is being a Guardian. You agreed to that when I accepted the fact that I was your mate."

"I never agreed to such a ridiculous thing," he yelled back at me. I was a little shocked—Drake never yelled—but I didn't have the time to mull over what that meant.

"You did, too! That night in my dream, the night we spoke the oath—I agreed to be your mate, and you agreed to me being a Guardian."

His eyes were so bright it almost hurt to look at them, but his voice dropped, to a low, angry tone. "You asked that I, and I quote, 'make no more snarky comments' about you being a Guardian. Further, you asked that I not say or do anything to ruin your chance with a potential mentor. I promised never to say anything to a mentor that could be interpreted as being against your plans. That is all you asked of me, Aisling. And I have fulfilled those terms wholly and completely."

I stared at him, too stunned, too filled with pain to comprehend what he was saying. "We swore an oath to each other," I whispered at last.

"Yes." His face was as hard as the edge to his voice. "You swore to uphold the well-being of the sept. I swore to protect, honor, and respect you."

He was a stranger. That wasn't Drake sitting there speaking in that cold voice. It had to be a stranger. Those were the thoughts that went around and around in my head with sickening regularity. "You knew how much I wanted this. You knew how important it was to me. You knew I was committed to being a Guardian. You agreed not to stop me."

"I agreed not to say anything to a potential mentor. I haven't. By no stretch of the imagination does that mean I endorse you being a Guardian. I never have, nor have I made secret my feelings."

I thought back to that night, to that dream, when I was so happy because Drake said he was willing to negotiate with me. The conversation we had repeated in my head, and again I heard his voice agreeing to something less than what I had intended.

He had betrayed me. He had fooled me into thinking he

was agreeing to my terms, when all along he was using me for his own purpose.

A little voice in my head pointed out that if I had been less lust-crazed, I might have noticed the difference in what I was saying and what he said. I acknowledged that as true. I acknowledged my own responsibility with the situation. I had sworn an oath to Drake and his sept.

But he had betrayed me.

My eyes sought his. They were cold, like green ice, and within them I could see the depth of his determination, his resolve, and his intent. He was fighting for the life of his clan, fighting against almost impossible odds to form a peace not for his own good, not for selfish reasons, but for the good of all people, dragon-born and mortal. I understood what he was doing. I understood why he did what he did.

But he had betrayed me, and I could not forgive that.

I closed my eyes on the tears that welled out from between my lashes and pulled hard on his fire, allowing it to fill me, consume me, burn every last tear inside me until it burst forth with a roar of anguish that filled the night sky — and that set fire to the limousine.

István slammed to a stop in the middle of a street, Pál already dragging Jim from the car. Drake swore and kicked open the door, yelling, "You foolish woman! You'll set the gas tank alight! This close to other cars you'll kill who knows how many people!"

I didn't wait for him to drag me out. I threw myself out the other side of the car, yelling an order to Jim as I ran along the median, dashing between cars, bouncing off a sedan to fall onto the pavement on the other side of the road, tears streaming down my face as I ignored the sound of Drake shouting after me. I knew him. He might be a thief, he might be a liar, he might be the sort of man who would betray the woman who loved him if he felt the reason was good enough, but he would not willingly walk away and allow innocent people to die.

"Fires of Abaddon, Aisling!" Jim panted as it reached my side. It took one look at my face and shut up, following me as I ran down streets, cutting through markets, dashing in front of cars, racing around corners until I had no idea where I was or where I'd come from.

At least I had lost Drake.

My heart, frozen in a block of disbelief, shattered at the realization that I had, indeed, lost Drake. I fell to my knees right there in the middle of the street, sobbing with the realization of what had happened. I had given Drake everything, I had sworn my allegiance to him, I had agreed to become his mate, I had fallen in love with the damned scaly lizard, and he betrayed me.

Tires squealed on asphalt as a car slammed to a stop a few inches away from me, the driver's swearing audible even over the hum of the engine.

"Ash?"

Jim's voice was unusually gentle.

"Ash, come on. You're in the street. I know you don't care about getting run over, but you're immortal now, and if one of these cars hits you and you crumple the bumper, you're going to have a hell of a lot of explaining to do."

"Aisling." Another voice spoke.

What was I going to do now? How was I supposed to fix things? Dammit, why was everything my responsibility? Why was I the only one who could make things right? Drake had betrayed me, but wasn't I guilty of the same thing by refusing him? It felt in my heart like betrayal, but I just couldn't see any other way out of the situation. There was more at stake here than just Drake and me—there was my promise to find the murderer before he killed another innocent Guardian. The dragon sept had my fealty, but how could I live with myself if the murderer struck again because I had been so busy with the dragons that I hadn't the time to stop him?

"Aisling Grey." I looked up at the sound of my name. Rene stood before me in the headlights of the car, his hand extended to me. "Come along. The street is no place for you."

I took his hand, clinging to the warmth of it, wanting nothing more than to throw myself into Rene's arms and beg him to take me to the airport so I could leave. "Drake betrayed me," I said.

He nodded. "I know what he has done. It is yet another bump in the road, *hein*?"

"No, Rene," I said, wiping the tears off my face with my sleeve. "This isn't a bump. It's a dead end."

"It seems that way, yes, but in time, I think, you will see things with the different eyes," he answered, getting into the front seat. Jim hopped up beside me, yanking the door handle with its mouth.

Rene didn't say anything else as he drove me to Margaret Island. I sat in silence, my thoughts so painful I couldn't stand thinking them, so I didn't. I pushed them all aside, idly watching the play of lights on the back of Rene's head. He was such a nice man. So unlike the people of the Otherworld. So normal.

I glanced down to where I my hand was clutching the

jade dragon talisman. Alongside it was the crystal Venus amulet. "Why aren't you affected by the amulet, Rene?"

His head turned a little so he could see me in the rearview mirror.

"What?"

I looked down at the amulet again, then back to him. "Why aren't you affected by this? Every other mortal man is. Everyone except you and . . ."

My mind snapped into place, just as if it had been dislocated and now pushed back into the proper position. One moment I was wondering why Rene wasn't affected by the amulet, the next I saw an image of György, the other man who wasn't affected by it. György the woodsman. György the hermit, the man who seldom left his claimed spot of land, but a man who had admitted to being at the hotel.

Jacob's voice played through my thoughts. "When we take human form, we are as humans."

György looked human to me. He felt human. But he smelled like a campfire   smoky.

I rubbed my head. No, that wasn't right. Jacob had named all of the other eleven incubi in his order. "Twelve brothers, twelve sisters . . ." I repeated, my eyes closing when I realized how stupid I'd been. "And one leader. The morpheus. That has to be György. Mother Mary and all the saints . . . Rene! Screw the traffic laws—get me to the hotel as soon as you can! I know who the murderer is!"

What was probably a ten-minute drive seemed to me to take aeons. By the time Rene pulled up in front of the hotel, I was shouting orders to Jim. "The final dinner has already started. You can run faster than me—go to the ballroom and find Nora or Monish. Tell them I know who the murderer is. Tell them to watch out for Marvabelle. And Tiffany, for that matter!"

Jim was off in a black flurry. I ran after the demon, Rene beside me as I raced down the stairs to the conference level. "You don't have to be here!"

"I am your friend. I will stand by you. You might need me as before, *hein*?"

"I will always need you, Rene." I leaped off the last step, haring down the long hallway to the double doors at the end that marked the main entrance to the ballroom.

I threw the door open, racing inside, praying that I wasn't too late. Jacob had said that the morpheus was the only one who did not need to be summoned to arrive—which meant he could attack anytime he chose. A group of people stood in a clutch before me, blocking my path. I shoved my way through them, scattering apologies behind me as I burst out into the center of the floor, cleared for the evening's presentation, and came to a skidding halt.

Dr. Kostich was at the podium, holding a piece of paper, reading a list of names into the microphone. He turned to look at me. I stared back at him, then slowly turned my head and saw that all two thousand of the Guardians, oracles, Diviners, Theurgists, and Mages were watching me with hushed disbelief.

I realized at that moment that my brush with Drake's fire, subsequent race through the city, and occasional contact with vehicles as I rebounded off them had not left me untouched. The thin gauze dress I wore was dirty, smeared with oil and grime from the road, torn along one side where I'd caught it on the edge of a car, and scorched black on the hem. My hands were black with soot and dirt. My hair had come loose and was flying around in clumps. My nose was running from crying.

Regardless, I was a professional. I had a job to do, and I had just sacrificed any chance of happiness with Drake to do it. I straightened my shoulders, brushed a hand down my dress, and stepped forward.

Dr. Kostich backed away from the podium. I leaned toward the microphone. "Has anyone seen Nora Charles or Monish Lakshmanan?"

My voice echoed through the huge ballroom. There were several gasps that I put down to using full names. I shaded my eyes against the big spotlights that were on the podium, scanning the audience for sign of Monish or Nora. Two thousand disbelieving, shocked, horrified pairs of eyes stared back at me. "No one has seen Nora? Or Monish? Has anyone seen a demon in Newfie form, answering to the name of Jim?"

You could have heard a cricket snore in the room, so silent was it.

"Um. How about Marvabelle O'Hallohan? Is she here?"

Dr. Kostich, keeping his distance, said in a voice that just about made my blood freeze, "If you are quite through with this farce, we would be glad to continue announcing the apprentices who have been accepted by their chosen mentors."

"Oh. Sure. Sorry." I stepped away from the podium, relinquishing it to him. "Um . . . I don't suppose my name is anywhere on that list?"

He just stared at me.

"Right. I didn't think so. Sorry to interrupt. I'll just go now."

I walked quickly to the back of the ballroom, worry about György overwhelming the mortification I felt at embarrassing myself in front of a ballroom full of my peers. Or people I had hoped would be peers. I doubt if they'd had any such hope. Rene was waiting for me by the door, but before I could reach him an arm reached out to stop me.

"Aisling, you look so very sad. Your eyes make me want to weep. You are having troubles?"

Tiffany, at least, was safe and sound. The people at the table hissed at us to be quiet as Dr. Kostich read out the next name on the list. Tiffany followed me to the door, smiling beatifically at Rene. "Good evening, Rene. Your eyes are not sad, I am happy to see."

"Have you seen Monish or Nora? Or Jim?"

"Yes, all three. Jim burst in a few minutes before you. They all left out the side door, there." She indicated a door that led to a smaller room of the ballroom.

"Thanks." I started to leave but stopped. "Rene, maybe you should stay here with Tiffany. The guy I'm after has a bit of a crush on her."

"Which one?" Tiffany asked.

"We will come with you," Rene announced, opening the door and pushing Tiffany out. I looked at him for a moment, wanting to protect him in case things got dicey, but his chin was as obstinate as Drake's.

"Fine, but don't blame me if you see some stuff that'll give you nightmares for years to come," I warned, walking through the doorway.

Straight into a mob of naked incubi.

27

"We have come to help you," Jacob said. "I have told my brothers what you said about taking charge of our own lives, and they agree with me that no more will we be used as sexual playthings. We have rights! We have needs and desires the same as other beings. Piotr wishes to become a musician." Piotr, standing behind Jacob, waved at me. I waved back. "Stefan wants to write novels. We are revolting from the tyranny that has long held us prisoners."

"Uh . . . well, that's good. Really good. How the heck did you get here?"

"Nora summoned us. Was that not clever of her? She said that you would tell us what to do. Since you have helped us throw off the shackles of our bondage, we have decided to help you."

I looked around at the group of twelve handsome, well-formed, extremely well-endowed men.

Tiffany approached a dark-haired incubus with rippling washboard abs, pectoral muscles that probably could have withstood a blow from a sledgehammer, and nether regions that would do a pony proud. "You have a lovely smile," she told the incubus.

"How can we help you?" Jacob asked.

I thought of suggesting they put on some clothes, but that would take too much time. "You can answer a question. Your leader, the morpheus—is his name György?"

Jacob nodded. "Yes. How did you know?"

"He's the one who murdered the two Guardians. Where is he?"

Jacob's mouth dropped open. "He left earlier. He said the signs were right for him to revenge his name and claim the Light of Chastity."

"The *what*?"

"Me," Tiffany said.

Twelve heads nodded their agreement.

"Oh, god. He's going to kill Marvabelle and kidnap Tiffany. Why can't I ever meet normal people?" I asked, waving the men aside. "Where's Nora?"

"Unconscious," Jacob said. "The demon Jim said she had it knock her out so she could summon us all. She could not summon more than one of us in a meditative state, but unconscious or asleep she could."

"Oh, great! What about Monish?"

"Who?"

"Never mind. I think I know where they went." I pushed past the incubi, running down the length of the ballroom to the small room that served as a meeting place for speakers and the like. Tiffany, Rene, and the gang of incubi followed. I resisted the temptation to ask them how they could run naked without at least a hand cupped around dangly parts. The door to the annex was locked, but gave way after a couple of the bigger incubi kicked it.

"Keep her back," I told Rene, gesturing toward

Tiffany before I raced into the room. "Well, well, fancy meeting you here, György the hermit. Or should I say György the morpheus?"

The walls of the left side of the room were made of fabric over wood, the kind of walls that were on a track and could be accordioned back to increase the size of the ballroom. Slumped in a corner, Nora lay in an extremely uncomfortable position, Jim sitting protectively beside her.

György had Marvabelle pinned by her throat against a wall on the opposite side of the room, held a couple of inches off the ground, her legs kicking madly as she tried to pull his hand from her throat. His eyes narrowed as the incubi followed me into the small room. "What are you doing here?"

Jacob came forward, shoulders back, chest out, the personification of righteous manhood. "We have revolted! I wish to raise horses. Piotr wishes to play violin. James wishes to work at a McDonald's and make the big hamburgers."

György sputtered something in Hungarian that had a couple of the incubi stepping back in fear.

"Looks like your days of being head stud are over," I told him, strolling forward. "Your boys don't want to be women's playthings anymore."

"Actually . . . I would like to. I don't mind the job, and the hours are good."

Jacob hushed the younger incubus who had spoken.

"Marvabelle's turning purple," I pointed out, nodding toward her. "Why don't you let her down, and we can talk about this?"

"She will die for her crime."

"Ya think? OK, how about this—you may have your ex-girlfriend, but I have Tiffany. Rene?"

Tiffany and Rene entered the room. György gasped and dropped Marvabelle, who hit the ground like a sack of anvils. She coughed and gagged, clutching at her throat. I wanted to go over and make sure she was all right, but I didn't dare leave György.

"Beauteous one! Has the she-devil harmed you?"

Tiffany gave him a haughty look. "Hello, György. I did not know you were an incubus. You must be a very bad one to kill women. I do not like bad men. I will not give you my virtue."

György groaned and went onto his knees, Marvabelle forgotten for the moment. "My darling, my beautiful goddess, do not believe the lies you hear about me. You alone possess the purity that can salvage my soul. You are my savior, my mother, the woman who will bring me back to life."

"Jim?" I said quietly.

"Got it right here," it answered, dropping the bag of supplies I'd bought earlier.

"How's Nora?"

"OK, although she's going to have a sore head in the morning."

"That's very pretty," Tiffany told György, pausing to give one of the incubi a smile. "But I do not wish to be your mother. To be a mother would mean I would no longer be a virgin. That is what I do best. It would be a shame if I stopped."

I pulled a spool of red thread from the bag, slowly, carefully making a circle around György, allowing the thread to trail on the floor behind me.

Marvabelle clawed her way to her knees, clutching the wall in an attempt to get to her feet.

"You will give me your virtue, for without it I am damned," György cried, pointing to where Marvabelle was still partially slumped against the wall. "She stole my manhood from me! She took it when she rejected me. Me! The most renowned lover of all the House of Balint! I offered her endless bliss in my arms, asking only for her soul in exchange, but she refused me, cast me aside, laughed at me, and called me a poor lover."

"Whoa! This is all about your feelings of inadequacy?" I asked. "You killed two innocent women and attacked a third simply because one of the thousands of women you've had sex with didn't think you were the best?"

"I was the best! There was no one better than me! Until she spurned me. Then I could not function as a man. I have waited many years, knowing that the day would come when she would return to beg my forgiveness."

"Never!" Marvabelle croaked, clutching an extra podium that had been stored in the room. She hauled herself upright, then collapsed against the dividing wall. "I will never beg you! You aren't half the man my Hank is. Not one third!"

I dug the four containers out of the bag, placing them at compass points around György. He didn't pay me the slightest bit of attention, intent as he was on pleading his case with Tiffany. "You will return me to my former power. Only a virgin's purity can restore me, and you, my glorious one, my flower, my blossom, will make me once again whole."

I flipped open the lid of the container to the south. "Frankincense for fire."

"I told you before that I would not give you my purity," Tiffany said. "It is too priceless to give away, and although I am sorry that you are not whole, perhaps if you tried smiling more you might feel happier. Sharing a smile always makes me feel better whenever I am sad."

The container to the west was next. "Mercury for water."

"No. I will not allow this," György said, getting to his feet. "You are my salvation. Just as she must die, so you must give to me that which will make me powerful again. I thought the amulet would restore my manhood, but now I know the truth—only you can do it."

"Incense for air," I said softly, opening the third container.

"No one can save you because there is nothin' to save," Marvabelle crowed, on her feet at last, although she lurched drunkenly to the side. She took a couple of steps toward György. "You were a useless, pulin' piece of turd then, and you're the same now. Useless and impotent!"

"No!" György roared, slamming his arm into Marvabelle, who spun backwards until she slammed into the wall. An electric hum started up somewhere.

I scooted to the side and reached behind György to the container marking north. "Gold for earth."

"Enough of this. Poppet, my fragile one, leave the room while I take care of this hag, this castrating harpy. Then we shall be together, and you will restore me."

I stepped back, out of the circle that was now cast

around György. Behind Marvabelle, the retracting wall started folding in on itself, accordioning back into recesses on either side of the walls, revealing a couple of extremely surprised faces of the people sitting nearest it.

Lovely. I got to have an audience. Just what I needed. I sighed. "Thread of crime, evil in design. Cord go round, your soul be bound. Earth, air, water, fire, by my will the elements conspire."

György looked at me in surprise. "What did you say?"

I backed away, unsure if there was anything else to the spell. The nuns didn't seem to think there was. "Um. Bright as fire glow, deep as water flow?"

His eyes widened with genuine puzzlement as he tried to step forward. The nuns must have been dead on with their binding spell, because his feet were evidently stuck to the floor. "You did this to me? I gave you my amulet. I thought you were my friend."

"You're a psychopathic, cold-blooded murderer. I'm a bit choosier in my friends," I answered, stepping to the side and beckoning Monish, who had appeared holding up a sagging and bloodied Hank. Marvabelle shrieked and threw herself forward, lunging onto her husband. Their heads collided with an audible *thunk,* both of them slipping to the floor.

Monish stepped over their inert forms. "You have him?"

"Yup. Where have you been?"

"Jim told me your suspicions. I went to find Marvabelle, but found her husband unconscious. By the time he told me what had happened, people were already talking about your appearance. I knew you must be close by." He looked down at the red thread and the four elements binding the incubus. "Excellent work. Has he confessed?"

"Not really. The rest is up to you." I turned to the doors to the ballroom, which were more than half open. Everyone was watching us, identical expressions of disbelief on their faces. "Hi again. Is there a doctor in the house? We've got one unconscious Guardian, an oracle who's had a couple of knocks on the head, and a half-strangled . . . uh . . . Marvabelle."

The audience rippled uneasily, looking around. A woman in a lovely peach power suit stepped forward. "I am a physician."

"Good. Could you look at the Guardian first?"

She nodded and knelt by Nora. I waited a moment to be sure Nora would be all right, then walked out of the room. The people in the ballroom started shouting something, applauding for some insane reason, but I didn't wait around to see what it was all about. My heart was destroyed, my future finished before it had a start, and not much was waiting for me other than a trip back home, where I would have to explain to my uncle why I had failed my job as a courier for the second time, and probable banishment from the Otherworld.

Drake stood at the end of the hallway.

"You want me to run interference for you?" Jim asked as I stared at the man who had so easily broken my dreams. "If I got a running start, I might be able to knock him down long enough for you to get past him."

"I, too, will run this interference," Rene said. "We will both tackle the dragon. You will escape without him bothering you further, *hein*?"

I thought for a long moment about asking Jim and Rene to do just that, but decided it wasn't any good. I had to face Drake one last time.

He waited until I was within a few feet before he spoke. "You cannot unmake what is, Aisling. You are bound to me, to my sept. You are my mate. No desire on your part can change that."

I thought of all the things I wanted to say to him, all the screaming and yelling and crying and pleading, but all that stayed bottled up inside me. Instead I leaned forward and kissed him. Very gently. Very lightly. "You're wrong, Drake. There is a way for me to change what happened. There is a way for me to cancel the fealty to you and cease being your mate."

His eyes, green and deep and so treacherous it made my heart bleed to look at them, asked the question he wouldn't allow past his lips.

"Lusus naturae," I answered. "If another wyvern challenges for me and wins, I cease to be your mate."

For the second time in my life I walked away from Drake, away from everything he was, and everything we could have been together.

This time, however, I left my heart behind.

The e-mail was waiting for me when I staggered into the tiny apartment I shared with Jim. Beth, my friend who was also Uncle Damian's secretary, had printed it out and left it on the cans of dog food that sat on the table in the kitchenette, where, driven by Jim's demands for food the second it got home, I would be sure to see it.

I have a three-room flat in London near Green Park,

the e-mail read. *If you have no other commitments, I would consider it the greatest honor if you would consent to being my apprentice. I believe there is much we can teach each other.*

The e-mail was signed *Nora Charles*.

Read on for a preview of
Katie MacAlister's
contemporary romance

BLOW ME DOWN

Available from Signet Eclipse

It was the sheep snuffling my face that woke me up. I didn't realize it was a sheep at first, not having the habit of keeping sheep in my house, where my last conscious moment was, but when something moistly warm blew on my face, followed by a horrible stinky scent of wet wool, my eyes popped open and I beheld the unlovely face of a sheep staring down at me.

"T'hell?" I said groggily, pushing the sheep face out of mine as I sat up, immediately regretting the latter action when the world spun around dizzily for a few seconds. As it settled into place I blinked at the hand I'd used to shove away the sheep—it tingled faintly, as if I had whacked my funny bone. I shook it a couple of times, the pins-and-needles feeling quickly fading . . . but that was when my wits returned.

"What the hell?" I said again, a growing sense of disbelief and horror welling within me until I thought my head was going to explode.

I used the rough wood wall behind me to help me get to my feet, my head still spinning a little as I looked around. I was in a short alley between two buildings, half-hidden behind a stack of what looked like whiskey barrels, the sheep who'd been snuffling me now engaged in rooting around through some garbage that slopped over from a wooden box. Sunlight filtered down through the overhang of the two buildings, spilling onto a lumpy cobblestone street behind the alley. Vague blurs resolved themselves into the images of people passing back and forth past the opening of the alley.

The game . . . the virtual reality game. I was seeing images from the game. I put my hand up to my face to pull off the VR glasses, but all my fingers found were my glassesless face. Had they gotten knocked off when I got the shock from the computer? If so, why was I still seeing the virtual world? I lurched my way forward down the alley, stumbling once or twice as my legs seemed to relearn how to walk.

"What the . . . *hell*?" As I burst out into the open, I staggered to a stop.

Two men in what I thought of as typical pirate outfits— breeches, jerkins, swords strapped to their hips, and bandannas on their heads—walked by, one giving me a leer as I clutched the corner of the nearest building.

Beyond them, a wooden well served as a gathering place for several women in long skirts and leather bodices, each armed with a wooden bucket or two. Pigs, sheep, chicken, dogs . . . they all wandered around the square, adding to the general sense of confusion and (at least on my part) disbelief.

A couple of children clad in what could only be described as rags ran past me, each clutching an armful of apples. A shout at the far end of the square pierced the general babble, what appeared to be a greengrocer in breeches and a long apron evidently just noticing the theft of some apples.

It was like something out of a movie. A period movie. One of those big MGM costume movies of the 1950s where everything was brightly colored and quasi-authentic. I expected Gene Kelly to burst singing from a building at any minute.

Instead of Gene, two men emerged from a one-story building across the square, both staggering and yelling slurred curses. One man shoved the other one. The second man shoved the first one back. Both pulled out swords and commenced fighting. The first man lunged. The second screamed, clutched his chest, and fell over backward into a stack of grain sacks. The first man yanked his sword out, spit on his downed opponent, and staggered away around the back of the building, wiping his bloody sword on the hem of his filthy open-necked shirt. A wooden sign hanging over the door he passed waved gently in the wind—a sign depicting a couple of mugs being knocked together beneath the words INN COGNITO printed in blocky letters.

No one bustling around the square gave the dead man so much as a second look.

"*WHAT THE HELL?*" I shouted, goose bumps of sheer, unadulterated horror rippling along my arms and legs as I ran toward the body lying sprawled on the dirty grain sacks. I was about to go into serious freak-out mode when I remembered that none of this was real—it might look real, and sound real, but it was just a game. No one had actually been murdered in front of me. It was just a bunch of computer sprites and sprockets and all those other techno-geeky things that I didn't understand. "OK, stay calm, Amy. This is not a real emergency. However, I'm not willing to lose points or bonus power chips or whatever this game hands out for acts above and beyond the norm. Let's approach this as a non-life-threatening emergency, and go for the next power level. Yeargh. How on earth did they manage that?"

As I squatted next to the dead man, the stench from his unwashed body hit me. I pushed down the skitter of repugnance as it rippled down my back, and rummaged around the dusty recesses of my brain for any knowledge of first aid techniques. "Let me think—a sword wound. CPR?"

A glance at the sluggishly seeping hole in his chest had me eliminating that option. There was no way putting pressure on that would help matters. "Mouth-to-mouth?"

The man's smell took care of that as a choice. "Hmm. Maybe something else. Okay. What's left? Er . . . raise his feet higher than his head? That should stop the flow of blood or something."

I scooted down to grab the man's mud-encrusted tattered boots, intending on swinging them around to a stack of grain bags, but was more than a little disconcerted when one of his legs separated from the rest of his body.

"Aieeee," I screamed, staring in horror at the limb that hung stiffly from my hands.

Just as it was dawning on me that the leg was a crudely fashioned wooden prosthetic and not the ghoulish severed limb I had first imagined, a whoosh of air behind me accompanied the loud slam of a wooden door being thrown open. Before I could do so much as flail the false leg, a steel-like arm wrapped around my waist and hauled me backward into the inn.

Air, warm and thick and scented heavily with beer and unwashed male bodies, folded me in its embrace as I was dragged into a murky open-beamed room.

"Found me a wench, Cap'n," a voice rumbled behind me. "Toothsome one, too, ain't she? Don't look like she's been used overly much. Can I keep her?"

Now, this was taking virtual realism a bit too far. I pushed aside the issue of how a game could make me smell things and feel the touch of another person, and beat the hand that clutched me with the booted end of my fake leg. "Hey! I am not a wench, and I am not a puppy to be kept, and how dare you invade my personal space in such a manner! Do it again, and I'll have you up on charges of sexual harassment and physical assault so fast, your . . . er . . . hook will spin."

The man whom I'd surprised into releasing me stood frowning at me for a second before glancing to the right, where tables—some broken into kindling, others rickety, but mostly whole—lurked in a shadowed corner. The dull rumble of masculine voices broke off as the man asked loudly, "I don't have no hook, do I, Cap'n?"

"Nay, Barn, ye don't," a deep voice answered. One of the

darker shadows separated itself from the others and stepped into the faint sunlight that bullied its way through two tiny begrimed windows. The man who swaggered forward was an arrogant-looking devil, with thick shoulder-length blond hair, a short-cropped goatee and mustache, and dark eyes, which even across the dimly lit room I could see were cast with a roguish light.

He was a charmer through and through—I knew his kind. I'd divorced one.

The behemoth named Barn looked back at me, disappointment written all over his unlovely face. "But the wench—she's mine. I found her. Ye said we could keep what we pillaged."

"She's probably got the French pox," the arrogant blond said as he started for the door, giving me nothing more than an uninterested glance. "We'll find ye a woman a little less tartish at Mongoose."

"Oh!" I gasped, outraged at the slur. I wasn't going to stand around and let some cyber gigolo insult me. "I will repeat myself for those of you with hearing problems or general mental incapacity—I am not a wench, nor am I a tart. I do not have the pox, French or any other sort. And I would rather go without my PDA for an entire year than be with *that* man."

"PDA?" the pirate asked, an odd look of speculation on his face. "You said PDA?"

"Yes, I did. And that's a very big sacrifice, considering."

"You're a player," he said, starting toward me in a long-legged stride that I refused to notice on the grounds that I would not allow myself to respond to another love-'em-and-leave-'em charmer.

"I most certainly am not! I'm a woman, in case it escaped your attention, and even if I was a man, I'm not at all the sort to cruise the meat market for a little companionship. I enjoy meaningful relationships with men, not one-night stands."

"Are you?" he asked, a slight smile quirking one side of his mouth.

"Am I what?"

"Are you enjoying a meaningful relationship with a man right now?"

"No, not that it's any of your business. And don't you come any nearer, " I answered, backing up a couple of paces and leveling my wooden leg at him. "I have a leg, and I'm not afraid to use it!"

I backed up a couple of more steps until I bumped into the rough wall of the inn. I could have kicked myself with the fake leg. Everyone knew the thing a charmer loved most was a challenge, and I'd just presented myself as one. Still, he was a virtual Lothario, not a real one, so I could handle him. I'd just do a little defusing, and be on my way.

"I know your sort. You're a charmer, a man who thinks he can sweet-talk the pants off a nun. Well, I'm immune to your brand of charm, buster. So you can just take your sexy walk and those tight leather pants and the really cool pirate boots of yours—wow, is that a rapier? Very nice. I used to fence in college—and trot off to harass some other un-poxed, tartless un-wench, because I'm not buying any of it."